THE LINE

Also by Martin Limón

Jade Lady Burning
Slicky Boys
Buddha's Money
The Door to Bitterness
The Wandering Ghost
GI Bones
Mr. Kill
The Joy Brigade
The Iron Sickle
The Ville Rat
Ping-Pong Heart
The Nine-Tailed Fox
GI Confidential

Nightmare Range

THE LINE

Martin Limón

SOHO
CRIME

Published by
Soho Press, Inc.
853 Broadway
New York, NY 10003

Library of Congress Cataloging-in-Publication Data

Limón, Martin, 1948– author.
The line / Martin Limón.
Series: A Sergeants Sueño and Bascom novel; 13

ISBN 978-1-64129-089-0
eISBN 978-1-61695-967-8

Subjects: 1. Sueño, George (Fictitious character)—Fiction. 2. Bascom,
Ernie (Fictitious character)—Fiction. 3. United States Army Criminal
Investigation Command—Fiction. 4. Americans—Korea—Fiction.
5. Korea (South)—History—1960-1988—Fiction. I. Title

PS3562.I465 L56 2018 813'.54—dc23 2018016742

Interior design by Janine Agro, Soho Press, Inc.

Printed in the United States of America

10 9 8 7 6 5 4 3 2 1

*To all the soldiers who have suffered and died along
the Military Demarcation Line.*

In the interest of stopping the Korean conflict, with its great toll of suffering and bloodshed . . . a military demarcation line shall be fixed . . . to prevent the occurrence of incidents which might lead to a resumption of hostilities.

—TEXT OF THE KOREAN WAR ARMISTICE AGREEMENT,
DATED JULY 27, 1953, AND SIGNED BY WILLIAM K.
HARRISON, JR., LIEUTENANT GENERAL, US ARMY, AND
NAM IL, GENERAL, KOREAN PEOPLE'S ARMY

THE LINE

-1-

The Imjin River rushed, gray and churning, toward the Yellow Sea. A South Korean soldier used his flashlight to check our emergency dispatch, then shouted back to his comrade, who in turn barked guttural phrases into a field radio.

"What's the hangup?" Ernie asked.

"They're worried about sabotage," I said. "All along the DMZ."

"Us?" Ernie asked. "Our motives are pure."

"Maybe they think we're Russian spies," I said.

Ernie crossed his arms. "Tell them I don't even like vodka. Makes me puke."

"Which designates it as unique amongst alcoholic beverages."

A convoy of M48 Patton tanks rumbled up behind us, adding a layer of urgency to the guards' discussion. Finally, the soldier on the radio walked toward us and waved his arm. "You go," he said, motioning toward the bridge.

"About time," Ernie grumbled. He shoved the jeep in gear and we rolled forward.

Freedom Bridge is narrow, only wide enough for one vehicle at a time, and the guards on either end of the bridge coordinate via field radio to control the flow of traffic. Armed soldiers in parkas, M16 rifles slung over their shoulders, paced the edge of the deck, studying us warily. In the muddy water below, basketball-sized chunks of ice swirled in the rapid current, smashing randomly into massive cement abutments. In the past, wooden boxes filled with explosives had been launched into the river from north of the Demilitarized Zone by our Communist brethren upriver. Sometimes the explosives floated harmlessly toward the Yellow Sea. Other times they hit something—or someone—and exploded, serving as a sort of North Korean forget-me-not.

My name is George Sueño. My partner, Ernie Bascom, and I are agents for the United States Army Criminal Investigation Division in Seoul, Republic of Korea. We'd been roused out of our bunks at oh-dark-thirty by none other than the headquarters command Staff Duty Officer. He said one word: "Murder." When I stood up, fully alert, he continued, "At the JSA. Get your butts movin'."

The JSA, or Joint Security Area, was also known as the truce village of Panmunjom. It was where Communist representatives of the Democratic People's Republic of Korea (DPRK), better known as North Korea, met with the American-allied representatives of the Republic of Korea (ROK), or South Korea. The purpose of the meetings was to make sure that war didn't break out again on the Korean Peninsula, as it had some twenty years ago. And that another two million people weren't slaughtered as a result.

When we reached the northern end of Freedom Bridge, the guards waved us on. I turned back and watched the first M48 tank in the convoy roll slowly onto the massive metal and cement edifice. On our right, we passed the US Army's Camp Greaves and then followed the two-lane road north through uncultivated land. It was only here, near the DMZ, that nature thrived unmolested. In the rest of South Korea, every square inch of arable land was ruthlessly cultivated, but here, near the most heavily armed border in the world, wildlife flourished. On lonely night patrols, GIs liked to kid one another that the nearly extinct Siberian tiger had made a comeback in the area. No one seriously thought it was possible. Even with their sensitive paws, the giant cats would never have been able to negotiate the acres of minefields that lurked beneath the soil on either side of the line.

I warmed my hands in front of the jeep's small heater. It valiantly pumped out a steady flow of hot air that dissipated quickly in the canvas-covered cab. Along the side of the road, splotches of snow and ice clung to ridges of frozen mud churned up by tracked vehicles during endless maneuvers.

A mile farther on, stanchions with signage on either side of the road warned us in English, Korean, and Chinese:

YOU ARE ABOUT TO ENTER THE JOINT SECURITY AREA.
AUTHORIZED PERSONNEL ONLY.

With both hands gripping the top of the steering wheel, Ernie hunched forward as if expecting to fall off a cliff. "Feels like the end of the world," he said.

And then, by the light of a naked bulb in a wooden guard shack, we saw them. North Korean guards, doing what they did best: glare viciously at imperialist running dogs.

"Assholes," Ernie growled.

The North Koreans were outfitted in fur-lined caps, brown tunics and brown trousers, black leather belts, holstered pistols, and faces that seemed hardened into stone. One of the guards studied us through binoculars, but they didn't try to stop us.

About fifty yards later, we spotted the two-story cement block building called Freedom House and beyond that the rectangular, single-story JSA conference rooms, each its own blue building. The Joint Security Area was a plot of land some 800 meters in diameter. It was accessible to designated allied and Communist soldiers under a supposed flag of truce. An American soldier used the beam of his flashlight to guide us into a parking space.

We were climbing out of the jeep when he said, "Are you CID?"

We answered in the affirmative.

"We've been waiting for you. I'm Lieutenant Colonel Brunmeyer, Battalion Commander." He was tall and lanky and had the blue and white JSA patch sewn onto the left shoulder of his fatigues. He was also dressed for combat, with a camouflaged steel helmet secured by a leather strap that hugged his chin. Unconsciously, his right hand sat atop the .45 automatic strapped to his web belt.

He turned and motioned for us to follow. "He's over here."

As we walked, he whistled to a group of about a dozen soldiers standing on the edge of the parking area. They hoisted M16 rifles, spread out, and arrayed themselves behind us in assault formation.

Lieutenant Brunmeyer spoke as we walked. "You are to show no hesitation. When we reach the body, I want you to do your jobs as if you're alone and there's no one watching you. Any sign of weakness and the North Koreans will pounce. Be efficient, be purposeful, and be bold. Any questions?"

"Yeah," Ernie said. "What do you mean, 'the North Koreans will pounce'?"

"I mean they've been watching the body since it was discovered, just prior to zero four hundred. So have we. Right now, it's what you might call a standoff. They won't touch the body because we have guns pointed at them, and we won't touch it because they have guns pointed at us."

"And you want us to walk into the middle of *that*?" Ernie asked.

Colonel Brunmeyer turned and studied him. "That's your job, isn't it?"

Before Ernie could respond, I said, "Who's the victim?"

"One of our KATUSAs," Brunmeyer replied. Korean Augmentation to the US Army. "From Alpha Company. About half the men of the Joint Security Battalion are Americans, the other half KATUSAs. His name is Corporal Noh Jong-bei."

"Noh Jong-bei," I repeated, writing it down in my notebook.

"The GIs call him Johnny No-Go."

"No-go," Ernie said. "As in, when you don't pass a training requirement?"

Some years ago, the US Army had adopted a "go" and "no-go" standard for military training. You were either competent in a skill—say, firing an M16 rifle or jumping out of an airplane—or you failed; that is, received a "no-go." If you were given a "no-go," you'd be retrained until you were competent enough to earn a "go."

"Yes," Colonel Brunmeyer answered. "But Corporal Noh wasn't a no-go. Nicknames are just the men's way of needling one another. Noh was an excellent troop."

"So what happened?" Ernie asked. "How was he killed?"

"We're not sure. He was out here alone, we think. Late."

"Was he on duty?" I asked.

"No. At night, we only man the observation posts." The towers around the perimeter of the JSA.

"So what was he doing?"

Brunmeyer shrugged. "No one knows."

We approached the long rectangular buildings where North Korea and South Korea actually meet. Ice crunched beneath our feet.

Four JSA guards stood at the southern edge of two parallel buildings. All wore black helmet liners with the letters "MP" painted in white on the front.

Colonel Brunmeyer spoke to the ranking man. "Any movement?"

"No, sir. They haven't tried to approach the body."

Brunmeyer frowned. "What the hell's wrong with them?"

"I don't know, sir. Usually they'd be all over something like this. Remember when that South Korean reporter argued with one of the guards and the North Koreans took him into custody?"

"Yeah, and we played hell getting him back." Brunmeyer placed both hands on his hips, exhaled slowly, and whispered, as if to himself: "But for some damn reason, they're staying away this time."

"Maybe it's superstition," the guard offered. "They could be afraid of the dead."

Brunmeyer shook his head resolutely. "It's not that."

It wasn't my place to say so, but I thought the North Koreans might be avoiding the victim because they didn't want to be blamed for his death. Whether they'd actually committed the murder or not, they knew that being charged with such a flagrant violation of the armistice could result in war.

The guards who patrolled the Joint Security Area were armed only with pistols, per the official armistice agreement. The infantry squad that lurked in the shadows behind us, however, was armed with M16 military assault rifles. A hell of a lot more firepower. Exactly what Colonel Brunmeyer had in mind, I wasn't sure. He turned to his men and raised his voice so all could hear.

"These are the CID investigators from Seoul. We're going to give them cover while they inspect the body. Nobody fires except on my command. Is that understood?"

A few mumbles were heard from the tense men.

Lieutenant Colonel Brunmeyer stepped toward us. "I'll walk out first. Junior Lieutenant Kwon, the Night Watch Officer over there on the North Korean side, knows me. Do your jobs without hesitation. The North Koreans respect one thing and one thing only, and that's complete fearlessness. This Joint Security Area is open to all of us, on both sides of the MDL." The Military Demarcation Line. "But during times of tension, we have a tendency to return to our own lines of scrimmage. Remember, the JSA is truce territory. We can cross the MDL if necessary." He pointed into the distance. "But about fifty yards north of here is the Bridge of No Return.

Don't go anywhere near there, because if you step onto that bridge, you're officially in North Korea, and heaven help you then." He glanced at each of us in turn. "You ready?"

"Wait a minute," Ernie said. "You want us to walk out to the middle of that no-man's-land and examine a crime scene like we're in the middle of a park on a summer's day?"

Brunmeyer nodded. "That's exactly what I want."

"And if we're shot?"

"That's our department." He paused for a moment. And then he said, "Your death would be avenged."

Ernie twisted his head to one side like a man who'd just been sucker-punched. For once, he wasn't sure what to say.

"When was the last time," I asked, "that you had a shooting incident here at the JSA?"

Colonel Brunmeyer thought about it. "There've been plenty along the DMZ. Dozens every year. But here at the JSA, near the conference rooms? None. Fistfights, yeah, and clubbings and stabbings, a few people hurt seriously—even disabled—but no one's been killed by gunfire. Not yet. Not since the truce was signed more than twenty years ago."

I turned to Ernie and raised an eyebrow, asking without words, "What do you think?"

Ernie turned toward the JSA guards standing in the snow and glanced at the assault squad hovering about ten yards behind. Slowly, he twisted his head to look back at the North Koreans. Then he looked at me and grinned.

"About time we earned our pay." He took a step toward the JSA guards and said, "All right, you guys, stay the hell alert. Our butts are on the line here."

Brunmeyer asked, "Ready now?"

"Roger Wilco," Ernie replied.

I hadn't said anything. My stomach convulsed, and if there'd been food in it I probably would've upchucked. I thought of the people I owed something to. My mother had died when I was very young, and shortly thereafter my father had disappeared into the endless mystery that is Mexico. My four-year-old son, Il-yong, was in hiding with his mother. Any move I made to be a part of his life would expose them both to danger, even death, at the hands of the Park Chung-hee regime. So despite the dull ache that never left my heart, I stayed resolutely away. The woman I'd been seeing most recently, Doctor Leah Prevault, had been transferred—as part of a concerted effort by the army to keep us apart—from the 121st Evacuation Hospital in Seoul to Tripler Army Medical Center in Honolulu. Despite our attempts to maintain intimacy, it was becoming increasingly clear that breathing life into a long-distance romance might be impossible.

So at that moment, the only person I owed anything to was myself.

The armed GIs were waiting. When Colonel Brunmeyer looked at me, I nodded. "Ready, sir," I told him.

"Okay," he replied. "Let's go."

-2-

Brunmeyer turned and walked out into the ten-yard-wide corridor between the two narrow buildings. We followed. At the far end of the pathway, a dozen North Korean guards stood with their hands on their holstered pistols.

"If anything goes wrong," Brunmeyer whispered, "dive for cover."

Which struck me as inane because there was no cover. Just the wooden sides of the buildings, painted blue and lined with frost-smeared windows.

The first few steps were the hardest. I expected that at any moment a North Korean bullet would plow through my flesh into the folds of my large intestines. Ernie sauntered forward as if he didn't have a care in the world, arms swinging, the flaps of his jacket flailing in the morning breeze.

"There," Brunmeyer told us, pointing at the ground another

five yards ahead. "That raised cement strip marks the MDL." The line separating North and South Korea.

The North Koreans were still watching us when the beam of Lieutenant Brunmeyer's flashlight crept along the snow. And then a boot. Brunmeyer's light traveled up a leg and finally revealed the body of a man clad in fatigues, lying faceup, staring sightlessly into the sky. His lower left combat boot was in South Korea, but the rest of his body lay in North Korea.

I pulled out my own flashlight and knelt and studied the body.

His name tag was in English, standard for KATUSAs; not *hangul*, the Korean alphabet, as would be standard for an ROK Army soldier. Just the single word: NOH.

Both of his eyes were open. Gently, I touched the frigid lids and pulled them shut. Now his expression seemed calm, and one would've thought he was sleeping if it hadn't been for the halo of blood that had spread from the back of his skull. In the cold morning air it no longer ran, having coagulated into a thick purple gel.

"Has anyone touched the body since it was found?" I asked Colonel Brunmeyer.

"No, I made sure of that. The guard I posted kept everyone away."

"Who discovered him?" Ernie asked.

"The change of guard," Brunmeyer said. "On their way to replace the graveyard shift."

"What time was that?"

"Zero four hundred." Four in the morning.

"And you immediately called it in?"

"Yes. By field radio back to Camp Kitty Hawk. They relayed the message to Seoul."

The SDO had woken me just prior to four-thirty. Things had moved fast.

"What did the graveyard shift say?" Ernie asked. "Did they see anything?"

"Nothing," Brunmeyer replied. "The two guys who spotted the body backed away immediately. In fact, they pulled their weapons and covered each other's retreat."

"They figured the North Koreans had done this?"

"Who else?"

We stared at Corporal Noh. He had been unarmed. No web belt around his waist, which meant no holstered pistol attached to that. Instead of an MP helmet, a standard-issue winter cap lay nearby in the snow. I looked around. Dark figures shuffled beneath the eaves of the conference buildings. Watching us.

"Why would they do this?" I asked.

"I don't know." Brunmeyer shrugged. "The North Koreans hate our guts, but they *always* hate our guts. There's nothing different about tonight."

Ernie and I used our flashlights to carefully check the area near the body. Nothing but hard ice, which crunched yet left indistinct footprints. There were plenty of footprints here, but that could've been said for the entire grounds of the JSA. Except in the wee hours, it was heavily patrolled.

"Here," Ernie said. I stood up and joined him. Beneath one of the windows of the main conference room, spattering the snow, spread a fan-like array of dark spots. I studied them closely.

"Could be blood," I said.

Ernie nodded, then moved his flashlight. "And here." Two lines, barely visible under the dim beam, wobbled their way toward the body. "Heels?" Ernie asked. "Being dragged?"

"Could be," I replied.

Between the two lines was a thin trickle of what appeared to be blood. But in this poor lighting, I couldn't be sure. I walked back to the body. We checked Corporal Noh's hands for defensive wounds. Nothing. No visible flesh or blood beneath his fingernails.

"He was caught by surprise," Ernie said.

I nodded.

"Killed here, close to the wall, on the southern side," Ernie continued. "And then dragged a few feet to the northern side of the MDL and left there."

"Those bastards," Brunmeyer said. He repeated it, lower this time and with more menace. "Those *bastards*." He glared at the North Koreans. "One of them hit him from behind and dragged him north. Probably planning to take him into their territory to hide the body, but then dropped him when they heard our men on their way to relieve the graveyard shift."

I thought through Colonel Brunmeyer's theory. It fit with the evidence, though we didn't have much to go on. Brunmeyer stood a few feet away from us, face twisted in hatred. He spit onto the ice before his feet. "They were trying to humiliate us," he said, "and embarrass my command."

Ernie and I looked over at him for a moment. He had every right to be angry. We were angry, too. But he acted as if the North Koreans were after him personally. As if it were Brunmeyer they hated, not the entire Western world. Gradually he calmed down, noticing us staring at him. We turned back to our work.

The US Army had no military police forensic team in Korea. The 8th Army honchos claimed there wasn't enough crime to justify the expense. And there was a twisted element of truth in that. The less effective we were in our investigations and the fewer prosecutions there were, the better 8th Army's crime statistics appeared. If we wanted a forensic examination, we had to package up any evidence we had and ship it to the designated medical center in Camp Zama, Japan. Consequently, Ernie and I generally took matters into our own hands. One of the unwritten rules in the Army is that if you want to do something, don't ask permission, because you'll never get it. On the other hand, if you just go ahead and do what you want, more often than not you'll get away with it.

A dim predawn light gradually began to suffuse the area. Ernie knelt and grabbed Corporal Noh's shoulders. I grabbed his hip, and on the count of three, we rolled him over.

Brunmeyer's eyes widened in horror. A line along the center of Noh's skull had been crushed in. Dented, as if he'd been shoved against the whirling blades of a giant buzz saw. Gray brain matter puffed out, shoving aside crushed bone and clumps of oozed blood. Brunmeyer stepped toward one of the conference rooms, leaned against it, and after dry-heaving a couple of times, barfed his guts out.

An ominous pounding shook the ground. I stopped my examination of the wound and looked up. A party of North Korean guards goose-stepped toward us; swinging their arms rhythmically, boots stomping into the snow. Brunmeyer pushed himself upright, wiped his mouth with the back of his hand, and pulled his .45. Holding it pointed toward the ground, he yelled weakly, "*Chongji!*" Halt!

They kept coming.

Brunmeyer pulled back the charging handle of his .45. He raised the pistol and aimed it unsteadily at the man leading the North Korean detachment.

"*Chongji!*" he ordered again, like he meant it this time.

Taking one last hard stomp into the snow, the soldiers came to a halt. The man in front pointed and gestured with his forearm, shouting something in Korean. Maybe I was in shock or he was just speaking too fast, but I couldn't understand what he was saying. Brunmeyer seemed to have no such problem.

"This is *our* patrol area, Kwon," he said, motioning in a large circle with his hand. "*Ours!*" He jabbed his thumb into the center of his chest. "You *arra*?" You understand?

It was an impolite way to use the verb. The ideal pronunciation would've been *arraseiyo*. But this seemed like the wrong time for a Korean grammar lesson.

The man Lieutenant Colonel Brunmeyer had addressed as Kwon appeared infuriated. He barked another order in Korean that I didn't understand, and his men spread out in a semicircle. All were outfitted with pistols, but so far they were keeping them holstered.

Ernie and I were the only two unarmed players in this drama. Before leaving Seoul, we could've checked out a couple of .45s from the MP Arms Room, but not only had we not had the time, we didn't think they'd do much good. Not with a 700,000-man North Korean army on one side of the Military Demarcation Line and a 450,000-man South Korean army on the other. Not to mention untold numbers of artillery pieces and tanks.

It soon became clear that the man Brunmeyer had previously briefed us on, Junior Lieutenant Kwon, planned on taking possession of Corporal Noh's body. Two of the guards pulled out wooden poles that I hadn't noticed before, lay them near the body, and unrolled a canvas stretcher. They rapidly assembled it and began to move toward Noh until Lieutenant Colonel Brunmeyer fired a shot into the air. The bullet cleared the head of Junior Lieutenant Kwon by about three feet.

Immediately, all North Korean soldiers present reached for their pistols.

Footsteps rumbled toward us. At the southern end of the conference room, the infantry reinforcements Brunmeyer had put in place earlier rounded the corner. They spread out, knelt, and took up firing positions. Within seconds, there were a dozen M16 rifles pointed at the North Korean detachment.

Junior Lieutenant Kwon was beside himself with rage. In broken English, he said, "This man is *Korean.* Not like you dirty Americans. He come to *us.* He come to *real* Korean army."

Hand steady, Brunmeyer held his .45 pointed directly at Kwon's red face.

"No *touchy,*" he said. "You *arra*? No touchy."

Apoplectic now, Kwon pointed at Corporal Noh's corpse. "He in North Korea. *This* side."

He had a point. There was probably a rule buried somewhere in the armistice agreement permitting each government to treat the wounded—or collect the dead—on its respective side of the MDL. If we lost the body now, we would never see it again. Or if the North Koreans did return it, that could take years.

Brunmeyer turned to me and ordered, "Pull it back here!"

I hesitated, staring at the North Koreans' guns.

"*Now!*" Brunmeyer hissed.

Perhaps it was my military training or the urgency to his command, but without thinking it through further, I knelt and took Noh's left leg, then began to pull. Some of the material beneath his body must've already frozen, because the corpse didn't move right away. I put more of my weight in the direction opposite the dead man. Ernie reached down to grab his other ankle, and soon what was left of Corporal Noh Jong-bei slid toward us until it lay in a crumpled heap on the southern side of the Military Demarcation Line.

Satisfied, Lieutenant Colonel Brunmeyer turned back to the North Koreans.

Junior Lieutenant Kwon snapped open his holster and pulled out his pistol. As the men behind him followed suit, Colonel Brunmeyer shouted a command and a volley of M16 automatic fire exploded into the night. I dove to the ground; so did Ernie. When we dared to look up, we realized that the North Korean soldiers were kneeling, their pistols pointed at us, but they hadn't returned fire. No one was hurt. The volley from the Americans had been aimed over their heads.

As if he were made of steel and had no need to fear bullets, Brunmeyer turned his back on the potential firing squad and shouted orders to his men. Two of the JSA guards approached with a stretcher, and Brunmeyer ordered them to pick up Noh's body. They did, despite Junior Lieutenant Kwon screaming invective at them while they worked. Still, with a row of M16 rifles pointed at him, Kwon didn't tell his men to fire. I watched their eyes. One or two sets glanced furtively at our own line of M16 barrels. The North Korean contingent was outgunned, and they knew it. And it was unlikely all of them were as willing to commit suicide, or to start another Korean War, as their commander was.

Finally, Noh's body was hoisted onto the stretcher, and stumbling their way across pounded snow, the two bearers carried him back through our lines.

"So much for our crime scene," Ernie whispered.

Brunmeyer motioned for us to stand behind him. We did. Then, maintaining good order and discipline, the entire contingent of infantry soldiers rose to their feet, keeping their rifles pointed at Kwon and the other North Koreans. Along with Colonel Brunmeyer and the four JSA guards, we performed an orderly retreat.

Kwon continued to barrage us with curse words, most in Korean. Walking forward, waving his fist in the air, he and his comrades trampled on what was left of the blood-spatter evidence. I understood what he was saying. Some of it colorful, as in "born of a female canine." His hectoring voice faded as we made our way back to the staging area.

-3-

Once we were out of the line of fire, Ernie asked me, "You okay?"

I took a deep breath. "Yeah, I think so. You?"

"I'll be fine. As soon as I change my shorts."

I turned to Brunmeyer. "What the hell was that all about?"

He shrugged. "Routine."

"What do you mean 'routine'?"

"I mean the North Koreans just wanted to make sure we knew they were watching. Junior Lieutenant Kwon knows what happened—what they did. Before you arrived, they probably took plenty of photographs of Noh's body for propaganda purposes. They'll claim an innocent Korean soldier was murdered by bloodthirsty American imperialists. Try to make us look bad."

"So that bit about them not wanting us to take the body," I asked, "that was all for show?"

He squinted. "Nothing's ever easy up here at the JSA."

"I'm beginning to see that."

"Why would they do that?" Ernie asked. "Now? When things have been quiet for a while?"

Colonel Brunmeyer shrugged. "Could be part of some broader strategy. Trying to cause tension on the Peninsula. Maybe bring foreign attention to the US-South Korean military exercises that are coming up in a couple months."

"They'd kill just for that?" Ernie asked.

"They've killed for less," Brunmeyer replied.

The 8th Army Coroner's van arrived and two medics climbed out. Ernie ran over and helped to hoist Corporal Noh into the back of the van. Then he returned to us, rubbing his gloveless hands together for warmth.

"So, Colonel," Ernie said, "we have a few questions for you."

"Why?" Brunmeyer asked. "You know who did it."

"Just routine," Ernie replied. "For our report."

We asked him the usual: who Corporal Noh's friends and enemies were, whether he'd had any professional or personal problems that had been weighing on him. Brunmeyer was helpful, elaborating where he could, but the picture his answers painted was one of a good soldier doing his duty, not one involved with anything that could've led to his death.

"It was them," Brunmeyer said, turning north. "Those goddamn Commies."

"You think we'll retaliate?" Ernie asked.

"That's a decision made above my pay grade. But if we don't, I can tell you who will."

"Who?"

"The ROK Army. They're probably preparing a few high-explosive artillery rounds as we speak."

Instead of pronouncing South Korea's official name letter-by-letter, R-O-K for Republic of Korea, he pronounced the acronym "rock." Standard here in Korea—the "rock" army, the "rock" government, a "rock" soldier. The only time GIs spelled out the acronym verbally was for poetic effect. As in the GI lament, "*Just another day in the R-O-K.*"

A loud scream pierced the air. It took me a moment to realize it wasn't a person, but an air raid siren.

"Alert," Colonel Brunmeyer told us. The call for every soldier to immediately report to his unit and prepare for combat. GIs ran in every direction. Brunmeyer nodded toward us. "If you'll excuse me." He strode off quickly to take command of his battalion.

Ernie and I trotted briskly back to the jeep. As we did so, an F-4 Phantom jet fighter swooped low over our heads.

Ernie ducked. "That one of ours?" he asked.

I watched wings wobble and a trail of exhaust linger in a somber gray sky. "If it wasn't," I said, "we'd be toast already."

"You mean Crispy Critters," Ernie replied.

Because of the area-wide alert, masses of military traffic jammed the MSR—the Main Supply Route—which stretched between the DMZ and Seoul. It was almost noon by the time we made our way back to the southern edge of the capital city; to Yongsan Compound, the home of 8th Army headquarters. At the back gate, a bored MP checked our dispatch. Suddenly, his eyes widened.

"CID, right?" he asked.

"Yeah," Ernie replied.

"Message for you." He stepped back into the guard shack, grabbed a clipboard, and returned to us, thumbing through sheets of paper. "Here it is," he said, pointing to an entry. "You're to report to Colonel Peele at the Military Armistice Commission headquarters immediately. You are to talk to no one until you see him." He lowered the clipboard and held it at his side, appearing pleased with himself.

After what we'd been through this morning, wrestling with more brass at the MAC headquarters was the last thing we felt like doing. Ernie grinned at the MP. "Why don't you do me a favor, buddy, and forget you ever saw us?"

"No can do," the MP said, shaking his head resolutely. "I'm supposed to call it in as soon as you're identified."

Ernie was about to say something more but the MP turned his back on us, stepped inside the guard shack, picked up the phone, and started dialing. Ernie let out a whoosh of air. "That's the problem with this man's army. Everybody's a brown-noser."

He shoved the jeep in gear and we rolled forward.

"Where to?" he asked.

I shrugged. "I guess we're going to have to comply."

"Can't we get some chow first?"

I checked my watch. "Noon hour," I said.

"Snack bar?" Ernie asked.

I nodded.

At the 8th Army Snack Bar, Sergeant First Class Harvey—better known as Strange—surveyed the room from his usual table against the wall.

Strange was a pervert. He loved nothing more than hearing detailed stories of others' sexual exploits. Instead of ignoring a guy like that, as most people did, Ernie and I catered to him, treated him like a pal. As the NCO-in-charge of the 8th Army Classified Documents Distribution Center—and a notorious gossip—he managed to poke his nose into everything of importance that was going on at the head shed. The information he provided was invaluable. But there was always a price.

After sliding our trays down the chow line, Ernie and I joined Strange at his table. Me with a bowl of chili and saltines on the side, Ernie with tuna salad on toast.

"I thought you guys would be dead by now," Strange said. He wore opaque sunglasses, his thinning hair slicked straight back. A plastic cigarette holder—with no cigarette—dangled from lips that looked like greased rubber bands.

"Why's that?" Ernie asked.

"Because you were trying to start a war this morning up at the JSA."

"Says who?"

"Says everybody. The MAC commander is furious."

The head of the Military Armistice Commission, the United Nations Command representative who negotiated with the North Koreans.

"We recovered a body," Ernie said, chomping into his sandwich and taking a bite so big that it made his cheek bulge. "What's wrong with that?"

"Don't chew with your mouth open."

"Who are you? Mother Superior?"

"I'm a senior NCO and you're grossing me out."

"*I'm* grossing *you* out?"

I figured Ernie's next sentence was "You're the pervert," or something just as complimentary, so I interrupted.

"The JSA commander felt he needed to bring an infantry squad for the North Koreans to let us take possession of the body," I said. "I don't see that he had a choice."

"Of course he had a choice," Strange replied. "He should've received permission before taking that kind of action. It's a clear violation of the armistice agreement. There aren't supposed to be any combat units in the Joint Security Area, and the North Koreans are already raising hell."

Ernie and I looked at one another. "Okay," I said, dipping a cracker into the steaming chili broth. "It's a violation. What's that have to do with us?"

"What's it have to do with you? You caused it. It's *your* fault."

"Hey," Ernie said. "We were just there to look at a crime scene. Nothing more."

"Doesn't matter," Strange said. "You were the enlisted pukes on site, so you take the blame."

"What about Lieutenant Colonel Brunmeyer?"

Strange smirked and sipped his hot chocolate. "*He* has connections." Then he paused, knowing he had us enthralled, and said, "When he finishes up his JSA assignment, he's slated for promotion to full colonel. And he's still under forty. That means he's on track to make general. The honchos at the MAC can't afford to be too angry with him. Might come back to haunt them. So they have you." Strange set down his mug and smiled broadly. "It's been nice knowing you two."

Ernie scoffed. "They can't do anything to us."

"Wanna bet?"

"Like what?" Doubt had already crept into Ernie's voice.

"Like a court-martial for creating an international incident."

"We didn't create an international incident."

"Oh, yeah? Who dragged the body from the North Korean side of the line to the South Korean side?"

Ernie and I glanced at one another. So Lieutenant Colonel

Brunmeyer had already dimed us out, blaming us for moving the body even though it had been under his orders. But we said nothing, knowing better than to provide Strange with any more information than we had to.

"There's no provision for 'creating an international incident' in the UCMJ," I said.

Strange laughed. It was hideous, like a hedgehog choking on phlegm. "That's never stopped them before."

He was right. The UCMJ, or the Uniform Code of Military Justice, was the law that every member of the US military lived under. And it was a flexible document. If you found yourself in violation of loosely worded passages like "disruption of good order and discipline" or showing "silent contempt" toward a senior officer, you could find yourself staring at the interior of four walls in a federal penitentiary.

Strange leaned toward us and spoke in the low, creepy voice that he used for such things. "Had any *strange* lately?"

Ernie had just polished off his sandwich, his mouth still full. Chomping on the last bite of tuna salad on rye, he said, "Why? You have information for us?"

"I've already given you information."

"Huh. Some information. We could've figured that out ourselves."

"But you didn't."

"Didn't have to. Everybody knows that a GI is toast if the honchos decide to burn him. Nothing new in that."

We both stared at Strange. From his smug expression, it was clear he had more information to trade.

"What is it?" I asked.

"Him," Strange said, nodding toward Ernie. "When he's finally done with that goddamn sandwich, I want him to go to the latrine and rinse his mouth out, then come back here and talk at me." Meaning tell him a story about the "strange" Ernie'd gotten lately.

"No way," Ernie said. "Not unless you have something good."

"Oh, it's good," Strange replied.

"Okay, then," I said. "Tell us."

Strange stared down at his empty cup of hot chocolate. After a brief silence, I said, "I'll get you another."

At the stainless-steel serving counter, I pulled a steaming cup of hot chocolate, and when I placed it in front of the middle-aged Korean cashier, she looked at it and said, "No marshmallow?"

So even the cafeteria staff was familiar with Strange's peculiarities. I retreated down the line and plopped two marshmallows into the hot drink, then returned to her cash register. She smirked as I handed her my quarter.

When I set the hot chocolate in front of Strange, he smiled, which was unpleasant to see. But then he leaned in closer, glancing around to make sure no one was listening.

"There's been some weird shit going on up at the JSA. One

document making the rounds in the head shed says that Colonel Brunmeyer was getting too chummy with the Commies. Especially the head honcho on the North Korean night watch."

"Junior Lieutenant Kwon?" I said.

"Yeah." Eyebrows lifted from above the shades. "How did you know?"

"We're not stupid," Ernie said. "Go on. What else did the document say?"

Strange waggled his cigarette holder and continued. "There were even reports of the North Koreans bringing a couple of bottles of Red Star soju and Colonel Brunmeyer and this joker Kwon sharing a tipple or two."

"They had a détente," I said.

"Yeah. Like Kissinger. But the JSA guards aren't diplomats. They're there to hold the line against those Red bastards, and instead they're smoking and joking with them."

"But they're supposed to communicate, aren't they?" I asked. "To make sure there are no misunderstandings. That nothing flares up into an incident serious enough to ignite a war."

Strange shook his head. "No, they're not supposed to talk. That's the MAC's job." The Military Armistice Commission. "The MAC officers decide on what positions to take in those meetings. It's their job to deal with the North Koreans. The JSA guard unit's only job is to protect the physical integrity of the JSA and anyone we send up there. It's not their job to make nice with the North Koreans."

"And the MAC doesn't want them doing that," Ernie said.

"The MAC doesn't want anybody making nice," Strange said. "They want to keep the North Koreans back on their heels. They want them afraid of our superior airpower and naval power, and most of all our overwhelming nuclear power. They want those Commies shivering in their boots. And they sure as shit don't want anybody at the JSA having happy hour with them."

He paused for hot chocolate while Ernie and I absorbed this. I averted my eyes as he slurped up a half-dissolved marshmallow.

"Because if the North Koreans are worried about our military strength," I said, "and in the dark as to our intentions, they're more likely to come to the table and accept our terms."

"Exactly," Strange said.

"So why didn't the MAC speak directly to Brunmeyer?"

"I told you, he's going to be a general one day. They don't want to step on his toes. An officer of his rank and his responsibility is supposed to *know* how to conduct himself at the JSA. Nobody should have to tell him."

Strange was silent again.

"There's more," I said.

"Yes. That's why the document was classified Top Secret." Strange's gaze moved slowly around the Snack Bar. The crowd was starting to thin out, with lunch hour almost over. "The report speculated that Lieutenant Colonel Rudolph M. Brunmeyer might have communist sympathies."

"Rudolph?"

"Yep. Rudy to his friends."

"We didn't get that close," Ernie said. "But you're kidding, right? About 'communist sympathies'?'"

"No." Strange shook his head.

"So what?" I added. "Everyone has political views. It's a free country, even in the Army. As long as those views don't interfere with you doing your job."

"It's worse than that," Strange said. "The head shed is starting to worry about his courage."

"Courage?" Ernie said, incredulous. "This morning, he walked right in front of a line of pissed-off North Korean guards who were armed with pistols."

I nodded in agreement.

"Not *that* kind of courage," Strange said.

"There's another kind?" Ernie asked.

"Yes. The kind where you don't buckle under pressure."

"What kind of pressure?"

"The ever-present North Korean threat to incite war if you don't do what they want you to do."

"And the head shed thinks Brunmeyer was playing nice with the North Koreans because he was afraid they'd cause trouble if he didn't?"

"Exactly."

"Sounds to me," Ernie said, "like he was trying to protect his men."

"How'd that work out for him?" Strange asked.

Ernie looked away. "Not well. At least for Corporal Noh."

"So maybe they were getting too chummy," I said. "Maybe Noh had a buddy on the North Korean side, and when he went by himself to talk to him, totally unarmed, Lieutenant Kwon took advantage of the opportunity and offed him."

"That's what they're thinking at the head shed," Strange said. "That something went wrong. Too much fraternization. Brunmeyer let his guard down."

"Maybe," Ernie said.

"Apparently," Strange continued, "the Noh family is taking the news pretty hard."

"Who wouldn't?" I asked.

"Yeah. The Korean officer who officially informed them of their son's death was trapped at the family home for over an hour, and one of the uncles was so enraged that ROK Army MPs had to be called in to fight him off."

"Did the officer get out okay?"

"Just a few bruises and cuts," Strange replied, sipping his hot chocolate. "And a concussion." He set the cup down. "Should've worn a helmet."

When we left the Snack Bar, Ernie asked me, "Ready for the MAC?"

"Not yet."

"They'll be angry if we put it off."

"Yeah, so what else is new? We're in the middle of an investigation. That comes first."

"Yeah," Ernie replied. "They can bite me." We climbed into the jeep. "First stop?"

I pulled out the piece of paper Strange had slipped us just as we'd left. On it, written in English, was a Korean address. Since the English alphabet doesn't correspond directly with the Korean alphabet, it's sometimes difficult to glean the meanings of Korean words written in English and vice versa. I pulled out my map of Seoul and located Inui-dong, the district where the address was.

"It's on the way to East Gate," I told Ernie. "Let's go there and I'll ask around."

"And what's the family going to tell us?"

"Maybe nothing," I said. "Maybe everything."

Ernie switched on the ignition and shoved the jeep in gear. "Sort of an awkward time for a visit. Especially considering what they did to the notifying officer."

I couldn't argue with that. The Noh family was probably suffering the single worst day of their lives. They'd just lost a son; their only son, according to Strange. Still, when you're investigating a murder, the first twenty-four hours are vital. The culprit can't be allowed time to gather his wits or tamper with evidence. I still wasn't convinced that the North Koreans had perpetrated this murder, although everyone was in a rush to say so and close the book on it. We had to talk to Corporal Noh Jong-bei's family—*now*.

And that's what we would've done if three jeeploads of MPs hadn't pulled up in front of us. The senior man, Staff Sergeant Grimes—whom I'd worked with before—climbed out and pulled his .45 from its holster.

"Don't make me use this thing, Sueño," he said.

"What the hell's with you, Grimes?" I asked. "Threatening us?"

"No, I'm promising you. You were already told at the back gate, so we're not playing games this time: I'll pop a cap in your butts if you don't come along right now."

"Where to?"

"MAC headquarters," he said. "The Military Armistice Commission wants to have a little chat with you."

"Tell them to go screw themselves," Ernie said.

Grimes raised his .45 and pointed it at Ernie's forehead. "You tell 'em," he said.

Ernie grinned. "Okay, since you put it that way."

-4-

Ten minutes later, Ernie and I walked through the big swinging double doors of the Military Armistice Commission building. After our presence had been so desperately sought, we were made to wait.

"Payback," Ernie whispered as we sat in two folding metal chairs in the center of the entrance foyer. A field table had been set up a few feet in front of us with a vinyl-upholstered swivel chair behind it. Odd, I thought. Why wouldn't we be ushered into someone's office? But the Army was the Army. You did what you were told, unless you could get away with *not* doing what you were told.

It was almost thirteen-hundred hours, one P.M., when a bald man in dress-green trousers and a brown poplin shirt loosened at the tie trundled out of a back room. He dropped down heavily in the swivel chair and placed his elbows on the flimsy table, showing off rolled-up cuffs that revealed hairy arms. He leaned forward, eyeing us as if we were a particularly loathsome specimen of insect larvae.

"Do you know who I am?" he asked.

Ernie shook his head.

"I'm Colonel Peele, Executive Officer here at the MAC. I've just been in conference with General Armstead, the MAC Commander himself." He glared at us for a moment, letting that sink in. And letting us know how tough he was, judging by the glower above his sagging cheeks.

A clicking sound emerged from Ernie's mouth.

"Are you chewing *gum*?" Peele asked.

"I was," Ernie replied. "Now I'm just grinding it between my teeth."

"Get rid of it."

"Yes, sir." Ernie continued to stare at Colonel Peele, not moving, and then a lump slowly convulsed down his throat. He finished swallowing and stared at the colonel as if nothing had happened.

Colonel Peele's bulldog expression remained unmoved, but I noticed that his bald pate had turned red. He cleared his throat before continuing.

"Do you have any idea," he asked, "the shitstorm you caused up at the JSA this morning?"

When Ernie didn't speak, I ventured, "It was a difficult situation, sir."

"*Difficult*? Is that what you're calling it? You damn near caused a war."

"We were ordered to investigate a crime, sir. And that's what we did."

"You don't investigate crime at the JSA."

I was taken aback until I realized where he was going with this.

"Why not?" Ernie asked. "Murder is murder."

"Crimes at the JSA," Colonel Peele said, "and all along the DMZ are to be investigated by the Neutral Nations Supervisory Commission. Not Eighth Army CID."

I looked at Ernie, who looked back at me. "We didn't know that, sir," I said. "The Staff Duty Officer told us to go, so we went."

"Don't make excuses. You were operating outside of your jurisdiction. Do you realize that's a court-martial offense?" When neither of us replied, Peele went on. "And while you were up there, you pissed off every North Korean in the DMZ." His fists were clenched, and leaning in toward us with his large head and round face, he resembled a rottweiler about to break its leash. All he lacked was fangs. "You didn't have to," Colonel Peele continued, "make the North Koreans put seven of their divisions along the border on combat alert. There are two tank battalions rolling toward Panmunjom, thanks to you. And this only a week before our next MAC meeting—"

Ernie stretched, arching his spine. Usually, he didn't mind getting chewed out. Letting hot air go in one ear and out the other was something most junior enlisted men had turned into an art form. But this guy had set up a little impromptu stage and preplanned a speech systematically blaming Ernie and me for every sin perpetrated along the DMZ that morning, rather than acknowledging who was truly responsible.

Ernie cut him off. "You can't pin any of that stuff on *us*, sir."

Colonel Peele's eyes widened, and after taking about two seconds to recover from shock at Ernie talking back, he banged his fist so hard on the field table it almost broke. "Well, goddamnit, *some*body caused it!" He closed his eyes for just a second, and then they popped open again, blue and bloodshot. "Those goddamn Commies murdered one of our boys, and by God we're going to rub their noses in it. They're going to pay for it however *we* want them to, at the time and place *we* say." He pointed a forefinger at us. "And you two are to stay away from the Joint Security Area. Is that understood? You are to go nowhere near Panmunjom, nowhere near Colonel Brunmeyer, and nowhere near the troops at the JSA." He paused to catch his breath. "I'll put that in writing if I have to."

"You should, sir." He seemed surprised that I'd responded. But I'd pictured Corporal Noh, a good soldier, and the hideous divot in the back of his head. "When we're investigating a murder," I said, "no one can pull us off that investigation except the Provost Marshal himself." When he didn't answer right away, I pushed on. "The officers on the Neutral Nations Supervisory Commission are from Switzerland and Poland

and other countries that don't know the lay of the land here. What do they know about tracking down a killer locally? If they assume jurisdiction of this incident, it will turn into a political exercise—an attempt to keep both sides from going to war again, not a murder investigation."

He stared at me, dumbfounded, as if he'd just seen an orangutan recite the Declaration of Independence. Then he reclenched his fists and bowed his head, putting on a show of valiantly trying to compose himself. In a low voice, he spoke again. "You two are just like so many of the troops nowadays. You think you're smart, too smart for the army. You think you don't have to follow the orders of those above you. Well, I have news for you. The army and the patriots within it have been around for a lot longer than you've been alive. And we'll be here long after you're ground up into dust and flushed down the goddamn latrine." He stood up, grabbed the field table by the edge, and lifted it about six inches into the air. "You got that?"

Sweat glistened on his flushed face. His moist lips sputtered, but no more words came out. Instead of tossing the table at us, which I knew he was tempted to do, he let it drop to the floor with a loud thud. Peele straightened himself, and without waiting for our salutes, he turned and marched out of the room.

Ernie and I looked at one another. He shrugged, his tongue worked along the inner edge of his teeth, and then he started clicking his gum again.

"Did you just bring that back up?" I asked.

"Never went down." When I just stared at him, he said, "Hey, ginseng gum is expensive. No sense wasting it."

Ernie had read an article once about the health benefits of the ginseng plant, especially how it increased the metabolism and acted as a tonic for the smooth functioning of the body, including lowering blood sugar, reducing stress, and curing sexual dysfunction. Ever since, he'd been a fanatic for the stuff, occasionally chewing on the raw root but more often popping the slightly bitter chewing gum in his mouth. It being dried out, ground down, and stuffed in mass-produced packaging probably eliminated any and all benefits of the original root, which grew feral in parts of North Korea and Manchuria. But that didn't faze him. He claimed that ginseng gum kept him revved up. "Like a new pair of spark plugs," he'd told me.

Since our little lecture was over, Ernie and I rose from our chairs and walked outside. After crossing the gravel parking lot, we climbed into the jeep's canvas seats and Ernie started the engine. He let it idle for a moment. "Displacement," he said.

"What?"

"Displacement," Ernie repeated. "Your girlfriend, what was her name?"

"You forgot?"

"It's been a while."

"Three months." The fact that we'd worked with her on an important murder case didn't seem to jog his memory. "Captain Leah Prevault," I said.

"Yeah, her. The shrink. That's what she called it. Displacement. When you're mad at one person but you take it out on somebody else."

"A whipping boy."

"Yeah. That's us. The whipping boys. Lieutenant Colonel Brunmeyer was the one who engineered for us to go up there before any of his superiors were aware of it, even though he probably knew the JSA wasn't under our jurisdiction. He's also the one who brought a squad of combat infantry onto JSA grounds, violating the armistice. But the Eighth Army honchos don't want to blame him. Not a fellow officer. Not one of their own. So they blame us."

And it was hardly our fault that the North Koreans had mobilized seven infantry divisions and two tank battalions on their side of the border. But that was the way it was in the army: shit rolled downhill.

"Colonel Peele says he's going to make the Commies pay," I said. "What do you suppose he means by that?"

"Accuse them of the murder," Ernie said. "Keep them on the defensive during the MAC meetings."

"For that he'd need proof, wouldn't he?"

Ernie shrugged. "The dead body of Corporal Noh is probably proof enough for him. It had to be the Commies. Who else?"

"You don't believe that."

"Right now," Ernie said, "I don't have an opinion one way

or the other. Maybe it was them, maybe not. But that's not going to stop Eighth Army from forming all the opinions they want. Especially if those opinions are useful to them."

Ernie shoved the jeep in reverse, backed out of the parking spot, and stomped on the clutch and shifted into first. As we rolled forward, he said, "I guess that's what us enlisted pukes are good for."

"For what?"

"For taking out frustrations on." He thought about it for a moment. "It must be nice to have somebody to take out your frustrations on."

"I guess it is. Who do you take your frustrations out on?"

"Me? I don't have any frustrations."

"Maybe because when you want to do something, you just do it."

"Yeah," he replied. "Peele ought to try that sometime."

"What he wanted just now," I said, "was to launch that table at us."

Ernie turned the corner, still pondering what we'd just seen. Then he said, "Probably would've done him a world of good." After cruising for a while, Ernie said, "So are we going to do what he said and drop the case?"

I remembered the bloody divot in the back of Corporal Noh Jong-bei's head. "Not on your life," I replied.

"Yeah," Ernie said. "Not on your life."

■　■　■

Ernie missed the turn and we ended up circling Dongdaemun, the Great East Gate. The ancient stone and tile-roofed edifice stared down at us as we made a one-eighty. During the Chosun Dynasty, Seoul had been much smaller and an actual wall had enveloped the city, extending from West Gate to South Gate to here at the East Gate. The northern approaches to the city had been guarded by fortifications that lined the precipitous mountains beyond. At night, constables with pikes, bows and arrows, and swords patrolled the walls, bearing oil lanterns. On the peaks above, lines of bonfires had been lit and doused according to a code that relayed messages up and down the spine of the Korean Peninsula. In those days, the country had been united. There had been no military demarcation line between north and south in centuries prior. No one had even imagined such a thing. The few times Korea had been conquered, it had been conquered whole. And then it had regained its freedom again, still whole.

I spotted a sign pointing us toward Inui-dong. Ernie turned right into a narrow lane wide enough for two-way traffic but populated with pedestrians and bicyclists and men with A-frames strapped to their backs, hauling loads of charcoal briquettes. We slowed to a crawl. Twice we stopped, and the second time, I read the address splashed with white paint onto the side of a *kagei*, an open-fronted shop. Most of the people inside were busy and ignored me, but I found a kind-looking shopper who listened as I recited the address. She said we were heading in the right direction, then pointed and told me that before the small temple on the hill straight ahead, we should turn right and wind up the narrow lane.

"When you get close," she said, "you won't be able to drive."

Many of the older neighborhoods in Seoul had been built before automobiles were popularized. Merchants pushing two-wheeled carts wandered through the lanes selling produce, fish, pulled taffy, secondhand clothes, and other sundries a busy housewife might need. The more resilient women would grab their own baskets and wander downhill toward the open-air markets that dotted the tightly packed city.

Before we reached the pagoda of the temple, we found a place to park near a bicycle repair shop. I paid the proprietor a thousand *won*—two bucks—to watch the jeep for us, which was really just meant as a way to compensate him for the inconvenience.

The address was 15-*dong*, 36-*ho*, and I had to ask for directions a couple more times. The lanes were a twisting maze lined with ten-foot-high walls of brick and stone. Every few feet, a metal gate led into an individual family home behind the wall. Finally, we spotted a wooden stand with a circular wreath of white flowers atop it, a black ribbon hanging from that. The gate was open.

"That's it," Ernie said. And it was: 15-*dong*, 36-*ho*, the home of the Noh family. I knocked on the edge of the gate. No one answered, so we stepped into the flagstone courtyard. From inside, a woman wailed.

In the courtyard in front of the house, a line of people stood before a blown-up black-and-white photograph of Corporal Noh Jong-bei. He stared impassively ahead and wore the black high-collared uniform of a high school boy. Somebody chanted a few words and everyone bowed. The smell of incense wafted through the air. Finally, an older man in a black suit and white gloves noticed us. He strode forward and said, "Yes?"

"We're from Eighth Army," I said, motioning toward myself and Ernie. I pulled out my badge and showed it to him. "We'd like to talk to Corporal Noh's parents or to anyone who knew him well."

"We all knew him well."

The man's English was polished; I figured he dealt with foreigners often.

"We'd like to talk to someone who knew if he'd had any problems lately. Any arguments, any enemies. Especially up at the JSA."

"JSA?" the man said, not familiar with the military acronym.

"Panmunjom," I corrected.

He nodded. "Oh, yes." Then he looked at me, studying my face. "You are trying to find Jong-bei's killer?"

"Yes."

He nodded again. "I will see if my brother, Jong-bei's father, will talk to you."

He gestured toward a covered area with some stools and a metal table with an old radio sitting atop it. "Wait here. I will return."

Ernie sat down heavily on one of the three-legged stools. Pained crying continued to emerge from inside the large single-story home.

"They're rich," Ernie said.

"Yep. That's why they could afford to pay for their son to become a KATUSA."

Every able-bodied young man in the Republic of Korea is required to serve two and a half years in the military. No exceptions. Even the president's son had done his service. However, the system of under-the-table payments still thrived in Korea, and a wealthy family could pay to have their son assigned to a relatively cushy job rather than being part of the infantry tromping through the mud and snow on the DMZ and worrying about his throat being cut by a North Korean commando. Being designated a KATUSA, Korean Augmentation to the US Army, was considered one of the cushiest positions to be

in. Mainly because you were assigned to an American army
unit, and the barracks and other facilities were much more
comfortable than they were on the ROK Army compounds.
Also because a young KATUSA was under US Army discipline, which was less hard on soldiers than the unforgiving,
often torturous ROK Army discipline.

So the parents of Noh Jong-bei had paid to keep him safe.
But though they'd succeeded in landing him the best assignment, he'd still been brutally murdered.

The man who'd been talking to us, apparently Jong-bei's
uncle, returned with an older man at his side. He wore traditional mourning garb: hemp cloth trousers, a hemp cloth
tunic, and a peaked cap sewn with the same ragged material
atop his head. The man seemed weak, barely able to walk. But
the two of them hobbled resolutely toward us.

When they stopped in front of us, I was about to speak,
but the older man gasped out something in garbled Korean. I
didn't understand and looked to the man in the suit support-
ing him.

"When," he translated, "are we going to get the body?"

I shook my head. "I don't know. That's up to the coroner."

The younger man translated. Then the older man spoke
again. This time I understood.

"Then why are you here?"

I answered in Korean, trying to remember the verb endings I'd learned in the night classes I'd taken on base; the

deferential ones that showed respect for an older person. It felt unnatural compared to the verb endings used in the bars and brothels of the GI villages outside American army compounds, where I'd developed most of my conversational skills, but I did my best. I asked about his son's friends and enemies. And whether Noh Jong-bei had had any problems recently.

If I'd made any grammatical mistakes, or mistakes in decorum, they were overlooked. The old man studied me.

"My son had no enemies. He was a good boy, dedicated to his work in the army. He had no problems. He was always on time, always prepared to do his best."

I tried to formulate more questions, but something told me that all this man wanted to talk about—or hear—at this painful time was how wonderful his son had been. Faults and other imperfections were off the table. Three women walked quickly through the crowd in front of the house. They wore identical cotton gowns—in white, the Korean color of mourning. One of the women was more distraught than the others, her face red and slathered in drying tears.

"*Weigurei no-nun?*" she said, pointing her forefinger at me. What's the matter with you?

Apparently, she'd overheard the conversation. Even though the two women at her side tried to pull her away, she held fast and continued her tirade.

"You come to my home, asking if my son has done

something wrong? Asking if he has enemies? Why would you do this? How dare you bother us and call him names? You should be out there trying to catch the person who killed him. He was a good boy. A good boy. Do you understand?"

She broke free from the other women and lunged at me. Her sharp nails would've reached my face if it hadn't been for Jong-bei's uncle, who stepped between us and moved her aside at the last minute. She grabbed the lapels of his suit, clinging to him, barely standing and still screaming.

"*Weigureino-nun*?" she repeated. What's wrong with you?

Both of Corporal Noh's parents were pulled away by his uncle and the others in the crowd. Ernie and I stood there under the overhang, feeling awkward now.

"Any more bright ideas?" Ernie said out of the side of his mouth.

"No," I replied. "Let's go."

We walked back to the entrance of the compound and ducked through the gate. Without talking, we walked down the narrow lane. I wasn't sure how Ernie felt, but for me, it was as if I'd been rammed in the gut with a tire iron.

"Hey," Ernie said, "at least they didn't beat us up like the last guy."

We'd almost reached the bottom of the hill when footsteps clattered on flagstone steps behind us. Ernie and I turned.

It was a girl. Or rather, a young woman, either in her late teens or very early twenties. Tears streamed down her face.

"I'm sorry," she said in English. "About my parents. They are very sad."

"It's okay. I understand they're upset," I said.

She nodded vigorously. "Yes, upset."

Her black hair fell to her shoulders, longer than the short bob required of high school girls. So my first impression had been right—she'd been out of high school for maybe a couple years.

"I'm sorry about your brother," I said.

She bowed her head but didn't reply. Then she looked at me. "I have to talk to Teddy."

Ernie knew enough to keep quiet.

"An American?" I asked gently.

"Yes. He worked with Jong-bei. Up there." She glanced north toward the DMZ.

"Do you want me to have him call you?" I asked.

"No. My parents would be very upset." She stepped forward and handed me a sheet of lined notepaper tightly folded into the shape of a flower. "Please, give him this." She started to walk away.

"I don't know his name," I said.

She stopped and turned. "Teddy."

"His family name."

She paused for a moment and said, "Fusterman." And then she spelled it for me, pronouncing the F with two syllables— "epp-uh"—and the U like the "ooh" in *ooh and aah*.

"Your parents don't want you to see him?" I asked.

"No. They think Americans something bad." Then she looked at us, remembering who she was talking to, and her face flushed slightly red.

"I understand," I said. "And your brother, too, he didn't want you going out with Teddy?"

She saddened again at the mention of her brother but managed to say, "How do you know that?"

"Was your brother the one who brought Teddy here to your home?"

"Yes. Many times."

"But when he started seeing you, they argued."

"No. They don't argue. Jong-bei don't think it's bad. Only my parents."

"But your brother sided with your parents."

She lowered her head again. "Supposed to."

"Okay," I replied. "What's your name?"

"Marilyn."

Many Korean students adopted a Western name in their English conversation classes. Sometimes, they also used them outside of the classroom.

"Your Korean name?" I asked.

"You don't need."

"Okay," I said, slipping the note into my pocket. "I'll deliver this for you."

"When?"

"Maybe tonight." The truth was, I couldn't deliver it until the alert was over and maybe never, since Colonel Peele had barred us from the JSA. But I didn't tell her that.

She bowed slightly to both of us and turned and ran off.

Ernie let out a breath of air. "Cute."

"Yeah. Plenty cute enough to attract a JSA GI."

"And cute enough to fight over."

"I'll say. But cute enough to kill for?"

Ernie didn't answer. We hustled downhill to where we'd left the jeep.

By the time we made it back to the Main Supply Route and began fighting our way through midafternoon traffic, it seemed like everyone in Seoul was on the road. And that was when the air raid sirens sounded. From nowhere, civil defense cops in white uniforms appeared out of side alleys, driving white jeeps painted with red *hangul* lettering on the side. They set up road-blocks and waved off vehicles to the side of the road.

A civil defense alert. Everyone was supposed to get out of their cars and trucks and taxis and take cover in the under-ground shelters—or if you couldn't reach a shelter, any place that would provide protection from incoming enemy artillery. Reluctantly, Ernie pulled the jeep over, and after securing the steering wheel with the chain welded to the floorboard, we crouched against a brick wall bordering a small Catholic uni-versity.

"Is this a drill," Ernie asked, "or are we actually under attack?"

"A drill," I said. "If this were a real attack, the rounds would already be landing."

"Why'd they call this now?"

"The ROK government must be worried about what's happening at the JSA. They probably think the North Koreans will overreact. Who knows? I bet they're preparing for war up there."

Ernie nodded. I pulled out the note Corporal Noh's sister had given us.

In local Korean custom, folding a missive into an origami-like shape indicated that it was personal and not intended for anyone but the addressee. But this was no time for niceties; we couldn't afford to miss something important regarding Noh Jong-bei's murder to preserve the privacy of his lovestruck sister. Carefully, I unwrapped the note. It was written in English, a flowing cursive neater than my own. When I finished reading it, I handed it to Ernie. He glanced through it quickly. As he clumsily attempted to refold it, I took it from his hands.

"I'll ask Miss Kim to fix it for us." The CID Admin secretary was the only person who had a prayer of putting the note back into its original orchid shape.

"Are we going to deliver it to this guy Teddy," Ernie asked, "or are we just going to arrest him?"

I didn't answer. What we had was motive for murder.

Teddy Fusterman had been seeing Marilyn against her family's wishes. As the oldest and only son, it was Corporal Noh's filial duty to uphold his father's wishes. Confucian tradition still held in principle here, even if not always in practice. But if Corporal Noh had followed these dictates as a good son and tried to stop his sister from seeing Fusterman, that might've been enough to drive the guy into a rage. We'd have to sweat the young trooper and see if their disagreement had spiraled into an argument serious enough to lead to murder.

I reread the note.

At the bottom, Marilyn had drawn a happy face.

When the all-clear siren sounded, Ernie and I ran to the jeep, and with some very aggressive driving, he managed to make it about a mile along the road before traffic bogged us down again. A half-hour later, we reached Yongsan Compound. We pulled into the narrow parking lot next to the two-story brick building that housed the Criminal Investigation Detachment.

After turning off the engine, Ernie took a deep breath. "Prepare for heavy swells," he said.

"What are you, a swabbie?"

"I feel like one," he said, "in the middle of a typhoon."

Inside, Staff Sergeant Riley, the admin NCO, was waiting for us.

"Where the hell you guys *been*?"

Ernie ignored him and checked the coffee urn in back, which was unplugged, cold, and empty.

"We've been investigating," I told Riley.

"Is that what you call it?"

"Yeah," I replied. "What would you call it?"

"Goofing off. It doesn't take all day to question a few GIs about what they saw or didn't see."

Frustrated, Ernie returned from the dormant urn. "What the hell would a pencil-pusher like you know?" he asked.

"I know that those North Korean Commies murdered one of our KATUSAs, and by God, we're going to make them pay for it."

"Relax, tiger," Ernie said. "I'm sure the Great Leader is shaking in his boots."

Miss Kim, the statuesque admin secretary, stopped typing and looked up at me, worried. When Riley wasn't looking, she asked in a soft voice, "Was the young man murdered by the North Koreans?"

She, like the rest of the eight-million-plus people living in Seoul, was terrified by the prospect of another war breaking out. North Korean artillery along the Demilitarized Zone was powerful enough to reach not only the city limits, but into the heart of downtown Seoul itself. Over the years, the North Korean army had moved entire battalions of heavy weaponry into hidden mountain caves and beneath heavily fortified positions. By now, 8th Army analysts predicted that within the first few hours of an outbreak of hostilities, the capital city of Seoul would be engulfed in fire.

"*Kokjong hajima,*" I said, patting the back of her hand. Don't worry.

Then I showed her my notebook, dog-eared from a few cases' worth of bookmarking. "From what we've found, it's possible that Corporal Noh wasn't harmed by the North Koreans at all."

Her eyes were wide. "No?"

I shook my head.

"Then who?" But she caught herself and placed her fingertips to her mouth as if to retract the question. I pulled out the note Corporal Noh's sister had given us and asked Miss Kim if she could refold it. She did. Her long, deft fingers accomplished the task in under thirty seconds. It looked just as it had when Marilyn had handed it to me.

"Thanks," I said, slipping the note into my pocket.

I sat down at a field desk and started to type up my report.

"No time for that!" Riley shouted.

"What the hell are you talking about?" Ernie said. "All you ever do is nag Sueño for reports so you'll have more paper to push."

Riley bellowed at me. "You were supposed to have been over at the MAC headquarters two hours ago."

Ernie sauntered toward Riley's desk, grabbed the wrinkled copy of this morning's *Stars and Stripes*, and began searching for the sports page. "What do they want to talk to us for?" he asked, apparently having decided to mess with Riley a little.

"To chew your butts," Riley replied. "Now get over there and report to Colonel Peele. I'll call and let them know you're on your way."

"Does the Provost Marshal know about this?" I asked, joining in on Ernie's game.

"Of course he does."

"And he doesn't mind another officer telling off the men who work for him?"

Riley's eyes widened. "Why should he?"

I shrugged. "Just thought he might want to provide us a little protection so we can do our jobs without interference."

Riley scoffed. "Who the hell do you think you are? A reporter for the *Washington Post* or something?"

I hadn't actually thought our boss, Colonel Walter P. Brace, Provost Marshal of the 8th US Army, would stick his neck out to protect us in a situation like this. In the army, everything was a power play. This was usually based on rank, but almost as often on who in the broader power structure you were connected to. The Military Armistice Commission had a direct line to Washington, DC. The conundrums they ran into when negotiating with the North Korean government were addressed not only by the Secretary of Defense, but sometimes the president himself.

Nobody messed with the MAC. And if a couple of

low-ranking enlisted men had to be sacrificed on their altar, so be it.

"Relax, Riley," Ernie said, snapping the paper open to the comics. "We've already had our butts reamed."

"You've already been to the MAC?"

"What'd I just say?"

Interrupting, I asked Riley to call his buddy Smitty over at 8th Army Personnel and check whether there was a Teddy Fusterman assigned to the JSA security unit.

"Why should I?"

"Because I'm asking nicely."

Riley always acted as if Ernie and I were a couple of screwups. But the truth was, he respected our work. And he knew that unlike the other CID agents, who only handled cases on base, we could roam around outside the walls of the US military compounds and get results, something no other investigators in country could claim. I was the only American law enforcement officer in 8th Army who spoke Korean, and Ernie had a knack for mingling with the lowest of the low and earning their trust. Staff Sergeant Riley also knew from experience that when we went after a criminal, we never gave up.

He lifted the phone and dialed.

After he got through, Riley waited on the line while Smitty looked up the requested information for him. Thirty seconds later, he started jotting furiously on a notepad, thanked Smitty, and read off the intel to me.

"Fusterman, Theodore H, Private First Class, Infantry. He's been in the army a little over a year and assigned to the Joint Security Area for almost six months."

"Thanks, Riley."

I also asked him to look up Fusterman's ration control records. He grumbled but placed a call to his contact over in 8th Army Data Processing. As he waited again to be transferred, he covered the receiver and said, "Anything else I can get for you? A new Corvette?"

"No," I said. "That'll be plenty."

Somebody came back on the other end of the line. Riley listened and mumbled a couple words of affirmation, then told the number cruncher that this was top secret and the guy needed to keep this request under his hat, but the information had something to do with the incident up at the JSA. By now, everyone on compound had heard about it. Finally, Riley said thanks and hung up.

"He'll try to have the printout for me by tomorrow, even if it means he has to work late tonight."

So we weren't the only GIs who were nervous about seven North Korean divisions being mobilized just thirty miles north of Seoul.

-6-

When the seventeen-hundred close-of-business canon went off, I waited for the office to empty out, something I occasionally did. I liked being in the office alone. It gave me a moment of peace. I didn't mind coming in early in the morning, which was also a quiet time, but Riley was often in early too, and there went my calm. But at close of business, Riley usually didn't stick around long. During the last few hours of the workday, he could already hear the siren call of the bottle of Old Overholt lounging seductively between the folded cotton drawers and rolled T-shirts in his footlocker in the barracks.

Finally, with everyone gone, I could hear only the low hiss of the ancient steam radiators that lined the hallway.

I sat down at my favorite Olivetti typewriter and rolled in a sheet of white paper and two carbon onionskins, a green and a pink. The green copy for the CID files, the pink copy for the accordion file folder I kept in my wall locker. I started typing. Remembering that morning, reproducing it in as much detail as I could muster. I wrote of us being ordered to the Joint Security Area, meeting Lieutenant Colonel Brunmeyer there, seeing the body, our confrontation with the North Korean army, and the subsequent area-wide alert. But I left out the part about me and Ernie dragging the corpse back to the south.

I pictured the wound to the back of Corporal Noh's skull and described it. Deep, as if he'd been split open with an axe, but by something with a longer blade. I wasn't sure if Ernie had thought of the same thing when he'd first looked at the cracked bone and oozing brain matter, but I had. An item that every GI was issued in his field equipment: an entrenching tool. Civilians would call it a shovel; short-handled, with a metal blade capable of being folded over so it fit more easily into a canvas sheath. Entrenching tools are heavy, sturdy, and made to be used by troops to claw out a foxhole in the middle of a battle. The edge of the iron shovel itself was about twice as long as the cutting edge of an axe. In the part of the report reserved for planned actions, I typed: *Finding and examining Private Teddy Fusterman's entrenching tool.* Even if he'd cleaned it, lab techs might be able to find traces of blood; if it had once been there.

I wanted to look at Corporal Noh's body again. I made a note to do that first thing in the morning. It was at the Eighth Army Morgue now, but would soon be turned over to the ROK Army and then to the Noh family in Inui-dong.

Eventually, it would be taken to what the bar girls in the GI villages called Happy Mountain. A burial mound atop a hill. Graveyards in Korea were in elevated areas, the fertile valleys below reserved for agriculture.

It was stupid to speculate, in writing, about the entrenching tool. Telling the US Army what you're thinking or planning to do was never a good idea. Somehow, they'd turn it back on you like a weapon.

When I finished the report, I dropped it with the green file copy attached into Staff Sergeant Riley's inbox. The pink copy I kept in my coat pocket as I trudged uphill in the dark toward the barracks.

First thing in the morning, Ernie and I stopped by the 8th Army Morgue.

At the front counter, a clerk checked his clipboard. "Noh Jong-bei," he repeated. "Corporal." Then he stopped riffling through the paper and looked up at us. "The KATUSA," he said, "the one from the JSA."

"Yeah. That's him."

"The ROK Army took his body last night."

"That quick?"

The clerk shrugged. "High priority. That's what they told us."

"Where did they take it?"

He shrugged again. "To their morgue."

"Where's that?"

"Hell if I know."

We continued to bother him until he checked with one of the civilian morticians in the back. He returned and told us, "ROK Army headquarters. Just down the road, across from the Ministry of National Defense."

We thanked him and left.

The ROK Army denied us permission to view the body. We argued with them for almost half an hour but in the end the only promise they made was to forward black-and-white photographs along with the autopsy report.

Out in the parking lot, Ernie said, "*Mox nix.*"

"Doesn't mean nothing? Why?"

"When you mentioned this morning that it looked like a wound from an entrenching tool, I realized you were right. What else would they have up there at the JSA that could cause a wound like that?"

"Still, it would be nice to examine the body more closely. See if there's anything like chipped paint or splintered wood that could help us match it to an entrenching tool."

"The autopsy guys are supposed to do that."

"I hope so."

"Better," Ernie said, "to find Noh's blood type on Teddy's shovel."

"That would be good."

"So let's go up to the JSA. Go through his field gear. We have to question him anyway."

"But Colonel Peele told us the JSA was off-limits."

"Screw him."

When we returned to Yongsan Compound, we noticed that there were fewer armed MPs at Gate Five. As we were about to be waved through, Ernie slowed and talked to the guard.

"Where's all your backup?" he asked.

"Gone. The alert was called off."

"When?"

"About twenty minutes ago."

"No more crisis up at the JSA?"

"So they tell me."

Ernie waved in acknowledgment, and we rolled through the gate and past the two-story redbrick buildings of the 8th Army headquarters complex.

"Odd," I said.

"What?"

"Peele said he planned to keep the pressure on the North Koreans, at least until the next MAC meeting, by blaming them for Noh's murder. That meant he was supposed to keep our side on combat alert."

"Yeah," Ernie said. "Maybe he was overruled."

"I don't think so. Not by the MAC. Squaring off with the North Koreans is the reason the US Army is here in Korea in the first place."

"Keeping the pressure on like that could literally blow up in everyone's face."

"Maybe," I said. "But I don't think Peele gives a damn. You saw how he acted when he talked about the North Koreans."

"He practically popped a valve. Hates them almost as much as he hates us enlisted pukes. So there must be another reason Eighth Army pulled the plug on the alert."

"Yeah."

"Like what?"

"I'm not sure." But I was worried about it.

At the CID office, Riley waved us over as soon as we walked in the door. "The Colonel has another job for you."

He was referring to Colonel Brace, our boss and the Provost Marshal of the 8th United States Army.

"What job?" Ernie asked. "You have something more important than the murder of a soldier at the Joint Security Area?"

"If the Colonel says it's more important, then it's more important."

"Like what?"

"Like this." Riley tossed a handwritten note toward Ernie. Ernie glanced at it but then handed it to me. "I can't read this chicken scratch."

The writing was indeed barely legible. It said something about "I can't take it anymore," and "Take care of Jenny."

"What's this bullshit have to do with us?" Ernie asked.

"Missing person. Evelyn Cresthill. Wife of Major Bob Cresthill, Army Corps of Engineers."

"Bob?" Ernie asked sarcastically. "You know this 'Bob' personally?"

"I don't. But Colonel Brace does. He wants this kept off the books. Mrs. Cresthill disappeared. He wants you two to talk to Major Cresthill and then go find her. ASAP."

"Sorry," Ernie said. "As much as I'd love to, we're all booked up. We have to go to the JSA."

"To check Fusterman's entrenching tool?" Riley asked.

Ernie froze, for once allowing himself to show surprise. "How'd you know about that?"

Riley glanced at me. Ernie stared at me also.

"I mentioned it in my report," I said.

Ernie turned back to Riley. "What the hell did you do?"

"Nothing," Riley said. "I turned the report in to Colonel Brace. He called the Eighth Army Chief of Staff and then he called the MAC, talked to Colonel Peele."

Now I knew why the alert had been called off. Once 8th Army believed that someone other than the North Koreans might've been guilty of the murder of Corporal Noh Jong-bei, the flame beneath the boiling pot of water could be lowered. Colonel Peele's rationale for keeping a heightened alert status along the DMZ—that the North Koreans had murdered a KATUSA—was gone. Not completely. The guilt of Private Fusterman had yet to be proven—far from it—but just the possibility was enough for the 8th Army Commander to overrule the MAC and lower the level of tension at the Joint Security Area.

"Next thing I knew," Riley continued, "two JAG officers are on their way to the JSA, to interview this Private Fusterman and to check his field gear for an entrenching tool."

"The yes-men at the Judge Advocate General's office," Ernie said. "They've taken our case from us."

"They've *elevated* it," Riley corrected. "The honchos will be handling it from now on."

"And making sure," Ernie told him, "that nobody in the chain-of-command is embarrassed."

"Which is something you two guys don't usually give a shit about." Riley tossed a memo he was holding into his out-basket. Then he said, "And another benefit of the Judge Advocate General taking over the case is that the North Koreans are no longer being accused of murder."

"That's why the alert was called off," Ernie said. "They're assuming, without having proved *anything*, that this guy Fusterman is guilty."

"Hey," Riley said, shrugging his narrow shoulders. "Better for everybody."

"Except for Colonel Peele," I said.

Riley chuckled. "Yeah. He's pissed to the max."

Ernie wanted to barge into Colonel Brace's office and confront him about being pulled off the JSA case. I grabbed his elbow and pulled him into the hallway, out of earshot of Sergeant Riley. "If we confront the Provost Marshal now," I said, "he'll probably comply with Colonel Peele's wishes and pull us off the case, officially, in writing. First, before they have a chance to do that, let's look around on our own."

"Look around for what?"

"To make sure these JAG officers accuse the right person."

"They don't want it to be a North Korean," Ernie said. "Less trouble if the killer is a GI. They can court-martial him, send him to Leavenworth, and close the book on the whole thing."

"Maybe the killer *is* a GI," I said. "But we'll be on their butts. Raise hell if something seems wrong."

"I don't like it," Ernie said.

"Neither do I. But searching for a missing wife could take us anywhere—and give us time to do whatever we want."

"Yeah," Ernie said, calming down, seeing the possibilities. "Anywhere." He grabbed the chicken-scratch note back from me. "So what's she look like, anyway?"

Major Bob Cresthill wasn't at the office of the 8th Army Corps of Engineers. A helpful secretary told us he was at a construction site near Soyang Lake.

"Where the hell's that?" Ernie asked.

The secretary was a middle-aged American woman, almost certainly married to an officer or enlisted service member and working this job to supplement the family income. She walked us over to a map of South Korea that covered the entire wall. It was dotted with some red pins, a few green ones, and a lot of blue ones. "The red pins are sites where we're actively building roads, bridges, dams, canals or other types of infrastructure. This one's on the Soyang River."

The US government had contributed to the rebuilding of South Korean infrastructure since the end of the Korean War. Part of that was in order to facilitate military operations. Without good roads, bridges, and dams in place to prevent seasonal flooding, the Army would become bogged down, which would hurt us tactically since one of our biggest advantages over the Korean People's Army was mobility. It was also thought that good infrastructure would bolster the South Korean economy, thereby strengthening the position of one of our most dedicated allies in the fight against international Communism. South Korea was so aligned with us, in fact, that they'd sent two infantry divisions to assist in the Vietnam War—a total of 50,000 soldiers in country at any time. And those soldiers saw plenty of combat and suffered mass casualties. This made US politicians happy, since Korean boys dying instead of American ones eased their paths to reelection.

I studied the map. The construction site was on the western slopes of the Taebaek Mountains, northeast of Seoul by about forty miles.

"Near Chuncheon?" I said.

"Yes. There's been periodic flooding in the Chuncheon

area. The Soyang River dam project should help to alleviate that."

"And protect the tactical missiles we have at Camp Page." An 8th Army antiaircraft artillery and helicopter base located near the city limits of Chuncheon.

"I wouldn't know about that," she said.

"Does Major Cresthill drive back to Seoul at night?"

"No. I don't believe so. They have temporary quarters up at Camp Page, at least for the next few days."

"No wonder his wife left him," Ernie said.

The secretary flushed red, turned away, and looked back at us, angry now. "Is there anything else I can help you with?" she said curtly.

"That should do it," Ernie replied. He doffed an imaginary hat, and we walked out of the office and down the long corridor.

The drive to Camp Page in Chuncheon took less than two hours. It was easy to find, with ample road signage guiding us. Once we arrived, our first objective was to locate the construction site along the Soyang River. On base, we drove to the 8th Army Engineers temporary office and asked for assistance. The NCO in charge was Sergeant First Class Bonneville, a big man with a bushy mustache. We explained that Major Cresthill had requested our assistance and we were there to talk to him.

"I'm transporting noon chow right now. Lend a hand and I'll give you a lift."

We did. He backed his three-quarter-ton truck to the loading dock behind the Camp Page Dining Facility. While Sergeant Bonneville signed a hand receipt for the storage and serving equipment, Ernie and I tossed a stainless steel urn of coffee and a pair of Mermite hot-food containers into the back of the vehicle. On strips of masking tape, one container was marked BEEF STEW and the other RICE.

"Creative menu," Ernie said.

"Three Michelin stars," I agreed.

It was a rocky ride into the mountains, but after sliding around a few corners slick with mud, Sergeant Bonneville got us there in one piece. Apparently, the engineers were working on some sort of drainage channel to divert excess river water. Over the edge of a nearby cliff, the view of the valley stretched to the city of Chuncheon, which floated eerily in a distant mist.

"If I didn't know Chuncheon was full of bars and whorehouses," Ernie said, "I'd almost say it looked enchanting."

Somebody had told Major Cresthill we were looking for him. He approached and shook our hands.

"Sorry about the mud," he said, pointing to the dried crust on his fingers. "Coffee?" he offered.

"That'd be good."

In the mess tent, we poured lukewarm java into paper cups. Then Major Cresthill led us toward a larger engineering tent. He wore fatigues and a fur-lined cap with the earflaps tied above his head. The top of a set of thermal long johns peeked up beneath the collar of his army-issue fatigues. He dropped heavily into a canvas chair and we sat opposite him.

"Thank you for responding so quickly," he said.

Normally, a missing person's case—one involving the missing Korean wife of an enlisted man, for example—would be handled by the Military Police, not the Criminal Investigation Division. And the MPs did pretty much nothing more than file the report and order subordinate units to notify them if the missing person, or their corpse, turned up. I didn't bother telling Major Cresthill that his status as a fellow field-grade officer had led Colonel Brace to prioritize his case. Officers liked to believe they weren't receiving special treatment.

Cresthill was average height—about five-foot-nine or -ten—but his face seemed small, as if he'd reached adolescence and his bone structure hadn't changed since. He was probably best described as "cute," with curly black hair falling over blue eyes. The kind of "cute" that might work well with women, but earned you less respect among military men. His eyes darted away as I analyzed him, as if sensing this disadvantage.

"I won't waste your time," Cresthill said. "My wife and I have had our difficulties. Back in the States, she was always busy. Working full-time. And her parents lived nearby, close enough that she could drive to see them on weekends."

"You're command-sponsored," Ernie said.

Meaning the army had paid for him to bring his family to

Korea. A prime benefit, with tens of thousands of enlisted men stationed near the DMZ on "unaccompanied tours," meaning that not only had they not been allowed to bring their families, they couldn't ship over a car or even a household pet.

"Yes. We share a duplex on south post. Comfortable quarters, and my wife seemed happy with them at first. My daughter Jenny is attending Seoul American Elementary School."

"How old is Jenny?" I pulled out my notebook and started jotting down details.

"Ten," he replied. "She's in the fifth grade."

"So what went wrong?" Ernie asked.

"My wife couldn't find work," Cresthill said. "The Civilian Personnel Office said they had a few positions open, but they were all secretarial. Filing clerk, receptionist, things like that. Evelyn—my wife—didn't want to accept the downgrade. Back in Texas, she was a frontline manager in marketing and sales. Making good money, used to being in charge. She didn't want to take orders from some uneducated bozo or get pawed at by a lonely officer far from home."

Cresthill glanced toward the sound of workmen's hammers on the cliff below.

"A lot of women go into charity work," I said, "with the Officers' Wives Club."

"She hates the military social whirl, the one-upmanship. The way some of the wives wear their husband's rank on their collars."

"Overall," I said, "it sounds like she's not too happy with the life of a military dependent."

"She's not," he said. "And she hates these field deployments." He spread his fingers at the encampment around us. "Too much time apart."

This was a familiar tale of woe to me and Ernie. We both sat silent, waiting for him to go on.

"She started going out. To the Officers Club. She'd get all dolled up and be there by happy hour. She would leave Jenny with one of the neighbors who had a daughter in the same class." He gave me the name of the neighbor, which I wrote down. "Then the O'Club became too small for her. She started going out somewhere off base."

"Do you know where?"

He shook his head. "No. All I know is that there was some Korean woman who used to go to the O'Club regularly. About Evelyn's age, someone said. They'd sit together and chat and laugh and eventually go off somewhere together."

"In a PX taxi?" I asked. The ones that wait outside the front of the club.

"I'm not sure," he replied. "I guess so." I made another note. "After Evelyn found her new friend, she stopped going to the O'Club altogether. She'd just leave home without a word."

"Do you think she was meeting this same woman?"

"Maybe. I'm not sure."

It figured that if an American woman decided to venture

into the city nightlife of Seoul, which was vast and varied, she would need either a male escort or a female guide. She wouldn't know where to go on her own, especially if she didn't read or write or speak Korean. Ending up at the wrong joint could be dangerous. Mobsters frequented and sometimes owned the nightclubs, and they weren't known for their chivalry.

"This Korean woman who befriended Evelyn, do you know her name?"

He shook his head again.

"So who told you about her?"

"Quincy."

"Who?"

"Randy Quincy. Captain. He's the CO of the Honor Guard and seems to spend about half his life over at the Officers Club. Somebody told me they'd seen him talking to my wife, so I confronted him." I nodded and kept writing. Then I paused, which seemed to spur Major Cresthill on. "He's a known womanizer. Hits on the nurses from the One-Two-One hard, I'm told."

The 121st Evacuation Hospital, located just a few hundred yards from the 8th Army Officers Club.

"What'd he tell you?"

"He claimed he'd never had anything to do with Evelyn. That he was just being polite, seeing a woman alone and all. Once she'd made friends with the Korean woman, he let her be."

"And then she disappeared?"

"Yes. You saw the note."

I pulled it out of my right pocket. "It's sort of incoherent."

"I thought so."

"Is she on prescription drugs?"

"I'm not sure."

"But she could be?"

"When I get home, I'll search our medicine cabinet."

I didn't tell him not to bother. If she was hooked on uppers or downers, she would've taken them with her. I made a note to check with the medicos over at the 121.

"So when did she disappear?" Ernie asked.

We pinned down the time. Major Cresthill had gone to work as normal three days ago, and when he'd come home that night, she was gone.

"And this note was on the table?"

"Yes."

"Who's taking care of Jenny now?"

"The same neighbor."

I made a note to talk to her. And to Jenny.

"When are you leaving Camp Page?" I asked.

"We wrap up this afternoon. After that, I'll go pick up Jenny and head straight home."

He gave me his quarters address and phone number.

"Anything you want to add?" Ernie said.

Cresthill shook his head negatively.

"Don't give this a lot of thought," I said. "Just say the first thing that comes to mind. If you were to go looking for Evelyn right now, where would you go?"

"The BOQ of Captain Randy Quincy."

In military parlance, BOQ meant Bachelor Officer Quarters.

"And if you found her there?" Ernie asked.

"I'd murder the son of a bitch," Cresthill said.

We both leaned back, surprised. Ernie asked, "You'd murder Quincy?"

Major Cresthill nodded, a grim expression on his face. Then he seemed to come to his senses, looked at the two of us and said, "Well, you asked me for the first thing that came to mind."

-7-

When we walked through the door of the CID office, Riley said nothing and kept busy with his pile of paperwork. Miss Kim similarly ignored us, pecking industriously away at her *hangul* typewriter.

Something was up. Ernie sensed it too. He sat down in front of Riley's desk.

"What happened?" he asked.

"What?" Riley looked up suddenly as if surprised to see us.

"What happened when the JAG officers went north to question Fusterman at the JSA?"

"Nothing." His voice rose at the end.

"Not nothing," Ernie persisted. "Come on, you can tell me. I won't slap the shit out of you. Probably not, anyway."

Riley shoved the stack of paperwork to his side, sighed, and looked at Ernie.

"They arrested him."

"Fusterman?"

"Yeah. They found his entrenching tool hidden behind his wall locker. It has stains on it that look like blood."

"But they can't be sure."

"Which is why they packaged it up and are sending it off to Camp Zama for analysis."

"Did Fusterman sing?"

"No. He denied everything. Even said it wasn't his entrenching tool. The JAG officer read him his rights and a couple of MPs arrested him. They've already transported him to ASCOM."

ASCOM is the military acronym for the Army Support Command, a logistical base southwest of Seoul near the city of Bupyong. It was where 8th Army housed its stockade.

"Do you have a copy of Fusterman's statement?"

"Not yet. JAG is working on it, but according to them, he didn't say much."

"Smart guy."

"I'll say."

"Has anybody notified the Noh family of the arrest?"

Riley shrugged. "I don't know. You'd have to ask the ROKs about that. They're responsible for notification."

"What does the Provost Marshal think?" Ernie asked.

Riley lowered his voice. "I think Colonel Brace is relieved."

"Because Noh wasn't murdered by a North Korean?"

"Yeah. And now the Eighth Army Chief of Staff has the MAC under control."

"Convenient," Ernie said.

"Yeah. Except Colonel Peele is still claiming the North Koreans did it. He wanted to keep the pressure on the NKs for negotiating purposes, and he blames you two for muddying the waters."

"That's what we're here for," Ernie replied. "To stir shit up."

Riley pointedly grabbed his pen and returned to his paperwork. I said nothing. Ernie looked at me and raised an eyebrow, as if to ask, "What now?"

I jerked my head to the southwest, toward ASCOM.

Ernie nodded, and without further conversation, we got up and left. For once, Riley didn't ask where we were going, probably because he didn't want to know.

As far as 8th Army was concerned, everything was going fine: a crisis had been defused, a bullet dodged. The only flies in the ointment were a recalcitrant Teddy Fusterman, who wouldn't confess to the murder of Corporal Noh Jong-bei, and two notoriously uncooperative criminal investigators. Namely, me and Ernie Bascom. Plus a colonel at the Military Armistice Commission named Peele.

A half-hour later, we walked toward a ten-foot-high chain-link fence topped with coiled razor wire. After checking our identification, an MP pulled back a gate and let us through. Across a narrow courtyard, a metal door led into a cement-block building, where we walked down a tiled hallway until we reached a room marked

INTERROGATION. Inside, there was a long table separated by dividers. We sat down.

Five minutes later, an armed MP led in the shackled Private First Class Theodore H. Fusterman from a different door and shoved him into the chair opposite us.

His blond crewcut was so closely cropped that splotches of pink shone from the side of his scalp. His eyes were wide and blinking, throat pulsing as if he were about to start crying. Knotted fists sat in his lap, with metal bracelets welded to an iron chain that looped toward his ankles.

"Who are you?" he asked suspiciously.

I showed him my badge and introduced Ernie. Without further preamble, I slid the orchid-shaped note across the counter. He stared at it, helpless with his hands shackled.

"Do you want me to open it for you?"

He nodded. I unraveled the note, flattened it with my palm, and slid it to his edge of the counter. He leaned forward and read it.

"It's from Marilyn," he said, seeming to soften upon seeing the name of Corporal Noh Jong-bei's younger sister.

"You were seeing her?" I said.

He lowered his head, as if in shame.

"Tell us about what happened," I prodded.

"At work, up at the JSA, No-Go and I hit it off." He glanced up at us. "That's Corporal Noh." We nodded. "He reminded me of a friend I had in high school. Always smiling and joking around and laughing. At least he was when we were off duty, when we weren't being stared at by those North Korean guards. He invited me down to his house in Seoul. I went. I met his parents and they served me Korean food. Kimchi and everything, the first time I'd ever had it. You know, sitting on flat cushions around the low table, me fumbling with chopsticks. That's when I met Marilyn. She showed me how to use chopsticks. She liked practicing her English with me, and her parents approved—at first. But when we started going out alone, without No-Go, they ordered her to stop seeing me."

Fusterman glanced around the room. The MP had left, but the shadow of his helmeted head occasionally appeared through the reinforced window in the door.

"Mostly we stopped," he continued. "I didn't want any hassles with No-Go or with his family. But then she called me."

"At the JSA?"

"Yeah. Must've taken her an hour to get through from the Korean telephone exchange to the military one. But a call came through to the Orderly Room at Camp Kitty Hawk, and the CQ runner came and found me. I was worried something had happened, but she just said she wanted to see me." Fusterman shrugged. "I said okay. After that, we saw each other every time I got an overnight."

An overnight pass, which had to be approved by both his squad leader and company commander.

"You signed out on the overnights and took the bus to Seoul?"

He nodded.

"Where'd you meet?"

"At first at a teahouse near her family's home, but she said that was too dangerous—somebody might recognize her. So we switched to a Korean inn near Mia-ri."

"The army bus runs through there."

"Right. There's a stop right by the inn, which was why we chose it."

"What then?"

Fusterman looked down. "No-Go found out. He was really angry, demanded that I stop seeing her. I felt guilty for causing trouble. I loved her, but I didn't want to cause rifts within the family. Or to hurt our mission here at the JSA." He paused, realizing his mistake. "I mean up there."

"So you stopped seeing her?"

"Sort of."

"What do you mean?"

"I stopped seeing her for almost a month. And then, maybe a week ago, she called again."

"And you met again in Mia-ri?"

"Yes."

"Did Corporal Noh find out?"

"I think he did. He wouldn't look at me or talk to me."

"Did you argue?"

"No."

"Did you kill him?"

"*No!*"

"Then who did?"

"The freaking North Koreans. Who else?"

"Did you see anything?"

"No. I was in the barracks the night he was killed. Asleep."

"According to that note," Ernie said, "Marilyn wants you to meet her tonight at the usual place."

"Yeah."

"What's the name of the inn?"

"I'm not sure, it was written in Korean. But I'd know it if I saw it."

"Describe it to us."

"At the Mia-ri bus stop, I'd get off and walk about two blocks east. Then I'd take a left, and about fifty yards up on the right side of the road, there was a neon sign with mermaids swimming in water."

"A public bathhouse."

"Yeah. Above that, there were rooms. That's where we stayed."

"Did you take baths together?" Ernie asked.

Fusterman flushed red. "Why's that important?"

Ernie shrugged.

"Yes," Fusterman said. "As a matter of fact, we did. She scrubbed me with one of those rough pads, and black stuff came out."

"*Ddei,*" I said.

"What?"

"Dirt and oil emerging from the pores of the skin. In Korean, it's called *ddei*."

"Yeah, that. Marilyn told me that Americans were never clean, but she'd keep me clean."

"That's nice of her," Ernie said.

Fusterman wasn't sure whether or not to be offended.

"You told JAG the entrenching tool they found wasn't yours," I said. "How do you know?"

"They showed it to me. I'd scratched my initials on the wooden handle right below the knob that adjusts the blade, but they weren't there."

"What'd they say?"

"Well, I'm in here, so they didn't believe me."

"So somebody stole your entrenching tool and replaced it? Possibly with one that's got bloodstains all over it."

"That's what happened."

"Who do you think made the switch?" Ernie asked.

"Hell if I know," Fusterman replied.

"Someone who hates you," Ernie said.

"Yeah, I already figured that part out."

"So who hates you?"

"Other than Corporal Noh, nobody. And he's gone now."

Without warning, Fusterman began to cry. Ernie reached over and tapped him lightly, almost tenderly, on the cheek. "No time for that," Ernie said. "JAG's gonna railroad you if we don't come up with an alternative theory for the murder."

"Not an alternative theory," Fusterman said, pulling himself away from Ernie. "The *truth*. I didn't murder No-Go."

"Okay," Ernie continued. "So tell us who did."

"I told you, I don't *know*."

"You have to give us something, Fusterman," I said. "You lived up there, you pulled duty with him, you knew what was going on. You must have some idea of what happened."

Private First Class Theodore H. Fusterman's head lolled on his neck. "There is one thing," he said. He glanced around the barren room. "I don't know if this has to do with anything, but I mentioned that No-Go was a happy-go-lucky guy. Or at least he was, until he met me. He was a talker. And somehow he started chatting with the officer in charge of the night shift, the one on the North Korean side."

"Junior Lieutenant Kwon?" I asked.

"Yeah, him. I don't know how it happened. We were out there on a quiet night, nothing much going on, and at first it was taunts, you know, back and forth, and then all of a sudden they were talking about soccer. North Korea had played an international game somewhere and No-Go knew about it. The North Koreans lost because of a bad call, and both No-Go and Lieutenant Kwon agreed that since the referee was a foreigner, he probably had it in for Koreans."

"How'd you know what they were talking about?" Ernie asked. "You don't speak Korean."

"No-Go told me later."

"Was that it? The only time?"

"No. There were others, and word got around that No-Go could talk to the North Koreans. We weren't supposed to, but there it was."

"Do you think No-Go talked to Junior Lieutenant Kwon when he was posted alone?"

Fusterman shrugged. "How would I know?"

"But he never said anything about it?"

"No. When he told me the first time and word got around, I think he was embarrassed."

"Or maybe he was afraid he'd get in trouble."

"Yeah. Anyway, he kept quiet about it after that. And when Marilyn and I started seeing each other, No-Go and I drifted apart."

The MP came in. "Time," he said.

"We want five more minutes," Ernie said.

"Talk to the Confinement Officer. As of now, this boy goes."

He grabbed Teddy Fusterman by the collar, yanked him to his feet, and dragged him from the room. As they exited, Ernie said, "Demand a lawyer! And only talk to him. No one else."

After the door slammed shut, I raised an eyebrow at Ernie.

He stiffened. "Hey," he said. "Somebody had to tell the poor slob what to do."

"We're supposed to be on Eighth Army's side," I said.

"Since when?" Ernie asked.

"Since they appointed us as Criminal Investigation agents."

Ernie rose from his seat. "I must've missed that part."

Sometimes, I missed it too.

We made our way through the cement catacombs, and once outside, both of us breathed in the air of freedom deeply.

"Riley says we'll end up in there someday," Ernie told me, "if we keep going the way we're going."

"He might be right."

We climbed in the jeep. Ernie turned to me and said, "What do you think?"

I lifted the clipboard that held our emergency dispatch and idly thumbed through the four sheets of onionskin. "I think we need to talk to Junior Lieutenant Kwon."

"No *way*. Colonel Peele would have our butts skinned alive if we went back up to the JSA."

I slipped the dispatch between the canvas-covered seats. "Kwon's a material witness," I said. "He knew Corporal Noh, they used to talk, and he was on duty on the night of the murder."

"If we go up there," Ernie said, "we're as good as making sure Riley's prediction comes true. They *will* throw us in the stockade."

"We have to figure out a way," I said.

"Like what?"

"I'm working on that."

"Take your time," Ernie said, starting the jeep. "I'm in no hurry."

-8-

The 8th Army Honor Guard was an infantry unit with two missions. The first was to protect Yongsan Compound and 8th Army headquarters, should they ever come under enemy attack. The second was to represent the US Army in the numerous ceremonies and parades held for the United Nations Command, the Republic of Korea, and of course, the United States Forces Korea. As such, Honor Guard soldiers had to keep their shoes shined, their brass polished, their uniforms perfectly pressed, and their hair cut so short it was barely more than stubble. They had to spend hours a day practicing marching and drilling and twirling their rifles in the air, all in synchronized precision. In other words, it took a lot of hard work and discipline. But to see the Bachelor Officer Quarters of Captain Randy Quincy, the Commanding Officer of the Honor Guard Company, was to see chaos. Clothes were strewn everywhere, along with ashtrays and chewed cigar butts and nearly empty pints and fifths of liquor, from Old Grand-Dad to Gilbey's Gin with just about everything in between.

"What the hell do you want?" he asked, tilting on the back legs of a wooden chair, hairy legs propped atop a half-sized refrigerator. He wore beige shorts and an old football jersey from Texas A&M.

I showed him my badge.

"You going to read me my rights?" he asked.

"Are you guilty of something?"

"You name it," he said, puffing a lit cigar, "I'm guilty of it."

"Evelyn Cresthill," I said.

He blew smoke and started coughing. "Her again." He slid his feet off the refrigerator and the chair plunked down as he turned to face us. "Did her old man send you?"

"She's missing," Ernie said.

Quincy studied Ernie, holding his cigar between two fingers a foot from his ear. The smooth flesh of his forehead wrinkled. "Missing?" he asked.

"No one's heard from her for three days."

Quincy turned away and sighed. "Not good," he said.

"No," Ernie agreed.

Quincy regained his composure and asked, "You guys track down dependents, too?"

"Sometimes," I said. "How did you meet her?"

"She was sitting at a cocktail table at the O'Club. Alone. She looked unhappy. I don't like that. I like to see women happy. So I sat down."

"Did you succeed in making her happy?"

"You better believe I did."

"Did you bring her back here?"

"Wait a minute." Quincy flicked ash from his cigar into an old tin can. "You guys seriously expect me to admit to the crime of adultery? With a fellow officer's wife? Are you nuts?"

According to the Uniform Code of Military Justice, adultery is a court-martial offense.

"I didn't say anything about adultery," I said. "All I asked was, did she come in here?" I indicated the small room that surrounded us.

"Would a gentleman bring a lady into a dump like this?"

"I don't know. Would you?"

"If I were going to do such a thing—and that's *if*, mind you—I'd be more inclined to take her off post somewhere. Like maybe the Tower Hotel. Or if I was flush with cash right after payday, maybe the Cosmos Hotel downtown."

"So?" Ernie asked.

"So what?"

"Did you take Evelyn Cresthill to the Tower Hotel or to the Cosmos Hotel?"

He spread the fingertips of his left hand across the center of his chest. "What? Do I look like an adulterer?"

"What does an adulterer look like?"

"You got me."

Quincy re-lit his cigar. Once he had it going, he lowered his voice, suddenly serious. "The last time I saw her was three days ago. At the Officers Club. I didn't speak to her. She was busy talking to that Korean broad who's been showing up in the last few weeks."

"What Korean broad?"

"I don't know her. Not my type." He paused for a moment and said, "Not bad-looking, though."

"What's her name?"

"Don't know that either. But the Korean staff treats her like a little sister. She has a nice smile and makes them laugh, and the younger waitresses seem fascinated by her fancy hair and makeup."

"Like a fashion model?" Ernie asked.

"Yeah. Sort of like that."

"What's she up to?"

Quincy puffed on his cigar. "Well, the usual routine is to get somebody to escort you on base, and then sign you in at the O'Club and from there you catch the attention of a horny officer and either spend the night with him in his quarters or off base in a hotel. You know, make an honest buck. But actually, I didn't see her doing that. She was sort of innocent-like. Like she was just there because of the excitement of being in a nice place."

"How'd she become friends with Evelyn Cresthill?" I asked.

"I don't know exactly, but they were two unescorted women. There are a few of those in the O'Club, but women mostly arrive in groups. Like the nurses."

"I hear you're popular at the One-Two-One."

"My picture's hanging in the employees' lounge."

"That's nice. So, these two unescorted women somehow got to know one another?"

"Yeah. Before you knew it, they were friends. Chatting away like they'd known each another their whole lives."

"Chatting about what?"

"Beats me. I'm interested in only one thing, and it ain't talk."

"But you need talk to get what you want."

Quincy blew out a puff of cigar smoke. "Ain't that the way of the world."

"What do you think was bothering Evelyn Cresthill?"

"Bored," he said.

"With what?"

"With Korea. With being stuck here on base. It's not like in the States. When an American woman ventures off post alone, all the locals stare at her, wondering what in the hell she's doing. So she ended up staying on compound like some shut-in. And she hated being a military dependent. Especially an officer's wife, with everyone always watching and judging her in this incestuous little environment of ours. You probably know she didn't work, either. She was going stir-crazy. To her, Yongsan Compound was some sort of glass cage."

"What was she going to do about it?"

"She wanted to break free."

"How?"

"One way was at the Tower Hotel."

"And the Cosmos?"

"Yep. Not that I'm admitting to anything."

"And this was until she met the Korean woman."

"Yeah."

"You're a man of the world, Captain Quincy. What do you think those two were up to?"

"I think the lady made her a proposition."

"Having to do with sex?"

"Maybe. But not between the two of them or anything like that. What I mean is sex in the Emerald City."

"Downtown Seoul?"

"Yeah."

"You think Evelyn found a way to make money?"

"I think so. That was a big deal to her. She didn't want to have to rely on her husband."

"What about her daughter, Jenny? Did she talk about her?"

Quincy's mouth dropped open, and his cigar butt slipped from his fingers to the floor. "She has a daughter?"

"Ten years old," I said.

"I had no idea."

After that, Quincy told us everything he could to help.

The name of the place was the In-oh Mogyok-tang. The Mermaid Bathhouse. We'd started at the Mia-ri bus stop, which was nothing more than a tin sign bolted to a pole on the main road that read UNITED STATES FORCES KOREA BUS STOP NUMBER 7 in English. Following Teddy Fusterman's directions, we'd headed east from there, and after a couple of blocks turned left until we spotted the neon sign with mermaids. Their long, illuminated hair seemed to float in the night.

Ernie hid across the street and I lurked in the shadows by the edge of the building. We'd met Marilyn before, so spotting her wasn't difficult. When she paused to survey the area for Teddy Fusterman, I stepped up next to her.

"Hello, Marilyn," I said and flashed my badge.

"Oh! It's you," she said in Korean, surprised. "You gave Teddy my note, right?" When I didn't answer, she said, "Where is he?"

I told her. She burst into tears and collapsed. Ernie and I caught her and held her up as we navigated the crowded streets of Mia-ri. We found a well-lit teahouse with a plastic-covered table in the far corner that allowed for some privacy. The three of us sat down and ordered ginseng tea.

"Why?" she said, her eyes rimmed in red. "Why do they think Teddy killed my brother?"

"It's complicated. They needed someone to blame."

She whimpered into a handkerchief as the waiter served our tea. Ernie paid him and told him to keep the change so we wouldn't be bothered further. I sipped the bitter brew. In more primitive times, ginseng had been sought exclusively in the wild, and the legend was that the rare plant would present itself only to those who were pure of heart. I sipped on the earthy mixture, indulging in its mythical power, but willed myself back to reality.

"Did Teddy ever buy things for you out of the PX?" I asked Marilyn.

Marilyn glanced down at the table. Black marketeering, though widespread, was often seen as shameful. At the end of the Korean War more than twenty years ago, what little had been left of the Korean economy was smashed to smithereens. With no one producing consumer goods, the items shipped in duty-free at US taxpayer expense to the military commissaries and PXs were highly sought after. A GI could buy almost anything out of the PX and sell it for twice what he paid for it. Some items, like American-made cigarettes or imported scotch, could bring in three or four times what it had cost on base. So if a Korean family had an American friend, it wasn't unusual for them to ask the GI to purchase something for them, like medicines that were difficult to come by or luxuries like granulated sugar, instant coffee, or canned milk. So it made sense that once he'd become friends with the Noh family, Teddy Fusterman would've purchased at least some small items for them.

"Yes," she said. "He bought medicine for my father's headaches and something for my mother's back. You know, hot." She made a rubbing motion. "And coffee and flour and salt." There was plenty of salt in Korea, but it wasn't finely granulated like the Stateside brands. "And sometimes *sokogi.*" Beef, which was far cheaper in the commissary and, because of generally spotty refrigeration in Korea, less likely to be tainted.

"Did he buy anything for you specifically?" I asked.

She blushed. "Nuts," she said. When she saw Ernie and I staring at her, she said, "Peanut Man. Big hat." She mimicked tilting a top hat.

"In a can?" I said.

"Yes."

The waiter came by again and Ernie told him we didn't need any more tea. After he left, I leaned closer to Marilyn. "Did Teddy and your brother sell anything from the PX? Were they trying to make money?"

"No," she said firmly. "My brother very, how you say?" Then the word came to her. "Honest. Very honest man. He don't like breaking rules, but what Teddy buy help my parents, so he say okay. But my brother, since he was little boy, he don't cheat. He don't steal. He don't lie."

Maybe, I thought. But the temptation to sell high-end items like imported cameras and wristwatches and stereo equipment and television sets on the black market for more money than you'd ever seen was strong enough to corrupt even some of the most honest men. A GI could only buy one each of these items in a twelve-month tour. And, to drive home the notion that soldiers weren't trusted by their superiors, these items were accounted for at the end of the GI's tour to make sure they hadn't been sold on the black market. Still, people came up with all sorts of creative ways to get around 8th Army's ration control regulations, like falsifying a shipment document or ordering additional items through the Sears catalogue. Could this have been the catalyst that had caused a rift between Private Teddy Fusterman and Corporal Noh Jong-bei?

I leaned in closer toward the young Korean woman.

"Did Teddy kill your brother?" I asked.

"No," she said firmly. "He's a good man."

"Then who do you think did it?"

She was crying again. "I don't know," she said. "*Na jinja moolah*." I really don't know.

Then she reached out and grabbed my hand. Through tears, she asked me, "Will you find the person who killed him?"

I nodded. "Yes."

"And will you free Teddy?"

"If he's not the murderer."

"He's *not*," she said. "I know."

She made Ernie make the same promise.

-9-

When we returned to Yongsan Compound South Post, the time was almost twenty-two-hundred hours—ten P.M. The MP at the gate checked our dispatch and waved us through. We wound through the command-sponsored housing on South Post past homes with well-tended lawns and cheap sedans in the driveways until we found the duplex at the address Bob Cresthill had given us. The lights were on, and muffled music seeped through the frosted windows. After Ernie parked the jeep, we walked up to the front door and knocked.

"Maybe Mrs. Cresthill is back," Ernie said. "Maybe they've made up and they're celebrating."

"Sure."

Major Bob Cresthill pulled the door open. He was smiling, his face flushed red. It took a moment for him to register who we were, and then the smile fell away.

"Did you find her?" he asked.

"No. May we come in?"

He opened the door wider. A song by the Rolling Stones blasted from stereo equipment down the hall. Cigarette smoke and the sound of conversation drifted into our faces.

"Having a party?" I asked.

"No," he said, ruffled. "Just invited a few friends over for drinks."

A few friends turned out to be about a dozen. A couple were officers I'd seen around compound and most were unknown to me, but everyone appeared to be military, with short haircuts and lean frames. Upwardly mobile young officers. Working hard, partying hard. The women seemed just as determined to enjoy the night, all of them wearing flattering dresses, puffing determinedly on cigarettes, highballs with rattling cubes clutched between polished nails.

He ushered us into a back room. A television set was on, tuned to the only English-language station in Korea: AFKN, the Armed Forces Korea Network. On the screen, a cross-eyed detective was questioning a witness. In front of the set, bathed in a flickering glow, a little girl with limp brown hair sat in a huge chair, staring at the screen.

I knelt next to her.

"You must be Jenny," I said.

She nodded. A whoop of laughter came from the front room.

"When did you last see your mom?"

"I told you already. I told my dad, I told everybody."

"What'd you tell them?"

"When I came home from school, she wasn't here."

"What'd you do?"

"I went over to Mrs. Bronson's."

"Have you heard anything from your Mom since?"

"*No.*" She stared stubbornly at the TV. I left her alone.

Cresthill walked us back through the house. "Why'd you come here?" he asked.

"Just to check on you. See if you'd heard from your wife."

"Well, I haven't. Maybe you should get busy looking for her."

"Maybe we should."

As we passed back through the partying crowd, a couple of the women gazed openly at Ernie. I'd never been able to figure out what his attraction was. He didn't put out the slightest bit of effort, but somehow they flocked toward him, as if finding his indifference a challenge to overcome. I'd tried Ernie's technique, feigning disinterest, but all I'd received was disinterest in return. Now I was back to that old standby: begging.

On the front porch, Major Cresthill stood with the door almost closed behind him.

"This isn't what it looks like," he said.

"What's that?" Ernie asked.

"It's not like I'm partying because she's gone. It's just that me and my friends and Evelyn's friends, we get together often. They came over to check on me, make sure I was all right."

"Are you?" I asked.

"I'm okay. As good as I can be under the circumstances."

"And Jenny?"

"She's a little trooper. She'll make it through."

We nodded to Major Cresthill and turned to head back down the walkway. He reentered the house. When we reached the jeep, Ernie said, "Poor guy. He's all broken up."

"Yeah. Wallowing in grief."

Inside, one of the women laughed like she'd been poked in the ribs. Wheels crunching on ice, we drove toward the Officers Club.

The place was closing down. On weeknights, by order of the 8th Army Commander, the Yongsan Officers Club shut its doors at twenty-three-hundred hours. Part of that was to make sure that all good officers returned to their quarters to get a good night's sleep. The other part was because the Korean staff had to clean up, count the money in the cash registers, punch out on the time clock, lock up, and arrive home before the nationwide midnight-to-four curfew.

Ernie and I found the night manager in his office. The nameplate on his desk said Cho. We flashed our badges to Mr. Cho, and I asked to talk to his head waitress. The middle-aged woman who was called in introduced herself as Mrs. Pei. She refused a seat and remained standing as I described Evelyn Cresthill and the Korean woman who'd befriended her.

"Yes," she said in carefully pronounced English. "I remember them."

"Did you serve them?"

"No. They sat in the cocktail lounge. Usually Miss Soh brings them drinks."

"Did you notice anything unusual about them?"

"Like what?"

"I don't know. Like maybe something strange?"

"No," she said. "Nothing strange."

"Is the Korean woman married to an American officer?"

"I don't know. I just see. We don't talk."

I thanked her and the manager ordered her to send in Miss Soh.

Ernie and I could've bypassed manager Cho and questioned the waitresses directly to figure out who used to serve Evelyn Cresthill and her Korean friend. But that would've upset the *kibun*, or the general contentment in a workplace. Korean societal structures were often hierarchical, from family to school and finally employment. These hierarchies were comfortable, especially when everyone knew their position within them. At the 8th Army Officers Club, the night manager was the "father," the head waitress the "mother," and the cooks and bartenders were the "older brother" figures. The cute young cocktail waitresses were called *yo dongseing*. Little sisters.

Within seconds, the younger, very pretty Miss Soh bowed

slightly to us. The night manager rose from his desk, ostensibly to supervise closing, but in reality to give us privacy. And to protect himself. Whatever was happening, he didn't want to know more about it than he had to.

Once he'd left, Miss Soh was visibly more nervous.

"*Choyong-hei*," I told her. Be calm. "We just have questions about some customers of yours."

She nodded, looking at us gamely.

I beckoned for her to take a seat on the small divan. Ernie grabbed a straight-backed chair and sat against a nearby wall. I stood a few feet in front of Miss Soh, leaning against the front edge of the night manager's desk as I described Evelyn Cresthill.

She nodded immediately. "Yes, Miss Evelyn," she said.

"Not Mrs. Evelyn?"

"No. She like Miss."

"Did any men sit with her?"

"No. Only Randy."

"Who?"

She thought about it. "Quincy." She folded her right arm across her chest and tapped two fingers on the top of her left shoulder. "Captain. I think he's captain. Captain Quincy, but everybody call him Randy."

Over the years, many of the young women who'd worked in the O'Club ended up marrying American officers. They paid close attention to rank, as well as to whether or not the young man was married and what his personality and temperament were like.

"Was Captain Quincy Miss Evelyn's boyfriend?"

"No." She waved her hand dismissively. "*Gaburo*." A joker. Someone not to be taken seriously.

"He plays around?"

"Yes. Talk to all woman. Don't mean nothing. Miss Evelyn, she laugh at him. Think he's funny."

"Did she ever leave the club with him?"

"Maybe. Maybe one time. But I don't think she like him." She thought about it some more. "When she first come in, she was sad. Randy Quincy, he made her laugh. After that, she don't pay attention to him."

"Why not?"

"He *gaburo*," she repeated, as if I were slow on the uptake.

"When was the last time you saw Miss Evelyn?"

Miss Soh's forehead creased slightly and she crinkled her nose. Finally, she said, "Maybe three—no, four days ago."

Most people had trouble remembering time frames, but this bright young Korean woman seemed to remember everything. I asked her about the Korean woman who'd become Evelyn's friend.

"Not good friend," Miss Soh said, shaking her head.

"No? Why not?"

"I think she want something."

"Like what?"

"Like she need woman. Young woman. Pretty woman. Like Miss Evelyn."

Ernie glanced at me but didn't say anything.

"Go on," I said.

"This Korean woman she not interested in man. Lot of trouble to get on compound, go to O'Club, but she not interested in man. She interested in woman."

"Korean women?"

"No." Miss Soh waved her hand dismissively. "Plenty of Korean women outside compound. She interested in American woman."

"Why?" I asked.

Miss Soh wrinkled her forehead. "I'm not sure. But not for good reason. For something bad."

I thought of asking Miss Soh if the Korean woman could have been interested in American women for her own sexual reasons, but I held back. In Korea, homosexuality was a taboo subject indeed. More than once, I'd heard Koreans say that homosexuality didn't exist in their country. I knew that to be wrong, but if I confronted Miss Soh with such a subject, she might clam up and stop talking completely. Instead, I asked, "What was this Korean woman's name?"

"She call herself Miss Shin."

"Do you think that's her real name?"

Miss Soh shrugged. "Maybe not."

"So why was this Miss Shin here at the Officers Club, talking to Evelyn Cresthill?"

Miss Soh swiveled to look at Ernie, then turned to look at me. She took a deep breath, as if bucking up her courage, and said, "I think she here to make money. She want American woman to make money."

"Make money how?" I asked.

"*Na moolah*," she said. I don't know.

"What does this Miss Shin do?"

"I don't know."

"But Evelyn Cresthill and this woman became friends. And Evelyn listened to this woman?"

"Oh, yes."

"Why?"

"Because Miss Evelyn need something."

"What?"

Miss Soh's forehead crinkled again.

When she didn't speak right away I said, "Did she need money?"

Waving her petite hand, Miss Soh dismissed my answer. "Everybody needs money."

"So what was it," I asked, "that Evelyn was hoping to receive from this Korean woman?"

Finally, Miss Soh spoke. "She want . . . How you say? Exciting."

"Excitement?"

"Yes."

"Nothing wrong with that," Ernie said.

Miss Soh turned toward him. "No," she said. "Exciting very wrong. Very dangerous. This woman, this Korean woman, she work for someone bad, I think."

"Bad?" I asked. "Who?"

She shook her head vehemently. "I don't know. But someone bad. I don't know how to say in English."

She was nervous and her language ability was deteriorating rapidly. "Say it in Korean," I said.

She looked up at me, eyes wide, and said, "*Gampei*." Gangsters.

Even Ernie knew that word. We'd dealt with them often enough.

"Which *gampei*?" I asked. There were numerous gangs in Seoul.

"I don't know," she said, rubbing her fingers together now; twisting and turning them until I was afraid she'd wrench a knuckle. Suddenly, she stood, straightening her shoulders. "I'm worried about Miss Evelyn. Some Korean people not good. You go find." She shook her forefinger at me. "You go find Miss Evelyn."

Without bowing, she turned and walked out of the room.

Ernie had parked the jeep toward the back of the O'Club's gravel lot. As we approached, the floodlight from the building revealed that somebody had tilted the front passenger seat forward. Since there was no rear door, this allowed someone to climb into the backseat, but instead of sitting there waiting for us, our visitor had left us a personalized calling card.

"What the *hell*!" Ernie said.

A combat jeep usually had a canvas-covered bench-like seat in back. But some months ago, Ernie'd splurged at the motor pool and paid the dispatcher two quart-sized bottles of imported Johnny Walker Black to have the rough Army-issue canvas replaced with black vinyl tuck-and-roll upholstery. This luxury, coupled with daily washing and first-class main-tenance, which Ernie also paid for, meant he probably had the classiest jeep in 8th Army.

"Money talks," he always told me.

"So does imported scotch."

"That too."

Ernie gazed at the seat in horror. "Who in the hell would do this?"

Somebody had slashed the tuck-and-roll. Thick, deep cuts, maybe two or three dozen of them, where white cotton puffed out of the vinyl. And then we both smelled it. Ernie recoiled.

"Piss," he said. "That son of a bitch pissed all over my seat." Even if he could get the vinyl repaired, the smell might not wear off for months.

In the wooded area behind us, something rustled as a clump of bushes wobbled. Ernie swiveled in time to see it and yelled, "You *bastard*."

Before I could stop him, he took off running, covering the length of the parking lot in about ten strides and plowing headfirst into the thick shrubbery. There was a hill here, fairly steep, that was undeveloped and covered in trees. On the far side were more individual officer quarters, and beyond that Gate Seven, which led off of Yongsan Compound South Post. I ran after Ernie, wishing he'd at least slow down. Whoever had done this to his jeep had a cutting implement—a sharp one, we could be sure—and in that thick shrubbery without any ambient light from the O'Club, Ernie was running blind. I shouted at him to stop, but he ignored me.

By the time I reached the edge of the shrubbery, I began to navigate cautiously through leaves and under branches. Ahead of me Ernie grunted, plowing through the greenery enveloping him. I wanted to stop and allow for my vision to adapt to the darkness, but there was no time. Instead I forged ahead, my hands in front of my face, pushing aside what seemed like acres' worth of massed foliage. I'd only made it about ten yards into the thicket when I heard a zing, a whoosh, and another grunt. A loud one this time, filled with pain.

On the far edge of the copse of trees, Ernie lay on the ground, both his hands stuck between his legs, curled up, moaning and writhing in agony. I looked around; light came in from all directions, from the small barracks below to the surrounding perimeter fence, which made it clear to me that we were alone. Whoever he'd been chasing was either still lurking somewhere in the small Sherwood Forest behind us or far enough ahead to be beyond our reach. I knelt down next to Ernie.

"What happened?"

Through gritted teeth, he said, "Booby trap."

I checked. A low hanging branch swung freely but upon closer inspection, I saw that it had been partially denuded of leaves in one spot where a hemp rope tied it to a wooden peg. I groped around and found an almost invisible strand of piano wire. The branch had been tied back, and when Ernie tripped the wire, the peg had been released, allowing the branch to swing forward at crotch level.

Well, at least there'd been no explosive device attached to it.

Ernie's forehead was slathered in sweat. I helped him sit up.

"Looks like somebody wanted your attention," I said.

"Whoever this psycho is," Ernie replied, "he has my attention now."

When Ernie was feeling better, I told him to sit for a few more deep breaths until he was able to clamber back to his feet. Once he was up and moving, we scoured the area and found nothing. The perp was long gone. I suggested calling for an MP patrol to expand the search, but Ernie nixed the idea.

"I just got hit in the balls," he said. "If you think I'm going to let every MP in 8th Army know that, you're sadly mistaken."

Instead, we trudged back to the jeep to find that whoever had slashed and urinated onto the tuck-and-roll had doubled back while we were on the other side of the hill and slashed all four tires.

Ernie's supply of four-letter words failed him. He leaned against the hood of the jeep, rubbed his crotch again, and squeezed his forehead with his free hand.

Finally, he said, "I'll find this *kei-nom sikki*." Born of a dog. "I guarantee, I'll sure as hell find him."

-10-

I used the phone in the Officers Club to call for a motor pool tow truck. It took them the better part of an hour to show up, and I didn't believe the guy on duty was exactly sober. But he managed to tow us back to the motor pool, where we left the jeep and hiked back to the barracks—a march of about two miles.

In my bunk, I thought for a while about who might've sabotaged Ernie's jeep, and a whole array of faces flashed before me. Some from past cases, but most of the enemies we'd made had received transfers back to the States, and a few had made the duffle-bag-drag off this mortal coil. Whoever it had been had to have followed us or known where we were going—could it have to do with the Cresthill case, or Corporal Noh's murder? Before I reached any conclusions, exhaustion overtook me.

The next morning at the 8th Army CID office, Staff Sergeant Riley issued more bad news. "Fusterman's court-martial has already been scheduled."

"They're moving fast."

"Yes. It's two weeks from today."

"For a capital murder case?" Ernie said. "What are they, nuts?"

"Hey," Riley responded. "You chop a guy in the back of his head with your entrenching tool, how complicated is that?"

Ernie snatched Riley's copy of the *Pacific Stars and Stripes* out of his hand. "Hey," Riley said, "what do you think you're doing?"

"You have work to do," Ernie said. "Get busy."

"What about you?"

"I'm on break." Ernie sat down and opened the paper.

He'd already called the 21 T-Car dispatcher and arranged for new tires. As to the slashed seat, the dispatcher said he'd have the whole thing removed and try to find a replacement, although it might take a while to get the parts.

I greeted Miss Kim and took a seat next to her admin secretary desk, breathing in the scent of the fresh *mugunghua* flower, Rose of Sharon, she kept on the corner in a glass vase. Then I grabbed the magazine-sized US Forces Korea phone book, looked up a number, and asked her to make a call for me.

"To who?" she asked.

"The PX Taxi Dispatcher's Office," I replied, pointing at the number. I explained what I wanted to find out.

I often asked Miss Kim to make calls for me because her sweet voice and pleasant demeanor—especially in Korean-to-Korean conversations—usually received cooperation that I couldn't have enlisted on my own. I would simply listen in as she spoke. On this call, the first person to answer transferred her to someone up the line. *Jibei-in* was the word I heard. Manager. She spoke for a while, he responded with a long string of words, and Miss Kim thanked him in a high, lilting voice and hung up. She jotted something on a slip of paper and handed it to me.

"Mr. Rhee. Go to his office. He will be waiting for you."

"Did you tell him what we're looking for?"

"No. Just some records from a few days ago."

I thanked her and slipped the note with Rhee's name and direct phone number in my pocket. She stopped me before I left.

"This American woman you're looking for," she asked. "Is she married?"

I nodded.

"And she has a daughter?"

I nodded again.

"*Ohttokei*?" A term that translates to "How?" but a bit stronger. As in, how could Evelyn Cresthill have abandoned her child?

I didn't have an answer for her, but I knew it was possible.

Ernie and I called a military taxi, one of the ones that were for official use only and operated strictly on base. We did it without asking Riley because Ernie was adamant that having his backseat slashed and pissed on, not to mention his balls being busted by a booby trap, was too humiliating to tell anyone, much less the blabbermouthed Sergeant Riley.

Mr. Rhee met us at the door of the PX Taxi Dispatch office and led us past a row of a half-dozen employees wearing headphones, all rapidly poking metal probes into telephone consoles with blinking red lights. They were speaking English for the most part, but a few spoke to Korean customers. In my experience, if a person who spoke Korean called for a PX taxi, the service was faster. Why? Because some Americans had a tendency to be overbearing, too demanding. They treated Korean phone operators and drivers like their personal servants. Servants who just couldn't do anything right.

Rhee led us down a short hallway into a records room that smelled of musk. In the center, a narrow, six-foot-long table was piled with stacks of paper that had been clipped together by metal hasps. "Last week's records," he told us. "They haven't been filed yet."

Ernie groaned.

"How many cabs do you have, anyway?" I asked.

"Almost fifty. We provide service for USFK personnel, military and civilian, in the entire Seoul area. All told, almost ten thousand customers."

Most of who didn't have their own cars, since 8th Army allowed only the command-sponsored elite to ship their vehicles over. I took off my jacket, sat down on a wooden chair, and got to work.

PX taxis were imported Ford Granadas, much larger than the Hyundai "kimchi cabs" that operated outside military gates. Kimchi cabs weren't allowed onto American bases, so the PX taxis picked up the slack. All the PX taxi drivers were Korean. They fell under the FOEU, the Foreign Organizations Employees Union—the only union legally permitted to exist in South Korea. All other unions had been outlawed by the Park Chung-hee regime; this stricture was ruthlessly enforced. When overworked and underpaid coal miners had gone on strike recently, President Park sent an infantry brigade to quell their protest. The miners armed themselves. The shootout lasted the better part of two days and in the end what had become a violent insurrection was put down. The exact number of casualties was never released.

Every PX taxi driver had a clipboard with a stack of forms. On it, he was supposed to record the time and place he picked up a passenger, plus the destination and time of arrival. Rhee explained that about four dozen PX taxis had been operating the day Evelyn Cresthill disappeared; it was our task to isolate those records and peruse every line of every entry to see if we could find out which driver had picked her up and where she'd been dropped off.

We started by narrowing down the timeframe. According to the employees at the 8th Army Officers Club, Evelyn had been there from late afternoon to early evening on the night of her disappearance. So Ernie and I skipped all the morning and late-night pickups and concentrated on entries from between 5 and 8 P.M. We were also scanning for starting points from the Officers Club. Korean drivers were required to make their entries in English, but usually weren't too careful about their handwriting. And they used abbreviations: "8O" was most common for the 8th Army Officers Club. We found numerous entries for the O'Club, but most had gone to rather mundane destinations. Quarters addresses on South Post, the Niblo Barracks in Hannam-dong, or the UN Compound about four miles from Yongsan. It took us less than an hour of going through the records line-by-line before Ernie found an interesting entry.

"Here," he said, handing the sheaf to me. The driver had departed the O'Club at 7:45. On the column for number of occupants, he had written the number two. Next to that, although it wasn't a required entry, he had scribbled something in *hangul*. I moved the form into the light and peered at it carefully.

"*Yo*," I said.

"What's that mean?"

"*Yoja*. Women."

"So he picked up two women at the Eighth Army Officers Club at seven forty-five," Ernie said. "Where'd he take them?"

Again breaking regulation, the driver had written his entry in Korean. It was scribbled hastily, so I had to study it for a while before I'd deciphered it. I sat up.

"Where?" Ernie asked.

"Myong-dong," I replied. A name that translated to Bright District.

"Bingo," Ernie said. "They arrived a little after eight in Myong-dong, the fanciest party district on the peninsula. Perfect time for the nightclubs, especially for two broads on the make."

"Yeah," I said, unhooking the sheet from its hasp. "No surprise there. Evelyn Cresthill wanted adventure in her life. A classy Korean woman promised to show her around. Show her a little excitement." I carefully folded the sheet and stuck it in my pocket. "But what sort of excitement were they after? And once she had her fun, why didn't Evelyn Cresthill go home?"

Ernie nodded. "That's the question."

We found Manager Rhee and showed him the handwritten record, and in seconds he was speaking into a shortwave radio mic, ordering a driver named Young Kim to return immediately to the Dispatch Office.

Rhee turned to us, his expression grim. "Young Kim is delivering a passenger now. He will be here in twenty minutes."

We waited. When he walked in, we were mildly surprised. Young Kim was half African-American.

During and after the Korean War, many children were born to Korean mothers and GI fathers; fathers who, for the most part, abandoned their new families. The children were often turned over to orphanages, who endeavored to find homes for them overseas. Some mothers kept their half-American children. While they faced harsh discrimination in school and by the broader Korean society, most of these young people managed to find their niche by the time they reached adulthood. More than a few gravitated toward American military compounds, perhaps because they felt accepted there. Or perhaps because they were looking to make up for missing relationships with fathers they'd never known.

Young Kim wore the high-collared black tunic standard for all PX cabdrivers. He sat with his hands folded in his lap, staring at us with bright, wide eyes; completely guileless. I showed him the dispatch.

"Do you remember them?" I asked, pointing toward the entry. "The two women you picked up at the Eighth Army Officers Club?"

He studied the entry for a moment and said, "Oh, yes. Two beautiful ladies."

"Where did you take them?" Ernie asked.

"Myong-dong," he replied without hesitation.

"Where in Myong-dong?"

He thought about that for a moment. "Near Shinsegae." He meant the Shinsegae—New World—Department Store, a landmark in Seoul. "Maybe one block past."

Ernie turned to me, rolling his eyes. The area Young Kim was describing just might be the busiest business district in the entire country. High-rises lined the main road of Myong-dong, pocked with lavishly expensive spas and boutiques. Behind the line of modern buildings, narrow pedestrian lanes spread, lined with neon, into a massive spider's web of restaurants and bars and nightclubs and *kisaeng* houses where modern-day courtesans catered to the whims of very wealthy men.

"All right, Mr. Kim," I said. "Thank you for that. You let them off in Myong-dong. Do you know where they were going? Did they mention a specific shop or nightclub or restaurant?"

"Specific?" he asked.

I held up my forefinger. "Yes, one place where they wanted to go. One *specific* place."

He pulled out a small spiral notebook from the breast pocket of his tunic, along with a pen, and prepared to jot the word down. "Spelling, please?" he asked.

I told him.

When he was finished, Young Kim put the notebook and pen away and considered my question.

"Not specific," he said slowly. "They didn't say name of one place. But the Korean woman, I think she speak English very well. She told American woman about a place with music and singers. A beautiful place. They were going to go there."

"But they didn't mention the name?"

He shook his head. "If they say, I don't remember."

The alleys where most of the Myong-dong nightclubs were located were too narrow for a big Ford Granada to squeeze through. It was standard in the area for even the smaller kimchi cabs to let off passengers on the main drag so they could walk to their destination.

"Do you remember which shop you let them off in front of?"

"No. Too many shops," he said. "I only remember Shinsegae." It was hard for the huge, multilevel department store not to overwhelm its surroundings in the eyes of an observer.

"Who paid?" I asked.

"Korean woman."

"The American woman didn't offer to split the fare?"

"She offer." Young Kim seemed certain. "But Korean woman say she'll pay. She very kind to American woman."

"What do you mean, 'kind'?"

"She so happy to have American woman with her. Maybe, how you say? Proud."

"Proud of having an American woman with her?"

"Yes."

"Do you know why?"

Young Kim shrugged and shook his head.

"On the ride down there," Ernie asked. "What did the two women talk about?"

"They speak English too fast. Seoul traffic very bad. I can't listen."

"You didn't understand?"

"No."

"Were they laughing or serious or angry?"

"Laughing."

"About what?"

"I don't know. Korean woman mentioned man's name.

Rich man. She say something, they both laugh, but I don't understand much."

"A Korean man or American man?"

"Korean."

"He was in Myong-dong?"

"I think maybe but I don't know."

Ernie glanced at me. I said, "Did either one of the women talk to you directly?"

"American woman, she do. She very nice."

"What'd she say?"

Young Kim shrugged again. "Say, 'Thank you.'"

"How about the Korean woman? Did she speak to you?"

"No, I'm too low. She won't talk to me."

It saddened me that this man considered himself beneath one of his customers. After a lifetime of doubtlessly being bullied by others for his half-black background and taunted for his father having abandoned him, it was no surprise that his self-esteem had taken a hell of a beating.

Ernie filled the silence. "Sounds like she's one *specific* kind of bitch."

Surprised, Young Kim turned to Ernie. Then he grinned. So did Ernie. And then they were both laughing. So was I. Even Manager Rhee joined in.

It was a short walk from the PX taxi dispatch office to the 21 T-Car motor pool. Ernie went into huddled conversation with the Korean civilian dispatcher, and they finally nodded to one another and shook hands. Outside, Ernie said, "You got any booze left on your monthly ration?"

"Sure," I said. "All four bottles."

"The greedy son-of-a-gun wants two bottles for the tires and another two to have the backseat taken off post to the upholstery shop. He'll have the pissed-on stuff ripped out and replaced with new tuck-and-roll."

"Black again?"

"Nah, I ordered red."

"Red?" I asked. "Won't that attract too much attention?"

"Actually it's burgundy. Very classy."

The tires should've been free. All parts and equipment on a military jeep were Army issue. But going through normal channels would've taken days, if not weeks, for new tires. The lubricant of PX-purchased liquor made everything happen fast. And we were asked to pay in scotch instead of cash because every bottle we purchased for ten bucks in the Class VI store could be sold by the 21 T-Car dispatcher off post for two or three times that amount in *won*.

The jeep was already washed and waiting for us, and except for the missing backseat, in tip-top condition. We climbed in, Ernie turned the ignition, and the engine roared to life. As we left the motor pool, he stepped on the accelerator and the back tires squealed, laying rubber on about twenty yards of cement.

-11-

Back at the CID office, Riley tossed a three-page printout at me.

"Fusterman's ration control record," he said. "You owe me."

I picked up the printout and found a spot to sit and study it. Ernie proceeded to the back counter and pulled himself a mugful of over-roasted coffee. He loaded it with sugar in an attempt to conceal its bitter taste. He took a few sips, grimaced, and poured a couple more packets in.

Fusterman's record looked pretty routine. A single GI is allowed to spend ninety dollars a month, combined, in the PX and commissary. Every purchase over two dollars is anviled on an IBM card and dropped into a padlocked box that's delivered weekly to the 8th Army Data Processing Center. If a GI goes over his ration, or if he purchases too many controlled items, a report is sent to his unit of assignment. Once the unit commander receives the report of the overpurchase, he has the option to bring the soldier up on charges. Typically, non-judicial punishment is used—dubbed an "Article 15" since the transgression fell under that section of the Uniform Code of Military Justice. But if the black marketing was egregious enough, a soldier could be court-martialed and fined, or imprisoned, or both. Cases this serious usually resulted in a Bad Conduct Discharge after jail time was served.

But Fusterman hadn't come close to anything like that. He'd merely spent up to his ration, usually to within a dollar or two, every month. A common enough occurrence—and one that indicated a single GI, whose meals and uniforms were provided to him for free, was black marketeering to make an extra buck. Fusterman, however, had apparently tapped out his monthly ration limit not to resell the items, but to turn them over to the Noh family.

"What'd you get?" Ernie asked me.

"Fusterman was maxing out his ration every month, but not going over."

"Anything high-value?"

"None, according to this."

Ernie shrugged. "Dead end."

"Looks like it," I said. "We can rule out Corporal Noh being killed over some big-money black-market dispute."

"Drugs, then," Ernie said. "We should check Fusterman's medical record. And Noh's."

That was the logical next step. But from everything I'd

learned about Private Theodore "Teddy" Fusterman and Corporal Noh Jong-bei, neither of them had been a druggie.

"There's something else," I said.

"What?"

"Both of these guys are too clean. Everybody praises them."

"Right. Until they found blood on Fusterman's entrenching tool."

"Yeah," I said. "If the tool is his."

"Tough to prove. The Army issues tens of thousands of entrenching tools, and as far as I've seen, they all look alike."

And then it hit me where we might find another lead. "Noh and Fusterman went to Seoul a lot."

"Yeah, since Noh's family lived there and Fusterman was dating his sister."

"A lot of GIs stationed along the DMZ never make it to Seoul. Not in an entire tour."

"Why bother?" Ernie said, playing along with my reasoning. "You have all the reefer and booze and dollies you want just south across the Imjin River, in Paju-ri."

Paju-ri. One of the many villages in South Korea that had come to thrive by catering to the whims of young American GIs.

"You ever been there?" I asked.

"Too far north," Ernie replied. "Haven't bothered."

"Maybe we should bother now."

"Why? You not getting enough?"

I ignored him. "The other guys at the JSA—the ones patrolling the grounds, staring down those North Korean guards. I want to hear what they have to say about this mess. We're barred from entering the JSA, but no one said anything about Paju-ri."

"Do you think they sell soju there?" Ernie asked.

"They sell everything there," I replied. "Dried cuttlefish and hot pepper paste and rice liquor."

"All the necessities of life," Ernie said, standing up. "We ain't there yet?"

The lead on Myong-dong in Evelyn Cresthill's missing person's case would have to wait until the evening. No sense going out there in the afternoon, alerting people to our interest. Better to wait until nighttime, when things were busy and anyone who might've met with Evelyn and her Korean escort would be awake, alert, and ready to earn a buck. So we could head to Paju-ri first and be back in plenty of time. GI nightlife started early, right after evening chow. But the high-class nightlife in Myong-dong was more Continental. Only the hoi-polloi would be seen there prior to eight P.M.

We were about to walk out the door when Sergeant Riley stepped in front of us, his mouth twisted as he jabbed his thumb in the direction of the hallway toward the office of the Provost Marshal.

"Colonel Brace wants to talk to you."

"Tell him we're otherwise indisposed," Ernie said.

"*Now*," Riley replied.

We would've had to tromp over a determined Riley to escape. Ernie was about to, but I stopped him. "Might as well get it over with," I said.

Ernie shrugged.

We marched down to the Provost Marshal's office.

Riley went in first to announce us, and after he motioned us in, Ernie and I came to attention in front of the Colonel's desk and saluted. Still seated, Colonel Brace waved a half-hearted salute in reply. He didn't tell us to sit.

"I talked to the MAC Commander," he said. "No more JSA. You're officially off the case." Then he slid the paperwork across an expanse of mahogany. "Sign," he said.

I read the statement. It was dated and issued by 8th Army headquarters, directing us to cease and desist from any further investigation into the murder of Corporal Noh Jong-bei and specifically denying us access to the Joint Security Area or its environs. We'd seen this coming, and I saw no point in arguing. I stepped forward and signed the document.

Ernie said, "Who's taking over the case, sir?"

Bored, Colonel Brace answered, "You know the answer to that, Bascom."

"The JAG Office?"

Colonel Brace nodded.

"They won't do any investigating, sir, and you know it. They'll just go with whatever's shoved in front of them. Like Private Fusterman's supposed guilt."

This seemed to wake the Colonel. He sat up straight in his chair. "You two are the ones who first pointed the finger at Fusterman."

"Pointing the finger at him just meant it merited a closer look. It doesn't mean he's guilty."

"I don't know what army you're in, Bascom. You're sure as hell not in the same army I'm in. In *my* army, a soldier follows orders. And a soldier does not constantly question the motives of his superior officers."

"Their motive, sir, is to keep everything quiet up at the JSA. Even if Fusterman isn't guilty."

Colonel Brace stood up. "That'll be just about enough out of you." He stuck his finger about a foot from Ernie's nose. "You will *not* investigate this matter further. Is that clear?"

Ernie didn't answer.

"Is that *clear*?"

Finally, Ernie relented. Even he knew that the hammer of the US Army smashed whatever it hit completely and flatly. He'd seen the splatter often enough.

"Yes, sir," Ernie replied sullenly. "It's clear." He stepped forward and signed.

"All right then," Colonel Brace said, sitting back down. He made a show of fiddling with his pipe. Then he turned to me. "What progress have you made on locating Evelyn Cresthill?"

"We have a lead, sir, in Myong-dong."

"Myong-dong? She went out there?"

"Yes, sir. We believe so."

He tapped the loose contents of the bowl of his pipe into a crystal ashtray. "Myong-dong," he mused. "All by herself." He shook his head. "Brave woman."

We didn't bother correcting his assumption.

"What's your next step?" he asked.

"To go out there," I said. "Ask some questions."

"Who's your translator?"

"Me," I replied.

"Oh, that's right. You took night classes, didn't you?"

"Yes, sir."

Colonel Brace stared at me curiously. "How many units did you earn?" he asked.

"All they had, sir. Eighteen semester units."

"That's a lot of work," he said, impressed. When I didn't answer, he continued. "After you leave Korea, what good will it do you? It's not like Korean's an international language. Not like French or German."

I wasn't exactly sure German was considered an international language, but I'd seen Colonel Brace in lederhosen at the annual Oktoberfest on South Post, so I didn't argue with him. I figured his questions were rhetorical, but he surprised me by waiting for an answer. How could I explain to him how deeply complex I found Korean culture? How much more I'd gained from my classes than the language? A different way of thinking, one that was almost the exact inverse of the American ideal of personal freedom. Even Korean sentence structure reinforced this—I remember being shocked to first learn that the verb was placed at the end of a sentence, demoting action to an after-thought. And that the subject—the "I"—didn't have to come first. The object could come first, as in the object of our attention, our desires. These thoughts weren't common, I knew. I'd never encountered them in any treatise on East Asian culture. But I wrestled with them pretty much constantly, trying to tease out the true nature of Korean philosophy. I knew that sometimes—probably more often than not—they thought of Americans as mad. Not just because of our crude behaviors, but because from their point of view, what we cherished seemed almost criminal. Worshipping the self instead of the whole.

Ernie was staring at me. I coughed. "Yes, sir," I said, "I suppose it won't do me much good when I'm back in the States."

"Yes, well, I suppose it'll still come in handy in Myong-dong."

"Yes, sir," I replied.

He pulled some paperwork closer and shifted his attention to it. Behind us, Riley opened the door. Realizing we'd been dismissed, Ernie and I saluted, turned, and marched out of the office.

"Okay," Ernie said once we were back in the jeep. "We go to the barracks, change into our running-the-ville outfits, grab some chow, and head up to Paju-ri."

When I didn't reply, he looked at me. "Isn't that the plan?"

"Yeah. It is."

"So what are you moping about?"

"Something you said in there."

"What'd I say?"

"About the motive of JAG. To pin this all on PFC Fusterman in order to calm things down at the JSA."

"Yeah. The North Koreans are off the hook if Fusterman gets convicted. Nobody can blame them for the murder. You think I'm wrong about that?"

"No," I said. "You're right. That's JAG's motive."

"Then what?"

"I'm thinking about Colonel Peele up at the MAC."

"No wonder you're so bummed. Want a tranquilizer?"

"No. Remember what he was mad about?"

"The whole world?"

"He was angry because he wanted to make sure Corporal Noh's murder was pinned on the North Koreans. He seemed sure that the Commies had done it. And now he's signed an order to keep us away from the JSA."

"Yeah," Ernie said. "He's siding with JAG, who wants to make sure the North Koreans *aren't* accused of the murder."

I turned to Ernie. "So why did he do that?"

Ernie shrugged. "Like Colonel Brace said, we're the ones who pointed the finger at Fusterman."

"Exactly. In Colonel Peele's mind, we're the ones who let the North Koreans off the hook."

"So he doesn't want us messing up anything else in the future." Ernie paused. "Maybe this Neutral Nations Committee, or whatever you call it . . ."

"The Neutral Nations Supervisory Committee."

"Yeah. Them. Maybe Colonel Peele will try to go through them to throw suspicion back onto the North Koreans."

"Maybe," I said. "But good luck with that. The mission of the Neutral Nations boys is to keep peace along the DMZ. I doubt they'd ever find enough evidence to heighten tensions by making that kind of accusation."

"So Peele is on his own," Ernie said.

"He thinks he is."

Ernie studied me. "He's such an asshole he doesn't realize that you and me are his best bet at getting at the truth."

"Right. He just thinks we're a couple of screwups." I paused, getting to the heart of it. "In fact, I bet he thinks we're worse than that. He probably sees us as his enemies."

"He can't blame JAG," Ernie said. "So he's putting everything that's gone wrong on us."

"We're his targets."

"Right. The paperwork he threw at us was personal."

"Easier than going up against a bunch of freaking lawyers."

Ernie's eyes lit up. "The jeep."

I nodded.

"He's the son of a bitch who trashed my tuck-and-roll."

"He's got it in for us," I said. "Maybe he was working long

hours and came into the O'Club for a late dinner. He's sitting there and sees us parade into the back office with Manager Cho."

"So outside he pulls the switchblade he always carries and slashes some very expensive tuck-and-roll, then takes a leak on my backseat. But what about the booby trap?"

"He might've set that up ahead of time. Or planted it a while ago, in case someone pissed him off."

"You think so? Must be some kind of a serious nut."

"Yeah, that's what we need to find out."

"How?"

"Well, I have an idea."

"Don't you always."

We decided not to check with 8th Army Billeting to locate Colonel Peele's BOQ because we didn't need anyone to know we were stalking him. Instead, we drove over to Yongsan Compound South Post, where the senior Bachelor Officer Quarters were clustered in about a two- or three-block area. Each building was a small brick home with a whitewashed sign out front giving the full name of the officer inside and his unit of assignment. Most were shared, two colonels per house.

"Snazzy," Ernie said. "Beats the hell out of the barracks."

"Earn a college degree," I told him. "Then go to Officer Candidate School. In twenty years, you can be here too."

"I'll settle for a hooch in the ville."

At a quiet cul-de-sac, we found it: PEELE, NORBERT M., COLONEL, EXECUTIVE OFFICER, MILITARY ARMISTICE COMMISSION. Next to his name was that of another officer, his roommate.

"Norbert?" Ernie said.

"Well, someone's got to be named Norbert."

Ernie completed his U-turn, and we meandered through the neighborhood before parking on the street behind Colonel Peele's quarters. Most high-ranking officers worked during the day, with shift work reserved for officers lower on the totem pole. So the neighborhood was quiet, except for the Korean maids, mostly middle-aged women who worked cleaning house, doing laundry, and often preparing an evening meal before departing around midafternoon.

Ernie and I waited until no one was watching, then passed between brick quarters and approached Colonel Peele's house from the rear.

-12-

We listened for the sound of a washing machine or a dish-washer, but heard nothing. No one seemed to be moving inside.

"The maids usually work more than one house," I said.

"Shall we knock on the front door?" Ernie asked.

"No. Someone might spot us. Let's just take a chance and go in through the back."

Which we did. Ernie brought along the tool set he called his "passkey," wrapped in rolled felt. Deftly, he worked on the hasp of the sliding glass door while I paced back and forth behind him, keeping an eye out for anyone approaching. The latch quietly clicked open. Ernie entered first and I followed, sliding the door almost shut behind me.

The kitchen area was immaculately clean. Either the house-maid possessed some kind of magic, or the two officers who lived here didn't do much cooking. Down a central hallway was a small living room, which I imagined the two officers shared. I stepped forward and unlocked the front door. Ernie nodded in approval. On either side of the hallway behind us was a door leading to what could only be each officer's personal quarters.

"Which one?" Ernie whispered.

"Colonel Peele's name on the sign out front is on this side," I said, motioning to our left. "This is probably it."

The door was locked. Cautious guy. Of course, he worked with a lot of classified material, which probably had something to do with it. Ernie set to work, and in a little under a minute he opened the door. Inside, I switched on the light. The shades were pulled shut, and the first thing we saw was a bed, neatly made, and beyond that a tiled bathroom. We checked the room quickly, noting the highly polished boots and low quarters in the closet sitting beneath a row of dry-cleaned dress uniforms and a single set of fatigues.

"If that was him last night," Ernie whispered, "there'd be mud on these shoes."

"The maid probably already cleaned them."

"And the clothes he was wearing?"

"On their way to the laundry."

On the left side of the room was another door, this one padlocked from the outside. "What's that?" Ernie said.

"I don't know," I said. "More storage space or an office? Somewhere to lock up confidential paperwork?"

"Damn," Ernie replied. "These field-grade officers have it made."

Some enlisted barracks were "open bay." That is, thirty or forty men and their bunks and their wall lockers stuffed into one huge room. Here at 8th Army headquarters, most GIs had it better. Four men per room and the latrine down the hall.

But rank has its privileges, and Colonel Peele clearly enjoyed those privileges. So far, we'd seen nothing that told us anything about him, other than that he was a military officer with nice quarters and extremely neat living habits. The latter, most probably, thanks to the help of a civilian-hire housemaid.

"I'll bet the maid doesn't have a key to that," I said, pointing to the padlock.

"The inner sanctum," Ernie said.

He went to work on the lock. In less than five minutes, tumblers dropped and it popped open. He turned the knob, pushed lightly, and the door swung forward, creaking.

Sure enough, there sat a muddy pair of combat boots and a soiled set of fatigues. Ernie checked the mud on the boots. "Still fresh," he said. Above a desk was a row of wooden shelving, housing rows of nonfiction books, mostly on history and the military, plus a couple dozen Army Field Manuals. I grabbed one and slipped it out. Jungle Operations. I showed it to Ernie.

"Does it have a chapter on booby traps?"

I thumbed through it. "Yeah. It does, actually." I slid the manual back into place.

Arrayed on the wall nearest the door were photographs of a younger Colonel Peele, of lower rank and with hair, receiving plaques and awards from older officers who resembled what he would look like in future decades. There were a couple of Distinguished Service Medals and similar awards, plus the requisite ticket punch: the Republic of Vietnam Campaign Medal. What was interesting to me was the back wall, the one on the opposite side of the official photographs and the plaques and the Army Field Manuals.

Ernie gazed at the floor-to-ceiling display. "What a madman," he said. "This is like an art student's collage."

"A demented art student," I added.

"One that needs help. Serious help."

Pinned and taped and stapled to the wall was a massive collection of photographs and headlines and quotes and articles clipped out of newspapers, magazines, and even what looked like pages from books. Kim Il-sung, the Great Leader of North Korea, was featured prominently; sometimes smiling, sometimes waving to crowds, sometimes standing with both hands behind his back, gazing approvingly at rows of tanks and missiles and other military hardware. Also featured was Commander Lloyd Bucher, the skipper of the ill-fated USS *Pueblo*, a naval reconnaissance ship that was hijacked on the high seas by the North Korean Navy. Members of his crew, wearing prison uniforms, were also pictured, some of them crossing the Bridge of No Return in Panmunjom on the day they were finally released from captivity back in 1968. One of them had been carried back in a casket. A later photo showed a haggard Commander Bucher, slouching in a too-large dress uniform, sitting at the defense table during eventual hearings concerning the *Pueblo* incident. The Navy had accused him of abandoning his ship illegally, even though he'd been surrounded by North Korean gunboats and most observers believed that resistance would've been suicidal for Bucher and his crew. There were numerous black-and-white photos of the Korean War: refugees streaming south, women and children screaming as they looked up at the sky, mangled bodies laying in frozen mud.

But the most telling photo was more recent, and of Colonel Peele himself. I peered at it closely. He appeared to be wearing only the lieutenant colonel insignia on his shoulder, so it had been before he had been promoted to full colonel. He stood in a line with several other officers behind a two-star general who was somberly signing a document. Across from the general, fingers laced contentedly across his belly, sat a North Korean military officer.

"Peele worked at the MAC before," Ernie said, "on a previous assignment."

"Yeah," I said, "about six years ago, when the *Pueblo* crew was released."

"Doesn't seem like he's too proud of it."

Inked across the headlines and the articles and the photographs was a red hammer and sickle. And more photos of starving North Korean civilians and sailors floating facedown at sea, men screaming in anguish as they were being tortured. But the central document, clearly displayed most prominently, was a copy of the formal apology signed by the MAC Commander in order to obtain the release of the *Pueblo* crew.

A door slammed out front. Ernie and I glanced at one another. Without talking, we backed out of the inner sanctum, switching off the light and relocking the door. I stepped carefully past Colonel Peele's bed and, at the door to the hallway, stopped and listened.

"*Nugu-syo?*" a woman's voice said. "Who is it?"

The maid.

I spotted a clipboard with a few blank army forms atop Colonel Peele's dresser. I grabbed it and pulled out my pen and, holding them in front of me, I stepped into the hallway. A startled middle-aged Korean woman backed away.

"Inspection, *ajjima*," I said. "Let's go to the kitchen."

In my experience, a GI holding a clipboard can do no wrong. And the unlocked front door actually buttressed my story. An inspector from 8th Army Billeting would have a master key. The maid's eyes widened, but she acquiesced and we walked into the kitchen. I made a big show of checking the refrigerator and feeling for dust in the back of the cupboards, and I even turned on the oven and fiddled with its temperature control. All the while, I jotted down notes and asked the woman how often she cleaned the kitchen. Nervously, she replied that she came in five days a week and always made sure the kitchen was left spotless. I asked her how many years she'd been working here and she told me almost twenty, since the end of the Korean War. Down the hallway, Ernie relocked Colonel Peele's room and exited through the front door. Finally, at the completion of my "inspection," I smiled at the woman and said she'd passed with flying colors. I even shook her hand, bowed, and thanked her for her service to the US military. Relieved, she beamed in response.

On the way out, I shut the front door behind me and dumped the clipboard into the trash bin at the side of the building. Ernie had retrieved the jeep and swung it around to the front. I climbed in.

"She okay?" he asked.

"Yeah. Confused, but I don't think she'll call the MPs."

"Do you think she'll tell Peele?"

"Probably not. She'd be worried about it reflecting poorly on her. It's always the maid's fault."

"Or the butler's," Ernie said.

"What was that document?" Ernie asked. "At the center of the collage?"

"Only the most famous document in North Korea, after the *juche* philosophy of the Great Leader."

"What is it?"

"It's the one and only time the United States of America has apologized to a foreign country for something we didn't do."

"We *apologized* to North Korea?"

"In writing," I said. "For what the document called 'grave acts of espionage.'"

"Why?"

"It was the only way to convince them to release the *Pueblo* crew. We had to publicly admit that the spy ship had entered North Korean waters, which wasn't true. The USS *Pueblo* was assaulted on the high seas, in international waters. A clear act of war. As soon as the MAC Commander, Major General Woodward, signed the admission document, he made another statement renouncing it, saying the US had only cooperated to get the crew released."

"Bet the North Koreans weren't too happy about that."

"They didn't mind; they already had a legal document that admitted wrongdoing on behalf of the United States and abjectly apologized to the North Korean people, promising that we'd never do such a thing again. I've heard the original's on display in a museum somewhere near Pyongyang."

"And Peele was there for the signing."

"He must've been on staff at the time. For all we know, he's the one who drafted the false confession. Couldn't have been easy. A lot of officers had to swallow their pride for that. Not only their own, but their country's, too."

"No wonder Peele hates the North Koreans. And now that he's the Executive Officer of the MAC, he has the rank and authority to make them pay."

"Maybe he will," I said.

"Maybe," Ernie replied. "Or maybe he'll screw things up so badly he'll start another war."

"Please don't tell me that."

We encountered little traffic on the road to Paju-ri. A sign informed us that the city of Munsan could be reached by taking the next left, and that if we continued straight we'd reach Freedom Bridge and the Imjin River. Instead, at a small road with only a tiny sign in *hangul* script, Ernie turned right. The sign read: PAJU-RI, 2 KM.

We wound past rice paddies and tin-roofed farmhouses until the road was lined on either side with single-story wood-frame shops. Some sold feed, others farming equipment. At a main intersection, we turned left toward the river. At a rise, we had a good view of the rapidly flowing Imjin about 500 yards ahead. About two miles to our left loomed the heavily guarded Freedom Bridge.

A hundred yards below us on a steep incline sat a cluster of buildings, one of them two stories tall, most decorated with neon signs. The brightest one blinked red: The Lucky Seven Bar.

Ernie slowed, stepped on the clutch, and coasted downhill.

"Nirvana," he said. At precisely that moment, three more signs switched on. The Mini Skirt Club, the Rock Band Inn, and the Disco Club.

"Calling to me," he said.

"They've been waiting for you," I agreed.

"Rock and roll!" he shouted. Then he downshifted and the little jeep rumbled to a stop in front of the Lucky Seven Bar.

Her name was Ai-suk. Love-Chastity. When I asked for her family name, she clammed up. Apparently, that was too many questions too fast. She was a cocktail waitress at the Lucky Seven, and even though we were sitting at the bar she loitered next to us, her round stainless steel tray canted against shapely hips. She knew what time they would come.

"Bus leave after chow," she said. "Bring all GI south if they have pass. Drop them here." She pointed at the front door of the Lucky Seven. Her nails were painted red but gnawed close, probably from worrying. What else could a young woman do when she was estranged from her family and far from home, with her only source of income being what she could hustle from GIs barely out of their teens? The soldiers themselves were provided regular meals, dental care, a hundred percent medical, Serviceman's Group Life Insurance, a roof over their heads, and a complimentary bronze marker from the Veterans Administration if they were unfortunate enough to stop a bullet. Compared to Ai-suk, they didn't have a care in the world.

"Bus leave JSA eighteen-hundred hours," she said. "Arrive Lucky Seven maybe twenty minutes if bridge not busy."

If there wasn't a military convoy crossing Freedom Bridge.

"Does everybody have an overnight?" I asked.

"No. Nobody have overnight. Only on weekends if they get three-day pass. If they get, most GI go Yonjukol." A larger GI village about six miles south. "Or if they have *yobo* in Paju-ri, they stay here."

"Do any of them go to Seoul?" I asked.

"Most not. JSA GI afraid of Seoul."

"Afraid? Why?"

"Too big city. Too much they don't know. Too much trouble get there and get back. If they come back JSA late, *taaksan* trouble." She slashed the nail of her thumb across her slender throat.

"Do you have a *yobo* from the JSA?" I asked.

"No more. My last *yobo*, he go Stateside."

"How long ago?"

She thought about that. "Two, maybe three weeks."

"Do you miss him?"

Her eyes widened. "You *dingy dingy*?"

"No," I replied. "I'm not crazy."

"Paju-ri woman no can love GI," she replied, suddenly serious. "GI come. GI go. Always count days until go back Stateside. Go back wife. Go back girlfriend. Paju woman just make GI happy." She fluttered her fingers like a bird taking flight. "Then he go."

"What do you get in return?" I asked.

Her eyes widened once again. She was debating whether I was making fun of her. Apparently, she realized that I wasn't, so she answered seriously. "What Paju-ri woman get is we get to live."

"A little money," I said, "to pay for your hooch and your chop."

Instead of being sad about this, Ai-suk smiled. "And nice hair." She twirled her long black locks like a cresting wave in front of my face. I smelled the lilacs and watched her slender body as she twirled, giving me a good chance to look. Then she hit me lightly with the back of her tray.

"Seoul GI too smart," she said. "Seoul GI have too many girlfriend. Why you come play with poor Paju woman?"

Instead of answering, I said, "How much is a drink for you?"

"Me?" she asked surprised. "One thousand *won*." About two bucks. The beer I was drinking cost three hundred *won*.

"Here," I said, laying a thousand *won* note on the bar. "Before the JSA GIs come. One drink for Ai-suk."

Within seconds, the young male bartender set a pink concoction in front of Ai-suk. She clinked her glass against my brown beer bottle and sipped provocatively on the straw. I wanted to win her confidence now, and the confidence of the bar owner, before the JSA contingent arrived. I knew from experience that when the local GIs realized that a couple of

Seoul transplants had invaded their enclave and run up the prices by spoiling one of their bar girls with a sweetheart drink, the resentment grew out of proportion. They hated REMFs anyway—"rear-echelon MFs."

Ai-suk sipped again on her drink, then handed it to the bartender who hid it behind the bar just as the green Army bus from the JSA pulled up in front of the Lucky Seven Bar. GIs whooped and hollered, hopped out of the bus, and headed straight for the Lucky Seven's beaded curtain. They pushed through and, like a horde of pillaging Vikings, assaulted the pool cues and the green felt tables.

Before we'd left Seoul, Ernie and I had put on our running-the-ville outfits: blue jeans, sneakers, sport shirts with collars, and nylon jackets with fire-breathing dragons embroidered on the back. Still, we weren't fooling anyone. Every set of eyeballs flicked toward us as the GIs filtered into the club. They knew we were strangers, probably from Seoul, and their paranoia had almost certainly led them to believe we'd been sent to spy on them. Still, no one approached us. They just ordered beer, racked up billiard balls, and played grab-ass with the waitresses, pretending to be unconcerned by our intrusion.

After Ai-suk had served a couple of rounds, I called her over.

"Who works at the JSA?" I asked.

"All," she said.

"And who has the most rank?"

She nodded toward a thin black GI leaning over the far pool table, preparing to break. "Him," she said. "His name Gol-sun." She hustled off to serve more drinks.

The letter "g" in Korean is interchangeable with the letter "k." So I figured his name was Colson. His rank was probably buck sergeant, because if he were a corporal, he wouldn't be the ranking man in this group. And if he were any higher—say, a staff sergeant—he would've already reenlisted at least once, making him a lifer, and he wouldn't be hanging out in a bar with this group of young knuckleheads. Already two of them were squaring off in an argument over a bank shot.

I motioned to Ernie. It would be up to him to isolate Sergeant Colson so we could have a private conversation with him. Luckily, Colson wasn't much of a pool player. He lost the first game, replaced his cue in the rack, and slapped a coin at the end of the line of coins on the edge of the table. As he stood alone sipping his beer, watching the green felt action, Ernie sidled up to him.

They spoke. Colson eyed Ernie curiously. Apparently he wasn't buying anything Ernie had to say. Ernie reached into his jacket and pulled out his identification. When he flashed it, Colson seemed shocked, nervous. Ernie kept talking, apparently reassuring him that there was nothing to worry about. A couple of other guys noticed their conversation. Soon there was a small group surrounding Ernie, and two GIs stepped up to me.

"You with him?" one of them asked, pointing his thumb toward Ernie.

"Yeah," I said.

"Better get him out of here."

"Why?"

"We don't like REMFs coming up here and asking questions."

"Did Colonel Brunmeyer tell you to say that?"

Neither man answered, but the way they shuffled their feet answered my question. Voices were raised now. I didn't have much time.

"And what about Johnny No-Go?" I asked. "Do you really think he was murdered by Teddy Fusterman?"

Both GIs looked away. One of them hooked his thumbs into his front belt loops.

"You don't," I said. "So if somebody around here would answer our damned questions, maybe we could find out who *did* murder No-Go." I sensed I was making headway as they shifted their gazes to the floor. "I visited his parents today," I told them, "and his kid sister. You can't even imagine what it's like for them."

But it seemed they could. The more talkative of the two said, "We don't know nothing. Nobody saw anything until those two guys spotted the body. That's all we know."

Ernie had managed to turn the tide. The little gang of GIs surrounding him was now listening intently. A couple were even laughing softly.

"So why does the colonel want you to keep quiet?"

"JSA business is JSA business. We don't need nobody on the outside butting in."

"Are you going to put it to the North Koreans?"

Again they looked uncomfortable.

"But there's no reason to," I said, "if Teddy Fusterman goes away for life for the murder. Why not be nice to the NKs? Treat 'em like pals."

The GI shook his head, confused.

"What's your name?" I asked.

"Not your business," he said, mimicking the cadence of Korean bar girls.

Just then someone shouted. I swiveled and saw Ernie push past two GIs, who reeled backward from the impact. He started to sprint for the front door, but one of the men reacted quickly and was about to collar him. I stepped away from my interlocutors and grabbed the back of the GI's shirt just as his forearm arced toward Ernie's neck. He jerked back, and his forward momentum had been slowed enough for Ernie to make his escape through the beaded door curtain. I jerked the GI backward and tossed him to the floor, then followed Ernie out through the still-rattling beads. Behind me, a poorly aimed beer bottle smashed against wood.

-13-

Just as I surged through the exit, one of the JSA GIs raced after me. Ernie landed a roundhouse kick to his midsection and the GI groaned and went down. Then we were running up the street, probably a quarter mile before we slowed and looked back. A few of the GIs were milling about in front of the Lucky Seven Bar, but they were mostly just posturing and jacking their jaws. None of them seemed inclined to form a posse and come after us.

"Nice fellows," Ernie said.

"What'd Colson tell you?" I asked.

"He told me to perform an impossible biological task."

"Did you?"

"Not yet. Maybe when I'm more limber."

"Yoga might help."

Still looking back to make sure we weren't being followed, Ernie and I walked deeper into the village of Paju-ri. When we were sure no one was behind us, we started to breathe easy again.

In a back alley, I inquired at an open-fronted *kagei* as to where I might be able to buy military supplies. The proprietress shook her head, so Ernie took the opportunity to load up with three double-packs of ginseng gum. After he paid her, he asked again in a nice way, using English that I doubt she understood. There must have been something about his boyish charm that helped her to open up. Her wrinkled face smiled beneath her white bandana, and she pointed down the street and told us in Korean to turn left past the grain warehouse. Ernie thanked her and unwrapped a stick of ginseng gum as we left.

"She didn't understand a word you said," I told him.

"Sure she did," he replied. "I speak the universal language."

"You mean love?" I asked.

"No. I mean being open to the possibilities of the universe."

"You been smoking that shit again?"

"I'm high on life," Ernie said, grinning.

He loved Paju-ri.

The old man was happy to see us.

"You buy?" he asked, pointing at the web belts and ammo pouches and rubberized rain parkas arrayed on the tables in his store.

I shook my head, then mimicked a man digging with a shovel. "You have?" I asked.

His smile beamed wider as he nodded and motioned for us to follow him into the back room. It was dimly lit with rotted wooden walls, probably built with cheap material just after the end of the Korean War. Places like this existed outside just about every military camp in the country. In the States, we might call them Army and Navy Surplus stores. In Korea, they were considered black market operations, since they dealt in military supplies often pilfered from American compounds. They stayed open because they fulfilled a need, because there was a demand for their inventory. With South Korea not manufacturing much domestically in the way of consumer goods, rural communities could make good use of the canvas and plastic and sturdy metal tools that overflowed from US bases like fruit from a cornucopia. Even GIs bought items here. If your equipment was lost, stolen, or otherwise destroyed, it was cheaper to purchase a used replacement on the black market than something new from the military. The Army doesn't play around in this respect: every soldier is responsible for his own equipment, and if he loses it, even during the most hectic field maneuvers or the most trying weather conditions, the expense is on him.

The old man switched on a naked bulb that hung from a rafter. Next to a pile of rubber overshoes and a mound of camouflage netting sat about a dozen entrenching tools. Most were older models, clearly used—their wooden handles worn and their digging blades too rusted at the hinges to fold. Some probably dated back to the Korean War. I shuffled through them quickly, tossing aside the ones that weren't of use to me. After checking them all without finding what I was looking for, I turned to the old man and said, "*Seiro-nun kot issoyo*?" Do you have any new ones?

Ernie was watching the elderly proprietor closely and saw what I saw. The shift of his eyes away from us, a furtive shake of the head.

Ernie grabbed the old man by the upper arm and said, "New ones. You *arra*? New ones."

The old man looked up at Ernie, terrified. He probably thought he was being robbed. I took pity on him and pulled out my CID badge, waving it in front of his nose and speaking in Korean as I did so. Show us the new ones, I told him, and we won't bother you further. A shakedown by government officials was something he could deal with, something he was used to— just part of doing business; nothing dangerous like a robbery. The old man visibly relaxed and then nodded enthusiastically. We followed him to the front counter. He knelt down in the darkness and reached far back in a shelf, and for a moment I thought he might come back out with a shotgun. Instead, he stood up and dropped two pristine-looking Army-issue entrenching tools onto the counter. He slid them toward us.

As I examined the newer models, the old man shone a flashlight up and down the sturdy wooden handles and along the cutting blades. I spotted something just below the fat adjusting nut and gasped. Ernie grabbed the entrenching tool for a closer look. He screwed the nut into the fully locked position until two scratched-in letters revealed themselves.

"Initials," he said. "T.F. Teddy Fusterman."

"Just like he said."

"But how'd it get here?"

I turned to the old man and questioned him in Korean. At first, he was reluctant to divulge the shovel's provenance. But when I showed him my Criminal Investigation badge again and then reminded him for good measure that theft from a US military compound was not only a crime, but a breach of national security in the eyes of the Korean government, he began to quake in fear.

Those who pose a threat to national security in South Korea are not treated well. Criminals alone were sentenced to long terms in austere prisons, but anyone perceived to be weakening national defense could expect the harshest of punishments. Even execution by hanging. Stealing a single entrenching tool wouldn't warrant that, but if I pressed the issue and complained to the KNPs, the resulting embarrassment in itself would be enough for the Korean courts to come down hard on this virtually defenseless businessman.

Perspiration appeared spontaneously on the man's forehead. I pushed him for an answer. He wiped his face with the back of his hand and, stuttering, began to explain. One of his regular suppliers, he said, was a Korean man who worked on the US military compound. He was a contract trash collector, and he and his crew picked up north of the Imjin at Camp Greaves, Four-Papa-One, and Camp Kitty Hawk. It was there, at Camp Kitty Hawk, just yards from the JSA, that the trash collector had found the entrenching tool. It had been shoved deep into a trash drum, covered by refuse. Whoever had hidden it there probably hadn't realized that the Korean trash collectors routinely checked for items they could recycle, including aluminum cans and beer bottles. Or ones they could repair, like broken Stateside appliances. Or things that were still fully serviceable, like the entrenching tool. They later sold these outright on the Korean black market to shop owners like this man in Paju-ri.

I asked for the supplier's name. He gave it to me, and I jotted it down in my notebook using *hangul*. I then showed it to him to confirm that I'd spelled it correctly. He nodded, but I sensed by the confusion in his eyes that he wasn't really sure. Decades before, when he had been of school age, the Japanese Empire had annexed Korea and made it illegal to teach the Korean language in school. Only Japanese had been taught. As a result, many people his age could barely read and write their national language.

When I asked him how much for the entrenching tool, he simply bowed and told us there was no charge. The pervasive influence of the Korean National Police. Still, I knew he had paid for it, and I didn't want him absorbing the full financial loss. I thrust five thousand *won* on the counter, about ten bucks. Hesitating at first, he finally accepted the money.

When we left, he must have been happy to see us go.

▪ ▪ ▪

"How about fingerprints?" Ernie asked as we drove back to Seoul.

"We can try," I said, "but whoever crammed that entrenching tool into the trash probably wiped it down beforehand."

"At least we know it wasn't a North Korean. Camp Kitty Hawk is south of the JSA; there's no way a Commie could make it down that far."

"Well, somebody could've lifted it from the crime scene and taken it down to Kitty Hawk."

"Why?"

"Either to cover up their own crime or hide the fact that a North Korean did it."

"Why would anybody want to help the North Koreans?" Ernie asked.

"To prevent war," I said.

"Oh, yeah. That."

"The fact is," I said, "we don't really know how this entrenching tool ended up with that black market papa-*san*. All we have is his testimony. We can't be sure who took it there or whether it's Teddy Fusterman's. A lot of GIs must have the initials TF."

"You worry too much, Sueño. This'll get Fusterman off."

"I wouldn't be so sure."

▪ ▪ ▪

We locked the entrenching tool beneath the fold-up panel on the floorboard of the jeep beneath the passenger seat. It barely fit next to the jack and crowbar and two red flares that resembled sticks of dynamite. Ernie padlocked the steering wheel and we stared up at the bright lights of Myong-dong.

With our blue jeans and sneakers and embroidered nylon jackets, we weren't exactly dressed for the sojourn. However, the outfits provided us good cover. The local sophisticates would figure that we were just a couple of bumpkin GIs, drunk and out of our element. And maybe that was what we were— aside from the drunk part, which Ernie planned to remedy.

"Let's stop at that *pochang macha*," he said.

"For what?" As if I didn't know.

"For some pig's blood dumplings," Ernie said sarcastically as he trotted off.

Pochang macha literally translates to "linen-covered horse cart." In ancient times, merchants would wander from village to village with a cart pulled by a horse or ox, their shelves loaded with exotic products otherwise unavailable to the isolated farmers of the Korean hinterlands. Wares like cut glass or metal pans or nails or textiles milled in modern factories. The concept had since changed. *Pochang macha*s now sold food and drink, rather than durable consumer goods. The carts were on large rubber wheels, but instead of being pulled by a beast of burden, they were pushed by the owner or his or her spouse, and their activities were required to be formally licensed by the city. They wandered through the massive metropolis of Seoul and set up in narrow alleys, often near bus stops or train stations. On rough benches, protected from the elements by a canvas awning, tired businessmen would jolt back a few shots of soju, the country's fiery rice liquor, often accompanied by snacks to settle worried stomachs. Favorites included pig gut stew and diced bean curd bubbling in red pepper broth, which the owner cooked right there over a charcoal stove bolted to the center of the cart.

Ernie had no time to eat. He handed the proprietor a few coins and returned with a half-liter bottle of Jinro soju. He popped the cap with his teeth and offered me the first slug.

"You go ahead," I told him.

He did. Glugging back a mouthful, grimacing, blowing out air, and then chugging another.

"You on the wagon?" he asked.

"Have you ever known me to be on the wagon?"

"You were when Leah Prevault had you toeing the line."

I looked away. "She was worried about my health."

"And now she's gone. So you can drink as much as you like."

I went silent at this. Captain Leah Prevault was a psychiatrist who'd been stationed at the 121st Evacuation Hospital in Seoul. We'd worked with her on more than one case, and she and I had become acquainted. One thing had led to another, and suddenly we were breaking every non-fraternization rule in the book. When she was transferred, it had been tough to say goodbye. She was now at Tripler Army Hospital in

Honolulu, and we corresponded pretty much constantly. She'd even managed to swing some temporary duty orders and return to Seoul about two months ago, ostensibly working on the backlog of patients that had built up at the 121 but also spending time with me. Eventually, though, she'd had to return to Honolulu, and I wondered if the occasional reunions weren't more painful than not seeing her at all.

"Sorry," Ernie said. "Guess I hit a nerve."

"Never mind," I said. "So Evelyn Cresthill and this Korean mystery woman get out of the PX cab right about here." The huge edifice of the Shinsegae Department Store loomed above us. "Where do they go?"

Ernie sipped on the soju, glancing around at the shops and the neon as he pondered the question. Pedestrians, mostly middle-aged women with shopping bags and young couples clinging closely to one another, streamed past us.

"The driver, Young Kim," Ernie said, "he told us they planned to go to a nightclub."

"Yeah. Somewhere beautiful, with music."

"Two unescorted ladies," Ernie said. "Sitting alone at a table. If there were plenty of gentlemen around, it wouldn't be long until they had company."

"Gentlemen?" I said.

"Yeah. What else? They'd want guys with money. Not a bunch of dumb gigolos."

"Are you sure? Evelyn couldn't have much money, not since

her husband closed down their joint bank account. But maybe the Korean woman did."

"I don't think so," Ernie replied. "She sounds like a recruiter to me. Camped out in the O'Club, waiting for prey."

What Ernie said made sense, but I wanted to hear his take on it. "What do you mean, 'recruiter'?"

"A recruiter," Ernie repeated. "Targeting pretty young white women. Some Korean businessmen, and definitely Japanese ones, will pay a lot for a blonde."

"Evelyn Cresthill has red hair."

"Close enough," Ernie replied with a shrug.

"You think this Korean broad was trying to show Evelyn the ropes?"

Ernie nodded.

"In return for what?"

"A piece of the action."

"Okay," I said. "Or maybe it's worse."

Ernie waited.

"Evelyn didn't come home. If she'd just spent the night with a rich businessman, the next morning she'd at least head back to check on her daughter, even pick up some fresh clothes?"

"But she didn't," Ernie said.

"No."

"So maybe the Korean broad isn't just a pimp."

"No," I said. "She might be something worse. Something Evelyn Cresthill hadn't bargained for."

-14-

The Blue Heaven Nightclub was only two blocks in from the mouth of the narrow road that branched off from the Shinsegae Department Store. Ernie and I had already hit almost a dozen joints, all full of painted ladies hired to seduce men into opening their wallets. We doubted they were the types of places Evelyn Cresthill would feel comfortable.

"If the Korean woman took her into one of those," Ernie said, "Evelyn probably would've backed out and gone home."

"I hope so."

We kept searching and eventually stumbled through the front door of the Blue Heaven.

"This is more like it," Ernie said.

It was an expansive ballroom with plush red carpeting and a stage hidden behind blue drapes, surrounded by a small sea of tables with white linen tablecloths and flickering candles exuding a seductive glow. In front of us, an elegant Korean couple was greeted by a tuxedoed maître d' who offered, with his open palm, to escort them to a table. He pulled a chair back for the lady—an unusual gesture in Korea.

"Western courtesies," I said.

"Probably better than Quincy showed her," Ernie replied.

"Or her husband."

As the maître d' schmoozed with the couple, the curtains opened onto the stage, swishing silently. Lights clicked on, and a twenty-piece, all-male orchestra in white dinner coats launched into a Korean song. I vaguely recognized the melody.

"Class," Ernie said. "Shitty music, but class."

"Evelyn would've liked this," I said.

"Yeah. What's not to like? Being catered to by a guy in a tuxedo, swanky surroundings. Heaven for the bored house-wife."

"Except for the expense," I said.

"Not to worry. The Korean broad would find some sucker to pay for their drinks."

Around the ballroom, about half the tables were occupied. A good crowd of about fifty people, and it was still early. I pulled the photograph Major Cresthill had given us from my pocket. Evelyn Cresthill smiled at me. She was nice-looking—not a great beauty, but definitely presentable.

The maître d' finally finished with the couple at the table and walked toward us. As he approached, I saw his beaming expression droop, then crumble.

Ernie sneered. "They're only happy to see GIs when we're

standing between them and a communist invasion." He pulled the bottle of soju from his pocket and took a quick sip.

When the maître d' arrived, I spoke to him in Korean and showed him the photograph of Evelyn Cresthill. He shone a small flashlight on it, and something flickered across his face. Recognition. Still, he shook his head. I slipped the photo back into my pocket and pulled out my badge.

"I want to speak with your waiters," I told him. "I need to show this photo to all of them."

"I will show," he offered.

"No," I replied. "We want to talk to them ourselves."

Ernie sipped more soju. "This asshole's trying to get rid of us," he said in an audible half-whisper.

Several people were now lined up behind us at the entranceway.

The maître d' motioned for us to step aside. "*Jomganman kidaryo*," he said. Please wait.

Ernie understood that and shook his head. "No wait. We talk to your waiters *now*. You *arra*?"

Two men emerged from the darkness on either side. They weren't waiters, that was for sure. They were easily burly enough to be weightlifters, and the dim light from the lamp over the maître d's counter illuminated huge calluses bulging from their knuckles.

"All right," Ernie said, chugging more soju. "Here comes the muscle. I'm so scared."

His expression purposefully grim, one of the big guys motioned us aside with an open palm.

"No," Ernie said. "We're not going anywhere. Not until you take us to the waitstaff. My partner here would like to speak to them."

Flustered, glancing between us and the increasingly impatient customers, the maître d' spoke in rapid Korean to the bouncers. I caught part of it: Take them to the waiters. Let them talk.

The lead bouncer's face seemed to carry traces of disappointment amidst its impassiveness, but he bowed to the maître d' and gestured with his palm once again and spoke to us in English. "Waiter. We go."

I nodded and we followed. One bouncer in front of us, the other behind.

In a busy, well-lit serving area, thin-hipped young men in tight black trousers and white shirts and red vests grabbed glasses and bottles of sparkling wine and shouted food orders to a half-dozen white-capped cooks behind a stainless steel counter. The bouncer motioned for Ernie and me to enter. Then he and his partner stood, rough hands across broad chests, bookending the doorway.

"Frick and Frack," Ernie said.

"What's that mean, anyway?" I asked.

"Huh?"

"Frick and Frack? I hear it all the time for two guys who

look alike. But where's it come from? Who's Frick, and who's Frack?"

"Who gives a shit, Sueño? You're too damn curious."

I turned my attention back to the busy waiters. The young men, running back and forth between the kitchen and the service bar, projected barely controlled chaos.

"What's it like when they get busy?" Ernie asked.

"Must be like this, except more so. How are we supposed to get their attention?"

Ernie uncapped his soju and took a swig. He plucked a napkin from the bar, wiped off the rim, and gave the bottle to me. I made too large a swallow, coughed, wiped my mouth on my sleeve, and chugged another mouthful before handing the bottle back to him.

"You ready now?" he asked.

"Almost." Working the resulting air up through my chest, I burped. "Okay," I said. "Ready."

Some of the waiters had started to glance at us warily. They knew we were up to something, but weren't sure if it was their concern. I hesitated until another waiter pushed through the swinging double doors into the serving area and shouted out a food order. As he stepped toward the bar, I blocked his path.

"*Yoboseiyo*," I said, an all-purpose greeting. I showed him the photograph of Evelyn and asked him in Korean if he recognized the woman in it. He brushed past me, bemused as he looked back, shaking his head and smiling to himself, almost laughing. Then he shouted in Korean, "*E sikki weigurei?*" What's wrong with this so-and-so?

Ernie understood the vulgar part of the sentence. He stepped forward, grabbed the waiter by the arm, and jerked him back. "Look!" he shouted, pointing at the photo. "You see? You tell us about her!"

The waiter pulled away, and then they were struggling. Ernie pushed forward and the waiter reeled backward, trying to twist his body away and smashing into a short tower of precariously stacked tableware. The delicate porcelain teetered, leaned, and tipped over, crashing into thousands of pieces on the tiled floor. Curse words flew and everyone rushed forward, including the two bouncers.

I tried to tell everyone to remain calm, but before I could get even a few words out, one of the bouncers grabbed me from behind. I dropped to a crouch, elbowed him in the groin, and then rose abruptly, cracking the top of my skull against his thick jaw. He reeled away, and then one of the waiters smacked me in the head with his tray. When I swiveled, the second bouncer ran full force into me and tackled me to the ground. I rolled atop scattered shards of expensive china. The bouncer leapt off me, and in the swirling mass of faces and arms and cutlery, I spotted Ernie swinging something around that resembled a frozen leg of lamb. He clunked the bouncer upside the head, and the man went down. Ernie helped me to my feet, pulled me toward the swinging doors, and we were out of the kitchen, stumbling between linen-covered tables, women screaming as we passed. From behind his podium, the maître d' pulled what looked like a sawed-off shotgun. He pointed it at us and said, "*Umjiki-jima, sikkya!*" Which even Ernie could figure out meant: *Don't move.* With an off-color reference to our maternal ancestors thrown in for good measure.

We held up our hands.

"See," Ernie said, "I told you."

"Told me what?"

"They have a bias against Americans."

"And here we were, on our best behavior."

Five minutes later, the KNPs arrived.

I tried to explain to the officer in charge that it was all a misunderstanding, and that we were there to conduct witness interviews for an important case, but he wasn't buying it. Not until I showed him the calling card for Mr. Kill; that is Inspector Gil Kwon-up, Chief Homicide Inspector for the Korean National Police, or Mr. Kill. The card was printed in English on one side and Korean on the other. As the cop read it, he blanched. Within seconds he was on the phone, and a few minutes later, he was murmuring deferential responses to the person on the other end, who seemed to be barking orders at him. Each time he said, "Yes, sir, I understand," in Korean, he bowed as if his superior was standing right in front of him. Finally, he hung up, face red. His voice deepened and he barked orders at his fellow cops.

"We're in," I whispered to Ernie.

All the customers had been chased out of the nightclub, and now the employees sheepishly approached the officer in charge. He motioned for me to show them the photograph. I did. As it passed from waiter to waiter, everyone kept their face impassive, including the maître d', who was last to study the photo. The head cop took it back and returned it to me. Then he asked if anyone recognized the foreign woman. Everyone kept their heads bowed and their mouths shut.

The KNPs weren't exactly trusted by the general populace. Cops in Korea, like everywhere else, were overworked and underpaid. So underpaid, in fact, that if they ever planned to make a house payment or save money so their kids could go to university, they were forced to make a little extra on the side. Bribes were routine. A traffic citation could be avoided by paying the "fine" up front. If you were about to be dragged into the station for a one-off incident like brawling in public, a bow, an apology, and a small wad of folded bills could usually prevent the embarrassment and paperwork. Sometimes the KNPs were used by the authoritarian Park Chung-hee government to round up dissidents or other enemies of the regime. As such, people were wary of the police. Cooperation from the public was seldom forthcoming. At least, voluntary cooperation. When no one answered, the cop pounded his fist on a table, cursed, walked up to the stylish maître d', and slapped him across the chops. The sound reverberated through the empty ballroom. "*Iyagi hei!*" Talk!

The man grabbed his cheek and focused his gaze on the ground. "*An boasso,*" he said. I didn't see.

Ernie and I knew how brutal the Korean National Police could be, and we weren't happy with this tactic of group intimidation, but it was too late to do anything about it now. If we intervened, the Korean cop would lose face and things would get even worse.

The cop went to the next man in line and slapped him even harder. Again, a denial of having seen the foreign woman. The cop worked down the line, growing progressively more enraged, and pulling his arm back farther and making each slap ring out louder until he reached a slender young man who seemed to be the youngest of the lot. Most of these waiters were tough, cynical, inured to abuse. This one seemed like someone who'd never quite resigned himself to the cruelty in the human heart, never formed the hard outer shell of his colleagues, and thus stood before us raw as a nerve. Before the cop even hit him, the terrified young man was already crying.

"*Iyagi hei!*" the cop said.

When the man didn't answer, but just stood there quivering, the cop said, "*Boasso? Anboasso?*" Did you see her? Didn't you see her?

His answer was just a whisper.

"*Muol?*" the cop said. What?

"*Boasso,*" the young man said. I saw her.

The cop leaned forward and said "*Odi?*" Where?

The young waiter pointed toward a booth by the back wall.

We pulled him to the side and told the rest of the wait-ers and the maître d' and bouncers and cooks to wait in the kitchen. The cop then sat the young man down at a table and had some barley tea brought to him. The whimpering slowed, and the cop offered him a *Kobukson* cigarette. Soon, the two of them were puffing away on the Turtleboat-brand tobacco like old friends. Then the interrogation began in earnest.

I sat at the table with them and listened to everything, tak-ing notes as I did so. Ernie, meanwhile, wandered outside with his bottle of soju. When the cop had asked all the questions he could think of, he turned to me and said. "*Munjei issoyo?*" Do you have anything to ask?

I did. They both seemed surprised that I could speak Korean. However, when the young man answered, he prattled away too fast, and I had to slow him down and ask him to explain certain words and expressions. "*Kandanhan-mal hei-juseiyo,*" I said. Please speak simply.

The woman who'd brought Evelyn Cresthill into the Blue Heaven Nightclub was well known to the wait staff. I asked if she usually came in alone or with other people.

"Always someone else," he told me. "Another woman."

"Was this one at a time, or in groups?"

"One at a time. Never more than one. But different women over time."

"What kind of women were these?"

"Nice ladies."

"Rich ladies?"

He shook his head. "No. Nice ladies. Not rich ones."

"These women she came in with, were they Koreans or foreigners?"

His mouth twisted. "I can't be sure. They didn't usually talk."

"But some looked Korean?"

He nodded. "And others were Chinese," he said.

"Any Japanese?" I asked.

"No Japanese."

"How can you be so certain?"

"I know."

I paused. "How do you know?"

"Clothes," he said. "And the way they talked."

"They had accents?"

"Yes, the Korean ones weren't from South Korea. I'm sure."

"Where were they from? North Korea?"

"No. North Korean women are small. Skinny. These women were healthy, but spoke Korean with strong accents."

"Maybe from America?" I asked.

"No," he said. "From China."

Millions of Koreans lived in what was now the People's

Republic of China. There had been small enclaves of ethnically Korean people in the northern provinces of Manchuria
for centuries, but many more had joined them during Imperial
Japan's brutal colonization of Korea between 1910 and 1945.
More recently, in the early 1950s, many had fled to China to
escape the massive slaughter of the Korean War.

"So she brought in Chinese and Korean women from
China. Had she ever brought in an American or European
woman before?"

"No," the waiter replied. "This lady first *kocheingi*." Big
nose. He pointed at the photograph of Evelyn Cresthill, which
lay on the table.

"Was the American woman happy to be here? Was she
enjoying herself?"

"Yes, very much. They drank and ate snacks. Sliced fruit."

These joints in Myong-dong charged plenty for the drinks
and even more for what the Koreans called *anju*—de rigueur
plates of either fruit or dried peanuts or the higher-class
shrimp and assorted seafood.

I asked the waiter how long they'd stayed and whether
they'd been joined by anyone else. He told me they'd only
spent about an hour in the Blue Heaven Nightclub, no men
had approached them, and they'd left together.

I felt a partial sense of relief. Evelyn hadn't been picked
up by some guy out to hurt women, at least not here. This
left her female companion as the primary suspect. But where

had the pair gone after striking out? The waiter said he had no idea.

When I was done with the nervous young man, I told the KNP officer in charge that I wanted to speak to the nightclub's owner. He said he'd already checked on that angle and told me that the owner was no longer on the premises. When I pressed him, he flatly denied me permission to contact the proprietor on my own.

"You talk to Gil Kwon-up," he said. Inspector Kill. "He talk to owner. Not you."

I knew I was lucky to have received as much cooperation as I had. Without Inspector Kill's help, I would've gotten nowhere. There was no sense pushing it further. Not tonight. This door had been shut in my face, and would remain so unless I found the leverage to pry it open.

After we left, Ernie said, "The other waiters are going to beat the crap out of the guy who talked."

"Why?"

"For being a snitch."

"What's it to them? We're searching for a missing woman."

Ernie scoffed. "Working-class people don't talk to the cops. He broke ranks. The odd bird in the flock—they'll peck him to death. It's the way of the world."

-15-

When we returned to the 8th Army headquarters Yongsan Compound, it was dark except for yellow streetlamps and the flashing red light atop the commo tower. The occasional duty vehicle cruised by.

"What the hell we gonna do with this entrenching tool?" Ernie asked.

"We can't send it to Camp Zama," I replied, referring to the official Army lab in Japan. "We're supposed to be off the case."

"We have to hide it somewhere. At least until Fusterman is assigned a defense attorney. Then we can turn it over to him."

"Hide it where?" We both knew that the barracks wouldn't be secure. The company commander could inspect our rooms anytime he wanted—even pry open our wall lockers if he felt like it. "The safe in the CID office won't work either," I continued. "Riley pokes his nose in there all the time."

Ernie thought for a moment. "I've got it," he said.

"Where?"

"Where they'll never look."

"Where?"

"The heart of Eighth Army headquarters."

"What?"

"The main ventricle."

Then it dawned on me. "You mean Strange."

"Right. The Classified Documents vault. What could be safer?"

"And if they inspect his vault?"

"When's the last time they did that?"

"Years ago, probably. They're afraid of what they might find." I thought about it, considering the risk, and then said, "But what if it's due for a search?"

"Then Strange is just the man who'll know where to shove it," Ernie said. "A three-foot-long entrenching tool should fit just about right."

The next morning we caught Strange just as he left his quarters and told him what we wanted him to do.

"Why me?" he asked.

"Because you're our favorite Classified Documents honcho."

"I'm the *only* Classified Documents honcho you know."

"That too."

He pondered our request, or pretended to. Strange fancied himself a James Bond type, an international man of mystery.

"What do I get out of the deal?" he asked.

"Health," Ernie replied.

"Health?"

"Yeah. I don't beat the crap out of you."

He agreed to do what we asked.

We gave him a ride over to the 8th Army headquarters building. As Ernie drove, I leaned back and casually asked, "What do you know about Colonel Peele over at the MAC?"

"Everything," Strange replied. "What do you want to know?"

"Why's he hate the North Koreans so much?"

"You didn't know?"

"Know what?"

"He was one of the guys who drafted that phony apology to the North Korean people and the Great Leader himself."

"So?" Ernie said. "He was just doing his job. Somebody had to get the *Pueblo* crew out of there."

"But he took it hard," Strange said. "A lot of the officers did. That was the first time the United States ever apologized to a foreign government—and the charges they were apologizing for were a *lie*. Peele started drinking. They told me the constant reek of booze pissed off his wife. The Army promoted him to full colonel, but that was more or less compensation for what he'd had to do."

"But doesn't that put him in pretty good standing?"

"Word is that nobody involved in that fiasco will ever make it to general officer rank—they're 'tainted.' You know how the

Army is. They get you to do something, then hate you for it. I suppose Peele could've lived with never pinning a star on his shoulder, but then his son was turned down for West Point."

"A lot of people are turned down for West Point," Ernie said.

"Not when you're a straight-A student through high school and your dad's a regular Army colonel."

I shifted in my seat. "So Peele's 'taint' affected his son, too."

Strange shrugged. "Who knows? The Academy claimed it was just the unusual number of highly qualified applicants that year. But I imagine Colonel Peele assumed otherwise. Still, he's a tough old bird. He could've survived that, too. It was his son who didn't take it too well."

"What happened?"

"He committed suicide. Left a note. Considered himself a disgrace, a failure to his father and to his country. Shortly after they buried the kid, Peele's wife filed for divorce; hired a good lawyer and scored half of Peele's military retirement in the process."

"How do you know all this?" Ernie asked.

"Keep your eyes and ears open," Strange said, "and you can learn things too."

Especially if you worked cheek-by-jowl with the gossip-prone officers of 8th Army headquarters, evidently.

"So now Peele's returned to the scene of the crime," Ernie said. "The Military Armistice Commission."

"And this time," Strange said, "with a silver eagle on his shoulder and a hard-on in his pants."

"A hard-on for who?"

"The Great Leader himself."

When we arrived at the back entrance of the headquarters building, Strange climbed out of the backseat of the jeep, Fusterman's entrenching tool tucked under his arm.

"You owe me," he said, pointing to the tool. "And for the information. I don't give it out for free." He turned and waddled off into the building, the self-closing door shutting behind him.

"There goes a dedicated soldier," Ernie said.

"And a prime gossip."

"Wish there were more like him," he replied.

At the 8th Army CID office, Staff Sergeant Riley gave his usual cheerful welcome.

"Where in the hell you guys *been*?"

"Investigating," Ernie replied.

"Fooling around is more like it."

The coffee urn in the back was perking, and Ernie pulled himself a cup.

"It's not *done* yet!" Riley shouted.

"How do you tell the difference?"

Ernie returned to Riley's desk, plucked a pristine copy of today's *Stars and Stripes* out of Riley's inbox, and sat down in a chair with padded gray vinyl. Miss Kim hadn't arrived yet.

"You're at work early," Riley said, eyeing us suspiciously. "You're up to something."

"Dedicated soldiers," Ernie replied, flipping to the comics.

"You find Evelyn Cresthill yet?"

"We're working on it."

"I can see that." Riley pulled a stack of memos toward the center of his desk blotter.

"We need a favor, Riley," I said.

"Don't you always."

"Who's handling the prosecution at JAG?"

"You mean for Fusterman?" When I nodded, he said, "You're off that case. Didn't you read the statement you signed yesterday?"

"Yeah. We're off. So who's handling it?"

"Who do you think? Hot shit herself. First Lieutenant Peggy Mendelson."

"They gave her a murder case?"

"Yeah. She's moving up fast."

"And who's on the defense?"

He rummaged through some paperwork. "I've got it here somewhere." Finally, he said, "Hughes, Patrick C., Captain. Some officer in transit between assignments."

"A *dud*," Ernie said. An artillery round that didn't fire.

"Maybe," Riley replied. "At least, that's who JAG appointed.

But he might not be working alone. Apparently, Fusterman's parents are hiring a Stateside lawyer."

Ernie lowered the newspaper. "A Stateside lawyer?" He whistled. "They must be loaded."

"I don't know about that, but they're going all-out to save their son."

An unexpected stab of anguish flashed through me, wrenching the flesh from my throat to the pit of my stomach. I realized I was jealous. What must it be like to have parents who loved you so much? To have parents at all. My mother had died when I was very young, so I harbored no blame for her, but my father had run off to Mexico, never to return. I'd grown up in foster homes financed by the Supervisors of the County of Los Angeles. A few of my foster parents had been fine; some, not so much. Like the guy who'd locked me in a closet for making too much noise. I don't remember exactly how long I'd been in there, but to a seven-year-old, it had seemed like an eternity. I'd eventually fallen asleep. As a teen-ager, I grew quickly, and by the age of fourteen I was taller than most grown men. I made my foster fathers nervous. And well I should have. I was through taking crap from them, through being locked in closets. And I would force them to back off whenever they tried to scream at the younger kids.

As soon as I turned seventeen, I dropped out of high school and said my goodbyes to Mrs. Aaronson, my last foster mother and maybe the best. She'd made sure that I'd done my homework every night, and she'd even reviewed it to make sure it was correct. She was the woman who'd helped me to get as far as I had. Once I joined the US Army, the military became my family. A dysfunctional one, to be sure, but my family nonetheless.

"Sueño," Riley said, calling me out of my reverie. "You want the contact information?"

"Whose contact information?"

"The Stateside defense lawyer. Who else we talking about?"

"Oh, yeah." I pulled out my notebook and a pen.

He gave me the information, and without interrupting him, I jotted it down. When he finished, I said, "A *she*?"

"Yeah. They're allowed to be lawyers now. Ever since they got the right to vote."

"And she's coming all the way to Korea?"

"Yeah. Bold, I know. But she's on her way. Arrives at Kimpo this afternoon."

"You have the flight number?"

Riley sighed and gave me the information. "Don't tell anyone I told you. You're off this case. You got it?"

"Got it. But who knows, Evelyn Cresthill might be out at Kimpo International Airfield even now, as we speak."

"She could pop up anywhere," Ernie said.

Riley looked at us each in turn, shook his head, and turned back to his memos, muttering, "Hopeless."

I was about to start typing my report on what we'd done

yesterday when Miss Kim walked in. I stood and greeted her, and she smiled and returned the greeting. Just as she sat at her desk, stashed her purse in a drawer, and pulled the cover off her *hangul* typewriter, the cannon went off. Zero eight hundred, the start of the business day.

Shrilly, Miss Kim's phone rang.

Miss Kim answered in a high, lilting voice. "*Yoboseiyo.*" She listened and switched to English. "Just a moment." With the receiver covered, she motioned toward me. I stepped to her desk and took the phone.

"Sueño," I said.

"Get your ass over here. *Now.*"

I recognized the voice. It was Staff Sergeant Grimes, one of the MPs working the Yongsan Compound detachment.

"You at the MP Station?" I asked.

"Where else?"

"What have you got?"

"You'll see when you get here. You better bring that psycho partner of yours too. Something tells me you're gonna be busy today."

"What *is* it, Grimes?" I asked again, impatient now.

"You were looking for that broad Evelyn Cresthill, weren't you?"

"Yes."

"Well we've got a Korean national who says he saw her."

"Where?"

"Like I said, come ask him yourself."

He hung up the phone.

The 8th Army MP Station was a low, ramshackle building made up of Quonset huts hooked together by wooden hallways, interspersed with the occasional cement-block addition. It housed a warren of law enforcement activities, including the ration control and traffic sections, not to mention interrogation rooms and a fairly extensive row of holding cells.

At the front entranceway, Ernie and I shoved through the double swinging door and marched toward the Desk Sergeant. He was bent over fiddling with a field radio, but when he heard our footsteps, he swung his swivel chair around to face us.

"Okay, Grimes," Ernie said. "What've you got?"

Grimes pointed to the wooden bench along the wall behind us.

"Talk to him yourself. I can't make out his gibberish."

Sitting in a slump-shouldered heap, still in his black pants and his white shirt and his red vest from the previous night, sat the waiter who'd spoken to us. His collar was torn now, and his bow tie gone, probably ripped off and thrown away. His face was severely bruised.

"What'd I tell you?" Ernie said, sotto voce.

The young man sat up straighter, staring at me. I sat next to him on the bench and turned slightly to face him.

"*Weikurei-yo?*" I said. Why this way?

"I talk to you, big trouble," he said.

"Who hit you?"

He lowered his head, glaring darkly at his hands. I noticed they were cut and bleeding in spots. He didn't answer.

"I'm sorry we caused you trouble," I told him in Korean.

He shrugged. I waited patiently for him to speak.

"Those women who come in with the Korean lady, everyone else knows they'll end up working for her. Maybe the women don't know it yet. At first, she treats them well. Good drink, good food, good music. When I serve them, I always bow, always smile. But I know that soon they'll be stuck."

"There's nothing you can do about it," I told him.

"No. I'm a small bird in a big flock." He rubbed sore knuckles, then continued. "So when I talked to you last night, everybody was furious. I told them I hadn't said anything important, but of course they didn't believe me. Now they think you know everything."

"Know what?"

He took a deep breath, holding it for a while as he put his hands to possibly damaged ribs, and slowly let it out. Then he sat up suddenly, doing his best to keep his back straight. "The Korean woman who brought in the American woman," he said. "Do you know what we call her?"

"No. What?"

He leaned toward me and whispered the word into my

face. At first, all I could think about was his foul breath, full of cigarette smoke and stale kimchi.

"*Gampei,*" he said. Gangster.

"The one who brings in the young women, she's part of a gang?"

"Not her, but she works for gangsters."

"Do you know which gang she works for? Has she ever named anyone?"

"No. I just know her bosses are high up. They own many nightclubs, many *kisaeng* houses."

"High up in the government?"

"Who knows?" he said. "High up. That's all I know."

"What do they do with these women?"

"Make them work," he replied, as if it was the most obvious thing in the world.

"Are they paid well?"

He barked a laugh. "Women work," he said, "the gangs keep the money."

The waiters of Myong-dong changed employment often, he told me, sometimes working two or even three jobs, and were used to seeing young women plying their trade. After pouring drinks and lighting cigarettes for and laughing at the jokes of the wealthy businessmen, the young women were more often than not expected to return with them to their hotel rooms. There were even books of photographs of the young hostesses offered by agents to businessmen in advance of their visits so they could select what best suited their tastes.

"And an American woman," I asked, "would men pay extra for her?"

He nodded. "Some, yes."

"Are the women forced into this?" I asked.

"They're poor. And once they're in, it's very hard to get out."

"So why did the other waiters beat you up? It's not their business, is it?"

He shrugged again. "Because I talked to an American about a shameful thing. I made Korea look bad."

"And made them look bad for not saying anything."

"Yes. We serve these businessmen and their women, we smile and bow to them, but maybe we don't like them either."

"Will you be able to get your job back?"

"I'll go somewhere else. Maybe far away."

"So where is she now? The American woman?"

"I don't know." He waved his arm. "Anywhere. But I know where she'll be at night—in Myong-dong. Or some other place full of bright lights where rich men sit with beautiful ladies. Where men like me bow our heads and smile. Always."

He asked me if I had a cigarette. I told him I didn't smoke. Ernie, who'd been listening in, understood the word *tambei* and stepped across the wood-slat floor to the Desk Sergeant's counter. After borrowing two smokes from Staff Sergeant Grimes, he brought them over. The young waiter stuck one cigarette in his breast pocket, pulled a lighter out of his vest, and fired up the remaining cancer stick. He took a deep puff. As he allowed smoke to run out of his nostrils, his face crinkled. It seemed as if the pain of being beaten and ostracized by his friends, of losing his job, had suddenly caught up with him. Slowly, without making a sound, tears rolled down his face.

Before he left the compound, Ernie and I chipped in and gave him a few dollars.

-16-

By the time we reached Kimpo Airfield, the only flight from the States scheduled for the day had just landed. We parked the jeep in the military section of the lot and trotted toward the two-story cement-block terminal. From the second floor we looked down through the plate-glass windows onto passengers descending the staircases that had been rolled up to the side of the planes. A line of them made their way onto the tarmac.

"We won't be able to tell which one she is," Ernie said.

"A woman alone," I told him. "Can't be many."

Some twenty years after the devastation of the Korean War, the tourism industry in Korea was virtually nonexistent, except for Japanese businessmen flooding in on package-deal sex tours. So the only Americans who arrived in country were either missionaries or Peace Corps volunteers, or more likely those associated with the US military, either dependents or civilian contract workers. Since the vast majority of civilian workers who arrived alone would be men, an American woman traveling to Korea by herself was not something you saw every day.

And we didn't see one. Even after the last passenger had balanced himself carefully down the stairs, we hadn't seen anyone who looked like an American female lawyer by herself. I glanced at my notes. "Riley said her name is Corrine Fitch."

We hurried downstairs to the big double glass doorway that was the exit from Korean customs inspection. The first passengers emerged.

"We should've brought a sign," Ernie said.

"Yeah. I guess we'll just have to stick with deductive reasoning."

"Like what?"

"Ask any woman who seems as if she might be a Stateside female lawyer if her name is Corrine?"

"I like that name," Ernie said.

"Calm down. You haven't even met her yet."

As the travelers emerged from the customs area, I asked a couple of women who were clearly with their husbands if they were Corrine Fitch and received odd looks in return. Finally, it dawned on me that I was assuming too much. When I adjusted my expectations, I spotted her almost immediately. A slender woman in a conservative dark blue skirt and matching vest, pulling a suitcase on rollers. In her left hand she held a briefcase. I walked up to her.

"Are you Corrine Fitch?" I asked.

"Yes," she answered, surprised. "Who are you?"

I showed her my badge. She smirked. "Am I under arrest already?"

Her face was pure Korean, a long oval with inquisitive eyes and an expressive mouth. Black hair fell to her shoulders in a wave.

"No, not under arrest," I stammered. I introduced Ernie. "We're just here to give you a ride into town. And to show you something, a piece of evidence that might be pertinent to your case."

She eyed me carefully, trying to discern my intentions.

"Is the Army trying to set me up?"

"Not at all. We were originally assigned the Corporal Noh Jong-bei murder case. We were brought to the crime scene just an hour or two after the body was discovered. We've interviewed your client, Private Fusterman, and we subsequently discovered an item that we believe will be important to the defense."

"Why don't you give it to JAG?" she asked.

Apparently, she was familiar with the standard operating procedures in the military judicial system.

I fidgeted. She was right. That was what we were supposed to do. Of course, we'd have been in hot water no matter how you looked at it, because when we'd found the entrenching tool, we'd already been under orders to keep our hands off the JSA case. Still, the evidence should've been turned over to our side—the prosecution, not the defense. How could I explain to her our mistrust of 8th Army justice? Or about the times we'd seen enlisted men scapegoated for trivial offenses? And I certainly couldn't blurt out our suspicions concerning the larger forces at work, trying to pawn off responsibility for Corporal Noh's death onto PFC Fusterman. Nor could I admit to my suspicion that if we turned the entrenching tool over to JAG, it might very well never see the light of day.

I couldn't explain all that to a practical stranger, especially here in a busy airport.

Ernie jumped in. "You want to see the evidence or not?"

She crossed her arms, thinking. "What is it?"

"An entrenching tool," Ernie replied.

"A what?"

"A shovel."

"Okay," she replied slowly. "A shovel. What does this have to do with my client's defense?"

"It has his initials on it," I said. "A similar tool, according to JAG, was used as the murder weapon."

Her eyes lit up as she instantly processed the implications of this. "Do you have it here?"

"No," I replied. "It's somewhere safe."

"All right," she said, apparently having made a decision. "I'll be staying at the Cosmos Hotel. Call me when you have the evidence and you're ready to meet."

With that, she swiveled on her short heels, grabbed her suitcase, and began walking toward the taxi stand.

Ernie called after her, "You want a ride into town?"

"No thanks," she replied without looking back.

Ernie and I watched her disappear into the crowd.

"What a woman," Ernie said. Then he turned to study me. "I see you agree." He grinned.

I looked away. Ernie constantly teased me because every time I fancied a woman, my face flushed red. A childish trait I wished I could get rid of.

"Sounds like she's All-American."

"Yes, it does."

He slapped me on the back. "Come on, Sueño. We've got people to save."

The headquarters of the Korean National Police is a twelve-story, partly granite building in downtown Seoul, and in the middle of the workday, the traffic near it was maddening. Ernie somehow navigated through the honking kimchi cabs and three-wheeled trucks loaded with huge mounds of cabbage and small peaks of garlic and found a narrow alley with a *pochang macha*. We knew the old woman who ran it, and she was always happy to see us. We paid her two thousand *won*—about four dollars—for the privilege of parking our jeep right up against her cart, which she shoved over a few feet to make room. After thanking her, we trotted off through the swirling pedestrian masses until we reached the stone steps leading to the main entranceway of the KNP headquarters. Huge plate-glass doors wheezed as they slid open and allowed us into a world of slightly damp air. The unmistakable odor of fermented kimchi and burnt Korean tobacco glommed onto my face like a moist glove. I knew the Koreans imported their tobacco from somewhere, but exactly where I wasn't sure. It was a safe bet that wherever it came from, the proud planters of Virginia would hardly recognize it as the same weed.

At the information counter we were told to wait. Some two minutes later, Officer Oh, the assistant to Chief Homicide Investigator Gil Kwon-up, emerged from a narrow elevator and walked toward us. Both Ernie and I admired the sharp lines of her light-blue blouse and the formfitting navy blue skirt of the female KNP uniform. When she reached us, she bowed slightly, flashed a half-smile, and told us to follow her. Inside the elevator, all three of us were silent. This was Officer Oh's general state, speaking only in response to a direct question. The elevator doors opened onto the tenth floor, and we got out and followed Officer Oh down the tiled hallway. When we reached the door marked OFFICE OF THE CHIEF HOMICIDE INSPECTOR, she pushed it open and motioned for us to enter.

After passing through a small anteroom, we walked into Mr. Kill's office. He had gotten this name among GIs because his family name—Gil—was rare and the nickname fit well with his job title. In Korea, the death penalty was alive and well. And the Korean judicial system didn't fool around with lengthy appeals. Sometimes, within two weeks of sentencing, a condemned man would be marched up on a wooden platform, a rope looped over his head, and he'd be hanged by the neck until dead.

Since Mr. Kill tracked down and arrested murderers, it was often his testimony that determined the criminal's fate. The eight-million-plus population of Seoul kept Kill and his team busy, but on a per capita basis, there wasn't much crime in Korea, at least not compared to the States. Maybe it was because of the country's underlying hierarchical structure and the inflexibility of the Park Chung-hee regime—or, as some believed, the swiftness and inevitability of punishment.

The man who was responsible for much of what led to that punishment, Inspector Gil Kwon-up, sat beneath a green-shaded lamp, staring at us. His eyes burned like polished coals, sharpened eyebrows pointing toward spiked bristles of swept-back black hair.

"Have a seat," he said, motioning toward a low divan next to a rectangular wooden coffee table. Officer Oh bowed and left the room, closing the door behind her. Mr. Kill finished some paperwork, rose from his chair, and walked around his desk. He took a seat across the coffee table. Neither Ernie nor I smoked, which Mr. Kill knew, so he didn't pull out his cigarettes.

"Evelyn Cresthill," he said, as usual dispensing with

formalities. "A missing American Army wife. Apparently the case was elevated to your Ambassador, and from there to our Ministry of the Interior." He sighed. "And after that, down to me."

Mr. Kill spoke better English than most GIs. Not only had he received a university education here in Korea—highly unusual for those outside of the wealthiest backgrounds—but he'd participated in an anti-Communist program sponsored by the US Department of Defense, and been sent to an Ivy League school in the States for two years to study the latest techniques in law enforcement. Rumor had it that during the Korean War, as a very young man, he'd been sent north to act as a spy. He'd survived, even though eighty percent of the South Korean spies sent there didn't, and brought back valuable targeting information for allied bombing raids. This had caught the attention of powerful men in the government. After two more missions, which he'd also miraculously survived, he'd been conscripted into the Korean National Police force and put on a fast track to success.

"You do homicide," Ernie said. "How did Evelyn Cresthill land on your desk?"

"This case is sensitive enough that my government wants to make sure it doesn't become a homicide."

"Do you believe she's in danger?" I asked.

"We'll soon find out."

The report in front of him was from the KNP officer who'd assisted us at the Blue Heaven Nightclub.

"I've had my men," Kill said, "visit Blue Heaven and they re-interviewed the people you spoke to."

"Anything new?" Ernie asked.

Mr. Kill's eyes widened. "Of course there's something new," he said, as if it were the most obvious thing in the world. Inspector Kill continued. "Our chief interrogator, Mr. Bam, conducted the interviews. You are aware of his sophisticated ways of delving into the human mind."

Ways that typically included a gloved fist.

Mr. Kill paused and stared at his hands. "I believe that Evelyn Cresthill was turned over to a group of mobsters who run several of the fanciest nightclubs in the city. They need young women like Evelyn to work as hostesses for wealthy Japanese and Korean businessmen with Western tastes."

"Who exactly are these gangsters?" Ernie asked.

Mr. Kill ignored him. "They will be sending Evelyn to downtown nightclubs. Maybe even *kisaeng* houses."

Kisaeng were originally ancient female entertainers for Korean royalty, highly trained and educated women amongst whom numbered the greatest poets of *sijo* tradition. But nowadays the term had an almost unsavory connotation, referring to little more than attractive young women who catered to the whims of wealthy older men.

"An American woman," Kill continued, "confers status. Evelyn as a hostess represents a small victory—an economic one, at least—over the most powerful country on earth. She will be reserved for their richest, most powerful clients."

"Have they ever done this to an American woman before?" I asked.

"Not to my knowledge. They are becoming very bold."

"And if they have her," Ernie added, "they won't want to let her go."

"Exactly," Kill replied.

"So all we have to do," I said, "is figure out which joints cater to the biggest of the big shots. Then we go there."

Kill glanced toward Ernie, who nodded in agreement. Then he turned back to me. "Good. And how will you obtain such a list?"

"Through you," I said.

He nodded again. "Not me specifically, but yes." Then he rose and returned to his desk. "See Officer Oh on the way out. She has already prepared a list. I recommend you stick to it, starting with the nightclub at the top tonight. We believe Evelyn Cresthill will be there."

"What makes you think that?"

"She's new. The freshest are always reserved for the most prized clients."

"What if we don't find her there?"

"Contact me," Kill said, smiling.

Ernie rose to his feet. "And if we do find her and she refuses to return to her husband?"

Kill's smile widened. "Contact me immediately."

"One more thing," Ernie said, "when I asked who these gangsters were, you didn't answer. Why? You don't know?"

"We know," Kill replied simply.

"Well, then who are they?"

I frowned. Mr. Kill's refusal to answer likely had to do with embarrassment because he couldn't control corruption above his pay grade, but I knew Ernie wouldn't stop pushing.

"You're persistent," Mr. Kill said.

"If you know, you should tell us."

"They don't have a name," Kill told us. "They're not like some juvenile group of hoodlums. They're more than that."

"What?"

"They're connected at the top levels. All I can do is give you leads. You take action. Against the Americans, they are less likely to strike back. Your country has too much power and influence amongst the most important people in the Park Chung-hee government for them to do that."

"They really won't strike back because we're American?" Ernie asked.

Kill stared at him for a few seconds too long. And then at me. "I don't think so," he said finally. "But lately they've become reckless. Proceed with caution."

"Caution is our byword," Ernie said.

On the way out, Officer Oh gave us her list. It was typed

in both English and Korean *hangul*. I studied it briefly, then folded it and slipped it into my jacket pocket.

Halfway to the jeep, Ernie was agitated. "Why don't the KNPs just line the *gampei* up against a wall and shoot them?"

"They've tried," I said.

"And?"

"There are always more."

When we reached the *pochang macha*, Ernie waved to the old woman who ran it. She smiled and nodded, then returned to stirring her bean curd stew. We hopped into the jeep. Ernie started the engine. Winding through the heavy Seoul traffic, Ernie headed toward Namsan Tunnel Number Three.

"Before we leave compound tonight," he said, "we're stopping at the MP Arms Room. I'm not going into some gangland playground without a .45 under my arm. If these guys play rough, I'm gonna have something for 'em."

"Oh, joy," I said.

-17-

Back at the 8th Army CID office, I called Corrine Fitch at the Cosmos Hotel. She picked up on the second ring.

"I was just leaving," she said.

"Where are you headed?" I asked.

"Who is this?"

"George Sueño," I said. "One of the guys from the airport. I didn't get to properly introduce myself."

"George what-o?" she said.

I was used to this. Hispanic names often threw people, especially an unusual one like Sueño.

"Sueño," I said. "With the 'n' like the 'ny' in canyon."

"Oh. Are you the tall one?"

"Yes."

"I don't have time to chat right now," she said. "I'm on the way to meet someone. But I'm moving into office space on Yongsan Compound tomorrow." She riffled through paperwork. "JAG office annex number two. Do you know where that is?"

"Yes." It was in a redbrick duplex provided to defense attorneys under the rare circumstances that a GI—usually a senior officer—coughed up enough dough to hire a Stateside lawyer.

"Good. Let's meet there around nine?"

"Zero-nine-hundred hours?"

"If that's what you want to call it," she said.

"Nine it is," I told her.

"Okay. Bring the shovel."

With that, she hung up.

Ernie was sitting in a straight-backed chair, thumbing through the *Pacific Stars and Stripes*.

"Sounds like she's into you," he said.

I ignored him and returned to my report on our search for Evelyn Cresthill, which sat half-finished in my Olivetti. A half hour later, I had an idea—one that seemed to get better each minute I thought it over. I cornered Riley out in the hallway. "Who's your contact over at Ration Control?"

"Why?" he asked, squinting warily at me.

I towered over him, aware that I outweighed him by close to fifty pounds. Still, he acted like he was the toughest guy in three brigades.

"I need to access some data," I said, "without making an official request."

"Not if it's about the JSA murder. So is it?"

"Why do you care? Just tell me who to talk to."

"You've been ordered to leave this shit alone," Riley said.

"There's no airtight evidence that Fusterman killed anybody, especially not his best friend—the brother of the woman he wanted to marry."

"Hell," Riley scoffed. "That makes him the most likely suspect."

"I don't think so," I told him. "Look, I just want to check out some data. If nothing comes of it, nobody's the wiser. If there is something, I'll have JAG make a formal request for an official report."

"You're out of your gourd, Sueño."

"Maybe," I said. "You still dating that cashier out at the Statue Lounge?"

Riley stiffened. He had a penchant for older women, which embarrassed him, and Ernie teased him about it mercilessly.

"You're not going mention that to anyone, are you?"

"Me? Of course not."

His shoulders relaxed. "Okay. I'll make a phone call."

"Thanks."

"What should I ask for?"

I told him.

Two hours later, Ernie and I picked up the report Riley had requested. A guy named Rodney Porter, a Specialist Five in charge of recordkeeping at the 8th Army Ration Control Office, met us on a stone bench on the far side of the 8th

Army Library, a place not much frequented by men in uniform.

He handed over a manila envelope stuffed with a computer printout.

"What's it show?" Ernie asked, peering inside.

"More than usual," Porter said. "But that's expected from a unit in an isolated area like the JSA."

"How much more than usual?" Ernie asked.

We were talking about LOAs—Letters of Authorization. Battalion commanders and above had the authority to fill out an LOA, sign it, and purchase whatever was necessary for their unit out of the PX and commissaries, regardless of ration control restrictions. This was a list of every LOA submitted in the last quarter by the JSA security unit.

Porter glanced down at his notes. "Maybe three times the regular number of LOAs," he responded.

Ernie whistled. "That's a lot of TVs and stereos."

"No, nothing like that," Porter said. "Mostly consumables. Coffee, cigarettes, liquor, even a few female items."

"Like nylons?" I asked.

"Yep."

"So the GIs up at the JSA," I continued, "stay up late, smoke like chimneys, and get drunk a lot?"

Spec 5 Porter grinned, flashing his blue eyes and an even row of teeth. "They also wear nice hosiery."

"Who monitors LOAs?" I asked.

"Just me."

"Do you report it up the line if you believe a unit is purchasing more than what is reasonable?"

"No."

"Why not?"

"LOAs are made at field-grade level and above," Porter said. "Battalion commanders. Nobody wants to hear anything bad about them." He paused, frowning. "If I ever accused them of black marketeering, I'd be chewed out for impugning the integrity of a superior officer."

"So Eighth Army doesn't really give a damn how many rationed items are purchased, as long as it's one of the honchos doing the purchasing?" I asked.

Porter shrugged again.

"But if a PFC goes ten dollars over his ration, he's hammered."

Porter's eyes widened. "What are you? Some sort of communist?"

I pretended I hadn't heard that, but the word "communist" triggered an alarm bell. And not because I was worried about the House Un-American Activities Committee.

We thanked Porter for his help as Ernie and I got up to leave.

"Wait a minute," he said.

We both stopped and looked back at him.

"Riley told me I'd receive something in return."

"What do you want?" I asked.

"I don't know," he said, floundering. "Maybe an introduction to that secretary who works in your office. What's her name?"

"Miss Kim," I said.

"Yeah," he replied. "Miss Kim."

"You've seen her?" Ernie asked.

His face flushed red. "Entering compound a couple of times in the morning."

"How'd you find out where she works?"

"You know, I was heading in that direction. Just happened to notice."

"That direction?" Ernie said. "On the opposite side of the compound from where your office is?"

Porter didn't answer. He stood awkwardly, toeing the sod in front of him, probably regretting asking. Still, I knew that we might need access to more of his information in the future.

"Do you play badminton?" I asked.

"Badminton?"

"Yeah. Badminton."

"No. Why?"

"Miss Kim plays every day during the noon hour, out by the Buddhist shrine. If you're patient and respectful, maybe she and the other employees will let you join them."

"Badminton," he said again.

"Yes."

Ernie pointed his forefinger at him. "But you'd better be nice to her."

Specialist Porter nodded eagerly. "Okay," he said.

When we were out of earshot, Ernie muttered, "He doesn't stand a chance."

The first joint on Officer Oh's list wasn't in the bright-light district of Myong-dong, but in a nearby area known as Mugyo-dong, military bridge district, deep in the catacombs of Seoul. We wound through a few narrow streets before finding the address. It was a run-down three-story building with cement-block walls and a rotted wooden fence surrounding a small courtyard. Stone steps led up to an entrance door made of reinforced lumber. A neon sign flashed on and off with two stylized Chinese characters against a yellow background.

"What's the sign say?" Ernie asked.

"*Unwon,*" I said.

"Meaning?"

"Cloud Garden."

"Sounds depressing."

"Clouds are beautiful," I said. "They float."

He paused, thinking it over. Then he said, "Like the broads who work here."

I raised an eyebrow at him. "You're developing the mind of a poet."

"Is it a *kisaeng* house?" Ernie asked.

"Looks like it."

"But sleazy," Ernie added.

"Just how you like it."

"Yep," he said, rubbing his stomach. "How are we gonna get in?"

GIs were refused entrance into places that catered to Korean or Japanese businessmen. First, the proprietors knew we were usually stingy. Second, their free-spending customers didn't necessarily want a bunch of crass Caucasian men tromping on the stylized elegance of their evening respite, not to mention drunkenly pawing at their women.

"Maybe it's best to wait out here," I said. "See who comes and goes."

"If we do that, I'll need something to warm me up."

"I didn't spot any *pochang macha* on the way here."

"Maybe there's a *kagei* down that way," Ernie said.

"Maybe."

"I'll be back in ten minutes."

"Make it five," I said.

"Christ, Sueño. We're just gonna end up standing out here all night and have nothing to show for it."

"We'll see."

"Be back in a few." Ernie trotted off down the street.

I stepped back into the shadows, about twenty yards from the Cloud Garden's flashing neon sign. I thought of Evelyn Cresthill and wondered if it was possible for her to find a dump like this preferable to her cookie-cutter home in the dependent housing on Yongsan Compound South Post. Maybe she did. This was certainly more exciting than life as the wife of a field-grade officer. When a young hostess catered to the wealthy businessmen at these establishments, they would cater to her in return. She'd feel wanted, even prized. Perhaps that was better than being a neglected housewife suffering through yet another tea with the Officers' Wives Club.

A black Hyundai sedan pulled up. The doors popped open and three Korean men in suits climbed out. Then a woman. I could barely see through the gloom, but when the sign's red and yellow neon flashed onto her face, there was little doubt. It was Evelyn Cresthill.

I'd understood from the start that the "list" Officer Oh had given us was likely a ruse. The Korean National Police monitored these mob operations far more closely than they were willing to let on—my guess was that they had an operative planted near the beating heart of the local crime syndicate and had received intelligence that Evelyn would be here tonight. They'd risked compromising that agent only because Evelyn Cresthill was an American, and as such her welfare was crucial to preserving that precious relationship between South Korea and the United States.

These thoughts raced through my mind as Evelyn was helped out of the car and hustled toward the front gate of the Cloud Garden.

It would've been nice to have Ernie as backup, but he was still out hunting for a bottle of soju. I had a .45 tucked into the shoulder holster beneath my coat. I patted it to make sure it was still there, took a deep breath, and stepped quickly into the light.

The group of men surrounding Evelyn Cresthill had reached the gate leading into the courtyard and were about to head through it.

"Evelyn!" I shouted.

Startled, she stopped and turned to look at me, as did the three men.

I held out my badge. "I just want to talk to you—to make sure you're okay. It won't take much of your time."

The men must have realized I meant trouble for them, because one barked an order and another grabbed Evelyn Cresthill by the elbows and pulled her through the opening in the gate. The remaining two men, still blocking my way, pulled large folding knives from their pockets.

I approached the two men, holding my badge out like a crucifix against circling vampires. I shouted "*Kyongchal!*" Police!

For some reason, they weren't impressed. I shoved the badge back into my pocket and reached for my .45, but the men moved quickly, and there were two of them. One grabbed my wrist, and as we grappled, I felt a blow to my back. A shod foot had slammed into my left kidney, knocking the air out of my body, and I tumbled forward into the thug holding my wrist, the gun sliding away from both of us. When we were back on our feet, he aimed a side-kick at me, but he was slow enough for me to adjust, twisting my body and grabbing his collar. I swung him as hard as I could in an arc before releasing, and he slammed face-first into the gate and went down.

Inside the courtyard, a woman's voice rose in anger as she argued with someone.

"Forget it, Charlie," she said. "I'm not going in. I don't *like* him, and I'm not sitting with him again. I don't care how much he's paying."

I had to admit, Evelyn Cresthill had moxie. But that was probably because the mobsters hadn't found a reason to beat the crap out of her—yet.

I crouched down to feel around for the .45 and felt a fist glance off the top of my head. When I turned, another kick came toward my face from the guy who'd knocked the wind out of me earlier. I managed to deflect it with my forearm, but that stung nevertheless. Furious, I rushed forward like a bull charging a matador, planning to hit my attacker right in the gut. But I'd left my sharp horns in my wall locker, and my head found a knee coming at me full-force instead of its initial target. I staggered backward, dazed. But the collision must've blown out his kneecap, as he lay writhing on the ground and didn't pursue me. I stumbled away, collapsing against the wooden fence, and found my .45 on the ground, my vision so blurred that I was barely able to pick it up. As blind as I was I wouldn't be able to even aim it, but my intervention and Evelyn Cresthill's refusal to enter the Cloud Garden had screwed up any plans these guys had for the night. Brief, guttural shouts were exchanged, and the car started up again, its headlights flashing on brightly. Two bodies emerged through the gate—Evelyn Cresthill and a man dragging her along by the arm. She glanced at me for only a moment, horror in her face and a new bruise on her cheek. Had she just realized what type of people she was dealing with? I supposed even the hardest of criminals could be charming at first—the rough stuff always came later.

I tried to speak, but my head lolled to my side, and suddenly I was so dizzy that I used the varnished wooden slats to lower myself to a squatting position. The man shoved Evelyn Cresthill into the backseat and then lifted the guy I'd knocked unconscious earlier and tossed him in after her. The last thug with the injured knee piled in and the car sped off.

I struggled to remain alert, still woozy. Somehow, I got to my feet, staggering forward.

"Stop!" I shouted after them, not quite conscious that I'd spoken English. I knew the Korean command, too, but it was just beyond my mind's reach. I raised the .45 as a threat but didn't fire, as I was in no condition to do so. I looked down at the pistol, realizing I hadn't even pulled back the charging handle, when my right thigh trembled and the knee below it forgot how to lock. As I fell, taillights swerved and tires squealed farther and farther in the distance. I felt a thud and recognized pain, first in my hip, then in my shoulder.

And that was the last thing I remembered.

I came to with someone pouring soju on my face. I sputtered and sat up, wiping the burning liquid from my eyes.

"What the hell?" I shouted.

"Lying down on the job again," Ernie said. He slapped my cheeks lightly and shone a penlight into my eyes.

I sat up. "Where'd they go?"

"Who?"

"Evelyn Cresthill." I explained what had happened.

"Well, they're long gone now," he told me.

A light-blue KNP sedan, red lights flashing, pulled up next to us. Two cops emerged, both in standard issue blue uniforms. One was a man I didn't recognize, and the other was Officer Oh. Hands on her hips, she stared down at us.

"So you used my list," she said.

"Yeah," Ernie replied. "Sueño here swears by it."

"Glad I could help," she said.

I hadn't previously realized Officer Oh spoke English so well, since she was usually so taciturn. But perhaps that was because she deferred to Inspector Kill. Now, she had a subordinate of her own in tow. She told the male officer to help get me to my feet. He complied quickly. I needed the help, too.

With Ernie on one side and the KNP on the other, I managed to stand. I braced myself against the splintered wood of the courtyard wall, still groggy.

"So what happened?" Ernie asked.

"Like you said," I replied. "Got bored and nodded off."

"Cut the crap, Sueño."

"We need to search the building." I waved my hand toward the Cloud Garden.

"Why?"

"They were taking Evelyn in there. But she changed her mind and refused when they told her who the client was. I got the impression she's been here before."

"You sure it was her?"

"Yes."

"Why didn't you stop her?" Ernie asked.

I just stared at him, my eyes smoldering with anger.

"Okay," he said. "Never mind."

-18-

With Officer Oh taking the lead, we were allowed immediate access to the Cloud Garden *kisaeng* house. None of the workers inside even thought of resisting the KNPs, who never needed search warrants. Their judgment was all the authority they required.

We wandered down a short hallway, then past some empty booths upholstered in fake leather and a few cocktail tables covered in dingy linen. Upstairs, the rooms were closer in design to traditional Korean style. Raised wooden floors were covered in vinyl and a low rectangular table filled most of the room, surrounded by flat square seating cushions. When the room was in use, businessmen would sit cross-legged on the cushions and young hostesses would squat next to them, massaging their necks and wiping their brows with warm towels. Later, after coats were off and ties loosened, the women would pour them drinks—usually imported scotch in crystal tumblers—and use chopsticks to pop succulent snacks in their mouths, selecting from an array of raw squid, boiled quail eggs, and other overpriced delicacies on the table.

"I'd rather drink at a bar," Ernie said.

"Why? You don't like being treated like a king?"

"At a bar, there's less bullshit between me and the booze."

Koreans found it unnatural to sit alone at a bar. Not only was it considered unhealthy to drink without food, but spirits were seen as something to be consumed in a group setting—accompanied by friends, along with singing or other entertainment. Not amongst fellow morose drunks mumbling to themselves and falling off bar stools. The *kisaeng* house was the model for social drinking, and it put Korean men at ease, which is why its structure had been replicated—in both opulence and squalor—throughout the country.

A middle-aged woman in a billowing Korean silk dress bowed to Officer Oh. In rapid Korean, Oh asked the woman why there were no customers in the Cloud Garden.

"A party was scheduled," she replied, "but our guests had a last-minute change of plans." Involuntarily, the old woman cast a sidelong glance at me.

"Party pooper," Ernie whispered.

My head throbbed and I wished I had some aspirin.

Officer Oh asked the proprietress for the name and phone number of the man who'd booked the party, but the old woman pled ignorance. "We are very informal," she said. "Guests tell us they will be here, and then they arrive. No record is kept."

A scowl crossed Officer Oh's smooth complexion, which made me realize that she wasn't an unemotional operative. There was a silent ferocity to her that could come to the surface when she was being jerked around.

"Come," Officer Oh told the woman in a voice barely containing her rage. "Let's go downtown to police headquarters. We will question you there."

"Oh, wait," the woman replied, bowing again, more deeply this time. "Maybe we do have something written down. Let me check." She hurried off with Officer Oh following close behind. Downstairs, the woman pulled a ledger from beneath the bar's serving counter. She thumbed through it and finally pointed to an entry, turning the ledger around for Officer Oh to examine. "Mr. Lee," the old woman said. "A Mr. Lee made the engagement."

"Do you have his full name or phone number?" Officer Oh asked.

"No, ma'am," the woman said, shaking her head. "We are very informal here."

Exasperated, Officer Oh had her assistant order a van to escort the woman and the three other Cloud Garden employees on the premises to headquarters for further interrogation. The old woman began to cry, but Officer Oh ignored her.

We walked out into the courtyard.

"We probably won't get much out of her," Officer Oh told me, calm again. "Or the others, either, but we'll try. If we do find something, I'll leave a message with your secretary. What's her name?"

"Miss Kim," I responded.

"Right. She seems very nice." A pause. "About that list I gave you."

"Yes?"

"It's probably worthless. The *gampei* know you're looking for Evelyn Cresthill. They'll hide her much more carefully now."

Ernie spoke up. "Has an American woman ever been taken like this before?"

"Not in Korea. Everyone knows the Park Chung-hee government won't tolerate any actions that could hurt our relations with the United States."

"So why are these mobsters taking this risk?" Ernie asked.

She frowned. "They are challenging us directly. They think they can push the Korean National Police aside and run the world the way *they* want to run the world. But it's not going to work."

We watched her smolder until finally I broke the silence and said, "So what now?"

Officer Oh seemed to awaken from a dream. She looked at me. "Chief Inspector Gil will have a strategy ready, of that you can be sure. By tomorrow."

"What do you think he'll do?"

She looked me straight in the eye and answered, "He'll

mobilize every resource we have to round up and punish these gang members."

"Won't that compromise Evelyn Cresthill's safety?"

"That, I'm afraid, is of lesser importance."

"The power of the state comes first."

Her eyes widened. "Of course."

Ernie and I were in the office the next morning shortly after the start-of-duty day cannon went off. I pilfered a couple of aspirin from the First Aid kit, popped them in my mouth, and soon felt relief as the throbbing began to subside. We'd reached the same conclusion separately and agreed to take action. Without bothering to go through Staff Sergeant Riley, we marched down the hallway and barged into the Office of the Provost Marshal of the 8th United States Army. Colonel Brace sat behind his mahogany desk. When we knocked and entered without permission, he raised his eyebrows at us, surprised. We usually tried to avoid him and he knew it.

Ernie and I both saluted.

This time, he returned the salute. "Yes?" he said.

"It's about Evelyn Cresthill," I said.

"What about her?"

"We have reason to believe that her life is in danger." I recounted last night's incident, leaving out that Ernie had left to buy a bottle of soju, and did my best to explain the dynamics at play.

"The KNPs are planning to take direct action," I told him. "They'll be going all-out to find her and arrest and prosecute the mob members behind all this. Sergeant Bascom and I would like to be there when the rescue operation takes place."

"We want to make sure Evelyn Cresthill isn't hurt," Ernie added.

"There was a 'sir' missing from that sentence," Colonel Brace told him.

"Yes, sir," Ernie said.

"So you're telling me you'll be out of the office for a while."

"Yes, sir," I replied. "And we might need backup. We thought Staff Sergeant Palinki would be good—him and maybe three MPs. If they could accompany us, be on call for when we need them. That way, when we take on these gangsters we'll have additional firepower."

"Like you didn't have last night."

"Yes, sir," I replied as I looked down at my feet, embarrassed.

"Sounds like you're preparing to start World War Three."

"No, sir. We'll be careful."

"You've thought this all out."

"Yes, sir. The KNPs have good intentions, but when they strike, they sometimes use too much brute force. More than we would. Evelyn Cresthill could become the first dependent casualty Eighth Army's ever had."

"Or not," Colonel Brace said.

"Sir?" I asked.

He tapped his pipe into an ashtray made out of thick, amber-tinted glass. He grabbed a pipe cleaner, scrapped burnt tobacco out of the bowl, and reached for his can of Sir Walter Raleigh. He was stalling, preparing to spring something on us. Ernie fidgeted.

"Admirable," Colonel Brace said finally, after he'd lit the new tobacco and sent up his first puff of smoke. "I appreciate that you're so concerned about the welfare of one of the fine ladies under our care. Unfortunately, you're a little behind the times."

"Sir?"

"Maybe you should've checked the MP blotter report. Some interesting things have happened since last night."

Ernie knew we were being sandbagged, and he didn't like it. "So we stepped in it, sir. Is that what you're trying to tell us?"

"Stepped out of it is more like it." He paused, puffed contentedly on his pipe, watching the smoke rise lazily toward the ceiling. "Evelyn Cresthill," he said, "was spotted at Gate Number Twelve on South Post shortly after zero four hundred this morning. The Staff Duty Officer was notified and he drove over in his jeep and personally escorted her to her quarters.

"She's back with Jenny," I said. "And her husband?"

"Major Cresthill has returned to the construction site. But yes, according to the SDO, she and Jenny had quite the emotional reunion."

I was happy for them. Even if something didn't seem quite right about this.

Colonel Brace set his pipe down in the tray. "Report to Staff Sergeant Riley," he said. "You're back on black market detail."

We saluted and walked out of Colonel Brace's office. Once we were in the hallway, Ernie muttered, "Lower than whale shit."

"What do you mean?"

"That's us. Lower than whale shit. Getting the JSA murder investigation yanked away and Evelyn Cresthill wandering home on her own makes us look ridiculous."

I thought of how frightened she'd seemed the previous night. Had the mobsters done this as a last-ditch effort to cut their losses after realizing how hard the KNPs were going to come down on them? I needed to talk to Evelyn Cresthill. To make sure she was all right, but also to understand what the hell she'd been thinking. But contacting her might make our situation worse. Though I'd never met Evelyn Cresthill, the one thing I knew about her was that she was trouble. And that kind of trouble, especially when it came to domestic disputes, had a way of rubbing off on investigators. If we were going to have any chance of sneaking back into the JSA murder case, it would be wise to stay away from her. But I figured Ernie also wanted to talk to her, given the embarrassment she'd caused us, and I had to admit that my curiosity had the better of me, whether this was a wise move or not.

Staff Sergeant Riley was at his desk now. He looked up from last night's blotter report, saw our expressions, and realized something had gone wrong in the Provost Marshal's office. He was about to open his trap when Ernie fixed him with a murderous glare. Confused for a moment, Riley glanced at Ernie's knotted fist and, for once stifling his bravado, snapped his pie-hole shut.

I nodded to Miss Kim, who returned the gesture, immediately sizing up the situation. Instead of speaking, she relaxed her furrowed brow and resumed pecking away at her *hangul* typewriter.

Without even bothering to stop for a cup of coffee, Ernie and I grabbed our jackets and headed toward the door.

"Where do you guys think you're going?" Riley asked.

"Out," Ernie replied.

"You're on the black market detail. As of now," Riley shouted after us. "The commissary opens at ten hundred hours. I expect you to be there!"

We didn't answer. Outside, neither of us spoke as we marched toward the jeep.

Strange met us in the narrow street behind 8th Army headquarters. He had covered the entrenching tool in wrapping paper.

"Why'd you do that?" Ernie asked. "It just makes it more obvious."

"Hey, it worked for Lee Harvey Oswald—he wrapped his rifle before going into the Texas Book Depository."

"Christ, Strange," Ernie said. "Why would you want to imitate that?"

"The name's Harvey."

"Yeah, okay, Harvey. So what're you, his cousin?"

Strange ignored Ernie and leaned against the passenger side of the jeep, his head practically inside the open window. I pressed back into the canvas seat as far as I could, wondering what the hell Strange had eaten for breakfast. Limburger cheese came to mind. But the commissary didn't carry the stuff, and the mess hall damn sure didn't serve it. Must've been something else. I was afraid to ask.

"Stinky bean curd," Strange said.

"Huh?"

"You're wincing, wondering what I ate. The answer is stinky bean curd. Good stuff. You ought to try it. Does wonders for the health."

"Cut the crap," Ernie said. "What is it you want?"

Strange glanced along the row of parked cars, as if expecting someone to be lurking nearby. When he determined no one was, he lowered his voice and said, "You need to be careful." A blast of eau-de-old-socks emanated from his mouth.

"Careful?" Ernie asked. "Us? Why?"

"You fucked up the Evelyn Cresthill missing person's case."

Apparently, the entire compound already knew about her

return. Gossip traveled at the speed of light at 8th Army head-quarters.

"So she came home on her own. What of it?"

"She's going to divorce her old man. That's what everyone is saying."

"Maybe he'll leave her first," Ernie said.

"Maybe. But worse than that is the shit that happened up at the JSA."

I sat up straighter. "What about the JSA?"

"The North Koreans are still hopping mad. They've complained to the Neutral Nations Supervisory Commission, and those pukes have started their own investigation. The North claims an innocent Korean citizen, forced into the South Korean army against his will, was degraded by us American imperialists."

The Democratic People's Republic of Korea, or North Korea, claimed the entire Korean Peninsula was their sovereign territory. And therefore every Korean born on the peninsula—either in North Korea or South Korea—they considered a citizen of the DPRK, including the late Corporal Noh.

"They claim that Noh was murdered just to set an example for the other troops. To coerce them into never crossing the Military Demarcation Line and thereby stopping them from defecting to the land of freedom blessed by their Great Leader Kim Il-sung's shining light of socialism."

"You have that down pretty good," Ernie said.

"But it's not just talk this time. The NKs are fully mobilized. Plenty of petroleum for their tank divisions is being shipped down from Hamhung, and dozens of Soviet transports are waiting to unload in the harbor. It looks like they're getting froggy—ready to jump."

"All because one guy was killed?"

"Sure," Strange said. "Could just be a bluff or an excuse to spread propaganda, but they're making the most of it."

"So what is Eighth Army going to do about it?"

"Colonel Peele wants to slam them right back, pin the murder on them at the next MAC meeting." Strange glanced around again to make sure no one had approached. "But the North Koreans have let it be known that if he does that, they're going to take action next time we go to red-alert level." When we mobilized all the ROK and US divisions along the DMZ, as well as brought in the Seventh Fleet off the coast and our B-52 bombers from Okinawa. "In retaliation, the North Koreans are threatening to open fire on Seoul. They're calling it 'preemptive defense.' All because one KATUSA corporal had his head bashed in."

"And they lost face during our pre-dawn standoff at the JSA," Ernie said.

"Exactly," Strange replied. "You have no idea what you two started when you stole the body from their side of the line."

"We didn't *steal* anything," Ernie said.

"Sure, have it your way. But not to worry. Peele's being

overruled. Cooler heads have decided to burn this PFC whatshisname."

"Fusterman," I interjected.

"Yeah. Him. Make an example of him on the international stage. And the sooner the better. Pulls the rug out from beneath the North Koreans. Shows that someone's been convicted of and punished for the murder and the case is closed. Before some idiot pops a cap across the line and the Commies retaliate and we have a real war on our hands." He pointed at the entrenching tool. "What do you plan to do with this?"

"Get Fusterman off," I said.

"Fat chance."

"He didn't do it," I replied.

"What the hell's that got to do with it?" Strange asked. "PFC Fusterman is going down, and no power on earth can save him. Unless you'd prefer another Korean War?"

I didn't see those as the only two options. But apparently 8th Army did.

Ernie started the jeep's engine. "Thanks for hiding the entrenching tool for us, Harvey. See you soon."

"You two better hold on to your butts," he replied.

As we backed away, I let out a whoosh of air. Ernie waved his hand in front of his face.

"Where does Strange come up with this stuff?" I asked. "Stinky bean curd for breakfast."

"He hangs around in back alleys. Eats at the same mom-and-pop stands the taxi drivers do."

"Why?"

Ernie shrugged. "Looking for some strange, I guess."

I pulled the entrenching tool closer.

"Not getting cold feet, are we, Sueño?"

"Not a chance."

Paper rustled. I hadn't realized I was clutching the entrenching tool so hard.

-19-

We were a few minutes late for our zero nine hundred appointment with Corrine Fitch, Esq., but it didn't matter because she hadn't arrived yet. The door to JAG Annex Number Two stood locked. We cooled our heels on the sidewalk outside like a couple of dummies until First Lieutenant Margaret "Peggy" Mendelson emerged from a side door of the main 8th Army JAG office. She walked toward us, waving a pink slip of paper.

Ernie groaned.

Peggy, a stout woman in a dress-green uniform, was all smiles. "I have a phone message for you." She thrust it at me. "From Fusterman's defense attorney. She asked me to let you know she won't be able to make your nine o'clock."

Her smile stretched so wide across her face that I thought her cheeks might pop.

"Awfully neighborly of you," Lieutenant Mendelson continued. "Helping out the stateside gun-for-hire. Especially considering you're supposed to be on our side."

"Fusterman didn't kill anybody," I said.

Her eyes widened in mock surprise. "Please, do tell. Then we won't need to bother with this silly court-martial," she said, indicating with her hand the brick courthouse on the far side of the lawn. "I'll just inform the Eighth Army Commander that Buck Sergeant Sueño, himself, has determined that Corporal Noh Jong-bei was murdered by aliens from planet Jupiter. That should satisfy him. Save us a lot of fuss. I'm sure the North Koreans will be happy to hear the news, too. Maybe even call back some of those tank divisions they have rolling toward the DMZ."

During her little speech, she'd transformed from facetious to fuming. Hands on her hips, she stared at us like a Doberman searching for a jugular.

"What've you got there?" she asked, pointing at the package.

No sense trying to hide it now. "Evidence," I said.

She held out her open palms. I turned it over to her. She peeked beneath the paper wrapping. "An entrenching tool," she said.

When I didn't respond, she said, "Where'd you get this?"

"I'll make a formal report," I said.

"You'd better," she told me. "And you'd better have the report on my desk in less than an hour. Does the Provost Marshal know about this?"

"I don't know," I responded, falling into cover-your-ass mode.

"Have you informed him?"

I shook my head. "No."

She unwrapped the entrenching tool and examined it. After a few seconds, she spotted the scratched initials: TF.

"So this is the entrenching tool Fusterman claims was stolen from him."

"And then replaced with the one stained with what appears to be blood."

"How did this come into your possession?"

"I'll put it all in my report."

Peggy Mendelson narrowed her eyes at me. "If you think a trick like this is going to get him off, you're sorely mistaken."

"It's not a trick," Ernie said.

She looked back and forth between us. "Whatever happened to you two being ordered off the case?"

I shrugged. "We're still investigators," I said. "Something comes to our attention that might be pertinent, it's our duty to look into it."

"No, it's *not*!" she snapped.

She caught herself, took a deep breath, and seemed to think better of what she'd been about to say. She turned on her heel and began to march back to the JAG office. As she did, she raised her right forefinger into the air and said, "I want that report. One hour."

When she disappeared back through the doorway, Ernie

waited until the lock clicked tight, then said, "Screw your report." He glanced at me. "Not our day so far, huh?"

"Nope. And it's still early."

"Where to now?"

I thought about it. "The place we're both dying to visit."

"Yeah," Ernie said. "Yongsan South Post."

The Cresthill residence.

We pounded on the door for nearly ten minutes before someone finally glanced through the curtains of the front window. Seconds later, the inner doorknob turned. A woman's face—groggy, framed by red hair in disarray—peered out at us. She kept the chain latch secured, the cheap metal crossing her forehead like an extra set of eyebrows.

"You," she said. "I saw you last night."

"Yes," I replied.

She didn't ask if I was okay.

"Sorry to wake you, Mrs. Cresthill," Ernie said, flashing his badge. "May we come in?"

"For Christ's sake. What time is it?"

Ernie told her, taking her civilian status into account by using "nine-thirty" instead of "zero nine thirty hours."

She unlatched the chain and let the door swing free, hustling off as she did so toward the hallway. "Sit down," she shouted over her shoulder. "I'll be out in five minutes."

It took fifteen. When she returned, Ernie and I had taken

seats in the front room. She wore black leotard-like pants, a pullover sweater, and hair piled and pinned atop her head. She'd put on makeup, which had probably taken most of that time.

"Okay," she said, sitting down without bothering to offer us coffee. "What do you want?"

"How's Jenny?" I asked.

She seemed surprised by the question. "Fine. She's at school," she said.

"She must've been delighted to see you."

She reached for some cigarettes and a white ceramic ashtray. "You're not from Defense Youth Activities," she said. "You're cops. Why are you here?" She lit up, again without offering us any. "I don't like the Army much," she said. "It's come between me and my husband. And I don't like living on this base. It's so *freaking* boring. And the women all think that if their husband gets promoted, they get promoted. As far as I'm concerned," she said, "they can kiss my heinie."

Ernie was silent. Apparently, he'd decided to let me handle this interview. For the time being, anyway.

"That woman you met at the O'Club," I said. "The Korean one. What's her name?"

"Her Korean name?"

"Yes."

"Hell if I know. I can never keep them straight. I just called her Shin."

"Shin?"

"Yeah. Like the leg bone."

I jotted it down.

"What's this woman's story?" I asked.

Evelyn exhaled a long drag and eyed me suspiciously. "What do you want to know about her for?"

"Was she authorized to come on base?"

"Probably not."

"So how did she get into the O'Club?"

"The way most local women do, I think. Flashed a smile to some GI who could get her in; pretended to be grateful to a big strong man for helping her."

"So an officer escorted her into the club," I said. "As a guest."

"Probably. She had a lot of friends."

"And the staff treated her well?"

"The Korean staff, yes. Especially the young women. They liked her style. She was young and beautiful and smart—and friendly. It was nice to have someone to talk to who wasn't a prig."

"How'd you first meet her?"

Evelyn puffed again, thoughtfully. "She sent me a drink at the O'Club. And told the waitress to ask if I wanted to join her. So I did."

"You two got along?"

She shrugged. "Well enough."

"How's her English?"

"Better than mine," she said, chortling. "Bob's always telling me I embarrass him at social functions. That I talk like a gutter whore."

"When you drink?"

"Yeah. I like drinking. And speaking my mind. Anything wrong with that?"

"Not as far as I'm concerned." I paused, flipping through my notes. "So you went downtown with this woman?"

"Yes," Evelyn said. "That was the second or third night I saw her at the O'Club."

"Did you arrange to meet with her?"

"Not formally, no. I just figured she'd show up at happy hour."

"Why'd you agree to go downtown with her?"

"It sounded like fun, the way she described it. I told you, I was usually bored out of my mind."

"You went to the Blue Heaven Nightclub."

She raised an eyebrow. "Pretty good. How'd you know?"

"Trade secret," I said. "After that, you fell off our radar."

She gazed at me coolly. "And what radar is that?"

"When a military dependent vanishes without a trace, we get worried."

"Afraid I'll do something to embarrass the *command*." The last word was freighted with resentment. "You want me to tell you where I went?"

"That'd be nice," I said.

She took a last drag and stubbed out her cigarette. "I wanted a little excitement. With people who knew how to laugh and didn't look down their noses at me. And I found it out there in downtown Seoul in those fancy nightclubs. Shin was nice enough to show me the ropes. Introduce me to rich men. Sometimes, I'd sit in a booth with half a dozen of them, all of them focused solely on me, vying to light my cigarettes. They poured me scotch. Not cheap bar scotch like I used to serve back in Austin, but the good stuff. Chivas or Johnny Walker Black. I like that feeling of being catered to." She stared at Ernie and then at me, challenging us. "Anything wrong with that?"

I shrugged. "Not that I can see." Again I shuffled through my notes. "Where'd you stay?"

She shrugged again, more pointedly this time. "Here and there."

"Like where?"

"Shin has an apartment. Pretty nice place."

"Where?"

"How the hell should I know? A high-rise somewhere in Seoul."

"Did you two always go out together?"

"At first. Then I started going out on my own."

"Why didn't she come with you?"

"She's a businesswoman. Has responsibilities. Me, I was sort of on vacation, you know—a vacation from Bob. You

know he likes to be called Major Bob? Especially in the sack."
She chuckled. "Once I was familiar enough with the clubs and
had dates lined up with some of the businessmen, I'd just get
ready, go downstairs, and tell the cabdriver the name of the
place. Even though I don't speak a word of Korean, they always
got me there. Once or twice," she said, grinning devilishly, "the
guys sent a car for me. With a driver and everything."

"Nice," I said.

She glanced at Ernie. "Don't you talk?"

"Not when my partner here is doing such a good job."

"He smarter than you?"

"By a lot."

She laughed out loud and reached for her cigarettes. "You
want one?" she said, offering the pack to Ernie.

"Never touch the stuff," Ernie said.

She waved the pack toward me, but I shook my head. She
lit her cigarette.

"So are we done here?" she asked. "I have a lot to do. The
house is a mess."

"Don't you have a housemaid?"

"I fired her," she said.

"Why?"

"She was stealing."

"How do you know?"

"How do I know? Shit's gone, that's how I know."

"What'd she steal?"

"This and that."

Accusations were occasionally levied against the maids, but they rarely turned out to be true. Given the miserable state of the Korean economy, a steady job on base was far too valuable for a middle-aged woman to jeopardize with petty theft.

"Maybe you just wanted her gone," Ernie said. "Out of your way."

She seemed amused by Ernie. "Why would I want that?"

Now it was Ernie's turn to shrug. "For the same reason you don't like the other officers' wives. Catty competition."

She laughed out loud. "That old hag? Please. I just didn't like giving her the hundred dollars a month."

"You'd rather spend it on yourself?"

"Why not? It's my money."

"What about Jenny?" Ernie asked. "Do you love her?"

Evelyn Cresthill's face tightened, anger creeping into her expression. "Of course. What are you talking about?"

"I'm talking about leaving your daughter here, alone and afraid, while you were out having a good time, drinking in nightclubs, having rich men light your cigarettes."

"What would you know about it? Goddamn it, I have a right to go out—to *live* instead of staying cooped up in this dump day after day."

"Did Shin pay you," Ernie continued, "or did you take money directly from the men?"

She grabbed a nearby cushion and threw it at Ernie.

I stood. Evelyn was reaching for the glass ashtray, but I snatched it up before she could hurl it at Ernie's head. He was also standing now.

"When are you going back, Evelyn?" he asked. "When you've recharged your batteries? When you've been to the bank and taken out enough money? When you've convinced Mrs. Bronson to watch your daughter for another week or two?"

"Get out!" she screeched, pointing at the front door. "Get the hell out of my house before I call the MPs."

We did. And once we were on the porch, she slammed and locked the door behind us. As we walked to the jeep, I said, "You've been reading that book again."

"What book?"

"The one about how to make friends and influence people."

"I was hoping she'd tell us more about the gangs and how they operate."

"It sounds like she doesn't know much."

"What was the point of all this? How did Miss Shin profit from showing Evelyn Cresthill around town?"

"Maybe she took a cut for Evelyn's company from the businessmen without telling Evelyn."

"Maybe," Ernie replied. "Seems sort of penny ante."

"Maybe she just does it for kicks. Or to promote her business, whatever that is."

"Do you think Evelyn could find that apartment building?"

"Sure. She had to know the name of the place to tell cab-drivers. You want to go back and ask?"

"Probably not a good time." Ernie climbed in behind the wheel of the jeep. "Evelyn Cresthill stumbled onto a good thing. High living. Glamour. Beats the hell out of a bake sale at the Officers' Wives Club."

He started the engine.

"If you were in her shoes," I asked, "if you were a woman, would you do the same thing?"

"Hell no, I'd do *worse*. Those Nipponese businessmen would never know what hit 'em."

"And the daughter?"

"Well, yeah, that's different. Leaving a ten-year-old alone, that's the rough part."

-20-

The Cosmos Hotel was the newest in downtown Seoul. More fancy high-rise joints had been planned, but so far, the Cosmos was the most modern of available digs. At the marble-topped check-in counter, I asked for Corrine Fitch.

The Korean clerk thumbed through a card file.

"F.I.T.C.H.," I said, spelling it out.

He looked at me, slightly offended. "I know." He returned to his search. Finally, he pulled out a card, stepped away to a phone, and dialed. Ernie glanced around the lobby. Well-dressed young Korean women in high heels clattered to and fro. Three of them, holding each other by linked elbows, headed straight for the elevators.

"Pros," Ernie said.

"How can you tell?"

"Three young Korean women alone, dressed to the nines. No way they could afford one of these rooms. Those girls have been picked out of a catalogue and are on their way to see clients."

"Three together?"

"Japanese businessmen travel in groups."

Entire planeloads of Japanese men, usually from the same company, arrived at Kimpo Airfield practically by the hour, which was part of the reason so many new hotels were being built.

"No answer," the clerk said.

I showed him my badge. "What room number?"

"I'm sorry sir, I can't—"

I glanced at the card in his hand before he could shield it from me. Room 706. Ernie and I marched toward the elevator bank. Once inside, I hit 7.

The door to room 706 was locked, but I politely asked one of the maids to open it. Using English, I explained that I was a friend of the American woman staying there and we were supposed to pick her up, but she hadn't answered her phone, so I wanted to make sure she wasn't ill. The maid didn't understand a word of this. Still, she was intimidated by the presence of foreigners and impressed by my confident reasoning. She turned and knocked on the door. When there was no answer, I motioned for her to use her key. She looked worried, looking around as if someone else might appear to give her the right answer. I then flashed my badge and switched to Korean, asking politely until she finally slid the key home and twisted the lock. Ernie and I pushed past her into the room. She backed away and quickly disappeared.

"Do you think she'll call security?" Ernie asked.

"I doubt it. Better to pretend she never saw us."

To most Koreans who were just trying to make a living, Americans were much more trouble than they were worth. Who knew which powerful people she might offend if she complained about two US military cops?

The bed hadn't been touched, other than a slight muss in the coverlet where someone had sat down. A suitcase on wheels, the same one we'd seen her pulling behind her at Kimpo Airfield, sat next to the bed. It had been opened, but not much had been removed.

"When I called her yesterday," I told Ernie, "she answered like she'd been expecting a call from someone else. And she hung up in a hurry."

The business suit we'd seen her wearing was hung neatly in the closet, the heels below that on the floor.

"So she changed," Ernie said, "and went out."

"Yeah. But where?"

"Not another missing woman," Ernie said.

We searched the room and found nothing except for some notes jotted on a pad next to the phone. Doodles, really. I was trying to make sense of them when someone burst through the door.

I was expecting hotel security, but to my unexpected delight, it was Corrine Fitch.

"Oh, you're here," she said, almost relieved. "Sorry about

the nine o'clock. This Seoul traffic is worse than New York." Then her face clouded. "What the hell are you doing in my room?"

"You didn't make your appointment," I said, "and you didn't answer your phone. We were afraid something happened to you."

This seemed to mollify her somewhat. She wore corduroy pants, hiking boots, and a windbreaker over a T-shirt with the logo for some sort of hockey team.

"You're from New York?" Ernie asked.

"Yes. Well, I suppose you could say I'm originally from Korea." She slipped off her windbreaker, hung it in the closet, and said, "It's a long story. I'll be right back." She stepped into the bathroom and shut the door. As the fan whirred, Ernie sat on the bed and I sat at a chair next to a small table by the window.

"What do you think she's up to?" Ernie asked.

"Haven't the foggiest."

"She looked like she was ready to climb Mount Tobong." The peak north of downtown Seoul. "Not your typical criminal defense attorney."

She emerged from the bathroom, hair brushed back, and said, "Well. Let's talk. Shall we go to the coffee shop? I'm starving."

Ernie and I both stood. In the elevator, we were silent amid a crowd of Japanese businessmen in suits and heavily made-up young Korean women, seeming to prove Ernie's earlier theory. All of them stared straight ahead, no one touching or even talking. When the doors opened onto the main lobby, we stepped out and watched the occupants depart in two separate groups, the women following the men.

Corrine Fitch noticed Ernie and me staring after them. "Who are they?" she asked.

"No one," I said.

We found an elegant coffee shop downstairs and were escorted to a table next to a huge plate-glass window. I quickly scanned my menu, which was in English, Japanese, and Korean.

"That American breakfast sounds good," Corrine said.

"Yeah. Sausage and eggs," Ernie replied. "But the eggs will be overcooked and the sausage will be soft and gummy, like those Vienna sausages from a can. And there won't be any potatoes. For toast, they'll give you something that tastes like burnt Silly Putty."

She gazed at him. "So you wouldn't recommend it."

"No. And the Korean breakfast will be second-rate. Within two blocks of this hotel, there are probably fifty restaurants that serve better—and cheaper—Korean food. The best thing on the menu in these tourist hotels is usually the Japanese breakfast. Miso soup, steamed rice, and roast mackerel. You can't screw that up."

"Okay," she said. "The Japanese breakfast it is."

A chubby-cheeked waitress approached and Corrine Fitch

placed the order. After handing the young girl our menus, Corrine smiled at us. I admired the golden smoothness of her face and felt a small stab of jealousy at Ernie for hogging the conversation.

"So you guys must be old hands," she said to us.

"Yes," I replied. "Is this your first time in Korea?"

She smiled even broader. "Second. The first was when I was born."

"You were adopted?" Ernie said.

"Bingo," she replied. "I was a refugee of the Korean War."

She proceeded to tell us that some twenty years ago, with virtually everyone in the country either fleeing American bombings or Communist atrocities, she had somehow ended up in an orphanage and been shipped to safety, then adopted by the Fitch family. She'd grown up in upstate New York with two older siblings who were the natural-born children of Mr. and Mrs. Fitch.

"Why Corrine?" Ernie asked.

"That was the name of one of my great-aunts."

"Your adopted great-aunts."

"Same to me," she said. "I barely remember my Korean family."

"How old were you when you were adopted?"

"According to my mom, six."

"Which could mean five," I said. She looked at me curiously. "Here, a child is considered one year old when they're born."

"Hunh," she said. "I didn't know that."

The waitress brought a tray loaded with our breakfast and set the hot soup, steaming rice, and filleted mackerel in front of us. Corrine Fitch studied the fish and asked the waitress, "Is this caught fresh from the sea, or was it raised in a fish farm?"

The girl stared at her blankly. The question went beyond her facility with English. I translated.

"*Seingson*," the girl told me. "*Meiil Inchon hantei.*"

"Fresh fish," I told Corrine. "Every day shipped in from the Port of Inchon."

Her eyes widened. "You speak Korean?"

"A little."

"More than a little," she said. "That was pretty good. Ask her if she's ever heard of a city called Taean."

I repeated the question in Korean. The young woman answered. "*Nei. Seingak ei Chungchong-namdo ieiyo.*"

"Yes. She thinks it's in Chungchong South Province."

The girl bowed and hurried away.

"Do all GIs speak Korean?" she asked.

Ernie had just ladled a spoonful of soup into his mouth. He coughed and spit it about halfway across the table. Still choking, he wiped his mouth and said, "Hell no! Sueño here is a freaking *genius*. Most GIs know only enough Korean to pay for beer and bargain for . . . never mind."

Hearing Ernie praise my Korean language ability was a first, but a satisfying one. Corrine looked at me, a half-smile playing around her mouth. "By the way, you guys can call me Corrine."

We re-introduced ourselves; I figured she'd forgotten our names from our brief encounter at the airport the day before. I rose from the table, offered my hand, and said, "*Choum peip-keissumnida*."

She shook my hand and asked, "What does that mean?"

"Delighted to meet you."

"The high-class way," Ernie said, sneering. "That's all Sueño knows." He shoveled rice into his mouth.

When she tried to eat the mackerel, Corrine fumbled with her chopsticks. I called the waitress over and asked for a fork.

"No," Corrine said, "I don't want one. I need to practice."

She watched the way Ernie and I pulled bits of mackerel flesh off with our chopsticks and popped them into our mouths. She tried to emulate it, but each morsel would slip to the table before reaching her lips. I showed her an alternative: pulling the bits off and dropping them atop the steamed rice. After a few bits accumulated in the bowl, you could use your flat spoon to scoop mackerel and rice into your mouth.

After we finished breakfast, Corrine insisted on putting the bill on her hotel tab.

"Fusterman's parents must be loaded," Ernie said, "to hire you to come all the way over here to defend him."

"Loaded enough," she said. "They had a nice house, paid for, which they've mortgaged."

"Are they coming over?" I asked.

"No. His father has a heart condition. He could go at any time, and his son being charged with murder certainly isn't helping his prognosis."

"How do you know them?"

"My law firm has worked with them before. Only one of us could be chosen to come over here, and I was selected."

"Because you're Korean?" Ernie said.

She stared at him coolly. "I'm American."

"Yeah, I guess you are."

We walked out of the coffee shop and took seats in the lobby, and I began to explain to her what we knew about the case. But also how we weren't supposed to be helping her and the best we could do for Fusterman's case was make sure all evidence was made available to her.

"Isn't JAG supposed to do that?"

I shrugged. "They're under a lot of pressure."

"You mean the North Koreans. Along the DMZ."

"Yes. JAG is under pressure to resolve this case right away. Get everybody to chop off on it. There's no guarantee that the North Koreans will accept Fusterman's guilt, but as long as they see one of us imperialist running dogs punished, they'll save face."

"And withdraw their tanks?"

"That's the hope."

"But if he's not guilty?"

"That screws up the whole deal," Ernie said.

"And tensions continue," I said. "Meaning one miscalculation . . ."

"And we're back to refugees," she said, "and orphans."

"Right."

"So that's what we're up against," she said.

"What *you're* up against," Ernie corrected.

"Yes." She clasped her hands together. "Why are you trying to help me?"

"Free breakfast," Ernie told her.

Corrine Fitch raised an eyebrow and looked at me.

"We were at the crime scene," I said. "We saw Corporal Noh Jong-bei's body, blood and crushed skull and all. And then we met his family."

"And we went down to the stockade in ASCOM and interviewed PFC Fusterman," Ernie added.

"It's pretty hard to imagine him bashing somebody's skull in," I said.

"But you're cops. You're not supposed to work on intuition."

"No," I said. "But we suspect there's something else going on at the JSA."

"What?"

"We're not sure yet."

"I'll be going up there," she said. "To the Joint Security Area, to view the crime scene. And then down south to interview my client."

"When?"

"Tomorrow. JAG has scheduled a military vehicle for me. And a driver."

"Be careful at the JSA," Ernie said. "They see you're Korean, and they're liable to pull you across the line and keep you there."

"They can't legally do that."

"No. But they've done it before, to a South Korean journalist."

"I'll be careful," she said.

"Be more than careful," Ernie told her. "At all times, keep at least one American guard between you and the North Koreans. And don't step too close to the line."

"What line?"

"The Military Demarcation Line. The line between North and South Korea."

"You can't be serious?" she said. "They wouldn't really pull me across the line."

"Since you were born on the soil of the Korean Peninsula," I explained to her, "in their minds, you're a citizen of the Democratic People's Republic of Korea. And as far as being unpredictable, think about taking the USS *Pueblo* on the high seas, or shooting down the EC-121 reconnaissance plane which evaporated with thirty-one American sailors aboard, or sending a commando raid into the heart of Seoul to assassinate President Park Chung-hee. Nobody was expecting any of those things. It's important that you don't relax, that you don't assume they'll follow any rules. Be on guard at all times."

Corrine Fitch stared at us silently without speaking.

I described the entrenching tool to her, down to the initials *TF* scratched into it. And I told her how Fusterman had claimed somebody must've switched it for the one covered in blood. This time, she pulled out a pen and spiral notebook and started to write.

"JAG has the shovel now?" she asked.

"The entrenching tool," Ernie corrected.

"Yes," I said. "JAG has it. We were spotted waiting for you, so we had no choice but to turn it over to them."

"As long as I know it's there," she said. "Of course, they'll claim my client could've done the switching, so it doesn't prove anything."

Then I asked her the question I'd been holding back since we'd run into her again. "You're doing something else here," I said, "besides representing PFC Fusterman. You went somewhere yesterday, and you didn't return to your room until this morning."

She slipped her notebook back into her pocket. "What are you, my chaperone?"

"No. But my partner and I are sticking our necks out just by talking to you. And if we help Fusterman any further, we'll be violating a direct order. We could be court-martialed."

"Weren't you violating a direct order when you located the *entrenching tool*?" She glanced at Ernie.

"Not really. If evidence happens to fall into our lap, it's our duty to turn it into JAG."

"But you were going to show it to me first."

I shrugged. "You're also an officer of the court. We were going to let JAG know about it too."

"You're really stretching the rules," she said.

"Welcome to Eighth Imperial Army," Ernie said.

She turned back to me. "So you want to know what I'm up to."

"Yes."

Her eyes narrowed slightly. "You have no right to question me. What I do on my own time is none of your damn business, nor Eighth Imperial Army's." She rose to her feet. "Hope you enjoyed your breakfast. I'll see you gentlemen in court." She turned and marched toward the elevators.

Once she was out of earshot, Ernie said, "Why do I feel like we've been had?"

"Yeah," I said, "in terms of passing along information, that was strictly a one-way street."

-21-

That afternoon, Ernie and I staked out the Yongsan Commissary and made one black-market bust, hoping that would be enough to keep Riley off our backs. The perpetrator's name was Chong-ja Jaegerman. After making her purchase, she had the bagger load her groceries into the back of one of the big Ford Granada PX taxis that line up beside the commissary. From there, she made her way straight to one of the well-known black-market operations in Itaewon, the red light village less than a mile off compound. Ernie and I followed at a safe distance and waited nearby until money changed hands. Then we rushed in and made the arrest.

We were only allowed to arrest her, not the Korean black-market honcho she'd sold the goods to, because he was a Korean citizen and therefore outside our jurisdiction. We didn't bother to notify the local KNP office about him because they were already fully aware of his operation. And even if we'd made a fuss and embarrassed them into arresting him, they would've let him go within twenty minutes. Partly because black marketeering wasn't seen as the most serious crime in town, but mainly because the local station commander was almost certainly on the black-market honcho's payroll.

We escorted Mrs. Jaegerman to the Yongsan MP Station. By the time we finished the paperwork, she was in crying mode. I called her husband to come and pick her up. He was a tall Sergeant First Class with a slight paunch pushing over his brass belt buckle, and he signed for his wife with a grim resolve. I gave him the commercial. "You're responsible for the actions of all your dependents, twenty-four hours a day, seven days a week."

"I know that," he snapped.

And then I told him to report to the 8th Army Ration Control Office.

The worst part, other than the fine and reprimand he was likely to receive from his unit commander, was that his family rations would be cut to what the military called "health and welfare maintenance." This restriction—a reduction of what he could spend in the PX and commissary to only ninety dollars per month—would be in effect for the remainder of his tour in Korea. Once a military family was back in the States, nobody cared how much they spent in the PX because there was no black-market demand for items they could purchase there. Maybe that was why GIs called America "the Land of the Big PX."

That night, Ernie and I returned to our home turf: the red-light district of Itaewon. Neon flashed and rock and roll blared from behind beaded curtains. Young women wearing only hot pants and halter tops, goose-fleshed in the cold, waved and cooed at us, trying to lure us into their domain.

At the bar of the King Club, Ernie tossed back a double shot of watered-down bourbon, chasing it with a cold bottle of OB Beer.

"You're going to get wasted," I told him.

"Why not? I live in the Mad Hatter's world of the Eighth United States Army. Sometimes a guy needs to take a bite out of the psychedelic mushroom."

He ordered another double shot and a beer. I had a second beer too.

"It bothers you," I said, "that they're trying to railroad Fusterman."

"Damn right it does."

"So maybe we don't let them."

"How? We can't go up to the JSA or question anyone involved. It's not likely we're going to make much progress."

"Maybe there's a different way."

"Like what?"

I paused, trying my best to come up with some sort of method to pin this murder where it belonged, which I suspected might be on someone we hadn't even yet considered.

When I didn't say anything, Ernie asked, "Well?"

"How's the bourbon?" I asked.

"Shitty," he said.

I called the bartender over and ordered a double shot.

Just before the midnight curfew, Ernie and I staggered down Itaewon's hill toward the MSR. At the dark entrance to the open-air Itaewon Market, we decided to take a shortcut. We plowed into the darkness past empty wooden stalls that before dawn would be filled with piles of cabbage and turnips and garlic, interspersed with shimmering blue ice encasing various forms of wriggling sea life.

We were about ten yards in when a dark figure emerged from the shadows. Neon flashed from the main road, illuminating a pudgy hand squeezing the grip of a small pistol. Pointing the business end of the weapon toward us, the man behind it said, "Make a move, and I'll plug you where you stand."

Ernie and I put our hands in the air. The man took a halfstep forward, revealing his face—skin white, slathered in perspiration, the top of his head bald.

"Colonel Peele," I said.

"Be quiet," he told us. "Stand at attention."

Ernie and I lowered our arms to our sides, placed our feet together and stood up straight.

Colonel Peele glanced in either direction to see if anyone was approaching, which no one was. At this time of night, there was no reason for any pedestrians to cruise by this empty alleyway. Except for a couple of drunks like Ernie and me.

"You've been following us," I said.

"I told you to shut up."

"Yes, sir."

"For once, you're going to keep your traps shut and listen." He wiped his forehead with the back of his free hand. It was cold, maybe ten degrees above freezing, but he acted as if we were in the tropics. "I know about the entrenching tool."

We waited silently, per his instructions.

"It's a good thing. Enough to get Fusterman off and put the blame back on the Commies where it belongs."

"But?" Ernie said.

Peele swiveled the barrel of the pistol toward him. "I told you to shut the fuck up."

"Yes, sir."

"You're right," he conceded. "There is a *but*. When it comes to appeasing the North Koreans, the lily livers at Eighth Army always have a *but*. They're already saying the entrenching tool is phony, that it's just a plant to get this kid free. Maybe so, I don't know. And I don't care. All I know is that it was the North Koreans who murdered Corporal Noh, and by God they're going to pay for it."

"How do you know?" I asked.

This time, he didn't tell me to shut up. A good sign.

"Because I *know* the North Korean Commies. They're

two-faced, lying, devil-worshipping sons of bitches. They've gotten away with torturing and murdering our men for years, but they're not about to get away with it this time." He waved the business end of the pistol between us. "You two are going to prove that the North Koreans murdered Corporal Noh Jong-bei."

"And how are we supposed to do that?" Ernie asked. "You were the one who barred us from going up there."

"Yeah, that was a mistake. I figured you two were trying to let the North Koreans off the hook, dragging the corpse south and messing up the crime scene. Then making Fusterman look guilty by exposing his affair with Noh's sister in your report."

"And now?"

"You've found the second entrenching tool and turned it in to JAG. It could let Fusterman off."

"Maybe."

"Yeah," he agreed. "Maybe. We need definitive proof so Eighth Army doesn't pull any more shenanigans."

"Why don't you just rescind the order barring us from the JSA?" Ernie asked.

"Can't. Too many people chopped off on it, including the Chief of Staff. They can't back down now."

"So what do you want us to do?" I should've added a *sir* to that, but his pointing a pistol at me was sort of pissing me off. "Colonel Peele, you may want to quit waving that gun at us."

He glanced down at his hand, as if just remembering he was holding a firearm. "Oh, yeah." He lowered it to his side but didn't put it away or turn the safety off. "What I want you to do is come up to the DMZ with me."

"When?" I asked.

"I'm not sure. I have to set up a meeting."

"A MAC meeting?"

"No, nothing that out in the open. This meeting will be private."

"With who?"

"Commissar Han. He's the one who's really in charge up there."

"You work with him?"

"If *work* is the right word. More like I suffer insults from him. You know, *lackey of the mad-dog imperialists*. Stuff like that."

"He's a political figure," I guessed, "not military?"

"Right. The real power in the North Korean government lies with the Workers' Party, not the army."

"What good can he do us?"

"I'm going to convince him to hand over whoever murdered Corporal Noh."

"And how are you going to manage that?" Ernie asked.

Colonel Peele raised the pistol again, holding it closer to his chest this time. "With this," he said, running his hand over the burnished metal absentmindedly. "Any man will tell the truth with a gun pointed at him."

Ernie and I glanced briefly at one another.

"And you want us there . . . why, sir?"

"So you can make it official with your Criminal Investigation report and arrest the culprit."

"We can't arrest North Koreans, sir. That's definitely outside of our jurisdiction, and in any case, we're officially barred from this investigation."

"Don't be ridiculous," he said. "Eighth Army rules can always be bent. Leave that to me."

With that, he turned and disappeared back into the darkness.

Ernie looked at me. "Is he serious?"

"As a freaking heart attack."

The next morning at the CID office, Staff Sergeant Riley said, "Only one black-market arrest yesterday?"

Ernie shrugged and returned to reading Riley's copy of the *Stars and Stripes*.

"You should've had more than that," Riley said. "I *know* you'll do better today."

"We will?" Ernie said. "Why's that?"

Our policy was to make as few black-market arrests as we could get away with. The alleged purpose of the ration control regulations was to make sure that tax-free American-made products didn't flood the Korean market. The unfair competition—with transportation costs funded by the American taxpayer—theoretically made it difficult, if not impossible, for fledgling Korean companies to gain a toehold in the consumer market. This was the official rationale. But the real reason the 8th Army honchos put such an emphasis on curtailing the black market was much more visceral: flat-out racism. The men and women who ran 8th Army didn't like seeing the wives of enlisted men—almost all of them Korean or from other third-world countries—descend on *their* PX, *their* commissary. The checkout lines grew longer and the desirable consumer goods were gobbled up, leaving less merchandise available for "real" Americans. As Ernie used to say, we were just tools of the power structure. By making fewer black-market arrests than we were actually capable of, we'd turned ourselves into blunt instruments, which might have been a petty form of protest, but a form of protest nevertheless.

No matter what we did—or didn't do—black marketeering continued unabated. It was an easy way to double or even triple your money, and almost everyone involved had someone relying on them financially. Maybe a younger brother struggling to get through high school or elderly parents who could no longer afford to put a roof over their heads. There was no social security or welfare system in Korea. So the incentive to turn an illicit buck was strong. Undaunted, Eighth Army continued to shovel against a tide of unbridled capitalism, and for the most part, Ernie and I were the only ones getting wet.

"Today is end-of-month *payday*," Riley continued. "A clean slate on everybody's monthly ration limit. So after hubby brings home the loot, wifey will stuff her patent leather purse full of money and hit the bricks. The *yobo*s will be all over the PX and commissary."

"Let the good times roll," Ernie said.

Ernie hated the PX. When he was forced to shop, he'd pile up about three months' worth of soap and shoe polish and toothpaste and rush out as soon as possible. And even though he spent so little time inside, he'd complain about the perky announcements over the intercom. "'*Good morning, shoppers.*' What do they think I am? A *freaking* shopper? They can stuff it." Then he'd pause and take a deep breath, trying to calm himself. "This place is loaded with crap. What would anybody want this stuff for?"

I didn't have an answer.

The military package liquor store—unofficially called the Class VI—was a different matter. Ernie could browse the shelves in there for hours. Studying the labels, meditating on the difference between a blended scotch and single malt or the relative merits of virgin sugarcane honey versus raw molasses in the manufacture of Caribbean rum.

At the counter in back of the CID office, I pulled myself a cup of hot coffee from the large silver urn. Miss Kim ignored Riley and Ernie's banter, as per usual, focusing on her typewriter. I carried my coffee toward her desk and sat down.

"*Anyonghaseiyo?*" I said. Are you at peace?

"*Nei,*" she said, smiling. "*Anyonghaseiyo?*" Yes. Are you?

She was always stylish, wearing colorful cotton dresses that were modest but still managed to highlight her magnificent figure and show off her long legs from the knee down. A little over a year ago, she and Ernie had dated. Miss Kim seemed to think that the two of them were headed in a serious direction. At first, she ignored the comments that Riley and a few of the other law enforcement agents let slip. But eventually they became too much for her to pretend they weren't valid. She confronted Ernie with her suspicions and, to his credit, he didn't deny his infidelities. And he made no promises to her that the two of them would be anything more than friends. It was a friendship with what Ernie hoped would be continuing privileges. But right then and there, Miss Kim ended those privileges—and the friendship. She'd barely spoken to Ernie since, which was awkward since they still worked in the same office. However, that didn't seem to bother Ernie. Nothing ever seemed to bother Ernie.

"Sorry to interrupt your work, Miss Kim," I said. "But I have a question."

"Yes?"

She placed her hands in her lap and waited.

"Have you ever heard of an orphanage in the city of Taean?"

"Taean?" she asked.

"Yes. In Chungchong-namdo."

I suspected that Corrine Fitch might be using this trip to Korea to research her own past. She'd mentioned Taean; if there was an orphanage there that had operated around her time of adoption, that might explain her interest.

"I've heard of it," Miss Kim replied. "But if there's an orphanage there, I wouldn't know."

"Do you think you could find out if there are any? And send me the names and locations? I believe this one operated during the Korean War, but it might not be there any longer. If it isn't, maybe there are some old records."

"You want to look someone up?"

"Yes."

Miss Kim was very quick on the uptake. If she'd gotten the chance to earn something above a high school diploma, I knew she would've gone far. Unfortunately, the Korean War had hit her family hard, as it had millions all over the country. Her father had been a soldier in the South Korean army and had been lucky enough to survive until the armistice was signed in July of 1953. But during the war, while combat still raged, his unit had been cut off from resupply and many of his fellow soldiers died of malnutrition. Miss Kim didn't talk about it, but from other stories I'd heard, many soldiers had survived by eating frogs and lizards—until the reptiles and amphibians became scarce. When her father returned from the war, he'd been frighteningly emaciated and in generally terrible health. In those days, few people had enough money to see a doctor, but he'd eventually gotten an appointment at a free clinic set up by the United Nations. His prognosis was bleak: starvation had caused irreparable damage to his internal organs. The doctors gave him medicine to ease his suffering, but he died only a few months later. Miss Kim was an only child. Since then, she and her mother had barely gotten by—that was, until she'd graduated from high school and landed a secretarial job on the 8th Army compound. The US military was one of the few employers that provided health insurance, a steady paycheck, and even a retirement plan. Her mother had no marketable skills—other than taking in laundry—and in any case was now too sickly to work. As a result, Miss Kim held on to this tedious administrative job at 8th Army CID as if it were a lifeline out of the ninth circle of hell. Which, to her, it was.

"I'll make some phone calls," she told me. "Off base, to some of the children's welfare organizations. Maybe one of them can tell me."

"I'd really appreciate it."

Miss Kim's cultured tone could open doors that my broken Korean usually couldn't. She stared at me quizzically. "There's a young man," she said "who says he knows you."

"Who's that?"

"I don't remember his name, but he started showing up every day at noon. He says he loves to play badminton."

"Oh," I said, "Porter."

"Yes. That's his name." She studied me. "He's odd."

"Odd? Why?"

"He plays badminton poorly."

"Oh, that's all?"

"Partly. But he always wants to be on my team."

"Does that bother you?"

"Of course," she said.

"Why?"

"Because I've dropped to third place in our division."

"You mean when I see you guys outside playing every day, you're participating in a tournament?"

"Tournament?" she said, deftly thumbing through her onion-skinned English–Korean dictionary, her polished forefinger running down the right page before coming to a halt. "Yes," she said, "a tournament."

"What's the prize?" I asked.

"No prize," she said.

"Then what?"

"Pride," she said, as if it were obvious.

"So you don't want Porter to play on your team?"

"Not all the time," she said. "We do, what do you call it?" She swirled her forefinger in a circle.

"Rotation," I said.

She looked that word up, too. When she found it she said, "Yes. Mr. Porter is welcome to play with us but he must follow the *rotation*."

"I see. That way it's fair."

"Yes."

"And you don't want to have to explain that to him."

"No. It's very embarrassing. He always wants to be on my team."

"Okay," I said. "I'll talk to him."

She placed her cool palm atop my hand. She almost certainly realized that Porter was sweet on her. "Be kind," she said.

"Of course," I promised.

While we'd been talking, Riley had received a phone call that I'd ignored—he received dozens of phone calls during the day—but now I realized his voice had risen.

"You're shittin' me," he said. Then, "They'll be right there."

He slammed the phone down.

"Bascom! Sueño!" he shouted even though we were just a few feet away from him. "Hat up! Evelyn Cresthill has gone missing. Again."

We jumped in the jeep and headed for the on-post quarters of Evelyn Cresthill. Within minutes, we reached the South Post housing area. Major Bob Cresthill answered the door.

"You two," he said, eyes wide.

"Yes, sir," I replied. "We thought you'd be at the Soyang construction site."

"We got back late last night. I was about to get ready and go to the office. What is it?" he asked irritably, not inviting us in.

"What happened to your wife?"

"Who the hell knows?" He shook his head several times. "Last night when I came in, the house was empty. I went over to Madge Bronson's place and Jenny was there again. I begged Madge to keep her one more day because I have to work this morning. We're finally wrapping up the project. She said okay, but I can tell you she's at the limits of her patience. Can't say that I blame her."

He glared at us as if we were personally responsible for his childcare problems.

"Did your wife leave a note or say anything to Mrs. Bronson about where she was going?"

"Not a word."

"How about to Jenny?"

"She just told Jenny to be good and not give Madge any trouble."

"Did she tell Madge when she'd be back?"

"Yeah. It was supposed to be last night, sometime early enough to get Jenny home so she could get a good night's sleep for school today. As you can see, she didn't make it."

The Seoul-American school had opened an hour ago.

"That's why you called it in."

"That and what she left in the bedroom."

"Can we see?"

He opened the door wider and we followed him down the hallway to the master bedroom. He motioned toward the top of the dresser. On it sat a white paper napkin and in the middle of that a wedding ring. The diamond glistened in the overhead light.

"And her passport's gone," Cresthill said. "Plus two of her favorite dresses." He pointed toward naked wires hanging in the closet. "Along with a Pan Am travel bag she likes to use. I wouldn't be surprised if our checking account's been cleaned out."

"Much in it?" Ernie asked.

He shrugged. "Only a couple hundred bucks."

More than an infantry private made in a month, but we didn't say anything.

Major Cresthill promised to call us if his wife contacted either him or Jenny. We thanked him and walked next door to confirm his story with Madge Bronson. She told us that Evelyn Cresthill came to her home about noontime yesterday—shortly after Ernie and I had talked to her—and asked Madge to pick Jenny up from school. She promised she'd be home that evening early enough to take Jenny home and tuck her into bed, but she hadn't shown up. Mrs. Bronson wagged her forefinger at us as she said, "Evelyn Cresthill dumped her daughter on me a second time and had the nerve not to come back. If you see her, you tell that woman that I'm through being taken advantage of. I'm nobody's doormat."

"We'll pass that along," I promised.

On the way back to the jeep, Ernie whistled softly. "Think Evelyn Cresthill's abandoned her family for good?" he said.

"Maybe she had no choice," I said. "The *gampei* might've threatened her."

"They'd do that?"

"They've probably already made appointments with big shots to be entertained by a Western woman. Rather than lose face, I don't think they would hesitate to do whatever got her back."

"She should've come to us."

"I don't think she trusts Eighth Army much. Besides, she probably thinks she can work this out on her own."

"Good luck with that," Ernie said.

We stopped at the Honor Guard barracks and checked with Captain Randy Quincy. He claimed that since the last time we talked to him, he'd had no contact with Evelyn Cresthill.

"Are you *sure* you haven't seen her?" Ernie asked.

"Scout's honor," he replied, holding up two fingers.

-22-

Per our usual routine, we parked our jeep next to the old lady who sold *pindaedok* from her rolling cart a block behind the downtown Jongno headquarters of the Korean National Police. When Ernie handed her another two thousand *won*, she bowed and beamed a wrinkled smile.

"Parking's adding up," he said, checking his fold and stuffing it back into his pocket.

Officer Oh met us in the lobby and escorted us upstairs. Once again, Mr. Kill waved us to the seats opposite him across the wooden coffee table. This time, Officer Oh joined us. She pressed her knees tightly together and adjusted her skirt, her spine not even touching the back of the chair. I explained that Evelyn Cresthill had disappeared again, and that we believed she might've voluntarily returned to the *gampei*.

"I wouldn't call it voluntary," Inspector Kill said.

"What do you mean?"

In response, he nodded toward Officer Oh. During past

encounters, she had typically been quiet, not doing much more than serving coffee and tea, driving Mr. Kill's police sedan, and handing him reports. But it seemed he was grooming her for greater things.

Officer Oh said, "To the *gampei*, Evelyn Cresthill is valuable in more ways than one. Not only are they making money from her by using her as a hostess for very rich men, but they are also"—she paused and studied her notes—"putting their thumb in the eye of the American forces."

"Why would they want to do that?" I asked.

"To showcase their power. To prove to competing mob groups that they're not afraid of the United States."

"And therefore not afraid of the Park Chung-hee regime," I added.

"Exactly," she said.

"How long will they hold her?" Ernie asked.

"I don't think they'll let her return this time. Our sources say that she surprised them by running home the last time. They won't make the same mistake again. When they realized she was gone, they used their spies on base to find her phone number. They called her and told her that if she didn't return, and do as they wished, her daughter would be abducted."

"They'd do that?" I asked.

"The threat might not have been serious."

"But Evelyn Cresthill wouldn't know that," Ernie said.

Officer Oh nodded.

I turned to Mr. Kill. "Aren't these *gampei* playing a pretty dangerous game? Just so they can pimp an American woman? It doesn't make any sense."

Mr. Kill nodded. "On the surface, no, it wouldn't make sense."

Ernie and I glanced at one another. I turned back to Mr. Kill. "And under the surface?"

He reached for his breast pocket, as if he wanted to pull out a cigarette, and then thought better of it and stopped himself. He nodded toward Officer Oh.

She straightened herself and spoke. "We believe," she said, "that these *gampei* might be under the influence, or trying to gain influence, with the North Korean regime. If the American forces have to start worrying about their women and children being kidnapped and sold into sex slavery, they will hesitate to bring them here."

"Which will damage our commitment to the defense of South Korea."

She nodded. "And ultimately cause all foreigners to be afraid to come to South Korea, which will greatly damage our economy."

"Evelyn Cresthill," Mr. Kill said, "could be the first victim in a brutal campaign."

"So this time, you don't think they'll let her go?" I asked.

"Not alive," he replied.

■　■　■

On the way back to Yongsan Compound, Ernie honked his horn as we roared through Namsan Tunnel Number Three.

"Why do you always do that?" I asked.

"To hear the echo. Let people know I'm here." Then he said, "What do you think the *gampei* will do with her next?"

"I'm not sure. But Inspector Kill is right. They'll toss her away when she's not useful anymore. Which may be soon."

"That would be a damn shame."

"You liked her?" I asked.

"Yeah. She's bold."

"With any luck, the KNPs will turn something up."

"Let's go find her ourselves." Ernie said.

"All right. But where?"

Ernie thought it over, but he didn't have an answer. When the MP waved us through Gate Number Seven into Yongsan Compound, I said, "Let's stop at Data Processing."

"Why?"

"I need to talk to Porter."

Ernie shrugged. He turned left, then a right, and pulled up on the gravel incline at the rear of the 8th Army Data Processing Unit.

"Won't take long," I told him.

He reached into his pocket and pulled out a pack of ginseng gum. "Take your time," he said. "I'm not anxious to get back to the office. All they'll want to know is why we haven't found Evelyn Cresthill yet."

I strolled off into the DPU, a big open bay jammed with desks. In the back were whirring machines: punch card readers with flywheels swallowing IBM cards, digesting them, and spitting them back out again. As I stood at the front counter, I saw Porter sitting beneath a sign that read RATION CONTROL LIAISON. He looked up, a pretty bad shiner puffing his left eye.

I motioned for him to meet me outside. Looking slightly surprised, he nodded in acknowledgment.

Once outside, he said, "What now? More LOAs?"

"No, not this time. It's about the badminton."

"Badminton?"

"Yeah." I paused, waiting for him to talk.

He smiled. "I'm starting to like the game."

I pointed to his black eye. "What happened to you?"

He reached up and touched the bruise. "Oh, this? Nothing. So, is this about Miss Kim?"

I continued to stare at him, then realized that he had more bruises on his forearm. Defensive wounds.

"She's happy that you're so interested in badminton," I told him. "But they have two-person teams, one on each side of the net. There's a rotation."

"Yeah," Porter said, hand still resting on his eye. "They mentioned that."

"They switch partners to make it fair. Otherwise, the best players would always stay together and end up on top. It's an ongoing tournament. They keep track and everything."

"What's the prize?"

"No material prize."

"I like playing with Miss Kim. I'm learning a lot from her."

"Yes. But you have to play by the rules. You can't have her on your side all the time."

"To keep it fair," he said.

"Right."

"That's what she sent you to tell me?"

"Yes. She likes you as a partner, but the tournament has its rules."

"Okay," he said, "I won't insist on being on her side all the time."

"Good." I touched his shoulder. "Now, tell me about the shiner."

He paused. "It's a little embarrassing."

"Consider me a father confessor. It'll stay between you and me."

"It's no big thing, just Colonel Brunmeyer," he continued. "He's sort of an emotional guy. When he stopped in a couple days ago, I asked him why they needed so many LOAs up there at the JSA, especially after all the stuff that's happened with the dead KATUSA and the GI charged with killing him."

"And he hit you?" I said.

"Yeah."

"Are you going to press charges?"

"No. It's no big thing. He's under a lot of pressure. I should've kept my mouth shut."

"If you change your mind—"

"Yeah," he replied. "I'll let you know."

"Finished?" Ernie asked.

"Yeah," I said, sliding back into the passenger seat.

"What's wrong?" he asked, starting the engine.

"Nothing. Porter just gave me a lot to think about."

"Don't hurt yourself," Ernie said, starting the engine.

Back in the CID Office, Riley demanded another report on the status of the investigation into the second disappearance of Evelyn Cresthill. I told him to keep his khaki shirt on and sat down to type it up. The close-of-business cannon went off before I was done. Miss Kim covered her typewriter, locked her desk, and bowed as she said her goodbyes. Riley scurried out right at five as well, claiming he had a hot date.

"With anyone under seventy?" Ernie asked.

"Mind your own beeswax, Bascom."

When I finished the report, I slid the original and a carbon copy into Riley's inbox. The pink carbon copy I kept for my own accordion file.

"What about tonight?" Ernie asked. "Itaewon?"

"No. I'm thinking someplace better."

"Better than Itaewon? Is that possible?"

Itaewon was the most notorious nightclub and red-light district in Seoul, and by far the most popular with GIs.

"Yeah, better," I replied. "Or fancier, at least."

"Where?"

"The nightclub at the Cosmos Hotel," I said.

"Oh," he said, crossing his arms. "So George Sueño has the hots for Corrine Fitch."

"You could say that. But I also want to find out how things went for her up at the Joint Security Area."

"And at the stockade in ASCOM."

"That, too."

We drove to the 8th Army Dining Facility, ate our evening chow, and within a half hour had changed into our running-the-ville outfits again. We were the picture of your typical GIs: showered, shaved, short-cropped hair, and chomping on gin-seng gum, ready for anything.

In the basement of the Cosmos Hotel, we flashed our badges to the doorman and told him we were on police business and wouldn't be paying the cover charge. He didn't seem to under-stand, so we pushed past him. When a bouncer noticed and approached, I said, "*Kyongchal!*" Police. It was enough to get him to back off, at least for the moment.

Ernie and I each took a side of the ballroom, scanning for her, but after twenty minutes of getting our eyes daz-zled by the reflected lights from the rotating glass ball suspended over the expansive space, we met back at the entrance.

"No dice," Ernie shouted above the din of the disco music.

Young Korean men and women gyrated madly on the dance floor. A few drunken Japanese businessmen, accompanied by bored prostitutes, shook various parts of their bodies in seeming disregard to the pulse of what passed for music these days.

As we left, the bouncers glared at us. I waved my thanks.

"Nice fellows," Ernie said.

Upstairs in the lobby, we considered our options. "Okay," I said, "no answer in her room. She's not in the coffee shop and not in the nightclub. So where the hell is she?"

"The only time you can find a lawyer," Ernie told me, "is when they're trying to hand you their bill. Good thing one of our military benefits is full legal representation from JAG."

"If we're being court-martialed," I said. "And even then the representation isn't necessarily a lawyer, just an officer appointed by JAG."

Ernie's head swiveled, and the way he stopped and squinted, I knew he'd spotted something. "Don't look now," he said.

We moved casually behind a bank of leafy plants. On the far side of the lobby, Attorney Corrine Fitch, wearing a professional gray pantsuit, walked with a bag slung over her shoulder. At her elbow marched a man we knew.

"They're a *couple*," Ernie said, a hint of awe in his voice. "That was quick."

They smiled and laughed and looked longingly at each other like newlyweds on a honeymoon. Paying little or no attention to their surroundings, the two lovebirds reached the elevators and stepped in when the first doors parted. As they drew back together, I saw her smile up at him.

Ernie turned to me. "You okay, pal?"

"Yeah," I said.

He patted me on the shoulder. "Hey, don't be so glum. Can't win 'em all. Besides, you were too slow."

"Hey, we met her less than forty-eight hours ago."

"That's what I mean. You snooze, you lose. You should never be too busy to get a little. That's my motto." Ernie studied me again. Finally, he said, "Hey, let's find a *pochang macha*. Split a bottle of soju. It'll make you feel better."

It wasn't just that Corrine Fitch had found someone, and in record time. It was who it was that bothered me.

"How can he even afford to come down here?" I asked. "With all the tension up at the JSA?"

Ernie shrugged. "Nobody's indispensable."

"But he's ambitious. In line to be promoted to full colonel, and maybe general someday. He can't afford to be gone when the shit hits the fan. An incident could blow up at any minute."

"Some things are worth it," Ernie said, which didn't improve my mood.

"There's more to it than that," I said.

"More to it than getting laid?" Ernie scoffed. "Like what?"

"I think I know. I think it's been right in front of us all along."

I remembered Lieutenant Colonel Brunmeyer's grim expression when he'd led us to the corpse of Corporal Noh Jong-bei. And I compared it to his demeanor as he waltzed through the hotel lobby, laughing with Corrine Fitch.

"Come on, don't let jealousy get to you," Ernie said.

"I won't." And I hoped it was true.

-23-

The next morning, the Judge Advocate General's Office conducted the first preliminary hearing, or "Article 32 proceeding," for the murder of Corporal Noh Jong-bei. Ernie and I were present, since we'd been the first investigators on scene. Major Reginald Pintergast led the hearing, which was also attended by Corrine Fitch, representing the defendant, and Captain Brian Orbanick, appointed by JAG to prosecute on behalf of the 8th United States Army. Lieutenant Peggy Mendelson was still on the prosecution team but acting as Orbanick's assistant.

Corrine sipped on a Styrofoam cup of coffee she'd ladled with a packet of artificial sweetener and what I considered too much soluble creamer. She didn't so much as glance in my direction, studying the paperwork in front of her intently and occasionally scribbling a note in the margins.

Ernie whispered in my ear.

"Get over it, Sueño."

I was pretty sure he was enjoying himself.

"I have a girlfriend," I told him.

"Thousands of miles away." He waved his hands, imitating a hula dancer.

Major Pintergast pounded a gavel and said, "Okay, let's get started." He glanced around the small conference room, calling out everyone's names and asking each of us to spell ours out loud for the benefit of the recorder. When that was done, he turned to the clerk of court and told him to read off the charges. It was a long list that started with premeditated murder and ended with misappropriation of government property, namely the bloodstained entrenching tool.

When he was done, Corrine Fitch gave her opening statement. She said that there was no evidence offered by the prosecution that indicated her client had been anywhere near the crime scene when the murder had been perpetrated. She went on to argue that the evidence against him amounted to mere speculation regarding motive, which was completely unprovable. In addition, she claimed, the entrenching tool with Corporal Noh's blood on it could easily have been planted among his possessions, since he lived in an open-bay barracks with many other soldiers who had access to his gear. When she was through, she asked that JAG dismiss all charges. Major Pintergast took only enough time to grab his gavel and bang it on wood. Then, in no uncertain terms, he said, "Denied."

Ernie was called up first, then me. We both stuck to the

bare facts as we'd noted them at the crime scene. Orbanick made me repeat more than once that I had noted the similarity of the wound in size and shape to the edge of an army-issue entrenching tool. Corrine asked about the black-market operation at Paju-ri and how much I'd paid for the shovel. I told her, and she asked both Ernie and me if the initials had already been scratched into the shovel when we'd first seen it. We both confirmed that they had. Finally, we were through.

Several other witnesses took the stand, mainly guys who worked at the JSA and knew both Corporal Noh and PFC Fusterman. They testified that Noh and Fusterman had been good friends and had often gone to Seoul together. Then the 8th Army Coroner was called up to confirm that the cause of death had been blunt force trauma, and the head wound Corporal Noh had suffered was consistent with a blow by an army-issue entrenching tool.

With the exception of the few minutes I was on the stand, Corrine Fitch paid no more attention to me than your average faceless trooper. I told myself to forget it, that this juvenile crush was foolish anyway, but my mind unwillingly drifted back to the image of her and Lieutenant Colonel Brunmeyer smiling at one another after entering the elevator at the Cosmos Hotel.

Although we'd finished our testimony, Ernie and I had to stand by in case either side had further questions for us. By late morning, I was thoroughly bored and Ernie was getting fidgety. Finally, Staff Sergeant Riley knocked and peeked through the door. He apologized to Major Pintergast and tiptoed over to hand me a phone message. I pointed at it and motioned to Pintergast that Ernie and I had to go. Exasperated, he waved his hand dismissively and we left.

"What is it?" I asked once we were outside.

Riley thrust a phone message at me. "Both of you. They want you over at the MAC. *Now.*"

"Bald-headed Colonel Peele again?" Ernie asked.

"The same."

"Tell him to take a flying leap. We're in the middle of a missing person investigation."

"You can call and tell him yourselves," Riley countered. "I'm sure he'll be thrilled, since he's a paragon of patience."

Ernie snorted. "Okay," he said. "Better than being here."

"And more important," I said. "We're wasting crucial hours on this hearing."

"Standard procedure. But this whole Article 32 thing doesn't matter, anyway," Riley said. "Just a waste of time—Fusterman's toast."

The phone rang as we walked into the CID office. Miss Kim was down the hall, so I sprinted to pick it up. "CID," I said. "Sueño."

There was a long silence.

"*Yoboseiyo?*" I said.

Finally, a young woman at the other end spoke faintly. "*Nei. Yoboseiyo.*"

I recognized the voice. She was frightened, but I responded in Korean to reassure her she could talk to me. Finally, she told me that we had to speak in person instead of on the phone. We set the details, an hour from now in Mia-ri. Then I hung up.

"Who was that?" Ernie asked.

"Noh Myong-bei."

"Who?"

"Marilyn. Noh Jong-bei's sister," I said. "Fusterman's girl-friend."

Ernie glanced at the note I'd scribbled. "We've got a date with her?"

"Yep."

He thought about it. "Should I bring a corsage?"

"And a white sport coat."

Before leaving the compound, we stopped at the Military Armistice Commission. We were immediately ushered into Colonel Peele's office.

"Where the *hell* have you two been?" he asked, fuming.

"Trying to find a missing woman," Ernie said.

"Well, we have a more pressing situation on our hands." I doubted this, but remained quiet as Peele continued. "I've set up that meeting with Commissar Han. Tonight," he said in barely more than a whisper, looking over my shoulder at the

closed door, "you are to meet me at Observation Point Ouellette. Twenty-three hundred hours."

"Ouellette?" Ernie asked.

"Did I stutter?" Colonel Peele asked, staring directly into
Ernie's eyes.

"That's on the DMZ," Ernie said. And it was—right on the
line, just a few hundred yards from the JSA.

"Correct. This meeting is confidential, and anything that
goes wrong will have repercussions of the highest order. If you
don't show up or if you tell *anyone* about this, you can bet I'll
find a way to court-martial your sorry asses."

He stood and bulled his way to the door, showing us back out.

It was early afternoon when we met her at the same coffee
shop in Mia-ri where we'd spoken to her before.

"Do your parents know you're here?" I asked in Korean.

She shook her head and answered in English. "No way."

"Where'd you learn how to say that?" I asked. "'No way.'" I
didn't believe the phrase was in any of her English textbooks.

She lowered her head. "Teddy taught me."

Ernie elbowed me. "Knock off the language lesson, Sueño."

I turned back to the young Korean woman who called herself Marilyn. Her eyes were red around the edges.

"What happened?"

"I was on my way home from school. I'd just left campus.
You know, walking down one of those roads with a bunch of

coffee shops and noodle houses and stationery stores for students. A man stepped out of an alley and told me to come with him. I didn't want to, but a second man appeared and I was frightened, so I followed them down a side alley, where a woman was waiting for me in the backseat of a big car."

"You got in?"

"Yes. They told me I had to."

"Did they take you somewhere?"

"No, we just sat there. The woman took my hand and told me she was sorry about my brother and Teddy."

"She called him that? Teddy?"

"No. She called him my boyfriend."

"What did this woman look like?"

Her red-rimmed eyes widened. "Beautiful. Dressed very well, like a fashion model."

"How old would you guess she was?"

"Young. Not older than thirty."

"Tell us everything she said."

"She mentioned your name, Sueño. She told me to call you, but not to say anything about her over the phone. Just to meet you somewhere and pass along a message." We waited. Marilyn swallowed. "I'm not sure I'm supposed to tell him," she said, nodding toward Ernie. Without being asked, Ernie rose from the table and walked outside, standing in front of the plate-glass window, arms crossed as he surveyed the street scene.

"Go ahead," I told her.

"She said that her, what do you call it? Group of people."

"Organization?"

"Yes. Organization. Her organization wants to trade. Not with you, but with a man you know. You must set up the meeting with him tonight, at nine P.M. You must come alone with him, no police."

"Who is this man?"

"She said you'd figure it out."

I frowned. Who would a couple of lowly GIs know who had anything worth trading? Marilyn went on to say that the meeting was to be held in the outskirts of a city called Kumchon at a *kisaeng* house known as Chunhyang Lin. Kumchon was on the way to the DMZ, a mile or two before you hit Freedom Bridge.

"Tonight," I repeated, "at nine P.M?"

"Yes."

"I'm not sure that's enough time to set this up. Did she give you a way for us to contact her if something goes wrong?"

Marilyn shook her head. "No." She switched to Korean. "She says no second chances. That if you don't bring the man her bosses want, the woman you're looking for will die."

We arrived back at the CID office an hour later to find Corrine Fitch inside, waiting impatiently for us. She looked upset after the day's hearing. She took a big breath, let it out slowly, and looked around the office. She glanced at Miss Kim, who sat with her head bowed in front of her typewriter, and then at the three of us clustered nervously around Riley's desk.

"*This* is your investigative nerve center?" she asked.

For the first time in my life, I felt self-conscious about the gray army-issue desks, the dented metal file cabinets, and the splintered wooden field tables. She spotted the silver coffee urn in back. She smirked, appearing to enjoy my discomfort. Then she said, "Can a girl get a cup of coffee?"

I grabbed a metal chair near the back counter, unfolded it, and invited her to take a seat. After I pulled her a cup of coffee and she fiddled around with the low-cal sweetener and powdered creamer, she sat down, seeming somewhat calmer.

"How can we help you?" I asked.

"The hearing isn't boding well for us. I suspect we'll be forced into a court-martial in a few days," she said with a grim expression. "The only concrete proof we have in my client's favor is your second entrenching tool. Have you found anything new?"

I sat down opposite her and explained that we were still officially barred from the case and had been tasked with an important missing person investigation, but promised we would do whatever we could to help Private First Class Theodore Fusterman.

She sat silent, sipping on the lukewarm coffee. She grimaced at its bitterness and asked for another packet of the soluble creamer. I handed it to her and, daintily, she ripped it to shreds. As the white powder fell into blackness, I said, "Where is Colonel Brunmeyer?"

Her eyes widened. "Why?" she said. "What's he got to do with anything?"

"Private Fusterman was one of his men. And we didn't get to speak to him much before being pulled off the case."

She stared at me suspiciously. "Seems to me that all you're doing by questioning him," she said, "is taking a shot in the dark."

"Maybe," I said. "It's important that I speak to him. Do you know his whereabouts?"

She set her coffee down, thinking it over, then checked her wristwatch. I noticed the slenderness of her forearm and how smooth her skin looked. Ernie studied me, seemingly reading my thoughts as the side of his mouth curved into a half-grin.

"He told me he was heading back to the JSA," she said, "but he had to run a few errands first."

"Like what?" Ernie asked.

"Hold on, I'm trying to remember." After a brief pause, she said, "He told me he was going to stop at the—what do you call it?" She snapped her fingers. "The office where purchasing quotas are issued."

"Ration Control," I ventured.

"Yes. The Ration Control Office. Then he had to pick up a few things at the PX and the supermarket."

"The commissary," I corrected.

"Right. The commissary. Why do you have such odd names for everything?"

"Guess what we call the liquor store," Ernie said.

"What?"

"The Class Six."

She waved her hand. "I don't even want to know."

"Where else was he going?" I prompted.

"That was it." She thought for a moment. "No, there was one more place. He said he had to see Mac."

"Who?" Ernie asked.

"Mac. Not sure who that is."

"MAC," I said. "The Military Armistice Commission."

"Ah, okay. There's a colonel or someone he has to see there."

"Colonel Peele," I said.

"That's the one." She raised an eyebrow at me. "So why are you so interested in Rudy's schedule?"

"Who?"

"Rudy. Colonel Brunmeyer."

"I'm sure he'll want to do everything he can to help one of the men under his command," I told her.

We convinced Corrine Fitch to return to the Cosmos Hotel. She made me promise to keep her posted on any developments and to call her as soon as I knew something. "We don't have much time, and I have to make a long-distance call to his parents," she said. "I'm not looking forward to it."

"Blame it on us," I told her.

"You're damn right I will."

As I escorted her to the door, Miss Kim looked up from her typewriter, eyes wide; absolutely flabbergasted at Corrine Fitch's temerity. From a Caucasian woman, I believe Miss Kim would've accepted it—been shocked by it, but accepted it. But from a woman who was ethnically Korean, she was flabbergasted.

Ernie and I watched Corrine parade down the hallway in her tight skirt, and we both heaved a sigh of relief as she pushed through the exit door.

"A handful," Ernie said.

"Brunmeyer's covering his tracks," I said.

"What do you mean?"

"Corrine Fitch, Porter over at Ration Control, and Colonel Peele at the Military Armistice Commission. He's making sure they're all on his team."

"On his team for what?"

I didn't answer. "Let me make a call."

Using Riley's phone, I called Specialist Porter at the Data Processing Unit.

After he picked up, he said immediately, "Don't worry, Sueño, I got it. I'm going along with the badminton rotation from now on."

"That's not what I'm calling about."

"Then what?"

"Did Lieutenant Colonel Brunmeyer from the JSA stop by your office this morning?"

"*Did* he. With a whole slew of new LOAs."

"Have you processed them yet?"

"Sure. He's a battalion commander. They go right through."

"What's he buying?"

"The usual. Liquor, cigarettes, cases of canned meat, instant coffee. Stuff like that."

"Consumables," I said.

"Right. To while away the long guard duty hours up on Freedom's Frontier."

"It's unusual for a battalion commander to turn them in himself, isn't it?"

"Very. He actually brought them in last time, too, though."

"The time he punched you."

Porter paused. "Right," he said finally. "But before that, some JSA dog-face used to be his messenger."

"I need a name."

"Hold on, let me check the paperwork."

Two minutes later he came back on the line. "Somebody named Fusterman. A PFC."

I hung up. After briefing Ernie on what I'd found, he said, "So what? It figures that the guy at the bottom of the totem pole would make the runs to Seoul, since the commander wouldn't mind releasing him."

"But Corporal Noh went with him," I said, "which gave them both a chance to stop at his parents' house."

"Briefly. They still had to make it back to the JSA by close of business."

Ernie and I had made plenty of personal stops while running one official errand or another. It wasn't authorized, but it was common practice. As long as something didn't go wrong, like totaling your military vehicle in an unauthorized area or getting drunk and failing to return to compound on time, no one noticed.

"What's this have to do with the cost of stereo sets in China?" Ernie asked.

"You mean tea," I said.

"Okay, *tea*."

"I'm not sure yet," I said, "but Brunmeyer is also chatting up Colonel Peele at the MAC and Corrine Fitch, Fusterman's defense attorney. Everything is going fine for him."

"What do you mean, 'going fine'? Noh's murder was a huge embarrassment to Colonel Brunmeyer."

"Not enough to stop his promotion," I said.

"According to Strange."

"Have you known Strange to be wrong about these things?"

"Guess not. But what of it? I don't know where you're going with this."

"If a criminal organization wanted to talk to the battalion commander of the Joint Security Area, if they wanted something from him, how would they get it?"

Ernie's eyes glazed over. "I don't know."

"They could kidnap a female dependent," I said, "and coerce you and me into bringing the good colonel to them."

"Okay."

"And once they talked to him, they'd tell him what they wanted him to do."

"To do? Like what?"

"Set that aside for now."

"Why? Because you don't know?"

"I haven't got a clue. But there's one thing we do know now. We know who we're supposed to bring to that meeting tonight."

"How do we know that?"

"Because they contacted the victim's sister. And they know we can't bring Fusterman, because he's locked up. So it must be somebody else involved with her brother."

"His commanding officer," Ernie said. "Who else?"

Frantically, we searched the PX, the commissary, and even the MAC headquarters, but Lieutenant Colonel Brunmeyer had already come and gone.

Or as Corrine Fitch called him, Rudy.

-24-

Ernie and I sped north toward the city of Kumchon.

"We could call him," Ernie said.

"Yeah. But the military phone lines from Seoul take forever. And sometimes they're down. Better if we call from Camp Giant."

We knew from a previous case that the central phone exchange for the 2nd Infantry Division area north of Seoul was located at Camp Giant. About ten miles north of the Seoul city limits, we were stopped by armed MPs at the 2nd Infantry Division checkpoint. We flashed our CID badges and our emergency dispatch for the jeep and they waved us through. A few miles farther on, at the phone exchange on Camp Giant, the Korean civilian on duty connected us directly to the JSA. The Duty NCO answered the phone. I explained to him who we were and told him that I needed to talk to Lieutenant Colonel Rudolph Brunmeyer.

"He's not here," the guy told us.

"What do you mean he's not there?" I asked. "He was in Seoul earlier today and he told the MAC commander he was heading back to the JSA."

"Well, he never made it."

"When do you expect him in?"

"Probably tomorrow before morning formation. Never known him to be gone more than one day at a time."

I gave the Duty NCO my name and told him I'd call back later if I couldn't locate Colonel Brunmeyer. And if he showed up, to have him sit tight.

"Why?"

"It's an emergency. I'll explain it to him."

I hung up. I hadn't given the Staff Duty NCO a return number, since the only phone numbers I could be reached at were either the CID office, which would be closed soon, or the Charge of Quarters desk in the barracks, which wouldn't do us any good. We had to find Brunmeyer and convince him to go to the Chunhyang Lin *kisaeng* house before twenty-one-hundred hours, nine P.M. But how?

"So where'd he go?" I asked Ernie.

Ernie smirked. "Where would you go?"

For a moment, I didn't understand what he was getting at. Then it dawned on me. I reached for my wallet and pulled out a card I'd saved. First, I had to get through to the civilian phone exchange, where I gave the operator the number to the Cosmos Hotel. When it started to ring, I thrust the phone at Ernie.

"You talk," I said.

I didn't want to hear her voice, not if she was with him. Ernie snickered at my discomfort but took the phone.

Chunhyang Lin literally translates to Spring Fragrance Forest, or more eloquently, the Forest of the Fragrance of Spring. Most *kisaeng* houses had fancy names like this, written in Chinese characters and glowing from a neon sign hanging over the front gate, which would be barred metal or wooden gates made of thick lumber. Exclusivity was part of their appeal; *kisaeng* houses were reserved for the elite. Which was true, if you defined "elite" as anybody with enough cash to pay the fare.

It wasn't hard to find. In downtown Kumchon, which stretched about two blocks, I asked one of the idle kimchi cabdrivers for directions. He pointed and said, "*Ddok parro.*" Straight ahead. About a quarter mile out of town, we saw the sign.

We didn't see any point in being devious, so Ernie drove directly into the gravel-covered parking lot out front. He backed into a space on the edge of the elevated area, which dropped off into a half-frozen rice paddy.

"What now?" he asked, turning off the engine.

"We hope like hell Brunmeyer shows up." I checked my watch. Eight-thirty P.M.

"And if he doesn't?" Ernie asked.

"We have to try to negotiate with them ourselves."

Ernie patted the .45 in a shoulder holster beneath his jacket. "I'll negotiate with them all right."

About the last thing we wanted to do was start shooting if we wanted Evelyn Cresthill to have any chance of surviving. Ernie knew that, but it made him feel better to talk big. He'd been hanging around Riley too much.

Back at Camp Giant, he had spoken on the phone to Corrine Fitch, who'd admitted that Lieutenant Colonel Brunmeyer was with her in the hotel room before handing him the phone. Ernie explained the life-or-death nature of this meeting and assured Brunmeyer that we would be there, armed, to ensure his safety. Maybe because Corrine was sitting beside him, listening, Brunmeyer responded gruffly that he could take care of his own safety. Ernie repeated the stakes of the meeting to drive home its importance.

"These gangs don't mess around. If you don't show, they're going to murder an innocent Army wife."

"I *got* it," Brunmeyer responded.

"Okay."

Ernie laid out the precise location of the city of Kumchon, about halfway between the first 2nd Division checkpoint and the Freedom Bridge, which crossed the Imjin River leading to the Demilitarized Zone. "At the turnoff on the Main Supply Route, there's a big sign pointing toward Kumchon," Ernie said, "in English and Korean. You can't miss it."

Brunmeyer said he'd seen the sign before and promised he'd be at the Chunhyang Lin *kisaeng* house before twenty-one-hundred hours.

Ernie hung up, but not before I'd heard Corrine Fitch's voice in the background, emanating from the receiver. It didn't make me feel great, but I reminded myself that I had no claim on her. Just a stupid adolescent crush.

The night grew colder, and sitting in the parked jeep as we waited was becoming uncomfortable. Ernie pulled his collar up and glanced at the road.

"The sign for the *kisaeng* house isn't in English," Ernie said. "Do you think he'll be able to find it?"

"He'll be coming down this road," I said. It was the only thoroughfare heading west out of Kumchon. "If we see a jeep coming, we'll flash our lights."

Ernie started the engine and moved to a spot more visible from the road. There were a few Korean-made sedans in the parking lot, but we were the only jeep. After Ernie turned off the engine we listened to the sounds of the night. No crickets—it was too cold. Just a lonely breeze whistling across muddy rice paddies.

"What kind of a spot is this for a *kisaeng* house?" Ernie asked.

"Removed from Seoul," I said, "so wives are less likely to find their businessmen husbands. And the rent's low, which means a smaller bar tab."

"And the Kumchon police are pliable, easy to pay off."

I shrugged. "Like the KNPs in Seoul, but cheaper."

"Lower cost of living," Ernie said.

We often relied on the Korean National Police, from things like forensic support to Mr. Kill's backup on our investigations. But we knew that corruption was rampant among rank-and-file KNPs. At least, what we would call corruption in the States. In Korea, it was seen more as simply making a living.

A pair of headlights approached. Near the entrance to Chunhyang Lin, it slowed, then pulled into the gravel-strewn lot. As it passed Ernie said, "Sedan."

And a big one. It stopped toward the back of the lot, just out of the glow of the yellow neon sign. A door popped open and a Korean man in a suit walked toward us.

"Showtime," Ernie said.

We both climbed out of the jeep.

He stopped a few feet in front of us, staring at me. "We told you to come alone," he said.

"She didn't say that." And it was true, Marilyn hadn't, though I certainly hadn't been about to ask.

The man shrugged. There was a scar along his face that disappeared into his rugged facial hair. "We want to talk to you," he said. "Not him."

"What about Brunmeyer?"

"We stopped him up the road."

This wasn't good. They controlled the battlefield.

"What's your business with him?" I asked.

The man shrugged again. "We've told him. Now, we want to talk to you."

Ernie looked at me. "Don't do it," he said. "Don't go over there."

"Where's Evelyn Cresthill?" I asked the gangster.

"We still have her."

"When will you let her go?"

"That's up to my boss." Then he said indifferently, "You talking to him, or no?"

"Don't do it," Ernie said again, voice low.

"If I don't come back," I told Ernie, "keep looking hard at Brunmeyer. Something's off up at the JSA. I'm not sure what, but something. If the Provost Marshal doesn't back you, go see Kill."

"Sueño," Ernie said warningly.

"It's Evelyn Cresthill's only chance," I told him.

I stepped forward, hands at my side. The Korean thug frisked me, stood back abruptly, and pointed at my .45. I pulled it out of its holster and tossed it to Ernie, who caught it on the fly.

I stepped toward the sedan.

-25-

A nondescript man in an expensive-looking suit sat in the backseat. He waved at the open spot beside him and I sat down, keeping one leg outside of the car. In the dim light, his features appeared blurred. The white shirt under his suit was buttoned all the way up to his neck.

"Lieutenant Colonel Brunmeyer won't be harmed," he said. "In fact, we will be releasing him soon. My colleague is explaining our demands to him—she is quite persuasive."

His English was so clearly pronounced that I thought he might be from the States, or at least had lived there for some years.

"What do you want from me?"

"We want you to ensure that Private Teddy Fusterman is convicted of the murder of Corporal Noh Jong-bei."

"Why?"

"Not your business."

I paused, waiting, but he didn't elaborate.

"And how do you expect me to do that?" I said.

"That's your problem. I'm sure you'll figure it out."

And I could. There were a number of things I could do as a CID agent that would seal Teddy Fusterman's fate. I could recant my testimony about the entrenching tool with Teddy's initials, say it was a fake. I could end up in the slammer for a while for that, but I doubted it would come to that, given that the Army wanted a conviction, and it would definitely seal Teddy's fate.

"Why should I do this?"

"For Jenny Cresthill. If you want her to grow up with a mother, you'll do what we ask."

"You hurt an American dependent wife, and the Korean National Police will come down on you like an avalanche."

"Maybe," he said. "Unless it looks like she was killed by a jealous lover. Or in a car accident." He turned toward me and grinned. "These things happen."

Mr. Kill would see right through such a ruse. But if the right people in the government hierarchy were paid to go along with it, Kill might not be able to bring a serious prosecution—or even be allowed to investigate. Money talked in Korea, as it did everywhere else, and if this group of mobsters had enough to hire a man of this status to be nothing more than a messenger boy, they probably had plenty with which to bribe politicians. But why was this so important to them? Why go to such lengths to burn Private Teddy Fusterman? The only possible answer I saw was that they were trying to protect the North Koreans.

"Who do you work for?" I asked. "It's not just *gampei*, is it? You work for someone bigger than that, maybe Kim Il-sung himself."

He snorted a laugh. "You can go now," he said, dismissing me with a wave of his hand.

The gangster outside of the car grabbed my arm and pulled. I resisted and broke his grip, then backed out of the sedan and calmly shrugged my coat back into place. Or at least, as calmly as I could before walking back toward Ernie.

The *gampei* piled back into their sedan, turned around, and sped off.

"What'd they want?" Ernie asked.

"Just making a few threats," I said. "Against Evelyn Cresthill."

"Why?"

And then I lied. I told him they wanted us to make sure Brunmeyer didn't step out of line or give any indication that they'd made demands on him, but that they hadn't told me what those demands were. I mentioned nothing about Fuster-man's case.

"And if Brunmeyer does whatever it is they want, they'll let her go?"

"That's what they're telling me."

Ernie shook his head. "They're holding all the aces."

"For now."

■   ■   ■

Just prior to twenty-three-hundred hours—or eleven P.M.—we were bouncing up and down over a muddy lane in the dark because there were no streetlamps up here and we'd already been ordered by the guards at the South Korean army checkpoints to turn off our headlights and use our blackout lights; a dim yellow glow canted toward the ground. We passed a whitewashed wooden sign shaped like a thick arrow that pointed toward the top of a ridge. It read OBSERVATION POINT OUELLETTE.

At a gravel-covered area in front of a small fortress of bricks and sandbags, we parked the jeep and climbed out. From the darkness, a rotund figure appeared.

"Goddamn it, you're late."

"Nice to see you too, Colonel," Ernie said.

"Knock off the bullshit. Follow me."

Planks in the dirt led up the side of the ridge. At the top, Colonel Peele disappeared through an opening in a large wall of sandbags. We followed. Beyond was a level area about the size of a basketball court, encircled by sandbags and brick. On the left stood a narrow wooden guard shack that towered about twenty feet high, and to the right, more sandbags and bricks were piled into igloo-shaped bunkers. Interspersed along the outer walls were narrow slits for riflemen and a few slightly wider ones with M2 .50 caliber machine guns balanced atop wooden platforms.

"They could hold off a siege from Genghis Khan up here," Ernie said.

"Yeah, for about two minutes."

The firepower on the North Korean side of the border was so immense that the GIs stationed up on the DMZ knew no one expected them to last more than a few minutes in an all-out assault. They were here for one reason and one reason only: to make sure that the US was formally involved in any repeat of the Korean War. American forces were not only stationed right on the line, they were placed at the most likely invasion routes: the Western and Eastern Corridors, both of which led straight to Seoul. Were tensions to erupt into full-blown hostilities, a long list of American casualties would mean that the sitting US President would find plenty of political backing for us to enter into war on the side of our ally, the Republic of Korea.

The GIs called it—and themselves—the "tripwire."

My eyes had adjusted to the darkness by now, and by the light of a three-quarter moon, I could make out that Observation Point Ouellette sat near the edge of a gully. Across that gully, about as far as the average center fielder could throw a baseball, sat another fortification.

"That one belongs to the Commies," Colonel Peele whispered.

A few tiny red lights blinked within the North Korean position, and what was perhaps a night vision device stared at me, resembling the eyes of an owl.

As I stared back, a Korean man in combat gear appeared at Colonel Peele's side. The two men whispered to each other, then they nodded and shook hands. Colonel Peele turned to us and said, "Time to move out." He took a step toward the north.

"Hold it," Ernie said. "You want us to go over there?"

"Not there," Peele replied. "Right on the line. Someone will be meeting us."

"Who?"

Without replying, Colonel Peele approached the sand-bagged wall, lay prone atop it, and flipped himself over. Ernie took a deep breath, looked at me, and said, "What the hell." After he slid over the short wall, I followed, met with solid ground, and remained crouched and wary as we moved north. I hoped the pathway Peele was following had been cleared of land mines. In less than ten yards, the terrain dropped off into the gully. We descended rapidly, sloshing in mud at the bottom and shoving branches out of the way to reach the far side of the depression. And then we were climbing until we hit level ground again. A few yards into that stood a ten-foot-tall chain-link fence topped with concertina wire.

Colonel Peele crouched and motioned for us to come closer. He pointed to the lower links of the wall, which had been snipped cleanly by wire cutters. There was enough space for a man to pull back the edges of the fence and crawl through.

"I'm not going through there," Ernie said. Any thought of addressing Peele as "sir" or using other military decorum had left both of us. Ernie and I were frightened and had entered survival mode, none of which seemed to bother Colonel Peele.

"No," he whispered. "I don't want you to go through. But I'm showing it to you, just in case."

"Just in case *what*?"

Before he could answer, footsteps approached.

About ten yards on the other side of the fence, two figures walked toward us. One stopped, his AK-47 pointed at the ground. The other figure continued in our direction. Soon I could make out a North Korean combat uniform, and then the man's features came into view. A weathered, gaunt face with distrustful eyes staring at Colonel Peele.

"Han," Peele said.

Standing about five yards apart, the chain-link fence between them, Commissar Han and Colonel Peele stared each other down like two fighters just before a bout. Unfortunately, there was no referee here, no Marquess of Queensberry rules. Ernie and I had our .45s, but they wouldn't be much help in comparison with the man standing behind Commissar Han with an automatic rifle.

Colonel Peele stepped forward and laced his thick fingers around chain links. "We can get out of this, Han. You call off your alert, we call off ours."

"You've been overflying our capital," Han said.

His English was good, clearly enunciated with a vaguely British accent.

"Yes," Peele replied, "and we hope the sonic booms have woken up your Great Leader."

"Our Great Leader is unperturbed by your running-dog provocations. He is a strong man who will lead us to victory and the eventual reunification of the Korean Peninsula."

"Knock off the bullshit, Han. This is *me*," Peele said, thrusting his thumb into the center of his chest. "I hear this propaganda from you at every MAC meeting, but this isn't the time. We're here to try to find a way to *save* your goddamn Great Leader. To make sure we don't send our entire air force and navy fleet and army up there to make him apologize for murdering one of our men."

"How dare you accuse the peace-loving people of North Korea of committing such an act? Corporal Noh was killed by an American soldier! This Fusterman, or whatever his name is. You can't blame this on us when it was one of your own, rotten to the core with the greed and never-ending lies of capitalism. *You* killed him. Not us."

"No. Fusterman's innocent," Peele said. "Junior Lieutenant Kwon was the officer in charge that night. *He's* the one who's guilty. He either murdered Corporal Noh with his own hands or he ordered one of his men to do it. Turn him over to us, and the mobilization will be called off."

Colonel Peele waved his right arm in the air, indicating the entire length of the Demilitarized Zone.

"Prosecute Fusterman," Han replied. "Hang him by the neck, witnessed by the Neutral Nations Supervisory Committee, and show us the film. Then we will call off our alert. Otherwise, I warn you, the wrath of the North Korean people will descend on your occupying forces and sweep you from the homeland of the pure race of Korean people. We will watch you flounder and drown."

Colonel Peele placed his fists on his hips. "You just don't get it, do you, Han? You don't understand what's going to happen to you if we move in. Not just your Great Leader, but every single one of you Commies will be dragged out of your bunkers and punished by your own people, the ones you've starved and tortured."

I glanced at Ernie nervously, worried about escalation. He had a different reaction, making a face as if to ask, *Did we come all the way up here just to listen to these two entrenched ideologues trade insults?*

But then Commissar Han opened negotiations.

"What would you give us for Junior Lieutenant Kwon?"

Without hesitation, Colonel Peele said, "We'll return two of your spies. The ones you've been bitching about for the last three years."

"Your South Korean lackeys are holding six of our comrades. We want all of them."

"Three," Peele said.

They bickered for a while and finally settled on four spies being released in exchange for Junior Lieutenant Kwon. Apparently, two of the North Korean espionage agents had only been captured recently and were still too high-value for the South Koreans to turn over.

Once they settled on that, the two men argued about the nature of the turnover. Han insisted that Junior Lieutenant Kwon only be questioned at the Joint Security Area, with a representative from the DPRK standing by, and when the interrogation was finished, he'd remain in his homeland, where the penalty would be decided.

Peele shook his head. "No dice. We take him into custody, try him in a South Korean court and execute him down here."

Both were now omitting the possibility of Kwon being innocent. I kept my trap shut.

"Impossible," Commissar Han countered. "There is only one legitimate Korean government, and that is ours. We will not turn one of our citizens over to your . . . wallaby court?"

"Kangaroo court," Peele corrected.

"Right. We won't turn a Korean citizen over to your *kangaroo* court."

Colonel Peele breathed so rapidly I wondered if he might be hyperventilating. "No," he said in a low, menacing voice. "You took advantage of us during the *Pueblo* incident. You tortured our men, murdered one of them and permanently injured others, but you won't get away with it this time. One of your men killed Corporal Noh, and we're not going to stand for it. If you want to avoid war, you *will* turn Junior Lieutenant Kwon over to us. Do you understand?"

Han stared at Peele as if he were a strange specimen of beast. Finally, he said slowly, "*Bul kanung.*" And then repeated it in English. "Impossible."

Without warning, Peele dove forward nose-first into the mud. At first, I thought he might've collapsed, but then I realized that he was wriggling like an eel, his large skull already pushing through the sliced wires in the chain-link fence. Commissar Han stepped back quickly, and the man behind him with the rifle leveled it at Colonel Peele. Ernie and I both knelt, pulled our .45s and took firing positions. In seconds, we'd switched off the safeties, clanged back the charging handles and had them pointed straight at the rifleman.

Colonel Peele crawled as far into North Korea as his fat shoulders would allow, but some of the sharp metal was cutting into his shirt and even his flesh, slowing his forward momentum.

Commissar Han shouted a command. With a deafening blast, the rifleman opened fire. Ernie and I fired, too. I thought for sure that Colonel Peele was dead and we were next, but then I realized that the blast from the AK-47 had landed a few yards in front of him—a warning shot. Our bullets had been aimed high, wafting harmlessly into the night sky.

Even more enraged now, Colonel Peele dragged himself onward, his body now halfway into North Korea. Han and the rifleman backed off, giving me and Ernie the chance to reholster our .45s and leap at Colonel Peele. I grabbed his right foot, Ernie his left, and we pulled, yanking him back toward our side of the line. He kicked viciously, and as I struggled to maintain my grip on his combat boot, Peele howled: "They tortured and killed our men! They took our ship on the high seas illegally and made *us* apologize for it! They're pirates and murderers, and someone needs to bring them to justice!"

By the time we'd wrestled him back fully into South Korea, Peele was sobbing. "They killed my son," he said. "If it weren't for them, he'd still be alive." He buried his eyes in his palms. "I'll kill them all!"

Three soldiers from Observation Point Ouellette appeared out of the darkness. With their help, Ernie and I managed to half-carry, half-drag the distraught Colonel Peele farther onto the free side of Freedom's Frontier.

-26-

The next morning, we sat in the CID office as if nothing had happened the night before.

Evelyn Cresthill was still being held as collateral for an action that went against every organelle in my body: lie. And more than just that. Perjure myself. Under oath.

The instructions of the *gampei* had been clear and simple. Make sure that Fusterman was convicted for Noh's murder in the court-martial and sent away for who knew how many years to rot in the Federal Penitentiary at Fort Leavenworth, Kansas. I was trading his freedom for Evelyn Cresthill's life, and I wasn't sure I could live with that decision. But if I didn't, and if the *gampei* killed Evelyn, Jenny would lose her mother in a violent, irreversible way. She was only ten years old—if she never recovered from the trauma, that was two lives lost.

Two innocent lives against one. That was the calculus.

I tried to figure out how to reverse my earlier testimony. I could claim that the initials scratched on the entrenching tool hadn't been there when Ernie and I purchased the shovel from the black market dealer in Paju-ri, but appeared later under circumstances unknown to me. As to what I'd said previously, I'd simply claim that I'd misunderstood the question. And that I wasn't sure who scratched the initials on the entrenching tool, but it certainly wasn't me. Ernie could be called back up to contest whatever he wanted, but that piece of evidence would be muddied enough to be thrown out. The bloodstains on the second shovel—the one found amongst Fusterman's field gear—had been identified by the lab techs at Camp Zama as human blood, belonging to the same blood group as Corporal Noh. And since those results and other circumstantial evidence pointed to Fusterman's guilt—in addition to the pressure to convict him—he'd be found guilty of the murder. Then everything would go back to normal at the JSA, and Evelyn Cresthill would be a free woman.

I still didn't understand why the *gampei* wanted me to do this. Did they simply have a stake in international peace, or were they part of a broader scheme I couldn't see? I suspected it had to do with Lieutenant Colonel Brunmeyer, JSA commander. What kind of deal had they struck with him that night?

Selling out wasn't as hard as I thought. At least, it wasn't at first. Once you're telling 8th Army what they want to hear, any inconsistencies in your story are easily glossed over, either ignored or reinterpreted as needed to keep the narrative rolling.

I told them that the pressure of the JSA murder case, coupled with the disappearance of Evelyn Cresthill, had been too much for me. I'd gone on a bender, jolting back soju on the long nights Ernie and I had spent traipsing through Seoul. And then I'd often been separated from Ernie while drunk in several dives in a village on the outskirts of Seoul, a place I didn't even remember the name of.

Major Reginald Pintergast, the JAG officer in charge of the Fusterman hearing, seemed sympathetic to my testimony. His dark-brown face smiled from behind round-lensed glasses. "I know what you mean," he said encouragingly. "Half the time, you don't know where you are because you can't read the signs."

I nodded agreement, not bothering to inform him that I could indeed read the signs. I continued my testimony by reneging on the entrenching tool story and testifying that the initials had somehow appeared on the tool *after* Ernie and I had purchased it in Paju-ri. I said I was sorry, that my memory had been cloudy due to my binges, but I'd now realized my mistake. Corrine Fitch glared at me, her pencil poised over a yellow legal pad, lips pursed. Finally, having heard enough, she stood and said, "You *lied*?"

"I just . . . made a mistake," I said, nodding sheepishly.

As she paced the room in front of me, I inadvertently

noticed the alternating movement of her hips, the taut flexing of her calves.

"Oh, no," she said. "You didn't make a *mistake*. Let's call this what it is. You *lied* then, or you're lying now due to pressure from the Judge Advocate General's Office." Before I could answer, she continued. "Initially, you told the truth, didn't you? And when the truth wasn't convenient for Eighth Army, they made your enlisted life so miserable that you couldn't bear it. And now you've knuckled under to them and are lying to stay on the right side of the power structure in this goddamn military *nuthouse*."

Major Pintergast pounded his gavel.

"Counselor," he said, "I know you're unfamiliar with how we do things here, but allow me to inform you that under no circumstances—and I mean *no* circumstances—are you to impugn the integrity of officers appointed to positions of authority in the United States Army."

"*Integrity?*" Corrine bellowed. "Is that what you call it?"

In truth, I was proud of her, sticking to her guns like that and calling me out for my bald-faced lie. Maybe everyone in the debriefing room knew I was lying, but for them, that lie was convenient, even beneficial for their military careers. We'd come back from the brink of war on the Korean Peninsula and, more importantly, the piss-poor leadership of the 8th Army officer corps wouldn't be held responsible for Noh's death. Only Corrine Fitch had spoken out.

It wouldn't take long for word to trickle down to the stockade that her client, PFC Teddy Fusterman, was not only accused, but was about to be rightfully convicted of murdering a fellow soldier. I pictured him alone in his cell, being yanked by the hair and kicked around by his MP guards. Once the word comes down that a particular inmate is guilty, even if he was once a fellow comrade-in-arms, there's little limit to how much he can be abused, as long as you deliver him to court still breathing and with no marks obvious enough to cause embarrassment. The likes and dislikes of the military brass, though they always maintain deniability, are transmitted to the soldiers at the hands-on level, sometimes giving them license to release the most horrid of their pent-up sadist tendencies.

Major Pintergast continued to bully Corrine Fitch and deny every motion she made, and in the end, my testimony was accepted. It hurt to watch her sit there, simultaneously dejected and enraged, gripping the edge of the mahogany table. And I changed my mind about how easy it was to join the forces of evil.

When Fusterman's court-martial started, Ernie asked to have Corporal June Muencher assigned permanently as his partner on the black market detail. After putting in the formal request with the Provost Marshal, he confronted me in the hallway.

"Lost your nerve, Sueño?"

"Not sure what you mean."

"Don't play dumb with me. You know exactly what I mean. You knuckled under pressure from Eighth Army and lied up there on the stand. They'll probably reward you with some cushy job wiping the Provost Marshal's ass." He glared at me, waiting for me to retaliate. I didn't.

"Don't know what you're talking about," I said, trying to go around him.

He stepped sideways and rammed his shoulder into mine. "Watch where you're going."

I stared at him for a moment, then twisted to slide past him. "Yeah," I replied. "I'll do that."

At the court-martial, it was time for me to give my official testimony. This was no longer a hearing. The presiding officer called me as the first witness, and I gave testimony about what I'd seen and heard at the JSA the horrible morning we'd come upon the dented skull of Corporal Noh Jong-bei. And then I was asked about the entrenching tool. I told them about purchasing it at the shop of the Paju-ri military surplus dealer and the magical but belated appearance of the initials. Corrine Fitch was tough in her cross-examination, but there was no way for her to break my story. Finally, the presiding officer released me, and my parting footsteps echoed through a silent courtroom.

That night, I heard from Riley that a major KNP raid was taking place in the Mapo area of Seoul. I didn't want to ask Ernie to borrow his jeep, so I hotfooted it out the front gate, waved down a kimchi cab, and told him what I was looking for. We didn't have to cruise Mapo for long; an entire city block was alight with the red-and-blue flashing lights of KNP sedans and even an armored personnel carrier. It didn't take me long after paying the driver to find Mr. Kill.

"We received an anonymous tip from a laundry delivery woman," Mr. Kill told me, "about a Caucasian woman being held in a dingy apartment. The delivery woman suspected something was wrong and called us."

"Good for her. What'd you find?"

"Evelyn Cresthill," he told me. "She's alive and well. That's her in the back of the sedan with Officer Oh." We watched the sedan drive off to a nearby hospital. "We'll have her checked out, then turn her over to your people."

"Who was with her?" I asked.

"Just a couple of low-level punks. We'll interrogate them, but I doubt they know much. They were left here, with Evelyn Cresthill's presence not very well hidden, so whoever set this up wasn't too concerned about her being found."

Maybe, I thought, because I'd already given my testimony in the court-martial. The transcripts passed through a lot of hands, including numerous Korean employees. The *gampei* were probably being informed of the court proceedings—if not on a minute-by-minute basis, certainly by the hour.

He studied me. "I heard about your testimony." When I didn't respond, he said, "You're up to something."

Tears pricked at my eyes, but I fought them back. He was probably the only person on earth who knew I wouldn't perjure myself without serious reason. "Whatever you're up to, you should be careful."

Then he patted me on the shoulder and walked away.

The next day, Evelyn Cresthill was returned to her family.

She testified to the KNPs and subsequently to 8th Army JAG that the *gampei* had threatened Jenny's life if she didn't resume working for them. At first, they promised that she had only a handful of "dates" to attend, and then she'd be let go. But they'd lied. She'd suspected they would, which was why she'd left her wedding ring in her quarters. She knew it was possible she'd never come back. After the first few outings, they used her sparingly, but she still wasn't allowed to return home. Who her captors were, she couldn't be sure. Just men, she said. Shin, the woman who originally recruited her, seemed to have vanished off the face of the earth.

Since the involuntary servitude of an American dependent wife on behalf of known Asian gang members was more than 8th Army wanted to contemplate—especially from a public relations standpoint—her story was kept out of the newspapers. At her request, in hopes of avoiding more emotional trauma, further investigation into her missing person case was summarily dropped.

■　　■　　■

Later, I sat in the 8th Army Snack Bar alone at a table, sipping coffee. Sergeant First Class Harvey, my buddy Strange, joined me.

"Heard about your cop-out," he said.

Another time, I might've reached across the table and slapped the plastic cigarette holder from his lips. This time, I lowered my head and continued to sip the bitter java.

"I know you're holding out for something," he said.

I looked at him. "What do you mean?"

"I mean, you're lying low. Waiting to make a move."

"What makes you think that?"

He pointed to the side of his head. "Brains."

"I don't know what you're getting at," I said dismissively.

"I'm getting at Brunmeyer. Lieutenant Colonel, promotion-eligible. He's been boffing your girl."

I gripped my coffee cup tighter. Strange was a weird guy, but brilliant in his own way. There were a few NCOs like that, sitting like spiders in the web of the military bureaucracy, gorging themselves on secrets and washing them down with great drafts of rumor—processing data, often coming up with conclusions that no one else would've imagined. Without thinking, I said, "How'd you hear about that?"

Strange grinned. "I knew it," he said. "Brunmeyer and Corrine Fitch. From what I hear, old Brunny has just about camped out at the Cosmos Hotel." Strange grinned again, his thin lips stretching like greased vermicelli. Then he grew serious and leaned forward, glancing to his right and left to make sure no one was listening. "Some people are saying you're ready to check your .45 out of the arms room and shoot them both. Preferably in flagrante delicto."

When it comes to gossip, the soldiers at 8th Army headquarters make soap opera characters seem like monks who've taken a vow of silence.

"Bull," I responded, not wanting to let Strange know how accurately he'd read my innermost thoughts.

Satisfied with himself, he leaned back and crossed his arms. "And your partner, Bascom, is so angry with you that he hasn't even tried to tap that little piece he's working with. What's her name—June? Or should I call her Corporal Muencher?"

"Shut up about that," I told him. Still, I continued to sit there, listening to 8th Army's king of the dramatic arts. Partly because he might spill something that would be useful to me. Mostly because I was allowing myself to wallow in my grief. Then he surprised me.

"Why are you doing this to yourself, Sueño?"

He asked the question almost as if he were actually concerned, a real human being and not the pervert I usually encountered. I was so surprised by the question that I excused myself and went to the serving line to pull myself another cup of coffee from the huge stainless steel vat. After slapping a quarter on the cashier's counter, I returned to the table. I sipped on my newly hot coffee and leaned toward Strange.

"Can you keep a secret?" I asked.

His eyes widened. Or at least, I imagined they did behind his opaque sunglasses. "Me? Of course."

"I need to know the exact time Colonel Peele is having his next MAC meeting."

"That's classified."

"I know it is. That's why I'm asking you. You're the head of Eighth Army Classified Documents."

"I don't know," he said. "Maybe I can find out."

"You know how to reach me," I told him. "I need this info."

"What do I get in return?"

"This time, nothing."

"No stories?"

"I've got nothing to tell."

He eyed me cagily. "Hmm, we'll see about that." He started to rise.

"You'll find out for me?" I asked.

"Posthaste," he replied.

And I watched him waddle out of the 8th Army Snack Bar.

My next stop was the badminton field. Porter was there, playing alongside an elderly Korean gentleman who seemed to have telekinetic control of the shuttlecock. It floated back and forth across the makeshift net like a well-trained bird. Every now and then, a player swatted it ruthlessly and a point was scored. When the round was over, Porter joined me on the sidelines, breathing heavily.

"You're getting the hang of this," I told him.

"Yeah," he said, grinning. "I'm starting to like it even when Miss Kim isn't on my side."

Which was what she'd been hoping for, I think. That Porter would begin to enjoy the exercise and maybe even find someone who was interested in him so she could let him down gently.

"Question for you," I said.

"Shoot."

"Who's been picking up the JSA LOAs lately?" The Letters of Authorization for the Joint Security Area.

He whistled. "Funny you should mention it. I made a comment to our CO about those, and how much stuff they're purchasing these days. I was told to shut up and mind my own business."

"When's the next pickup scheduled?"

"There's no schedule, but they've been turning them in routinely on Fridays."

"And doing their shopping the same day?"

"I suppose. Colonel Brunmeyer has been bringing a three-quarter-ton truck and a driver with him."

"A GI or KATUSA?"

"ROK soldier," Porter replied. "Not a KATUSA."

"Odd," I said.

"I thought so."

His teammates were about to resume the game. Someone called Porter and he said, "Gotta go."

"Okay, see ya," I replied.

Fridays, I thought. And Colonel Brunmeyer had taken to having a South Korean soldier, someone not assigned to his unit, drive a three-quarter-ton truck for him. There were very few reasons he would do this. Soldiers in the ROK Army faced a much more severe discipline than American GIs, or even the KATUSAs assigned alongside them. If you wanted someone who would keep their mouth shut upon command, you couldn't do better than a member of the ROK Army.

"What?" Ernie asked.

I'd stopped him in the parking lot outside the 8th Army CID office.

"Tomorrow," I said. "Friday. There's a meeting of the Military Armistice Commission up at the JSA at thirteen hundred hours." One P.M.

"So?" Ernie asked.

"I want you to join me there."

"Why? You going to throw yourself at Colonel Peele's feet?"

I ignored the insult. "I want us armed and ready to make some arrests."

"Who the hell are we going to arrest?"

Bypassing the question, I said, "I've already talked to Staff Sergeant Palinki. He's on the dusk-to-dawn MP patrol in Itaewon, but when I told him what I planned to do, he told me that he wouldn't mind missing a little sleep. He's in. I don't know about Corporal Muencher. You've been working with her, so you know her better than I do. Maybe she'll come. But let her know that we could be landing feetfirst into a moist mountain of cow shit."

Ernie squinted. "What the hell are you up to, Sueño?"

I told him. He eyed me suspiciously at first, but gradually a grin spread across his face.

"*Bold*," he said, pronouncing the word with reverence. "So you're *not* a sellout to the power structure."

Now it was my turn to glare at him. He started to fidget, then said, "I knew it all along." When he saw that I wasn't buying it, he changed the subject. "I'll take the jeep in for an oil change. The backseat's already been replaced. Primo tuck-and-roll. One-hundred percent vinyl. And I'll make sure the tank is topped off with gas."

"Do that. And if Muencher decides to join us," I told him, "have her check out an M16."

"An M16?" he said, arching an eyebrow.

"Yeah. We might need some serious firepower."

-27-

"Joint Security Area," Palinki said. "That's the same as Panmunjom, where the North Koreans are?"

"Right," I told him.

"I never been up there. North Korean tough guys, huh?"

"Supposedly," Ernie said, "they're trained to break bricks with their bare hands."

"Tough guys," Palinki said.

Ernie swerved through traffic as we passed the city limits of Munsan on our left. Up ahead, the sign for Jayu Tari, the Freedom Bridge, loomed.

Corporal June Muencher was quiet. When I glanced into the backseat of the jeep, I noticed she was pinching the tips of her short fingernails together.

"How about you, Muencher?" I asked. "Ever been to the JSA?"

"First time." She clutched the M16 across her lap.

"It's exciting," I said.

"I'll bet."

After being stopped at the ROK Army checkpoint and showing our dispatch, we rolled onto Freedom Bridge and crossed the rushing expanse of the Imjin River. Once back on solid ground, we followed the two-lane blacktop north toward the Demilitarized Zone.

"So who we going to bust?" Palinki asked, leaning forward like a kid on his way to an amusement park.

I told him. "A black marketeer," I said, "like any other." I turned toward Corporal Muencher. "You've arrested plenty of them."

"Yes, in the last couple weeks under the instruction of Sergeant Bascom."

"Well, it will be the same up here. We find the goods, hopefully catch the culprits in the act of transferring them, and we make the bust."

"The only thing out of the ordinary," Ernie said, "is that we'll be surrounded by armed Communist soldiers who hate our guts."

Muencher punched him on the shoulder. "You're always so negative."

Ernie looked at me. "She's getting to know me."

We rolled beneath the wooden arch that read UNITED NATIONS COMMAND JOINT SECURITY AREA. One of the gate guards gave us a curious look, but after checking our emergency dispatch, waved us through. After we passed, he rotated the handle on his field phone.

"In a few seconds, Brunmeyer will know we're here," Ernie said.

"But with a MAC meeting just starting, he won't have time to do anything about it."

A line of polished military sedans sat in the parking area. Ahead, a small group of officers in Class A uniforms marched toward the central meeting room. Even from this distance, I spotted the beefy shoulders of Colonel Peele, the Executive Officer of the Military Armistice Commission, his head so polished that it shone.

Near the long narrow building that housed the MAC meeting room, an armed guard stopped us, holding out his hand. He wore a black armband that said SERGEANT OF THE GUARD.

"Colonel Brunmeyer's orders," he told us. "No visitors during the MAC meeting."

I showed him my badge. "We're here on police business."

"I don't care what business you're on," he said. "You can't interrupt the meeting."

The officers on the South Korean side had already entered the building. On the North Korean side, a boxy sedan pulled up, soldiers in brown uniforms smartly opened the doors, and military officers wearing round-brimmed hats two sizes too large for them climbed out. All of them were weighed down with enough medals on their chests to sink a battleship. They marched through the door on the northern side of the meeting room.

"We don't want to interrupt," I told the sergeant of the guard, "but this has to be served." I pulled out an official-looking document titled *Notice of Summary Indictment* that Riley had fixed up for me. Before he could study it in too much detail, I slipped it back into my pocket. "Tell you what. We'll wait until the meeting's over. Where's the break room? We could use a cup of hot coffee."

"Over there," he said, pointing toward a long Quonset hut. "But it's locked right now."

"If you open it," I told him, "we'll stay there during the meeting, out of your hair, and present this to Colonel Brunmeyer when it's over."

The sergeant of the guard paused, seeming unsure.

"Hey," Ernie said. "We'll keep a low profile. The Chief of Staff won't mind us waiting until the meeting's over."

Finally, the guard said, "Okay, come on."

At a trot, he led us two buildings down to the locked door. He pulled out a ring of keys, popped the lock, and told us to stay inside until he gave us the word.

"Not to worry," Ernie told him.

It was your typical military break room, with a flat, wooden picnic-style table in the center and a counter with a hot-water urn beneath a small cupboard. Plenty of sugar packets and soluble creamer and economy-sized jars of Folgers Freeze

Dried Crystals. Inside a small refrigerator were sodas and a punctured tin of canned milk.

"Not much here," Ernie said, opening and closing the cupboards. He found an old pistol belt and a torn pair of wet-weather-gear suspenders. The break room only occupied half of the building. A door led to the northern side, but it was padlocked shut.

"I wonder what's on the other side," Ernie said.

I pointed to the bottom of the door. "The MDL runs right here."

"The MDL?" Muencher asked.

"The Military Demarcation Line," Palinki answered. "The one that divides North and South Korea."

"So if we went through that door," Muencher said, "we'd be in North Korea."

"Yes. Although the entire JSA is theoretically open to both sides."

Palinki shuddered, his shoulders hulking. "I don't wanna go in no North Korea."

"Aren't you curious?" Muencher asked him.

"No way. Not about these things."

"It's not about curiosity," I said. "It's about a murder."

"What do you expect to find?" Muencher asked.

"We won't know until we look," Ernie told her.

"*Maestro*," I said, motioning with a flourish for Ernie to pick the lock. From his jacket pocket, he pulled out the special tools that he kept rolled in an old piece of felt. He knelt and I shone my flashlight on the lock to give him extra light. I'd asked Ernie a few times where he'd picked up these skills, but he'd been tight-lipped about it, mumbling something about a locksmith academy on the outskirts of Detroit where he'd grown up. Wherever he'd learned the art, it came in handy in our line of work. Five minutes later, the lock popped open and Ernie turned the handle. With a creak, the door swung open. The room was dark but seemed to be filled to the rafters with rectangular bulk. We stepped into the shadow.

"No cobwebs," I said.

"No. But plenty of dust."

With so many enlisted soldiers up at the JSA on both the North and South Korean sides, it seemed odd to me that such a room would've been left in this state of uncleanliness. I switched on my flashlight. Dust layered the floor and grime coated the woodwork.

"Guess no one brings work details in here," I said.

"Yeah." Ernie wiped his hand on a nearby cardboard box. It came away clean. "But these all look new. Probably stored here for no more than a few days."

We stepped farther inside as I played the beam of the flashlight across the boxes.

"God," Ernie said slowly, reading the labels. "There's so much stuff. It's like being in the commissary warehouse. Or the PX."

Cases of liquor: Johnny Walker Black, Old Grand-Dad, Tanqueray Gin, Courvoisier Cognac. Flatter boxes marked Spam, Folgers, Dole, and C&H pure cane sugar. Closer to the far door, stacked almost to the rafters, were boxes of Kool menthol cigarettes, filtered.

"Pallets full of this shit," Ernie said. We gazed at the wooden platforms on the cement floor. "No way the GIs stationed here could consume all this."

We checked the far door on the North Korean side. "Locked from the outside," I said.

"Let's go take a look," Ernie said.

"They'll see us."

"So? You told me you've already gone through the ration control records. The number of LOAs submitted by Lieutenant Colonel Brunmeyer and the volume of crap he's purchased out of the Commissary and the PX is huge. There is no way that he or his soldiers could've eaten, smoked, or drank all that on their own. You nailed it, Sueño. This is the answer to our case. This secret warehouse with a front door accessible only to the North Koreans, it makes sense. Brunmeyer's been funneling US-made goods into the back door of this warehouse and the North Koreans have been taking them out the front."

"But why?" Muencher asked.

"Why else?" Ernie said. "To make a buck."

"I'm not so sure," I said. "He's a Lieutenant Colonel, a single man making good pay, on his way to becoming full colonel and likely general someday. Even if he made ten or twenty thousand dollars per year on this deal, after a two-year tour he'd barely clear enough for a down payment on a house. Would that really be worth it to him?"

"People have sold their souls for less," Ernie responded.

"There has to be more," I said. "More than just the money." Then I paused. "It's possible he wasn't even making money."

"What?" Muencher said.

Palinki waved his arms. "All this Spam, he don't make money?"

"I mean, maybe Brunmeyer wasn't *selling* this stuff to the North Koreans. Maybe he was paying for it out of his own pocket and just giving it to them."

"Are you nuts?" Ernie said. "Why would he do that?"

"Yeah," Muencher asked. "Why would anyone do that?"

I turned slowly in the center of the small warehouse, taking it all in. With the light bleeding in from the break room, Palinki and Muencher cast long shadows.

"For peace," I said.

"A piece of *what*?" Ernie asked.

"Not *a* piece. Just peace." Ernie stared at me like I'd gone mad, but I continued. "Being the commander of the JSA US contingent is a prestigious job. Brunmeyer was handpicked by the Pentagon. What did he need more than anything to make colonel and have a running start on getting pinned with his first star? A successful tour here at the JSA. No issues. Nobody shot, nobody killed, nobody beaten up and put in a coma. Hard to do with the North Koreans because they're volatile and don't want peace. They've been looking for confrontation—their propaganda machine thrives on one incident after another. So how do you handle guys like that?" I paused, waiting for an answer. No one had it. "What's the best way to keep the peace in any situation?"

"Cooperation," Muencher said.

"Sure. But the North Koreans hate our guts. Their regime is built around the fact that their people have to be constantly prepared for war because of the bloodthirsty American soldiers occupying the southern half of the peninsula. Soldiers who they believe are ready at any moment to attack their peace-loving homeland."

"You sound like the guy on the loudspeaker."

"Yes. It's the justification for putting up with austerity and the oppression imposed on them by Kim Il-sung."

"So we'll never have peace at the JSA," Ernie said.

"Not unless we buy it."

Ernie glanced at the imported liquor and the salted pork in cans and the brightly colored fruit cocktail. "This is stuff no one can buy in North Korea," he said.

"Precisely. But can you imagine if Brunmeyer's North Korean counterpart had access to goods like these? Think of how many generals above him could be paid off. How many Communist Party apparatchiks he could bribe."

"So Brunmeyer wasn't black marketeering at all," Ernie said. "He was shelling out goods purchased with his own hard-earned dollars in order to bribe Junior Lieutenant Kwon into preventing any major incidents."

"And Kwon was low man on the totem pole," I said. "Just the conduit. If he tried to black-market this stuff on his own, he'd risk being caught and charged with treason against the revolution—and the Great Leader himself. You can bet he passed this stuff up the line to his superior officers."

We stood silent, gazing around the room filled with bounty from the American and European manufacturing cornucopia. What I didn't tell them was that I'd realized how the *gampei* fit into this. No time for that now.

"So what's our next move?" Ernie asked.

"Like you said, we technically have enough evidence to make a case. But Eighth Army won't be happy about it. JAG will blow holes in our theory three ways from Sunday."

"What we need," Ernie said, "is to catch somebody in flagrante delicto."

His favorite new term. I was sure he'd learned it from Strange.

There were no windows in the warehouse, but Muencher held up her hand for quiet. We stood still, hardly breathing. And then we heard it. Footsteps. A small contingent of North Korean soldiers marching in our direction. I hoped they'd keep going, but they stopped at the front door on the North

Korean side of the warehouse. Orders were shouted. A pause as metal slid into metal. We'd started to back away, but we were too late. The door burst open, sunlight streamed in, and two North Korean guards pointed the business ends of AK-47 automatic rifles at us.

"*Chong-ji!*" a voice shouted. "Halt!"

Lieutenant Kwon pushed past the two men, waving his pistol in our direction. "*Thieves!*" he shouted.

I stood perfectly still, hoping we could talk our way out of this. Instead, Palinki fired his .45.

-28-

The bullet exploded into the splintered rafter above Lieutenant Kwon's head. Ernie and I both leapt for cover. The AK-47s started spraying the small room with bullets. Glass exploded and the sweet smell of spilled liquor permeated the air. Muencher crouched by the open doorway and popped off her own burst of rounds. Lieutenant Kwon and the two riflemen stumbled backward. As they did, the door swung shut behind them.

"Let's get the hell out of here!" Ernie shouted.

I didn't argue.

Within seconds, we were out of the warehouse and back in the break room.

"Anybody hurt?"

Palinki patted his giant body. "I'm okay."

"Me too," Muencher said.

Palinki leading the way, we exited and made our way toward the main meeting room of the Military Armistice

Commission. As a determined cop, he knew exactly what our next objective was: Arrest JSA Commander Lieutenant Colonel Rudolph M. Brunmeyer. The problem was, there was a contingent of JSA guards who had other ideas. The sergeant of the guard blocked our path. "*Dammit!* I knew I shouldn't have let you into the break room."

"We were attacked," Palinki told him.

"I heard," he said. "And so did everybody else. The whole damn place is on alert." Soldiers crouched behind whatever cover they could find, every one of them with their pistols pulled and aimed toward North Korea. "We're evacuating the MAC building."

American and South Korean officers in Class A uniforms, paperwork in their hands or loosely stuffed into briefcases, filed out the southern side of the MAC meeting room. On the northern side, the boxy sedan had pulled up again and Communist soldiers were using their bodies to shield the high-ranking officers who were crouching and hurrying north toward safety.

Lieutenant Colonel Brunmeyer stood near the rear door on the south, waving the MAC Commission officers toward the safety of a line of armed guards. One of the last officers to emerge was Colonel Peele. He squinted into the sunlight as saliva bubbled on puffed lips.

"What kind of operation you running here, Brunmeyer?"

Lieutenant Colonel Brunmeyer stiffened and stood at the position of attention.

Colonel Peele continued. "Didn't I give you specific orders to maintain the peace up here? How the hell are we going to get anything done with these *goddamn* Commies if you can't keep people from shooting at each other every five minutes?"

Ernie stood next to me. "Asshole didn't even ask if anyone was hurt."

I leaned toward him and whispered, "Time for us to make our move."

He nodded, understanding what I wanted him to do. He pulled a fresh stick of ginseng gum and stuck it in his mouth, then stepped forward to the sergeant of the guard.

"Why you letting the brass go first?" Ernie asked. "What are we, chopped liver?"

"We'll be moving you out in an orderly manner."

"Orderly my *ass*," Ernie said. "You're not leaving *me* behind."

He tried to step past the sergeant of the guard, but the big man grabbed him, and then they were wrestling. While the other guards turned their attention to Ernie, I slipped past the melee and walked toward the bulky back of Colonel Peele, who was still waving his fat forefinger in front of Brunmeyer's nose.

"Excuse me, sir," I told him, stepping between the two men. "Police business."

I turned to Lieutenant Colonel Brunmeyer. "You're under arrest for transference of rationed items to unauthorized individuals. And for aiding and abetting the enemy. Step over here, Colonel, and place both hands against the wall."

Brunmeyer stared at me, flabbergasted. "Transference? Aiding and abetting? Who the hell do you think you're talking to?"

Although they knew who I was, I flashed my badge to both men, just to make it official. "Against the wall!" I shouted. When he didn't move, I shoved him and he resisted. I'd anticipated it and placed him in a reverse hammerlock before throwing him to the ground. As I handcuffed his wrists behind the small of his back, a half-dozen soldiers surrounded me. The sergeant of the guard, apparently through with Ernie, pointed his .45 directly at my head.

"Get off him!"

I ignored him and finished locking the cuffs. "Not just illegal transference and aiding and abetting," I said, pulling Brunmeyer to his feet. "We're also charging you with assault with a deadly weapon. Namely, an entrenching tool. Lastly, we're charging you with the murder of Corporal Noh Jong-bei."

The soldiers around me, including the sergeant of the guard, stopped, stricken.

"You knew what was happening," I said, turning to them. "But you were afraid, and you chose to look away. You knew Brunmeyer was purchasing tons of goods from the PX, coffee and liquor and cigarettes, and handing them over to

Lieutenant Kwon. You can't claim that you didn't see anything, not in an area this small. But it made your lives easier, and anyway, that was your commander's call, not yours. But No-Go didn't agree. He didn't like knuckling under to the NKs, and he confronted Brunmeyer about it. Threatened to turn him in." I waved my arm. "To turn all of you in."

"We didn't do nothin'," one of the guards said.

"But you *should've* done something," I replied. "You knew it was wrong. You looked the other way when your commander bribed the North Koreans, and worse, you looked the other way when No-Go turned up dead."

A few of the guys averted their eyes. The sergeant of the guard continued to stare at me with unmitigated hatred. "We could turn you over to *them*," he said, nodding toward the North Korean guards crouched in firing positions at the far end of the MAC building. "After all, you just fired on their men."

"No," I said, "you won't be turning us over." I nodded toward Ernie and Staff Sergeant Palinki and Corporal Muencher, all of whom had their weapons trained on the group surrounding Brunmeyer.

Brunmeyer knelt in the dirt, his head hanging down.

Colonel Peele's eyes bugged out of his flushed face. Moist lips sputtered and he shouted, "Back off, damn you! Let him go. Who the hell do you think you are? I'll have you court-martialed for this!"

"There'll be a court-martial all right," I said. "For him and maybe for you."

Ernie shoved through the crowd, followed closely by Palinki and Muencher. He lifted Brunmeyer by the armpits, and he and Palinki marched him past the dumbfounded JSA guards and toward the parking area. I followed close on their heels. As we left, Colonel Peele shouted after us, repeating his threat that we would be court-martialed.

"He needs a new catchphrase," Ernie said.

We had just about reached the jeep when Lieutenant Kwon, backed up by a contingent of armed North Korean soldiers, appeared around the corner of one of the single-story buildings. Without hesitation, Palinki stepped forward. "Get the hell outta here," he said, waving his big arm. "You got it? Get the hell outta here."

The North Koreans didn't move.

I stepped forward and addressed Lieutenant Kwon. "Back off, Kwon," I told him. "You'd better clear out that warehouse and take what you can. Your black marketeering days are over."

He pulled his pistol, a Russian-made Tokarev.

"They can't be," he said.

"Why not?" I asked.

"They just can't."

I switched to Korean so his men would understand. "Your bosses, the generals, they take all the liquor, they take all the cigarettes, they take all the food. They leave nothing for you or your men."

Kwon didn't answer, so I continued.

"Now it's finished, so the generals will be angry. They'll blame you. That's why you're frightened."

Again he didn't answer but his head lowered slightly.

"So come with us," I told him. "To the south. You'll be safe there. You and your men. There's room for all of you."

There wasn't room in the jeep, but if they decided to defect, I'd find a vehicle somewhere.

Kwon seemed to be seriously considering my words. He knew that as the lowest-ranking officer involved in this scheme, he would be punished for having botched a good deal. More than likely, none of his bosses would suffer anything more than embarrassment. And then one of the men behind him spoke up.

"The American is a *liar*. Don't listen to the big-nosed thief."

Everyone was armed—and frightened. Kwon stood up straighter, as if instantly remembering there was no way he could defect. It might be a nice dream, but an impossible one. When you ran from the worker's paradise of North Korea and the Great Leader could no longer lay his hands on you, he would lay them on your family. Often, they'd be executed. Three generations wiped off the face of the earth. That was the policy. If your family members were lucky enough not to be killed immediately, then they'd be thrown in a prison camp, facing hard labor for the rest of their lives; lives that figured to be short, painful, and brutish.

Kwon's face straightened back into that of the stern officer we'd seen a few minutes ago. He'd made his decision. He wouldn't be going with us. But would he try to save Brunmeyer?

Lieutenant Colonel Rudolph M. Brunmeyer seemed to have undergone the inverse transition. Unlike that of the brave, efficient officer who'd exited the MAC meeting room, his head now hung heavily, as if physically weighed down by his arrest.

Lieutenant Kwon studied Brunmeyer. The same soldier who'd just called us liars sidled up next to him and said in Korean, "We can't let him go." Kwon squinted and seemed to nod in agreement.

I tensed, my hand reaching toward the hilt of my .45. Although Ernie didn't understand what had been said, he sensed my alarm. So did Palinki and Muencher. Without being told, they stepped slightly away from us and started to raise their weapons. The North Koreans, outnumbering us, raised theirs.

Kwon pointed his pistol at Brunmeyer. "*Him!*" he said in English. "He stays with us."

"Not a chance," Palinki shouted. "He's our prisoner, brutha. Nobody takes him from our custody."

Words were exchanged in Korean so rapidly I didn't

understand them. Kwon's men stepped slightly apart, making themselves more difficult targets.

"*Now!*" Kwon said, pointing again at Brunmeyer. "I want him *now!*"

That's when we heard it. More gunfire. I flinched. Ernie swiveled, hesitated for a moment, and then shouted, "Colonel Peele!"

The big man had stripped off his green coat, loosened his tie, and rolled up the cuffs of his long-sleeved shirt, just as we'd seen him do in his office. But now he had a pistol in his hand and he was running toward Lieutenant Kwon and the contingent of North Korean soldiers.

"Kwon, you son of a bitch," he yelled. "Stop where you stand!"

He raised the pistol and fired. The bullet zinged wildly over their heads. The North Koreans crouched, swiveled, and one of them aimed his AK-47 and let loose with a burst of automatic fire. Bullets smashed into Peele's body. He stood tall, his face a mask of surprise; then slowly he twisted and tumbled forward, struggling to keep his feet as more of the flying metal rammed into his torso, twirling him like a top before he slammed face-first to the ground.

The firing stopped. We'd taken advantage of the distraction to drag Brunmeyer behind the jeep and take cover. Lieutenant Kwon now faced the barrels of our pistols and Muencher's M16 automatic assault rifle, which was pointed directly at his head. For a few seconds, he appeared to ponder the wisdom of immediate death versus an unknown fate. In North Korea, the choice between oblivion and survival can be a finely calibrated calculation.

After what seemed like a long time, he shouted an order. He and his men lowered their weapons, turned, and trotted quick time back to their command building on the northern side of the line.

Ernie and I reached Colonel Peele first. He stared up at us, saliva flowing in thick gobs from his mouth, blue eyes rolling wildly in his head.

"Did I get him?" he asked.

I patted his wrinkled forehead, not bothering to ask who he was talking about, knowing it didn't really matter. "Yeah," I said, "you got him."

"We should never have apologized," he croaked, "to the lying sons of bitches."

With that, he smiled, gulped a last spasmodic breath, and exhaled slowly. We waited a few seconds, and when he didn't move, Ernie reached forward and closed shut his open eyelids.

Ernie drove us hurriedly out of the JSA, and minutes later we were crossing Freedom Bridge. No one tried to stop us since we were heading south, and soon we were on Tongil Lo, Unification Road, speeding toward Seoul. Military convoys roared north.

"Somebody must've called an alert," Ernie said.

"I hope to tell ya," Palinki replied.

I checked my hands. They were still shaking. "You want to tell us, Brunmeyer?" I turned to the backseat and spoke to him. "About you and Corporal Noh Jong-bei?"

He looked up, startled by the mention of No-Go, Corporal Noh Jong-bei. He rattled his handcuffs, checking their strength, then relaxed, laughing to himself at some untold joke.

"It seemed harmless enough at first," Brunmeyer said. "A way to gain cooperation and get things done up at the JSA. Like oil on machinery, making it hum. After a while, the whole business became routine. Write up the Letter of Authorization, send No-Go and Fusterman to Seoul to pick up the liquor and Spam, and after they returned to the barracks, I shoved the newly purchased cases into the warehouse. Later, Kwon would take them away. Clean, easy, and simple. But then No-Go realized there was too much being brought up for our unit alone, and he must've heard the North Koreans talking about the stuff they were getting for free from the dumb Americans. He confronted me, threatened to blow the whole deal. I knew that once it became public knowledge, the MAC would claim that their constant carping at me to keep peace up here at JSA had nothing to do with my decision to grease the skids with the North Koreans. They'd take the easy way out. They'd lay the whole blame on me." He looked around at me and Ernie and Palinki and Muencher. "Don't you see? I had to do it. Everything was on the line."

Palinki patted him on the back. "I see, brutha. But you killed a guy."

"And the *gampei*," I said. "They went to all that trouble to talk to you because they wanted to be cut into the deal."

"More than just that," Brunmeyer said. "They wanted to use Lieutenant Kwon and his superiors to set up a much more extensive, more powerful network of contacts in the North Korean government. So far, the Commies up north have always dealt with the Chinese smugglers on their northern border. The Korean *gampei* wanted to set up something closer to home. Something we could transport across the border at the JSA."

"And you would've agreed to *that*?" Muencher asked.

Brunmeyer shrugged. "What choice did I have? They made it clear they had the goods on me. If I didn't play ball, they'd not only hurt that American woman they were holding, they'd also turn me in."

"No choice, brutha," Palinki said, jollying him along.

From the beginning, the *gampei* had seen the setup, probably before I did, with the information they were receiving from their Korean civilian contacts on base. And once they had Evelyn Cresthill, they had an additional lever they could use to pry their way into a potentially very lucrative smuggling operation into North Korea.

Brunmeyer explained how the scheme had evolved. A GI

on guard duty on a cold wintry night, offering an American-made cigarette to an exhausted North Korean soldier. The North Korean stealthily taking the cigarette, knowing he'd be punished if he were caught, and then not smoking it but hiding it in his pocket and later using it as currency to gain favor with his own superior.

"It started to take on a life of its own," Brunmeyer said. "There we were, in the middle of the Korean winter, cold, tired, exhausted and staring at one another, with no MAC meetings and no honchos from Seoul, or honchos from Pyongyang, anywhere in sight. American GIs are friendly. It was the North Koreans who let down their guard. They accepted what they couldn't get in their own country. A cup of hot coffee, sugar, and eventually a can of Spam, which made its way up to Kwon, the officer in charge on those long, lonely nights.

"He saw the possibilities immediately. Apparently, he was confident enough to approach one of his superior officers with the can of Spam as a gift. At first, he claimed that he'd stolen it—that is, 'liberated' it from the American imperialist running dogs. But when more Spam was forthcoming, and then fruit cocktail and instant coffee, the operation started to expand. The officer who was accepting the goods transferred part of the booty up the line, earning favors from his own superiors. Soon, the demand was greater than I could provide with my personal rations. I switched to LOAs." Letters of Authorization.

"Ingenious," Muencher said, possibly in awe of the first field-grade officer she'd ever spoken to in such a personal context.

"I thought so," Brunmeyer replied. "I figured we were subverting the North Koreans with proof of the superiority of our own capitalist system. It made things run smoothly up at the JSA, and I didn't see the harm."

"Weren't you worried about the LOAs?"

"Yes. But when nobody said anything after the first few, I worried less. And the demand from the North Koreans was growing. They offered me money to bring more things north, but I turned down any and all payment, telling them I had to keep the operation at least somewhat small or I'd be discovered. They seemed to understand."

"What about Colonel Peele at the MAC? Did he realize what you were doing?"

Brunmeyer thought about that one. "Yes and no."

"What do you mean?"

"Colonel Peele was Executive Officer at the Military Armistice Commission for three years, just now starting on his fourth. He must've been aware—in fact, he commented on it once—how smoothly things were running up at the JSA. How, other than posturing, the North Koreans hadn't really done anything out of line in quite a while. I'm not sure about this, but I suspect that Ration Control might've informed him about the Letters of Authorization and he told them to leave the issue alone. Other than troops in actual combat, the soldiers at the

Joint Security Area have the most dangerous assignment in the world, and they shouldn't be subjected to petty ration control restrictions. I think it was something like that." Brunmeyer spread his fingers, rattling his handcuffs. "Before I knew it, we had a full-fledged supply operation on our hands."

"And Corporal Noh?"

Brunmeyer's face clouded, then turned red. His eyes welled up with moisture. "My fault entirely. Noh and Fusterman were doing my runs to Seoul; turning in the LOAs, making the purchases at the PX and commissary, and bringing everything back to the JSA. I knew that No-Go's family lived somewhere in Seoul, and it didn't bother me that he would stop there with Fusterman and visit with his parents as long as they returned to the JSA by close-of-business. But then something went wrong. I don't know if he had a feud with one of the North Koreans or if he was angry with PFC Fusterman, but for whatever reason, he threatened to turn me in for providing American product to the North Koreans. He couldn't go to the KATUSA First Sergeant or even higher up in the South Korean Army chain of command. They'd beat the hell out of him, order him to mind his own business, and more than likely ship him off to some infantry division walking the line."

"Right along the DMZ?" Palinki asked.

"Yes. The more remote the assignment, the better. I'd seen the Koreans do that to other KATUSAs who caused trouble. That was the sword always hanging over their heads. The threat of losing their cushy assignment with the US Army and being banished to a regular army unit. That's what makes them such good troops."

"Convenient for you," I said.

"Yes. Except for Noh. When I talked to him, he said the issue was personal, and he didn't care what the risk to himself was. He said his father had fought against the North Koreans, and he had relatives he'd never met who were being held captive in North Korea, so he couldn't abide us cutting deals with the brutal, two-faced Communists. He told me that I couldn't stop him, that he and Fusterman were going to get word to an American newspaper reporter in Seoul. They were going to bust the entire thing wide open."

As I listened, I couldn't help thinking that blowing the whistle would not only get Corporal Noh transferred to the DMZ, but would also lead to the transfer of PFC Fusterman. Most likely, he'd be shipped back to the States, which would have the additional benefit of putting an end to Fusterman's romance with Noh's sister, Marilyn.

"So what did you do?" I asked. As the jeep raced down Tongil Lo, Ernie, Palinki, and Muencher were now barely breathing.

Brunmeyer hung his head, allowing it to loll listlessly, as if the muscles in his neck had lost power.

"I was so angry," he said. "Noh was ruining everything. Not only the sweet setup we had at the JSA, but also ruining my chance to make full colonel. Ruining my chance to advance my career, maybe even make general someday. It was all going down the drain. Maybe even a few of my troops would be implicated, who knows? Many of them were dedicated soldiers, had been in the army for years, but if our dealings with the North Koreans came to light, those good men might be kicked out of the army, even court-martialed, for their loyalty to me. I couldn't allow that to happen." He turned to Palinki, then to Muencher. "Don't you see? I couldn't allow it."

"So you talked to Corporal Noh?"

"Yes. Alone. I found him outside one night and ordered him to follow me to the area between the conference buildings where no one could see us."

"What about the entrenching tool?"

"I had it in my hand. I'm not sure why. I just brought it with me when I went to find him. I told myself I was going to clean off some of the frozen snow from the guard post viewing areas. I shouldn't have brought it. If I hadn't carried that damned thing with me, maybe things would have turned out differently."

"You lost your temper."

"Yes. He was so self-righteous. Lecturing me. Telling me I was wrong. Who was he, a lowly KATUSA corporal, to look down his nose at me, a field-grade officer in the US Army?"

"So what'd you do?"

"I bashed him," Brunmeyer said. "He hadn't been dismissed, and yet he turned his back on me. I ordered him to return to the position of attention, but he continued to walk away from me, ignoring me as if I were nothing. It was more than I could tolerate. I caught up with him and hit him on the back of his arrogant head. The wound was worse than I thought it would be," he said, staring blankly, as if at a distant memory. "The entrenching tool was so heavy. It swung forward on its own, faster and harder than I'd intended. When it hit, I heard something pop. Skin. And then the crunch of bone." Brunmeyer paused. He swallowed heavily, then said, "It was the worst sound I've ever heard. And there was blood gushing everywhere."

"He fell?"

"Like a sack of wet rice."

"And you left him there," I said, "and you slipped the entrenching tool into Fusterman's field gear?"

"First, I knelt down and checked Noh's body. He was already dead. I was sure of it. I looked around and no one had been watching. I had to get out of there. As quickly as I could, I walked away. The barracks was quiet. Everybody snoring. Asleep. And I was cautious."

"And Fusterman's entrenching tool?"

"After replacing it with the bloody one, I took it with me and hid it overnight. The next day, down at Camp Liberty Bell, I stuffed it deep into a trash drum."

"You didn't think it would resurface?"

"No. I certainly did not."

"Koreans recycle their trash," I said.

"So I've come to find out."

-29-

The next morning, all charges were dropped against Private First Class Theodore H. "Teddy" Fusterman. He was released the following day from the ASCOM stockade. At the CID office that afternoon, Corrine Fitch was delighted with me for having freed her client, but not so happy about me locking up her boyfriend. Before she could say anything, I handed her a three-by-five card with an address written on it in both Korean and English. She glanced at it.

"A Catholic orphanage?" she asked.

"Yes. In Taean. I think this might be the place you were looking for."

"How'd you know?"

I shrugged. "Just a hunch. You spent your first day in country wrestling with Korean officialdom and came up with the name of Taean in Chungcheong South Province. Our admin assistant, Miss Kim, made some phone calls and discovered that an order of Catholic nuns operated an orphanage there during and after the Korean War. In fact, it's still in business."

She clutched the paper to her chest. "Thank you."

"Don't mention it."

After sliding the notecard into her handbag she said, "You don't seriously believe that Rudy murdered Corporal Noh, do you?"

"I do," I told her. I tossed her a copy of the transcript of Lieutenant Colonel Brunmeyer's official statement.

As she read it, she pulled out a handkerchief and wiped her eyes. Shaking her head, she said, "Why didn't he talk to me?"

"So you could have advised him to take the fifth?"

She shot me a sharp look. "What's it to you?"

I stared at her for a while, pondering the smoothness of her skin, the angles of her long face, the intelligent eyes staring at me from beneath heavy lids. "Oh, nothing, I guess."

She stuffed the transcript into her briefcase, stood, and walked out of the room.

Evelyn Cresthill met us in the front room of her friend and neighbor, Madge Bronson. Madge, being the patient and considerate woman she was, excused herself to take a walk. The home was virtually identical to the one the Cresthills lived in, since all the field-grade family quarters had been built by the same contractor—using the same design—to save money. Because military families seldom stayed more than a year or two, modifications weren't allowed. No extra bedrooms, no treehouses out back, no extra workstations in the garage. On some people, sameness has a reassuring effect. I know it does for me, after a childhood of being bounced from one foster home to the next. Other people despise its drabness, but I like the uniformity of the US Army.

Evelyn sat on Madge's sofa, fidgeting because Madge didn't allow smoking in her house. Or her "quarters," as the Army called them.

Ernie started. "You got lucky," he said. "Very lucky."

"I know," she said nonchalantly. "Thank you for convincing them to release me." She stared at us unapologetically, and I wondered if she'd truly wanted to be saved. Maybe Evelyn Cresthill had been more than just an unwilling participant in her own disappearance.

"We only want to talk to you about some administrative things," Ernie said. "None of it is on the record. Okay?"

She didn't answer but turned to glare at him.

"You'll be going back to the States soon," he continued, "by order of the Chief of Staff. When's your household goods appointment?"

"The movers will be here tomorrow. Bob will be in the field, so he's letting me take care of it."

"And Jenny?"

"She's in school, but she'll be returning to the States with me."

"Tough for her to move like that in the middle of the school year."

Evelyn didn't answer.

Ernie continued. "So you have nothing to lose, Evelyn. But me and my partner here still have criminals to catch." He leaned forward, placing his elbows on his knees. "We don't want this gang threatening any more American dependents."

She shook her head vehemently. "I don't know anything about them."

"You know more than you *think*," Ernie snapped. "Besides the Cloud Garden in Mugyo-dong, where my partner roughhoused with those tough guys, where else did they take you?"

She thought about the question, then ran through a long list of joints where she'd met important men in suits. She didn't know the names of these places because she couldn't read the signs. All she could tell us was that she'd poured scotch for the men—using two hands, like they'd taught her—and lit their cigarettes and laughed even though she couldn't understand their jokes. She also couldn't tell us who was Japanese and who was Korean. Everything they said, apart from their broken English, was gibberish to her. When it came to geography, she was even worse. She had little comprehension of the layout of Seoul, and the only landmark she recognized was Namsan Mountain on the southern edge of the city. She said as far as she could tell, they stayed pretty far away from that.

"Did you keep the tips you earned?" Ernie asked.

"Yes, all of them. The men this time were even richer than before."

"So you didn't have to reimburse anyone for transportation or the introductions or security?"

"Nobody said a word about it. These were powerful men who wanted to meet an American woman, so Shin and her employees were doing them a favor and my guess is they were well paid."

"What we want to know," Ernie said, "is the location of Shin. Where does she live and run her operation?"

Evelyn Cresthill waved her arm. "You think she's at the head of this? She's smart, but she's still sort of a recruiter—she gets sent all over Seoul by someone else."

I pulled out a map of Seoul, spread it out on the coffee table, and showed Evelyn where we were now, then where the Cloud Garden club in Mugyo-dong was located. I also pinpointed the road that ran north out of Yongsan Compound toward Myong-dong. None of it helped. She shook her head vehemently. "It was all just a jumble to me."

"What were you taking?" Ernie asked.

She stared at Ernie, seemingly surprised at the accuracy of his guess. "Something to relax me."

"And you got them from Shin?"

"Yes."

"Weren't you worried about accepting drugs from her?"

"No. They were branded red capsules. They had 'Eli Lilly' stamped on the side."

"So they must've been okay?"

"I'd say so."

Ernie leaned forward again. "Somebody may have told you that you're off the hook, Evelyn, but that can change. Eighth Army wants to believe that all of you ladies are as pure as the driven snow. But you're putting more women at risk here. If more American women get taken by these criminals, you'll be facing more questions, either here or in the States."

"I've told you everything I know."

"Not everything. If you had to find this Shin, how would you go about doing it?"

"I'd hang out in the Officers Club."

"She won't be back there," Ernie replied.

Evelyn thought about it. "Then I suppose if I wanted to see her again, I'd go where very rich men hang out. Where international deals are struck. I do remember her telling me about the expensive gifts she received from foreigners."

"That doesn't narrow it down much."

"I know. Sorry, but that's all I've got." She glanced back and forth between us. "Do either of you have a cigarette?"

"Your reach," Staff Sergeant Riley said, "extends even beyond the Eighth United States Army."

We were back in the CID office.

"What do you mean?" I asked.

"Read this." He tossed me a blue-bordered coversheet marked CONFIDENTIAL with only two sheets of paper attached. An hour after we'd left the Joint Security Area, after Colonel Peele's body had been picked up by the 8th Army Coroner, Lieutenant Kwon was seen departing the JSA. It is believed that he was driven to the North Korean Army battalion headquarters, less than a quarter mile north of the Military Demarcation Line. Twenty minutes later, a single gunshot was heard. Then a second gunshot, this one muffled. Perhaps the coup de grâce. Thirty minutes later, a new North Korean lieutenant named Sohn arrived at the JSA to take over Kwon's duties.

I handed the report to Ernie.

"Summary execution," Riley said. "Just confirmed by South Korean intelligence. You've got to hand it to those Reds, they don't mess around."

Miss Kim grabbed a tissue from the box on her desk, rose to her feet, and hurried down the hallway.

Riley beamed like a proud father. "Nice work, boys."

Ernie let him know the dark, unholy place where he could shove it.

-30-

Cymbals clanged and a reedy flute wailed. Ernie and I stood at the bottom of a hill as the funeral procession slowly made its way up the incline. At the top, mourners fell to crying as workmen expertly lowered the casket into the ground via pulleys of hemp rope. Incense was waved, more prayers intoned, and then dirt clattered on wood. A woman howled in pain and was immediately surrounded by others who muffled her anguish.

Finally, as the procession started to return downhill, a young woman parted ways with the group and made her way toward us. She wore the traditional white cloth skirt and short blouse of mourning. She pulled a hemp scarf off her head. Noh Myong-bei, or Marilyn, the deceased man's younger sister. Her smooth cheeks were streaked with dried tears.

"Where's Teddy?" she asked.

"Gone," I replied.

"Gone where?"

"Back to the States," I told her. "The Army didn't give him a choice. After he was released from the stockade, they gave him just enough time to return to his barracks and pack up his stuff. Then an MP escort drove him to Osan." Osan Air Force Base, the main terminal in Korea for the Military Airlift Command.

"He's home now?" she asked.

"Yes."

"He doesn't even have my address," she said sadly.

"Write it down," I told her. "I'll send it to him."

I handed her my notebook and a pen. After scribbling a few lines, she looked at me, worried. "I don't know how to write it in English."

"I'll take care of that," I told her.

After handing the items back to me, she lingered, looking at both of us in turn. She said, "My parents regret having been so against me and Teddy. They understand now that if they had been more—how do you say?—'open-minded' about it, my brother might not have done what he did."

"Your brother was brave," Ernie said.

I agreed. "We investigated this case," I told her, "and your parents should know that this isn't their fault. A man driven by ambition and greed did a terrible thing to your brother. It's Colonel Brunmeyer's fault and no one else's. He'll be punished for it."

She nodded slowly as more tears started to flow. "Maybe it's no one else's fault. Maybe it's mine. Only mine."

Before I could respond, Marilyn turned and ran down the hill, disappearing behind a row of quivering birch trees.

The next morning, Ernie and I left the CID office and drove about twenty miles south to Osan Air Force Base. We wore our dress-green uniforms and stood at attention as an honor guard loaded a flag-draped coffin up the back ramp of a C-130. As the coffin passed, Ernie and I saluted.

One of the crewmen asked us, "You knew him?"

"Yes," I said. "Colonel Peele. XO of the MAC."

The crewman held an onionskin copy of the manifest fluttering in the breeze. "Must've been an asshole," he said.

"What do you mean?"

"We're shipping him back to Dover Air Force Base, but there's no forwarding address after that. Nobody wants him."

"No," I said. "There's no one back home for him."

"Too bad," he said, shaking his head and walking away.

Ernie and I saluted the casket one more time, then turned and walked back to the jeep.

ACKNOWLEDGMENTS

This book could not have been completed without the help and advice of Amara Hoshijo.

Continue reading for a preview from the next
Sueño and Bascom Mystery set in South Korea

GI CONFIDENTIAL

-1-

A rifle butt to the face neutralized the bank guard.

Teeth, saliva, and blood flew everywhere. Then, waving M16 rifles, the three American soldiers stormed across the lobby of the Itaewon Branch of the Kukmin Bank, shouting at the female tellers, male clerks, and gray-haired bank manager to get on the ground. They did, kneeling on the floor and raising their hands over their heads. Whether the Korean employees really understood these English commands or had just picked up on the men's frantic hand signals and the swinging barrels of their weapons, every one of them complied.

Two of the robbers hopped over the counter and began pulling 10,000-*won* bills and other cash out of metal trays, stuffing the loot into gunny sacks. The third man kept watch at the front door. Within less than two minutes, the thieves had emptied all the cash drawers, but instead of trying to enter the locked vault, they climbed back over the counter, still clutching their rifles and their gunny sacks now stuffed with ill-gotten lucre. Then, like a well-drilled infantry squad, they backed across the lobby, maintaining a two-arms-length distance and, in good military order, exited the building.

That quickly, it was over.

Some of the tellers and one of the clerks began to cry. Two of the senior women plucked up their courage, came around the counter, and tended to the injured door guard. The bank manager, hands shaking, dialed the Korean National Police. Then he called an ambulance.

When the authorities arrived, they were dumbfounded to hear that the thieves had been American soldiers. The first question they asked was, "How can you be so sure?" The answer was unanimous. The men had been tall and husky; they'd worn fur-lined headgear pulled down low over their ears, but despite the camo paint, they couldn't hide the contours of their faces.

"*Kocheingi*," the employees agreed. Big noses.

The captain of the Itaewon Police Station sighed and put in a call to Yongsan District Police Headquarters. They certainly wouldn't believe it. GIs had never robbed a bank before. Not in South Korea, not even during the chaos of the Korean War some twenty years ago. Of course, back in those days, none of the banks had had any money, at least, nothing worth more than the paper it was printed on. But now, a single ten-thou-sand-*won* note could be exchanged for almost twenty bucks US.

An amount worth stealing for. An amount worth taking a risk for. Maybe even an amount worth killing for.

■　■　■

"Had any *strange* lately?"

Strange leaned across a Formica-topped table in the 8th Army Snack Bar. His hair was slicked back, his eyes were hidden behind opaque shades, and a plastic cigarette holder waggled excitedly from thin lips.

"What's it to ya?" Ernie replied, looming over the table.

People in the dining area turned their heads toward us. My investigative partner, Ernie Bascom, was tall, slightly over six feet, with sandy-colored hair and green eyes behind round-lensed glasses. His pointed nose swiveled during his occasional visual sweeps, like radar homing in on an incoming missile. For some reason, women found him attractive. Why, I never had figured out. Maybe because he was nervous, fidgety, always looking for someone to arrest—or someone on whom he could focus all his formidable attention. I was even taller than Ernie. Dark hair, Hispanic, no glasses. People's eyes often followed me, too. Maybe they were afraid of getting mugged.

We pulled out chairs and sat opposite Strange.

Undaunted, Strange said, "That bank robbery this morning. How much did they get away with?"

"Ongoing investigation," Ernie said.

"Everybody's talking about it at the head shed. Even the Chief of Staff."

"They'll get their report in due time."

"But if I give them info now, that'll set me up for repayment later. See what I mean?"

Strange is a pervert. He likes to have other GIs—especially Ernie—recount their sexual exploits to him. His real name, according to the plate on his khaki uniform, is Harvey. His shoulder stripes indicate that he's a Sergeant First Class, a senior noncommissioned officer. Titles normally deserving of respect. Ernie and I don't have much of that for him, but we cater to him on occasion because he's the NCO in charge of the Classified Documents Section at the headquarters of the 8th United States Army. As such, he's privy to certain information that we need to conduct our investigations. Not to mention he's a notorious gossip, and despite his obnoxious demeanor, he knows everybody at the head shed. More importantly, he knows what their best-kept secrets are and keeps tabs on what they're up to.

My name is George Sueño. I'm an agent for the Criminal Investigation Division here at 8th Army Headquarters in Seoul, Republic of Korea. Ernie usually deals with Strange, telling him the dirty stories he wants to hear and using pressure and mind games to keep the information flowing.

Ernie reached forward and flicked the tip of the greasy holder dangling from Strange's lips. "How come you never have a cigarette in that thing?"

"I'm trying to quit."

"How can you quit when nobody's seen you smoke?"

"What are you, the chaplain?"

"Yeah. The Church of Ernie." He turned to me. "Pass the plate, Sueño."

"They took about two million *won*," I told Strange.

He whistled. The holder almost fell out of his mouth. "On the black market," he replied, "you could exchange that much *won* for about four thousand dollars. Easy."

Illegal money changers usually offered a better deal than the official conversion rate at a government-authorized foreign exchange bank.

"Not a bad haul for two minutes' work," Ernie said.

"That's all the time they were in there?"

"Precision raid," Ernie said. "The Green Berets would've been proud."

"Maybe it *was* the Green Berets."

"Nah. The Provost Marshal already checked. The Special Forces unit has been out in the field on a joint training exercise since last week."

"That only leaves about fifty thousand other GIs in-country," I said, "that we don't have alibis for."

"Then why are you sitting here?" Strange asked. "Get off your butts and start working the case." When we didn't respond, he looked back and forth between us. An epiphany lit up his eyes. "You aren't *on* the case." He grinned. It was a gruesome thing to see, like a rat having its teeth cleaned. "The Provost Marshal doesn't trust you," Strange continued. "He's keeping you on the black market detail."

Ernie shrugged.

The two CID agents officially handling the bank robbery,

Jake Burrows and Felix Slabem, were brownnosers from way back. They'd do what the 8th Army honchos asked, without exception. And what those honchos wanted was deniability. So far, the official party line was that it hadn't been established that the three men involved in the bank robbery were actually American soldiers. In the early seventies, there were few foreigners of any type living in South Korea who weren't either civilians or service members working for the US military. And there was virtually no tourism. So the thought that the three robbers might've been someone other than American GIs stretched the credulity of even the most gullible. Not to mention that each of the robbers carried an M16 rifle, standard weaponry issued to every American soldier in-country.

The United States military presence here was at the sufferance of the South Korean government, and more importantly, the sufferance of the South Korean citizenry. If the twenty-five million people of South Korea were to suddenly turn against us, the US would have to abandon its only remaining combat-capable presence in mainland Asia. The last of the major military units had withdrawn from South Vietnam just a few months ago, in accordance with President Nixon's policy of "Vietnamization." Leaving Korea as well was something the American government didn't want to contemplate. Not in the middle of a Cold War, the world divided between the Western powers and the Soviet Union and Red China.

Thus, until proven otherwise, the three men who robbed the

Kukmin Bank weren't Americans. A fiction that Agents Burrows and Slabem could tolerate, even pretend to believe. One that Ernie and I couldn't. And that was why we'd been ordered to stay on the black market detail, chasing down Korean military dependents who were buying cigarettes and freeze-dried coffee and imported Scotch at the 8th Army Post Exchange and selling it to black marketeers at twice what they paid for it.

Honest work for us. Sort of. But I doubted that Burrows and Slabem had the skill or tenacity to find these bank robbers, which was likely why 8th Army had assigned them to the case.

"So you two are just sitting on your butts doing nothing?" Strange asked.

"Nope," Ernie said. "I'm seriously considering reaching across this table and slapping you in your fat chops, then kicking *your* butt from here to the parade field."

Strange sat up taller. "I'm a Sergeant First Class," he said. "You can't do that to me."

"Keep mouthing off," Ernie said, pointing his forefinger at him, "and I'll eventually manage to override my respect for your exalted rank."

"That's more like it," Strange said, glancing back and forth between us, unsure if he liked that answer but willing to pretend it worked for him.

"Find out what you can," I told Strange, "about what the Chief of Staff is telling the Provost Marshal."

"Why?"

"Because Eighth Army policy can change direction as fast as a fart in the wind. We want to be ready for it."

Strange glanced at us slyly. "You're planning on investigating on your own, aren't you?"

"You don't have a need-to-know," Ernie told him. "Just do what the man says."

After I bought him a cup of hot chocolate with two marshmallows, Strange promised he would keep his eyes and ears open at the head shed.

"What about us?" Ernie asked, as we walked out of the snack bar. "We going to let Burrows and Slabem screw this thing up?"

"Not on your life. These guys, whoever they are, robbed a bank in Itaewon, and Itaewon might as well be our hometown."

"Can't let them get away with crap like that," Ernie said. "Not in our neighborhood."

"No way. We'll catch these guys and make 'em pay for what they did, regardless of whether the Eighth Army honchos like it or not."

"They definitely won't," Ernie said. "Not if it embarrasses the Command."

"We've embarrassed them before."

"Yeah. Which is why we hold an esteemed place on the Eighth Army shit list."

-2-

Night had fallen, and the lights up and down Itaewon's main drag sparkled with a neon glow. Drawn like moths to the bars and brothels and nightclubs, packs of GIs swarmed uphill, hands in the pockets of their blue jeans, nylon jackets with dragons and flames embroidered on the back glistening in the ambient light. Ernie and I watched them go, somehow managing to resist the siren call of debauchery ourselves. Instead, we stood at the base of Itaewon hill, along the edge of the four-lane road that fronted the Kukmin Bank. Crime-scene tape emblazoned with *hangul* script kept the public away, but inside, the bank's lights were still on, and beyond plate glass windows, shadowy figures milled about. Accountants, I figured, doing a precise inventory of what had been stolen.

On either side of the street, shops lined the road, lights on and doors open: Han's Tailor Shop, Kim's Sporting Goods, Pak Family Brassware Emporium, Hamhung Cold Noodles, Miss Shin's House of Leather. Their main source of income was the five thousand or so American GIs who worked on 8th

Army's Yongsan Compound less than a mile down the road. And since those GIs were typically working during the day, the establishments of Itaewon, especially the bars and brothels and nightclubs, did most of their business at night. The shops were open until about ten P.M, the bars and nightclubs until the government-mandated midnight-to-four curfew; the brothels, once they locked their front gates, were open twenty-four seven.

Ernie and I questioned the proprietors of every shop within a quarter mile of the Kukmin Bank. We weren't worried about missing the day shift and inadvertently questioning the night shift. In Korea, most shop owners and their employees worked from the early morning opening to nighttime closing, regardless of how many consecutive hours that was. There was no such thing as overtime; to have a job in this beat-up economy meant you held onto it like a hoard of gold. It had been just over twenty years since the devastation of the Korean War, when, as one American bomber pilot famously said, "All we're doing is bouncing rubble on rubble." During the ensuing two decades, circumstances had improved, but not much.

Everyone who worked in the nearby shops had heard about the robbery and was surprised and concerned by it, since the crime rate was so low in Korea. They were especially shocked to hear of the use of weapons.

The South Korean government exercised total gun control. Only authorized personnel, like the military or the Korean

National Police, were allowed to possess or utilize firearms. Penalties for the illegal possession of a rifle or a handgun, much less the use of one in committing a crime, were steep. As a result, even gangsters and other hardened criminals preferred to use cudgels, knives, and other such charming implements. GIs were known to commit the occasional crime with their Army-issue weapon—raping Korean business girls or mugging cab drivers—but no one had ever heard of them robbing a bank.

We found an eyewitness. The owner of Han's Tailor Shop, who oddly enough was named Cho. Because of his profession and the fact that most of his customers were American, he spoke English well. He walked us outside, and we stood in front of his window display of jackets and shirts.

"I was standing here," he said, then pointed two doors down the street toward the bank. "A jeep pulled up onto the sidewalk, there. American."

"How could you tell it wasn't a Korean Army jeep?" I asked.

The Republic of Korea Army, or ROK Army, was massive, almost ten times the size of the US presence, and they had American-made military vehicles swarming all over the country.

"Paint," Mr. Cho said. "Korean army use cheaper paint on their vehicles. Darker green. This jeep was American."

"You saw the soldiers get out?"

"Yes. Three of them. One man stayed behind the steering wheel. The driver."

Ernie glanced at me. So, there were four robbers, not just the three that had been mentioned in the preliminary report by Burrows and Slabem.

Cho lit up a Turtleboat cigarette and took a long drag, and I tried not to grimace at its pungent aroma.

"I wondered if any of them were my customers," he said. "You know, maybe some other time they came to Han's Tailor, bought a suit."

"Did you recognize any of them?"

"No. They wore hats, the winter kind, pulled down low, and their faces were covered with green . . . what do you call that?"

"Camo stick," I said.

"Yeah. Camo stick. Looked like crazy men. All kinds of lines. Black, green, everything. Anyway, they went into the bank."

"Carrying their rifles?"

"Yeah, rifles."

"Why didn't you call the KNPs?" Ernie asked.

Cho studied him for a moment, exhaling smoke through his nostrils. Then he turned and spit on the sidewalk. "I don't trust KNPs."

Under President Park Chung-hee's military regime, the Korean National Police, like most government employees, were severely underpaid. As such, they had to supplement their income somehow. That was usually done with payoffs, mostly minor ones. For example, if someone was caught with a bottle of scotch without an import stamp on it, they could avoid being taken down to the station and having an official report filed on them by paying a "fine" on the spot. A fine that the underpaid police officer would then stick in his pocket. After all, he had expenses, too—feeding his family, paying for his children's books and uniforms, not to mention the tuition charged even for high school. And the massive expenditure if the kid made it to college. Most Koreans didn't resent the police taking money. They'd probably do the same if roles were reversed. But they weren't foolish enough to get involved with the Korean National Police if they didn't have to.

"So the GIs went inside the bank," I said, "and a few minutes later, they came back out?"

Cho nodded. "Carrying bags." He mimicked gripping something heavy at his side.

"What else did you notice?"

"I wanted to see what unit they were in," he said, puffing once again on his cigarette.

I held my breath.

"You know," he continued, slashing a parallel line with his thumb and forefinger. "It's on the front and back of the jeep."

"Right, on the bumper," I said. They always stenciled the unit designation in white paint.

"Yeah. That."

"So what'd you see?" Ernie asked.

"Nothing."

"Nothing?"

"Yeah, nothing. Somebody covered it with black tape."

Damn. "So, we don't know their unit," I said.

"Right."

I supposed it made sense that the thieves didn't want anyone noticing that the vehicle was assigned to, say, C Btry 2/17 FA during the two minutes their jeep was parked outside the bank. According to military nomenclature this translates to Charlie Battery of the 2nd Battalion of the 17th Field Artillery Brigade and would lead us directly to their place of assignment.

After a long pause, Ernie asked, "Does anybody else know about this?"

"Like who?" Cho asked.

"Like the KNPs. Or like the American investigators."

"No. Nobody came. Nobody asked me anything. You're first."

"But there were cops down the street all day?" I said. "At the bank."

"Lots," Cho replied.

"Can you tell us anything else about the GIs?"

He shrugged and took another long drag on his cigarette, thinking it over. "They're smart," he said.

"Why?" I asked.

He looked at me like I was crazy. "Fastest way to get money."

"Why didn't you ever try it?" Ernie asked. "You work just a few steps from the bank."

Cho threw his cigarette butt on the sidewalk and stomped on it. "You give me a gun and a jeep, maybe I will."

He turned and walked back into Han's Tailor Shop.

I yelled a thank-you at him, and he shrugged and gave a desultory wave. I turned to Ernie.

"You pissed him off."

"How'd I do that?"

"By implying he was a thief."

"Well, he owns a shop, doesn't he?"

"That's not thievery."

"Seems like it to me every time I buy something."

Ernie hated capitalism. He also had no use for communism. I was never sure, really, how he thought the world should be run. Except maybe through playing it by ear, according to the thoughts of *der reichsführer* Ernie.

We walked back toward the lights of Itaewon. After a few steps, a slim figure hopped out of the darkness of a narrow alley. "*Hey!*" she shouted. We turned. She raised and pointed a rectangular object. Before we had time to react, a flash erupted into the night. Both Ernie and I reached for our eyes, blinded.

"What the *hell*?" Ernie said.

The slim figure fumbled with something, shoved it with a click into a metallic device, and the flash erupted again. This time I lurched forward and reached for the shadowy waif, but instead of grasping something solid, all I grabbed was air.

"Relax, big boy," a woman's voice called. "I'm done. Your vision will come back in a second."

"Who in the hell are you?" I asked, rubbing my eyes.

"Just a tourist."

"A tourist? There are no tourists here."

She let out a brief chortle. "There are now."

With that, she trotted briskly away. For a few steps Ernie ran after her, but almost immediately plowed into an electrical pole. I checked to see if he was all right. Embarrassed, he shoved my hand away. I could barely make out the retreating photographer, prancing off down the street, leaving us standing immobilized like two dumb giants.

"Witch," Ernie said, gallantly eschewing the B-word.

-3-

"Where in the hell you two guys *been*?" The next day, Staff Sergeant Riley, NCO in charge of the Criminal Investigation Admin Division, gave us his usual warm greeting.

"Doing what we're supposed to be doing," Ernie said. "All freaking morning. Chasing down dollies and busting them for black market violations. Where the hell you think we've been?"

A slight exaggeration. The truth was, after being accosted by our mystery photographer last night, we'd made our way into the heart of Itaewon and discussed the bank robbery case over a couple of beers, which led to a couple of shots of bourbon, which led to a bottle of soju. All of which inevitably led to a horrific hangover this morning that had made us both late for work. We rendezvoused at the barracks, and after driving the jeep through the empty parking lot of the Yongsan Compound Main PX, we could at least claim that we'd been doing our regular duty on black market patrol. After which we'd made it over to the office.

"Burrows and Slabem," Riley said, "are already briefing the

Chief of Staff on that bank robbery fiasco. Good troops. Doing their job."

"Brownnosers," Ernie said, making his way toward the back counter and the three-foot-tall stainless steel urn of hot coffee. Supposedly, some years ago, it had been hand-receipted from the 8th Army mess hall. Somebody had once tried to clean the brown crust that encased its innards, but Riley had ordered them to stop, afraid it would fall apart.

I sat down in front of Riley's desk and grabbed his copy of the *Pacific Stars and Stripes*. President Gerald R. Ford was having his usual headaches, and some were speculating that he was getting ready to pardon Nixon. Since those problems were all on the other side of the planet, I set the paper down. "Are the honchos still claiming the robbers weren't GIs?"

Riley had turned his attention to a stack of paperwork in front of him. "Yep."

"Pretty far-fetched."

"As long as it stays out of the newspapers, they're happy."

The Park Chung-hee government had total control over the South Korean press. More than a few reporters who'd crossed the line with anti-government rhetoric had been arrested and charged with sedition. The rationale was that with over 700,000 bloodthirsty North Korean Communist soldiers stationed thirty miles north of Seoul, ready to invade at the drop of a bayonet, the people of South Korea had more to worry about than freedom of the press. They had to think about survival. Niceties like James Madison's First Amendment would have to wait. And wait. And wait.

A snippet of pulp stuck out from beneath Riley's desk blotter.

"What's this?" I asked, reaching for it.

Riley slapped his hand down on top of it. "Nothing," he said.

"If it's nothing, why are you so nervous?"

"Mind your own business," he said.

High heels clicked down the hallway toward us. Miss Kim, the tall, elegant admin secretary, entered the office. She nodded to me and took her seat at her desk behind her *hangul* typewriter. After fumbling with some paperwork and propping it against a wire holder, she rolled a blank sheet into the platen and started typing away.

I joined Ernie at the back counter. He had gone silent—the uneasy truce between him and Miss Kim still ruled the office, sort of like the détente between North and South Korea. I supposed she'd never forgiven him for his wandering ways during their brief relationship. He hadn't bothered to apologize, after all.

I pulled myself a mug of hot coffee and sat with Ernie on the folding metal chairs at the wooden field table.

"Are we gonna tell 'em?" I asked.

"Tell who what?"

"Tell Riley and Burrows and Slabem and the Provost

Marshal about the fourth GI. The driver. And the fact that they covered up their jeep's unit designation."

"Screw 'em," Ernie said, before glugging down more coffee. "I say we keep working on the case ourselves without sharing anything."

"The information could be important to their investigation."

"They don't want it to be important," Ernie replied. "All they want is to be able to claim that our pure-as-driven-snow American soldiers had nothing to do with this. We tell 'em that it was GIs who robbed the bank, and they'll blame us for bursting their bubble. As if the entire robbery was our fault."

I watched Riley shuffling his documents and Miss Kim pecking at the keys of her typewriter. "These guys could strike again. After all, it was so easy for them this time."

"Except for the bank guard."

"Yeah. Except for that."

"Otherwise, they were pretty lucky," Ernie said.

"You know it and I know it. But they may not know it. This time, an old man lost some teeth and ended up with a broken jaw. Next time, it could be worse."

Ernie stirred his coffee.

"I still say screw 'em. They don't want our help, they don't get it. The KNPs didn't even bother to canvass the area. They know the deal. The Americans and, therefore, the higher-ups in the Korean government—their bosses—want deniability.

They want to be able to say it wasn't American GIs. Tens of millions of dollars in US aid are hitched to that story."

Actually, it was hundreds of millions. Both economic and military aid was provided by the US government to the South Korean regime in order to prop them up as our bulwark against Communist aggression. Bad publicity in the States could ruin all that, turn the American public and therefore Congress, which controlled the purse strings, against the US military presence on the Korean Peninsula. An eventuality that the honchos of the 8th United States Army would go to great lengths to avoid.

"So they're investigating with one hand tied behind their back," I said.

"Yes. Which is why they put those bozos Burrows and Slabem on the case. You're the only GI in Korea who speaks Korean. And you and I are the only two law enforcement officers with enough gumption to venture out into Seoul and ask questions. The other guys can't even read the signs, they think people are talking bad about them every time they hear a foreign language, they aren't limber enough to squat over a Korean toilet, and they hate the smell of kimchi. They're *morons*," Ernie said, warming to the subject. "The only two real investigators Eighth Army's got are you and me. And we're sidelined; they've relegated us to wandering around the PX and the commissary, busting housewives for selling a jar of maraschino cherries to black market mama-sans."

I sipped on my coffee, set it down, and said, "Yeah, yeah, *yeah*. But other than that."

Ernie sighed. "Screw you, Sueño."

Riley rose from his desk, hiked up his pants, and walked out into the hallway. I listened to his footsteps, figuring he was headed to the latrine.

"Hold on a minute," I told Ernie, as I rose and walked toward Riley's desk. There, beneath the blotter, was the little piece of pulp. I carefully slid it out. A newspaper. The *Overseas Observer*. It was a single fold tabloid type, like the *Stars and Stripes*, but this periodical was definitely not Department of Defense authorized. I held it up to the light. Covering most of the front page was a gorgeous young woman kneeling on a beach, beaming at the camera and wearing nothing but a leather bikini that accented her voluptuous curves.

Miss Kim glanced in my direction, saw what I was holding, and quickly turned back to her work. I liked her a lot and did my best to treat her well, especially after Ernie's betrayal. I quickly refolded the newspaper, carried it to the back of the room, and plopped it down in front of Ernie.

"All *right*," he said, ogling the bathing beauty. "The *Oversexed Observer*. I used to read this rag all the time in 'Nam. The honchos hate it."

"They won a court case against McNamara," I said. "So the PX has to sell it."

"I see Riley's a fan."

Ernie picked up the paper and thumbed through it. It was twenty flimsy pages with plenty of photos. And plenty of ads for liquor, hair cream, cigarettes, sports cars, even mail-order jewelry, complete with instructions on how to have the perfect engagement ring mailed to your girl back in the States. The headlines were salacious: COLONEL BOFF'S PRIVATE. TENNIS COURT FIRST, THEN PERIMETER DEFENSE. GI CONVICTED OF FRAGGING CO.

All the stuff that would never be covered in the *Stars and Stripes*.

"How do they get these stories?" Ernie asked.

"Shoe leather," I said. "And leaks from inside the military."

Plenty of GIs were pissed off at the Green Machine and willing to pass confidential information to the *Overseas Observer*, even though they could technically be court-martialed for violating a standing order. To wit, all reporters and other media inquiries were to be referred to the local command Public Affairs Office.

Riley stomped back into the office, surveyed his desk, noticed that his blotter was slightly askew, and glanced back at us.

"Hey," he said, "what are you doing with that?"

"Wrapping fish," Ernie said.

Riley marched toward us, holding out his palm. "Give it here."

"Ix-nay," Ernie said, still reading. "I'm improving my mind."

Riley snatched the newspaper, but Ernie held on, and a loud ripping noise tore through the office. Miss Kim stopped typing, stood up, grabbed a tissue from the box in front of her, and briskly swept out into the hallway.

"See what you've done," Riley said. "You've upset Miss Kim. And you ripped my paper."

"You're the one who ripped it," Ernie replied.

"I haven't even read it yet," Riley said.

"Sueño will buy you a new one."

Riley glanced at me.

"Sure," I said. "When does the next issue hit the stands?"

"Sunday," Riley replied.

"All right," I said. "The next *Overseas Observer* is on me."

That seemed to calm the waters. Working with Scotch tape, Ernie and Riley pieced the *Oversexed Observer* back together. It was great to see the boys cooperate. The girl in the bikini probably had something to do with it.

Three days later, on a Friday, Riley answered a call from the MP desk. He listened for a while, repeating, "Yeah." And finally, "Roger that." He slammed down the receiver.

"Bascom! Sueño!" he yelled, though we were only a few feet away.

"What?" Ernie said.

"Hat up! Your presence is required immediately, if not sooner."

"What are you talking about, Riley?"

"Another bank. This one ain't good."

"What do you mean, not good?"

"I mean somebody's dead."

Ernie and I looked at each other. "Somebody like who?"

"Korean civilian. That's all I know." He gave us the name of the bank and the district, grievously mispronouncing both. Still, I knew what he meant. The Daehan Bank in Dongsung-dong. Miss Kim stood up and helped me find it on the large office wall map of Seoul.

"Okay," I said. "Got it."

Ernie and I slipped on our coats and our headgear and left the office. In the parking lot on the way to the jeep, Ernie said, "Why are they sending us and not Burrows and Slabem?"

"Maybe they're through dicking around."

"That'll be the day."

Ernie started the jeep and we roared out of Gate Seven and into the overcast afternoon, heading north toward Namsan Tunnel #3, which would lead us to Dongsung-dong on the far side of downtown Seoul.

Other Titles in the Soho Crime Series

Michael Genelin
(Slovakia)
Siren of the Waters
Dark Dreams
The Magician's Accomplice
Requiem for a Gypsy

Timothy Hallinan
(Thailand)
The Fear Artist
For the Dead
The Hot Countries
Fools' River

(Los Angeles)
Crashed
Little Elvises
The Fame Thief
Herbie's Game
King Maybe
Fields Where They Lay
Nighttown

Mette Ivie Harrison
(Mormon Utah)
The Bishop's Wife
His Right Hand
For Time and All Eternities
Not of This Fold

Mick Herron
(England)
Slow Horses
Dead Lions
Real Tigers
Spook Street
London Rules
Joe Country

Down Cemetery Road
The Last Voice You Hear
Why We Die
Smoke and Whispers

Reconstruction
Nobody Walks
This Is What Happened

Stan Jones
(Alaska)
White Sky, Black Ice
Shaman Pass

Stan Jones cont.
Frozen Sun
Village of the Ghost Bears
Tundra Kill
The Big Empty

**Lene Kaaberbøl &
Agnete Friis**
(Denmark)
The Boy in the Suitcase
Invisible Murder
Death of a Nightingale
The Considerate Killer

Martin Limón
(South Korea)
Jade Lady Burning
Slicky Boys
Buddha's Money
The Door to Bitterness
The Wandering Ghost
G.I. Bones
Mr. Kill
The Joy Brigade
Nightmare Range
The Iron Sickle
The Ville Rat
Ping-Pong Heart
The Nine-Tailed Fox
The Line
GI Confidential

Ed Lin
(Taiwan)
Ghost Month
Incensed
99 Ways to Die

Peter Lovesey
(England)
The Circle
The Headhunters
False Inspector Dew
Rough Cider
On the Edge
The Reaper

(Bath, England)
The Last Detective
Diamond Solitaire
The Summons

Peter Lovesey cont.
Bloodhounds
Upon a Dark Night
The Vault
Diamond Dust
The House Sitter
The Secret Hangman
Skeleton Hill
Stagestruck
Cop to Corpse
The Tooth Tattoo
The Stone Wife
*Down Among
the Dead Men*
Another One Goes Tonight
Beau Death
Killing with Confetti

(London, England)
Wobble to Death
*The Detective Wore
Silk Drawers*
Abracadaver
Mad Hatter's Holiday
The Tick of Death
A Case of Spirits
Swing, Swing Together
Waxwork

Jassy Mackenzie
(South Africa)
Random Violence
Stolen Lives
The Fallen
Pale Horses
Bad Seeds

Sujata Massey
(1920s Bombay)
The Widows of Malabar Hill
The Satapur Moonstone

Francine Mathews
(Nantucket)
Death in the Off-Season
Death in Rough Water
Death in a Mood Indigo
Death in a Cold Hard Light
Death on Nantucket

Seichō Matsumoto
(Japan)
*Inspector Imanishi
Investigates*

Magdalen Nabb
(Italy)
*Death of an Englishman
Death of a Dutchman
Death in Springtime
Death in Autumn
The Marshal and
the Murderer
The Marshal and
the Madwoman
The Marshal's Own Case
The Marshal Makes
His Report
The Marshal
at the Villa Torrini
Property of Blood
Some Bitter Taste
The Innocent
Vita Nuova
The Monster of Florence*

Fuminori Nakamura
(Japan)
*The Thief
Evil and the Mask
Last Winter, We Parted
The Kingdom
The Boy in the Earth
Cult X*

Stuart Neville
(Northern Ireland)
*The Ghosts of Belfast
Collusion
Stolen Souls
The Final Silence
Those We Left Behind
So Say the Fallen*

(Dublin)
Ratlines

Rebecca Pawel
(1930s Spain)
*Death of a Nationalist
Law of Return
The Watcher in the Pine
The Summer Snow*

Kwei Quartey
(Ghana)
*Murder at Cape
Three Points
Gold of Our Fathers
Death by His Grace*

Qiu Xiaolong
(China)
*Death of a Red Heroine
A Loyal Character Dancer
When Red Is Black*

James Sallis
(New Orleans)
*The Long-Legged Fly
Moth
Black Hornet
Eye of the Cricket
Bluebottle
Ghost of a Flea*

Sarah Jane

John Straley
(Sitka, Alaska)
*The Woman Who
Married a Bear
The Curious Eat Themselves
The Music of What Happens
Death and the Language
of Happiness
The Angels Will Not Care
Cold Water Burning
Baby's First Felony*

(Cold Storage, Alaska)
*The Big Both Ways
Cold Storage, Alaska*

Akimitsu Takagi
(Japan)
*The Tattoo Murder Case
Honeymoon to Nowhere
The Informer*

Helene Tursten
(Sweden)
*Detective Inspector Huss
The Torso
The Glass Devil
Night Rounds
The Golden Calf
The Fire Dance
The Beige Man
The Treacherous Net
Who Watcheth
Protected by the Shadows*

Hunting Game

*An Elderly Lady Is Up to
No Good*

**Janwillem van de
Wetering**
(Holland)
*Outsider in Amsterdam
Tumbleweed
The Corpse on the Dike
Death of a Hawker
The Japanese Corpse
The Blond Baboon
The Maine Massacre
The Mind-Murders
The Streetbird
The Rattle-Rat
Hard Rain
Just a Corpse at Twilight
Hollow-Eyed Angel
The Perfidious Parrot
The Sergeant's Cat:
Collected Stories*

Jacqueline Winspear
(1920s England)
*Maisie Dobbs
Birds of a Feather*